FÉLIX J. PALMA

Félix J. Palma was born in Spain in 1968. A columnist and literary critic, his short stories have appeared in numerous publications and have earned him more than a hundred awards. *The Map of Time* won the prestigious University of Seville prize for literature in 2008 and will be published in more than thirty countries.

FÉLIX J. PALMA

The Map of Time

TRANSLATED FROM THE SPANISH
BY NICK CAISTOR

HarperCollins*Publishers*

HarperCollins*Publishers*
77–85 Fulham Palace Road,
Hammersmith, London W6 8JB

www.harpercollins.co.uk

Published by HarperCollins*Publishers* 2011
2

First published in Spanish as *El Mapa Del Tiempo* 2008

A catalogue record for this book
is available from the British Library

ISBN: 978-0-00-734412-3

Typeset in Janson Text by Palimpsest Book Production Limited,
Falkirk, Stirlingshire

Printed and bound in Great Britain by
Clays Ltd, St Ives plc

CONTENTS

PART ONE
1

PART TWO
199

PART THREE
377

'The distinction between past, present and future is an illusion, but a very persistent one.' ALBERT EINSTEIN

'Mankind's most perfectly terrifying work of art is the division of time.' ELIAS CANETTI

'What is waiting for me in the direction I don't take?'
JACK KEROUAC

The Map of Time

PART ONE

WELCOME, DEAR READER

AS YOU PLUNGE INTO THE THRILLING PAGES OF OUR

MELODRAMA

WHERE YOU WILL FIND

ADVENTURES

OF WHICH YOU NEVER

DREAMED!

If, like any reasonable person, you believe that time is a river sweeping away all that is born towards the darkest shore, in these pages you will discover that the past can be revisited, that mankind can retrace his footsteps, thanks to a machine that can travel through time.

YOUR DELECTATION AND ASTONISHMENT ARE

GUARANTEED

I

Andrew Harrington would gladly have died several times over if that meant not having to choose just one pistol from among his father's vast collection in the living-room cabinet. Decisions had never been Andrew's strong point. On close examination, his life had been a series of mistaken choices, the last of which threatened to cast its lengthy shadow over the future. But that life of unedifying blunders was about to end. This time he was sure he had made the right decision, because he had decided not to decide. There would be no more mistakes in the future because there would be no future. He was going to destroy it completely by putting one of those guns to his right temple. He could see no other solution: obliterating the future was the only way for him to eradicate the past.

He scanned the contents of the cabinet, the lethal assortment his father had lovingly assembled after his return from the war. He was fanatical about those weapons, though Andrew suspected it was not so much nostalgia that drove him to collect them as his desire to contemplate the novel ways mankind kept coming up with for taking one's own life outside the law. In stark contrast to his father, Andrew was impassive as he surveyed the apparently docile, almost humdrum implements that had brought thunder to men's fingertips and freed war from the unpleasantness of hand-to-hand combat.

He tried to imagine what kind of death might be lurking inside each of them, lying in wait like some predator. Which would his father have recommended he use to blow his brains out? He calculated that death from one of those antiquated muzzle-loading flintlocks, which had to be refilled with gunpowder and a ball, then tamped down with a paper plug each time it was fired, would be a noble but drawn-out and tedious affair. He preferred the swift death guaranteed by one of the more modern revolvers nestling in their luxurious velvet-lined wooden cases.

He considered a Colt single-action model, which looked easy to handle and reliable – but he had seen Buffalo Bill brandishing one in his Wild West Adventures: a pitiful attempt to re-enact his transoceanic exploits with a handful of imported Red Indians and a dozen lethargic, apparently opium-sated buffalo. Death for him was not just another adventure. He also rejected a fine Smith & Wesson, the gun that had killed the outlaw Jesse James, of whom he considered himself unworthy, and a Webley, specially designed to hold back the charging hordes in Britain's colonial wars; he thought it looked too cumbersome.

His attention turned next to his father's favourite, a fine Pepperbox with rotating barrels, but he seriously doubted whether this ridiculously ostentatious weapon would be capable of firing a bullet with enough force.

Eventually he settled on an elegant 1870 Colt with mother-of-pearl inlay that would take his life with all the delicacy of a woman's caress. He smiled defiantly as he plucked it from the cabinet, remembering how often his father had forbidden him to meddle with his pistols. But the illustrious William Harrington was in Italy at that moment, no doubt reducing the Fontana de Trevi to dust with his critical gaze. His parents' decision to leave for Europe on the very day he had chosen to kill himself had been a happy coincidence. He doubted that either of them would ever decipher the true message concealed in his gesture (that he had preferred to die as he had lived – alone), but for Andrew it was enough to imagine the disgust on his father's face when he discovered his son had killed himself behind his back and without his permission.

He opened the cabinet where the ammunition was kept and loaded six bullets into the chamber. He supposed that one would be enough, but who knew what might happen? After all, he had never killed himself before. Then he tucked the gun, wrapped in a cloth, inside his coat pocket, as though it were a piece of fruit he would eat later. In a further act of defiance, he left the cabinet door open. If only he had shown this much courage before, he thought. If only he had dared confront his father when it had mattered, she would still be alive. But by the time he had, it was too late. And he had spent eight long years paying for his hesitation. Eight years, during which his pain had only worsened, spreading its tendrils through him like poison ivy, wrapping itself around his guts, gnawing at his soul. Despite the efforts of his cousin Charles and the distraction of other women's bodies, his grief over Marie's death refused to be laid to rest. Tonight, though, it would all be over.

Twenty-six was a good age to die, he reflected, contentedly fingering the bulge in his pocket. He had the gun. Now all he needed was a suitable spot in which to perform the ceremony. And there was only one possible place.

With the weight of the revolver in his pocket comforting him like a good-luck charm, he descended the grand staircase of the Harrington mansion in elegant Kensington Gore, a stone's throw from the Queen's Gate entrance to Hyde Park. He had not intended to cast any farewell glances at the walls of what had been his home for almost three decades, but he could not help feeling a perverse wish to pause before his father's portrait, which dominated the hall. His father stared down at him disapprovingly from the gilt frame, a proud, commanding figure, bursting out of the old uniform he had worn as a young infantryman in the Crimean War until a Russian bayonet had punctured his thigh; the wound had left him with a disturbingly lopsided gait. William Harrington surveyed the world disdainfully, as though in his view the universe was a botched affair on which he had long since given up. What fool had been responsible for the untimely blanket of fog that had descended on the battlefield outside the besieged city of Sebastopol so that nobody could see the tips of the enemy's bayonets? Who had decided that a woman was the ideal person to preside over England's destiny? Was the east really the best place for the sun to rise?

Andrew had never seen his father without cruel animosity in his eyes so could not know whether he had been born with it or had been infected with it when fighting alongside the ferocious Ottomans in the Crimea. In any event, it had not vanished, like a mild case of smallpox, leaving no mark on his face, even though the path that had opened in front of him on his return could only have been termed a fortunate one. What did it matter that he had to hobble along it with the aid of a stick? Without having had to enter any pact with the Devil, the man with the bushy moustache and clean-cut features depicted on the canvas had overnight become one of the richest men in England. Trudging around in that distant war, bayonet at the ready, he could never have dreamed of possessing a fraction of what he now owned. How he had amassed his fortune, though, was one of the family's best-kept secrets, a complete mystery to Andrew.

The tedious moment is now approaching when the young man must decide which hat and overcoat to pick from among the heap in the hall cupboard: one has to look presentable even for death. This is a scene that, knowing Andrew, could take several exasperating minutes and, since I see no need to describe it, I shall take the opportunity to welcome you to this tale, which has just begun, and which, after lengthy reflection, I chose to begin at this juncture and not another – as though I, too, had to select a single beginning from among the many jostling for position in the closet of possibilities.

Assuming you stay until the end, some of you, no doubt, will think I chose the wrong thread with which to begin spinning my yarn, and that for accuracy's sake I should have respected chronological order and begun with Miss Haggerty's story. Perhaps so – but there are stories that cannot begin at their beginning, and this may be one of them.

So, let's forget about Miss Haggerty for the moment, forget that I ever mentioned her, even, and go back to Andrew, who has just stepped forth from the mansion suitably dressed in a hat and coat, and even a pair of warm gloves to protect his hands from the harsh winter cold.

Once outside the mansion, the young man paused at the top of the steps, which unfurled at his feet like a wave of marble down to the garden. From there, he surveyed the world in which he had been brought up, suddenly aware that, if things went to plan, he would never see it again. Night was spreading its veil over the Harrington residence. A hazy full moon hung in the sky, bathing in its soft glow the immaculate lawns surrounding the house, most of them cluttered with flowerbeds, hedges and oversized stone fountains – dozens of them – decorated with excessively ornate sculptures of mermaids, fauns and other mythical creatures. His father had accumulated such a large number because, an unsophisticated soul, his only way of showing off his importance was to buy a lot of expensive and useless objects. In the case of the fountains his extravagance was excusable, because they combined to soothe the night with their watery refrain, making the listener want to close his eyes and forget everything except their hypnotic burble.

Further off, beyond the neatly clipped lawns, stood the immense greenhouse, graceful as a swan poised for flight, where his mother spent most of the day marvelling at the exotic flowers that sprouted from seeds brought back from the colonies.

Andrew gazed at the moon for several minutes. He wondered whether man would ever be able to travel there, as had the characters in Jules Verne and Cyrano de Bergerac's works. What would he find if he did manage to land on its shimmering surface – in an airship, or shot out of a cannon, or with a dozen bottles of dew strapped to his body in the hope that, as it evaporated, he would float up to the sky, like the Gascon swashbuckler's hero? Ariosto the poet had turned the planet into a warehouse where lunatics' reason was stored in phials, but Andrew was more drawn to Plutarch, who imagined that the moon was where dead people dwelled. Andrew liked to picture them living at peace in ivory palaces built by an army of worker angels or in caves dug out of that white rock, waiting for the living to receive their safe-conduct to death and to carry on their lives anew, exactly where they had left off.

Sometimes he imagined that Marie was living at that very moment in one of those grottoes, oblivious to what had happened to her, and grateful that death had offered her a better existence than life. Marie, pale in that white splendour, waiting patiently for him to decide once and for all to blow his brains out and come to fill the empty space in her bed.

He stopped gazing at the moon when he noticed that Harold, the coachman, had followed his orders and was standing at the foot of the stairs with a brougham at the ready. As soon as he saw his young master descending the flight of steps, the coachman rushed to open the carriage door. Andrew had always been amused by Harold's display of energy, considering it incongruous in a man approaching sixty, but the coachman clearly kept in good shape.

'Miller's Court,' the youth commanded.

Harold was astonished by his request. 'But, sir, that's where—'

'Is there some problem, Harold?' Andrew interrupted.

The coachman stared at him for a moment, his mouth hanging ludicrously half open, then recollected himself: 'None whatsoever, sir.'

Andrew gave a nod, signalling that the conversation was at an end. He climbed into the brougham and sat down on the red velvet seat. Glimpsing his reflection in the window, he gave a sigh of despair. Was that haggard countenance really his? It was the face of someone whose life had been seeping out of him unawares, like a pillow losing its stuffing through an open seam.

In a certain sense this was true. Although his face retained the harmonious good looks he had been born with, it now resembled an empty shell, a vague impression in a mound of ashes. The sorrow that had cast a shadow over his soul had taken its toll on his appearance: he could scarcely recognise himself in the ageing youth, with hollowed cheeks, downcast eyes and unkempt beard, who stared back at him in the glass. Grief had stunted him, transforming him into a dried-up, sullen creature.

The brougham rocked as Harold, having overcome his astonishment, clambered up to his perch, and took Andrew's attention away from the blurred face sketched on the canvas of the night. The final act of the disastrous performance that had been his life was about to begin, and he was determined to savour every moment. He heard the whip crack above his head and, caressing the steely bulge in his pocket, he let himself be lulled by the vehicle's gentle sway.

The brougham left the mansion and went down Carriage Drive, which bordered the lush vegetation of Hyde Park. Gazing through the window at the city, Andrew thought that in less than half an hour's time they would be in the East End. This ride had always fascinated and puzzled him in equal measure: it allowed him to glimpse in a single sweep every aspect of his beloved London, the world's greatest metropolis, the giant head of an insatiable octopus whose tentacles stretched over almost a fifth of the Earth's surface, holding Canada, India, Australia and a large part of Africa in its vice-like grip.

As they sped east, the salubrious, almost countrified atmosphere of Kensington soon gave way to the crowded urban environment of Piccadilly, and beyond to the Circus, where Anteros, the avenger of unrequited love, is firing an arrow into the city's heart. Beyond Fleet Street, the middle-class dwellings seemingly huddled around St Paul's Cathedral gradually came into view, until finally, once they had passed the Bank of England and Cornhill Street, a wave of poverty swept over everything, a poverty that people from the adjoining West End knew of only from the satirical cartoons in *Punch*. It seemed to pollute the very air itself, as it mingled with the stench rising from the Thames.

Andrew had last made this journey eight years earlier, and had known ever since that, sooner or later, he would make it again, for the very last time. Hardly surprising, then, that as they drew nearer to Aldgate, the gateway to Whitechapel, he felt slightly uneasy.

He peered warily out of the window as they entered the district, experiencing the same misgivings as he had in the past. He was overwhelmed, again, by shame because he was spying on an alien world with the dispassionate interest of someone who studies insects – even though, over time, his initial revulsion had turned into compassion for the souls who inhabited this place, where the city dumped its human waste.

Now it seemed that there was every reason for him to feel compassion still: London's poorest borough had changed relatively little in the past eight years. Wealth brings poverty in its wake, thought Andrew, as they crossed the ill-lit, rowdy streets, crammed with stalls and handcarts, and teeming with wretched creatures whose lives were played out beneath the menacing shadow of Christ Church. At first he had been shocked to discover that behind the dazzle of the city's façade there existed this outpost of hell where, with the Queen's blessing, human beings were condemned to live like beasts. The intervening years had made him less naïve: he was no longer surprised that, even as the advances of science were transforming London – and the well-to-do amused themselves by recording their dogs' barks onto the wax-coated cylinders of phonographs or conversed via telephone under the glow of Robertson's electric lamps – Whitechapel had remained immune to progress, untouchable beneath its rotten shell, drowning in its own filth.

A glance was enough to tell him that crossing into this world was still like sticking his hand into a hornets' nest. It was here that poverty showed its ugliest face, here that the same jarring, sinister tune was playing. He observed a couple of pub brawls, heard screams from the depths of dark alleyways, glimpsed a few drunks sprawled in the gutter, gangs of street urchins stripping them of their shoes, and exchanged glances with a pair of pugnacious-looking men standing on street corners, petty rulers in this parallel kingdom of vice and crime.

The luxurious brougham caught the attention of several prostitutes, who shouted lewd proposals to him, hitching up their skirts and showing their cleavage. Andrew felt a pang of sorrow as he gazed upon this pitiful spectacle. Most of the women were filthy and downtrodden, their bodies bearing the mark of their daily burden of customers. Even the youngest and prettiest were stained by the misery of their surroundings. He was revisited by the agonising thought that he might have saved one of these doomed women, offered her a better life than the one her Creator had allotted her, yet he had failed to do so.

His sorrow reached a crescendo as the carriage rattled past the Ten Bells, emitting an arpeggio of creaks as it turned into Crispin Street on its way to Dorset Street, passing in front of the Britannia pub where he had first spoken to Marie. This street was his final destination. Harold pulled the brougham up next to the stone arch leading to the Miller's Court flats, and climbed off the box to open the carriage door.

Andrew stepped out, feeling suddenly dizzy. His legs were shaking as he looked around him. Everything was exactly as he remembered it, down to the shop with grimy windows run by McCarthy, the owner of the flats, which stood beside the entrance. Nothing he saw indicated to him that time also passed in Whitechapel, that it did not avoid it, as did the bigwigs and bishops visiting the city.

'You can go home now, Harold,' he told the coachman, who was standing at his side.

'What time shall I fetch you, sir?' asked the old man.

Andrew didn't know what to say. He stifled a laugh. The only thing fetching him would be the cart from the Golden Lane morgue, the same one that had come there to fetch what was left of his beloved Marie eight years ago. 'Forget you ever brought me here,' was his reply.

The sombre expression that clouded the coachman's face moved Andrew. Had Harold understood what he had come there to do? He could not be sure, because he had never given a moment's thought to the coachman's intelligence, or indeed to that of any servant. He always thought that at most they possessed the innate cunning of people who, from an early age, are obliged to swim against the current in which he and his class manoeuvred with ease.

Now, though, he thought he detected in old Harold's attitude an unease that might only have come from his having guessed Andrew's intention.

And the servant's capacity for deduction was not the only discovery Andrew made during that brief moment when, for once, they looked directly at each other. Andrew also became aware of something hitherto unimaginable to him: the affection a servant can feel for his master. Although he saw them as shadows drifting in and out of rooms, according to some invisible design, only aware of them when he needed to leave his glass on a tray or wanted the fire lighting, these phantoms could care about what happened to their masters. That succession of faceless people – the maids whom his mother dismissed on the flimsiest grounds, the cooks systematically impregnated by the stable boys as though conforming to some ancient ritual, the butlers who left their employ with excellent references for another mansion identical to theirs – made up a shifting landscape that Andrew had never taken the trouble to notice.

'Very well, sir,' murmured Harold.

Andrew understood that these words were the coachman's last farewell; that this was the old fellow's only way of saying goodbye to him – embracing him was a risk he appeared unwilling to take. With a heavy heart, he watched that stout, resolute man, to whom he would have had to relinquish the role of master if they had ever been stranded on a desert island, clamber back on to the brougham and urge on the horses, leaving only an echo of hoofs as the carriage was swallowed by the fog that spread through the London streets like muddy foam. It struck him as odd that the only person to whom he had said goodbye before killing himself should be the coachman, not his parents or his cousin Charles. Life was full of such ironies.

That was exactly what Harold Barker was thinking as he drove the horses down Dorset Street, looking for the way out of that accursed neighbourhood, where life was not worth thruppence. But for his father's determination to pluck him from poverty and secure him a job as a coachman, he might have been one more among the hordes of wretched souls scraping an existence in this gangrenous patch of London. Yes, that surly old drunk had hurled him into a series of jobs that had ended at the coach house of the illustrious William Harrington, in whose service he had spent half his life. But they had been peaceful years. He could admit as much when he was taking stock of his life in the early hours after his chores were done and his masters were asleep; peaceful years in which he had taken a wife and fathered two healthy children, one of whom was employed as a gardener by Mr Harrington.

The good fortune that had allowed him to forge a different life from the one he had believed was his lot enabled him now to look upon the wretched souls of Whitechapel with a degree of objectivity and compassion. Harold had been obliged to go to Whitechapel more often than he would have liked when ferrying his master there that terrible autumn eight years ago, a period when even the sky seemed at times to ooze blood. He had read in the newspapers about what had happened in that warren of Godforsaken streets, but also he had seen it reflected in his master's eyes.

He knew now that the young master had never recovered, that those reckless excursions to pubs and brothels, on which his cousin Charles had dragged them both (Harold had been obliged to remain in the carriage, shivering with cold), had not succeeded in driving the terror from his eyes. And that night young Harrington had appeared ready to lay down his arms, to surrender to an enemy who had proved invincible. Hadn't that bulge in his pocket looked suspiciously like a firearm? But what could Harold do? Should he turn around and try to stop him? Should a servant step in to alter his master's destiny?

Harold Barker shook his head. Maybe he was imagining things, he thought, and the young man simply wanted to spend the night in that haunted room, safe with a gun in his pocket.

He left off his uncomfortable broodings when he glimpsed a familiar equipage coming out of the fog towards him. It was the Winslow family carriage, and the bundled-up figure on the box was almost certainly Edward Rush, one of their coachmen. To judge from the way he slowed the horses, Rush appeared to have recognised him, too. Harold nodded a silent greeting to his colleague, before directing his gaze to the occupant of the vehicle. For a split second he and young Charles Winslow stared solemnly at one another. They did not say a word.

'Faster, Edward,' Charles ordered his driver, tapping the roof of the carriage with the knob of his cane.

Harold watched with relief as they vanished into the fog in the direction of the Miller's Court flats. He was not needed now. He only hoped that young Winslow would arrive in time. He would have liked to stay and see how the affair ended, but he had an order to carry out – although he fancied it had been given him by a dead man – so he urged the horses on, and found his way out of that dread neighbourhood where life (I apologise for the repetition, but the same thought occurred to Harold twice) was not worth thruppence.

Admittedly, the expression sums up the area's peculiarity very accurately, and we probably could not hope for a more profound appraisal from a coachman. However, although his life is worthy of recounting – as are all lives upon close scrutiny – the coachman Barker is not a relevant character in this story. Others may choose to write about it and will no doubt find plenty of material to endow it with the emotion every good story requires – I am thinking of the time he met Rebecca, his wife, or the hilarious incident involving a ferret and a rake – but that is not my purpose here.

And so let us leave Harold – whose reappearance at some point in this tale I cannot vouch for, because a whole host of characters will pass through it and I can't be expected to remember every one of their faces – and return to Andrew, who at this very moment is crossing the arched entrance to Miller's Court and walking up the muddy stone path to number thirteen while he rummages in his coat pocket for the key.

After stumbling around in the dark for a time he found the room, and paused before the door in an attitude that anyone seeing him from a neighbouring window would have taken for incongruous reverence. But for Andrew that room was infinitely more than some wretched lair where people who hadn't a penny to their name took refuge. He had not been back there since that fateful night, although he had paid to keep everything exactly as it had been, exactly as it still was inside his head. Every month for the past eight years he had sent one of his servants to pay the rent, so that nobody could live there: if he ever went back he did not want to find traces of anyone but Marie. The few pennies were to him a drop in the ocean, and Mr McCarthy had been delighted that a wealthy gentleman and obvious rake should want to rent that hovel indefinitely – after what had taken place within its four walls he very much doubted that anybody would be brave enough to sleep there.

Andrew had always known he would come back, that the ceremony he was about to perform could not have been carried out anywhere else.

He opened the door and mournfully cast an eye around the room. It was a tiny space, scarcely more sophisticated than a barn, with flaking walls and a few sticks of battered furniture, including a dilapidated bed, a grimy mirror, a crumbling fireplace and a couple of chairs that might fall apart if a fly landed on them. He felt a renewed sense of amazement that life could take place somewhere like this. Yet had he not known more happiness in this room than in the luxurious Harrington mansion? If, as he had read somewhere, every man's paradise was in a different place, his was undoubtedly here. He had reached it guided not by a map, charting rivers and valleys, but by kisses and caresses.

And it was a caress, this time an icy one on the nape of his neck, which drew his attention to the fact that nobody had taken the trouble to fix the broken window to the left of the door. What would have been the point? McCarthy belonged to that class of people whose motto was to work as little as possible, and had Andrew reproached him for not replacing the pane he would have argued that, since Mr Harrington had requested everything be kept just as it was, he had assumed that included the window glass. Andrew sighed. He could see nothing with which to plug the hole and decided to kill himself in his hat and coat.

He sat down on one of the rickety chairs, reached into his pocket for the gun and carefully unfolded the cloth, as if he were performing a sacrament. The Colt gleamed in the moonlight that filtered weakly through the small, grimy window.

He stroked the weapon as though it were a cat curled up in his lap and let Marie's smile wash over him once more. Andrew was always surprised that his memories retained the vibrancy, like fresh roses, of those first days. He remembered everything so vividly, as though no eight-year gap stretched between them, and at times his memories seemed even more beautiful than the real events. What mysterious alchemy could make these imitations appear more vivid than the real thing? The answer was obvious: the passage of time. It transformed the volatile present into a finished, unalterable painting called the past, a canvas that was always executed blindly, with erratic brushstrokes, and only made sense when one stepped far enough away to admire it as a whole.

II

The first time their eyes had met, she was not even there. Andrew had fallen in love with Marie without needing to have her in front of him, and to him this was as romantic as it was paradoxical. The event had occurred at his uncle's mansion in Queen's Gate, opposite the Natural History Museum, a place Andrew had always thought of as his second home. He and his cousin were the same age, and had almost grown up together; the servants sometimes forgot which of them was their employer's son.

As is easily imaginable, their affluent social position had spared them any hardship or misfortune, exposing them only to the pleasant side of life, which they immediately mistook for one long party where everything was apparently permissible. They moved on from sharing toys to sharing teenage conquests, and from there, curious to see how far they could stretch the impunity they enjoyed, to devising different ways of testing the limits of what was acceptable.

Their elaborate indiscretions and more or less immoral behaviour were so perfectly co-ordinated that for years it had been difficult not to see them as one person. This was partly down to their sharing the complicity of twins, but also to their arrogant approach to life and even to their physical similarity: both boys were lean and sinewy, and possessed angelic good looks that made it almost impossible to refuse them anything. This was especially true of women, as was amply demonstrated during their time at Cambridge, where they established a record number of conquests unmatched to this day.

Their habit of visiting the same tailors and hat-makers added the finishing touch to that unnerving resemblance, a likeness it seemed would last for ever, until one day, without warning, as though God had resolved to compensate for his lack of creativity, that wild, two-headed creature split into two distinct halves. Andrew turned into a pensive, taciturn young man, while Charles went on perfecting the frivolous behaviour of his adolescence. This change did not alter their friendship, which was rooted in kinship. Far from driving them apart, the unexpected divergence made them complement one another. Charles's devil-may-care attitude found its counterpart in the refined melancholy of his cousin, for whom such a whimsical approach to life was no longer satisfying.

Charles observed with a wry smile Andrew's attempts to give his life some meaning, wandering around in disillusionment, waiting for a flash of inspiration that never came. Andrew, in turn, was amused by his cousin's insistence on behaving like a brash, shallow youth, even though some of his gestures and opinions betrayed disappointment similar to his own. Charles lived intensely, as though he could not get enough of life's pleasures, while Andrew could sit alone for hours, watching a rose wilt in his hands.

The month of August when it all happened, they had both just turned eighteen, and although neither showed any sign of settling down, they sensed this life of leisure could not go on much longer, that soon their parents would lose patience with their unproductive indolence and find them positions in one of the family firms. In the meantime, though, they were enjoying seeing how much longer they could get away with it. Charles was already going to the office occasionally to attend to minor business, but Andrew preferred to wait until his boredom became so unbearable that taking care of family business would seem a relief rather than a prison sentence. After all, his older brother Anthony had already fulfilled their father's expectations sufficiently in this respect to allow the illustrious

William Harrington to consent to his second son pursuing his career of black sheep for a couple more years, provided he did not stray from his sight.

But Andrew had strayed. He had strayed a long way. And now he intended to stray even further, until he disappeared completely, beyond all redemption.

But let us not be sidetracked by melodrama. Let us carry on with our story. Andrew had dropped in at the Winslow mansion that August afternoon so that he and Charles could arrange a Sunday outing with the charming Keller sisters. As usual, they would take them to a little grassy knoll carpeted with flowers near the Serpentine, in Hyde Park, where they invariably mounted their amorous offensives. But Charles was still sleeping, so the butler showed Andrew into the library. He did not mind waiting there until his cousin got up; he felt at ease surrounded by the books that filled the large, bright room with their peculiar musty smell.

Andrew's father prided himself on having built up a decent library, yet his cousin's collection contained more than just obscure volumes on politics and other equally dull subjects. Here, Andrew could find the classics and adventure stories by authors such as Verne and Salgari, but still more interesting to him was a strange, rather picturesque type of literature many considered frivolous: novels in which the authors had let their imaginations run wild, regardless of how implausible or often downright absurd the outcome. Like all discerning readers, Charles appreciated Homer's *Odyssey* and his *Iliad*, but his real enjoyment came from immersing himself in the crazy world of *Batracomiomachia*, the blind poet's satire on his own work in an epic tale about a battle between mice and frogs. Andrew recalled a few books written in a similar style, which his cousin had lent him; one called *True Tales* by Luciano de Samósata, which recounted a series of fabulous voyages in a flying ship that takes the hero up to the sun and even through the belly of a giant whale; another called *The Man in the Moon* by Francis Godwin, the first novel ever to describe an interplanetary voyage. It told of a Spaniard named Domingo González who travels to the moon in a machine drawn by a flock of wild geese.

These flights of fancy reminded Andrew of pop guns or firecrackers, all sound and fury, yet he understood, or thought he did, why his cousin was so passionate about them. Somehow this literary genre, which most people condemned, acted as a sort of counterbalance to Charles's soul; it was the ballast that prevented him from lurching into seriousness or melancholy, unlike Andrew, to whom everything seemed so achingly profound, imbued with the absurd solemnity that the transience of existence conferred upon even the smallest act.

However, that afternoon, Andrew did not have time to look at any book. He did not even manage to cross the room to the bookshelves because the loveliest girl he had ever seen stopped him in his tracks. He stood staring at her, bemused, as time seemed to congeal, to stand still. Finally he managed to approach the portrait slowly to take a closer look. The woman was wearing a black velvet toque and a flowery scarf knotted at the neck. Andrew had to admit she was by no means conventionally beautiful: her nose was disproportionately large for her face, her eyes too close together and her reddish hair looked damaged, yet at the same time she possessed a charm as unmistakable as it was elusive. He was unsure exactly what about her captivated him. Perhaps it was the contrast between her fragile appearance and the strength that radiated from her gaze; a gaze he had never seen in any of his conquests. It was wild, determined, and retained a glimmer of youthful innocence, as if every day the woman was forced to confront the ugliness of life, and yet, curled up in her bed at night, still believed it a regrettable figment of her imagination, a bad dream that would dissolve and give way to a more pleasant reality. It was the gaze of a person who yearns for something and refuses to believe it will never be hers, because hope is all she has left.

'A charming creature, isn't she?' Charles's voice came from behind him.

Andrew jumped. He had been so absorbed in the portrait he

had not heard his cousin come in. He nodded as Charles walked over to the drinks cabinet. He himself could not have found a better way to describe the emotions the portrait had stirred in him, the desire to protect her mixed with the admiration he could only compare – rather reluctantly, owing to the inappropriateness of the metaphor – to that which he felt for cats.

'It was my birthday present to my father,' Charles explained, pouring brandy. 'It's only been hanging there a few days.'

'Who is she?' asked Andrew. 'I don't remember seeing her at any of Lady Holland or Lord Broughton's parties.'

'At those parties?' Charles laughed. 'I'm beginning to think the artist is gifted. He's taken you in as well.'

'What do you mean?' asked Andrew, accepting the glass his cousin was holding out to him.

'Surely you don't think I gave it to my father because of its artistic merit? Does it look like a painting worthy of my consideration, cousin?' Charles grabbed his arm, forcing him to move a few steps closer to the portrait. 'Take a good look. Notice the brushwork: utterly devoid of talent. The painter is no more than an amusing disciple of Degas. Where the Parisian is gentle, he is starkly sombre.'

Andrew did not understand enough about painting to discuss it with his cousin, and all he really wanted to know was the sitter's identity, so he nodded gravely, giving his cousin to understand he agreed with his view that the artist would do better to devote himself to repairing bicycles. Charles smiled, amused by his cousin's refusal to converse about painting – it would have given Charles a chance to air his knowledge – and declared: 'I had another reason for giving it to him, dear cousin.'

He drained his glass slowly, and gazed at the picture, shaking his head with satisfaction.

'And what reason was that, Charles?' Andrew asked, becoming impatient.

'The private enjoyment I get from knowing that my father, who looks down on the lower classes, has the portrait of a common prostitute hanging in his library.'

His words made Andrew reel. 'A p-p-prostitute?' he stammered.

'Yes, cousin,' replied Charles, beaming with content. 'But not a high-class whore from the brothels in Russell Square, or even one of the tarts who ply their trade in the park on Vincent Street, but a dirty, foul-smelling draggletail from Whitechapel upon whose ravaged loins the wretched of the earth alleviate their misery for a few meagre pennies.'

Andrew took a swig of brandy. There was no denying that his cousin's revelation had shocked him, as it would anybody who saw the portrait, but he also felt strangely disappointed. He stared at the painting again, trying to discover the cause of his unease. So, this lovely creature was a vulgar tart. Now he understood the mixture of passion and resentment that the artist had so skilfully captured in her eyes. But Andrew had to admit his disappointment related to a far more selfish logic: the woman did not belong to his social class, which meant he could never meet her.

'I bought it thanks to Bruce Driscoll,' Charles explained, pouring more brandy for them both. 'Do you remember him?'

Andrew nodded unenthusiastically. Bruce was a friend of his cousin whom boredom and money had made an art collector; a conceited, idle young man who had no compunction in showing off his knowledge of painting at every opportunity.

'You know how he likes to search for treasure in the most unlikely places,' his cousin said, handing him his glass. 'Well, the last time I saw him, he told me about a painter he'd dug up during one of his visits to the flea markets. A man called Walter Sickert, a founding member of the New English Art Club. His studio was in Cleveland Street, and he painted East End prostitutes as though they were society ladies. I dropped in there and couldn't resist his latest canvas.'

'Did he tell you anything about her?' Andrew asked, trying to appear nonchalant.

'About the whore? Only her name. I think she's called Marie Jeanette.'

'Marie Jeanette,' Andrew murmured. The name suited her, like her little hat. 'A Whitechapel whore . . .' he whispered, still unable to get over his surprise.

'Yes, a Whitechapel whore. And my father has given her pride of place in his library!' Charles spread his arms theatrically in a mock-triumphant gesture. 'Isn't it absolutely priceless?'

With this, Charles flung his arm around his cousin's shoulders and guided him to the sitting room. Andrew tried to hide his agitation, but could not help thinking about the girl in the portrait as they planned their assault on the charming Keller sisters.

That night, in his bedroom, Andrew lay awake. Where was the woman in the painting now? What was she doing? By the fourth or fifth question he had begun calling her by her name, as though he really knew her and they enjoyed a non-existent intimacy. He realised he was seriously disturbed when he began to feel an absurd jealousy towards the men who could have her for a few pennies when to him, despite his wealth, she was unattainable. And yet was she really beyond his reach? Surely, given his position, he could have her, physically at least, more easily than he could any other woman, and for the rest of his life. The problem was finding her.

Andrew had never been to Whitechapel, but he had heard enough about it to know it was dangerous, especially for someone of his class. It was not advisable to go there alone, but he could not count on Charles accompanying him. His cousin would not understand him preferring a tart's grubby charms to what the delightful Keller sisters kept hidden beneath their petticoats, or the perfumed honey-pots of the Chelsea madams with whom well-to-do West End gentlemen sated their appetites. Perhaps he would understand, and even agree to go with him for the fun of it, if Andrew explained it as a passing fancy, but what he felt was too powerful to be reduced to a mere whim.

Or was it? He would not know what he wanted from her until he had her in his arms. Would she really be so difficult to find? Three sleepless nights were enough for him to come up with a plan.

And so it was that while the Crystal Palace (which had been

moved to Sydenham after displaying the Empire's industrial prowess) offered organ recitals, children's ballets, ventriloquists' acts and the possibility of picnicking in its gardens with dinosaurs, iguanodons and megatheriums reconstructed from fossils found in the Sussex Weald, and Madame Tussaud's deprived its visitors of sleep with its famous Chamber of Horrors (in which madmen, cutthroats and poisoners huddled at the foot of the guillotine that had beheaded Marie-Antoinette), Andrew Harrington – oblivious to the festive spirit that had taken hold of the city – put on the humble clothes one of his servants had lent him, and examined his disguise in the cheval glass. He gave a wry smile at the sight of himself in a threadbare jacket and trousers, his fair hair tucked under a checked cap pulled low over his eyes. Surely, looking like that, people would take him for a nobody, possibly a cobbler or a barber.

Disguised in this way, he ordered the astonished Harold Barker to take him to Whitechapel. Before leaving, he made him swear to secrecy. No one must know about his expedition to London's worst neighbourhood, not his father, not the mistress of the house, not his brother Anthony, not even his cousin Charles. No one.

III

In order not to draw attention to himself, Andrew made Harold pull up the luxurious carriage in Leadenhall, and continued alone on foot towards Commercial Street. After wandering a good way down that evil-smelling thoroughfare, he plucked up his courage and entered the maze of alleyways that made up Whitechapel. Within ten minutes, a dozen prostitutes loomed out of the fog to offer him a trip to Mount Venus for the price of a few pennies, but none was the girl in the portrait. Had they been draped in seaweed, Andrew might easily have mistaken them for faded, dirty ship's figureheads. He refused them politely, a dreadful sadness welling up in him at the sight of those scarecrows, hunched against the cold, who had no better way to earn a living. Their toothless mouths, attempting bawdy smiles, were more repulsive than desirable. Would Marie look like that outside the portrait, far from the brushstrokes that had transformed her into an angel?

He soon realised he was unlikely to find her by chance. Perhaps he would have more luck if he asked for her directly. Once he was sure his disguise was convincing, he entered the Ten Bells, a popular tavern on the corner of Fournier Street and Commercial Street, opposite the ghostly Christ Church. When he peered inside the pub, it looked to him the sort of place whores would go in search of clients. As soon as he reached the bar, two came up to him.

Trying to seem casual, Andrew refused their propositions as politely as he could and offered them a glass of stout. He explained he was looking for a woman called Marie Jeanette. One of the whores left immediately, pretending to be offended, but the other, the taller of the two, accepted a drink. 'I suppose you mean Marie Kelly,' she said. 'That dratted Irishwoman, everybody wants her. I expect she's done a few by now and is in the Britannia – that's where we all go when we've made enough for a bed and a bit more besides so that we can get drunk quick and forget our sorrows.' She spoke with more irony than bitterness.

'Where is this tavern?' Andrew asked.

'Near here, on the corner of Crispin Street and Dorset Street.'

The least Andrew could do was thank her for the information by giving her four shillings. 'Get yourself a room,' he recommended, with a smile. 'It's too cold out there tonight to be traipsing the streets.'

'Why, thank you, mister. You're too kind, I'm sure,' said the whore, genuinely grateful.

Andrew said goodbye, politely doffing his cap.

'If Marie Kelly won't give you what you want, come back and see me,' she added, with a flash of coquettishness that was blighted by her toothless smile. 'My name's Liz – Liz Stride. Don't forget.'

Andrew had no problem finding the Britannia, a seedy bar with a windowed front. The room was brilliantly lit by oil lamps and thick with tobacco smoke. At the far end there was a long bar, with a couple of private rooms to the left. A crowd of noisy customers filled the large main area, which was cluttered with tables and chairs, the floor strewn with sawdust. A fleet of bartenders in filthy aprons squeezed their way between tightly packed tables, juggling metal tankards brimming with beer. In the corner, a battered old piano displayed its grubby keys to anyone wishing to enliven the evening with a tune.

Andrew reached the bar, which was laden with large jugs of wine, oil lamps and plates of cheese cut into huge chunks – they looked like bits of rubble from a tip. He lit a cigarette from one of the lamps, ordered a pint of beer, and leaned discreetly against the bar, surveying the crowd and wrinkling his nose at the strong smell of sausage that emanated from the kitchen. As he had been told, the atmosphere was more convivial than it had been at the Ten Bells. Most of the tables were occupied by sailors on shore leave and local people dressed as modestly as he, although he also noticed a few groups of prostitutes busy getting drunk. He sipped his beer slowly and looked for one who fitted Marie Kelly's description, but none did.

By his third beer, he had begun to despair, and wondered what on earth he was doing there, chasing an illusion. He was about to leave when she pushed her way through the pub door. He recognised her at once. There was no doubt about it: she was the girl in the portrait, but more beautiful still for being endowed with movement. Her face looked drained, yet she moved with the energy Andrew had imagined from seeing her on canvas. Most of the other customers remained oblivious to her. How was it possible for anyone not to react to the small miracle that had just taken place in front of them? Their complete indifference made him feel he was a privileged witness to the phenomenon.

He recalled when, as a child, he had seen the wind take a leaf between invisible fingers and balance its tip on the surface of a puddle, spinning it like a top until a carriage wheel had put an end to its dance. To Andrew, it had seemed Mother Nature had engineered that magic trick for his eyes alone. From then on he was convinced that the universe dazzled mankind with volcanic eruptions, but had its own secret way of communicating with the select few, people like himself, who looked at reality as though it were a strip of wallpaper covering something else. Taken aback, he watched Marie Kelly walk towards him as if she knew him. His heart started to pound. He calmed a little when she propped her elbow on the bar and ordered half a pint of beer without glancing at him.

'Having a good night, Marie?'

'Can't grumble, Mrs Ringer.'

Andrew was on the verge of blacking out. She was standing next to him! He could scarcely believe it, yet it was true. He had heard her voice. A tired, rather husky voice, but lovely in any case. And if he really tried, ignoring the stench of tobacco smoke and sausages, he could probably smell her, too. Smell Marie Kelly. Mesmerised, Andrew gazed at her, rediscovering in her every gesture what he already knew. In the same way that a shell holds the roar of the sea so this fragile body seemed to contain within it a force of nature.

When the landlady placed the beer on the counter, Andrew realised this was an opportunity he must not waste. He rummaged swiftly in his pockets and paid before she could. 'Allow me, miss.'

The gesture, as unexpected as it was chivalrous, earned him an openly approving look from Marie Kelly. He was paralysed. As the painting had already shown, the girl's eyes were beautiful, yet they seemed buried beneath a layer of resentment. He could not help comparing her to a poppy field where someone had decided to dump refuse. And yet he was completely, hopelessly enthralled by her, and he tried to make the instant at which their eyes met as meaningful to her as it was to him, but – my apologies to any romantic souls reading these lines – some things cannot be expressed in a look.

How could Andrew make her share in the almost mystical feeling overwhelming him? How could he convey, with nothing more than his eyes, the sudden knowledge that he had been searching for her all his life without knowing it? If in addition we consider that Marie Kelly's existence up to that point had done little to increase her understanding of life's subtleties, it should come as no surprise that this initial attempt at spiritual communion (for want of a better way of putting it) was doomed to failure. Andrew did his best, obviously, but the girl understood his passionate gaze just as she interpreted that of the other men who accosted her every evening.

'Thanks, mister,' she replied, with a lewd smile, no doubt from force of habit.

Andrew nodded, dismissing the significance of a gesture he considered an all-important part of his strategy, then realised with horror that his careful plan had not taken into account how he was to strike up a conversation with the girl once he found her. What did he have to say to her? Or, more precisely, what did he have to say to a whore? A Whitechapel whore, at that. He had never bothered speaking much to the Chelsea prostitutes, only enough to discuss positions or the lighting in the room, and with the charming Keller sisters, or his other female acquaintances – young ladies whom it would not do to worry with talk of politics or Darwin's theories – he only discussed trivia: Paris fashions, botany and, more recently, spiritualism, the latest craze. But none of these subjects seemed suitable to embark on with this woman, who was unlikely to want to summon some spirit to tell her which of her many suitors she would marry. So he simply stared at her, enraptured.

Luckily, Marie Kelly knew a better way of breaking the ice. 'I know what you want, mister, although you're too shy to ask,' she said, her grin broadening as she gave his hand a fugitive caress. It brought him out in goose pimples. 'Thruppence, and I can make your dreams come true. Tonight, at any rate.'

Andrew was shaken: she did not know how right she was. She had been his only dream the past few nights, his deepest longing, his most urgent desire, and now, although he was still scarcely able to believe it, he could have her. His whole body tingled with excitement at the mere thought of touching her, of caressing the slender body silhouetted beneath the shabby dress, of bringing forth moans from her lips as he was set alight by her eyes, those of a wild animal, a tormented, indomitable creature. That tremor of joy rapidly gave way to a profound sadness when he considered the unjust plight of the fallen angel, the ease with which any man could grope her, defile her in a filthy back alley, without anyone in the world uttering a cry of protest. Was that what such a unique creature had been created for?

He had no choice but to accept her invitation, a lump in his throat, distressed at being compelled to take her in the same way as her other clients, as if his intentions were no different from theirs.

Once he had accepted, Marie Kelly smiled with what looked to

Andrew like forced enthusiasm, and tilted her head for them to leave the pub.

Andrew felt odd following the whore, walking behind her with bird-like steps as though Marie Kelly were leading him to the gallows instead of to plunge between her thighs. But could their meeting have been any different? From the moment he had come across his cousin's painting he had been penetrating deeper into unknown territory, where he could not get his bearings because nothing around him was familiar. Everything was new and, to judge from the deserted streets they were going through, quite possibly dangerous. Was he blithely walking into a trap laid by the whore's pimp? He wondered whether Harold would hear his shouts and, if so, if he would bother coming to his aid, or use the opportunity to avenge himself for the offhand treatment he had received from his master all these years.

After guiding him along Hanbury Street, a muddy alley dimly lit by a single oil-lamp sputtering on a corner, Marie Kelly beckoned him down a narrow passageway leading into pitch darkness. Andrew followed her, convinced he would meet his death, or at least be beaten to within an inch of his life by a couple of ruffians much bigger than him who, having stolen everything including his socks, would spit contemptuously on his bloody remains. That was how they did things here, and his idiotic adventure richly deserved such an ending. But before fear had time to take hold, they came out into a filthy, water-logged backyard where, to his surprise, no one was waiting for him.

Andrew glanced warily about him. Yes: strange as it might seem, they were alone in that evil-smelling place. The world they had left behind was reduced to a muffled rumble in which a distant church bell's chimes rang out. At his feet the moon, reflected in a puddle, looked like a crumpled letter some unhappy lover had tossed on the ground.

'We won't be disturbed here, mister,' Marie Kelly reassured him, leaning back against the wall and drawing him to her.

Before he knew it, she had unbuttoned his trousers and pulled out his manhood. She did so with startling ease, without any of the provocative foreplay to which the Chelsea prostitutes had accustomed him. The matter-of-fact way in which she manoeuvred his sex beneath her hiked-up skirts made it clear to Andrew that what to him was another magical moment was to her no more than routine.

'It's in,' she assured him.

In? Andrew had enough experience to know the whore was lying. She was simply gripping him between her thighs. He assumed it was common practice among them, a trick to avoid penetration, which, if they were lucky and the client failed to notice or was too drunk, reduced the number of hasty intrusions they were forced to undergo each day, and with them the unwanted pregnancies that such might bring about. With this in mind, he began to thrust energetically, prepared to go along with the charade.

It was enough for him to rub himself against the silky skin of her inner thigh, to feel her body pressed against his for as long as the pretence lasted. What did it matter whether it was a sham if this phantom penetration allowed him to cross the boundary imposed by good manners and force his way into the intimacy that only lovers share? Feeling her hot breath in his ear, inhaling the delicate odour of her neck and clasping her to him until he felt the contours of her body merge with his was worth infinitely more than thruppence. And, as he soon discovered when he ejaculated into her petticoats, it had the same effect on him as other, greater, undertakings. Slightly ashamed at his lack of endurance, he finished emptying himself in quiet contemplation, still pressed against her.

Eventually he felt her stir impatiently. He stepped back, embarrassed. Oblivious to his unease, the whore straightened her skirts and thrust out a hand to be paid. Trying to regain his composure, Andrew hurriedly gave her the agreed sum. He had enough money left in his pockets to buy her for the whole night, but he preferred to savour what he had just experienced in the privacy of his own bed, and to persuade her to meet him the next night.

'My name's Andrew,' he introduced himself, his voice high-pitched with emotion. She raised an eyebrow, amused. 'And I'd like to see you again tomorrow.'

'Certainly, mister. You know where to find me,' the whore said, leading him back along the gloomy passageway she had brought him down.

As they made their way towards the main streets, Andrew was wondering whether ejaculating between her thighs entitled him to put his arm around her shoulders. He had decided it did, and was about to do precisely that, when they ran into another couple walking almost blindly towards them down the dim alley. Andrew mumbled an apology to the fellow he had bumped into, who, although scarcely more than a shadow in the darkness, seemed quite a burly sort. He was clinging to a whore, whom Marie Kelly greeted with a smile.

'It's all yours, Annie,' she said, referring to the backyard she and Andrew had just left.

Annie thanked her with a raucous laugh and tugged her companion towards the passageway. Andrew watched them stagger into the blackness. Would that fellow be satisfied with having his member trapped between her thighs? he wondered. He had noticed how avidly the man clutched the whore to him.

'Didn't I tell you it was a quiet spot?' Marie Kelly remarked, as they came out into Hanbury Street.

They said a laconic goodbye in front of the Britannia. Rather disheartened by the coldness she had shown after the act, Andrew tried to find his way back through the gloomy streets to his carriage. It was a good half-hour before he came upon it. He avoided Harold's eyes as he climbed into the brougham.

'Home, sir?' Harold enquired sardonically.

The following night he arrived at the Britannia determined to behave like a self-assured man instead of the fumbling, timid dandy of his previous encounter. He had to overcome his nerves and prove he could adapt to his surroundings if he was to display his true charms to the girl, the repertoire of smiles and flattery with which he habitually captivated the ladies of his own class.

He found Marie Kelly sitting at a corner table, brooding over a pint of beer. Her demeanour unnerved him, but as he was not the sort to think up a new strategy as he went along, he decided to stick with his original plan. He ordered a beer at the bar, sat down at the girl's table, as naturally as he could, and told her he knew of a guaranteed way to wipe the worry from her face. Marie Kelly shot him a black look, confirming what he feared: he had made a tactless blunder. Andrew thought she was going to tell him to clear off with a simple wave of her hand, as if he were an irritating fly, but she restrained herself and gazed at him quizzically for a few seconds.

She must have decided he was as good a person as any to unburden herself to because she took a swig from her tankard, wiped her mouth on her sleeve, and told him that her friend Annie, the woman they had bumped into in Hanbury Street the night before, had been found that morning, murdered, in the same yard they had been in. The poor woman had been partially decapitated, sliced open, her intestines pulled out and her womb removed.

Andrew stammered that he was sorry, as shocked by the killer's attention to detail as he was to have collided with him moments before the crime. Evidently that particular client had not been satisfied with the usual service. But Marie Kelly had other concerns. According to her, Annie was the third prostitute in less than a month to be murdered in Whitechapel. Polly Nichols had been found dead with her throat slit in Bucks Road, opposite Essex Pier, on 31 August, and on the seventh of that month, Martha Tabram had been found brutally stabbed with a penknife on the stairs of a rooming house. Marie Kelly laid the blame on the gang from Old Nichol Street, blackmailers who demanded a share of the whores' earnings.

'Those bastards will stop at nothing to get us working for them,' she said, between gritted teeth.

This state of affairs disturbed Andrew, but it should have come as no surprise: after all, they were in Whitechapel – the putrid dung-heap upon which London had turned its back, home to more than a thousand prostitutes living alongside German, Jewish and French immigrants. Stabbings were a daily occurrence. Wiping away the tears that had finally flowed from her eyes, Marie Kelly sat, head bowed, as though in prayer, until, to Andrew's surprise, she roused herself from her stupor, grasped his hand and smiled lustfully at him. Whatever else happened, life went on. Was that what she had meant by her gesture? After all, she, Marie Kelly, had not been murdered. She had to go on living, dragging her skirts through those foul-smelling streets in search of money to pay for a bed.

Andrew gazed with pity at her hand lying in his, the dirty nails poking through the frayed mitten. He, too, felt the need to concentrate for a moment in order to change masks, like an actor who needs time in his dressing room to concentrate on becoming a different character. After all, life went on for him, too. Time did not stop because a whore had been murdered. He stroked her hand tenderly, ready to resume his plan. As though wiping condensation from a window pane, he freed his young lover's smile from its veil of sadness and, looking her in the eye for the first time, said: 'I have enough money to buy you for the whole night, but I don't want any fakery in a cold backyard.'

This startled Marie Kelly, and she tensed, but Andrew's smile soon put her at ease. 'I rent a room at Miller's Court, but I don't know as it'll be good enough for the likes of you,' she remarked flirtatiously.

'I'm sure you'll make me like it,' Andrew ventured, delighted at the bantering tone their conversation had taken – this was a register at which he excelled.

'But first I'll have to turn out my good-for-nothing husband,' she replied. 'He doesn't like me bringing work home.'

This remark came as yet another shock to Andrew on an extraordinary night over which he clearly had no control. He tried not to let his disappointment show.

'Still, I'm sure your money will make up his mind for him,' Marie concluded.

* * *

So it was that Andrew found paradise in the dismal little room where he was now sitting. That night, everything had changed between them. When at last she lay naked, Andrew made love to her so respectfully, caressing her with such tenderness, that Marie Kelly could feel the hard shell she had carefully built around her begin to crack. To her surprise, Andrew's kisses, marking her body like a pleasurable itch, made her own caresses less mechanical, and she quickly discovered she was no longer a whore lying on the bed, but the woman crying out for affection that she had always been. Andrew also sensed his love-making was freeing the real Marie Kelly, as though he were rescuing her from one of the water tanks in which stage magicians immersed their beautiful assistants, bound hand and foot, or as though his sense of direction had saved him from getting lost in the maze, like her other lovers, allowing him to reach a secret corner where the girl's true nature survived intact.

They burned with a single flame, and when it waned, and Marie Kelly began to talk about springtime in Paris, where she had worked as an artist's model, and about her childhood in Wales and on Ratcliffe Highway in London, Andrew understood that the strange sensation in his chest must be the pangs of love: he was experiencing all the emotions of which the poets spoke.

He was touched by the tone her voice took on when she described the Parisian squares with their riot of gladioli and petunias, and how on her return to London she had insisted everybody say her name in French, the only way she had found of preserving intact the distant fragrance that softened life's sharp edges. He was equally moved by the hint of sadness in her voice as she described how they had hanged pirates from the Ratcliffe Highway Bridge until they drowned in the rising waters of the Thames. This was the real Marie Kelly, this bitter-sweet fruit, nature's flawed perfection, one of God's contradictions.

When she asked what work he did that could apparently allow him to buy her for the rest of his life, he decided to risk telling her the truth. If their love were to exist it must be nurtured in truth or not at all, and the truth (of how her portrait had sent him on his foolish quest to find her in a neighbourhood so different from his own) seemed as beautiful and miraculous to him as those stories about impossible love you read of in books. When their bodies came together again, he realised that, far from being an act of madness, falling in love with her was possibly the most reasonable thing he had ever done. And when he left the room, with the memory of her skin on his lips, he tried not to look at her husband, Joe, who was leaning against the wall, shivering with cold.

It was nearly daylight when Harold delivered him home. Too excited to go to bed, if only to relish the moments he had spent with Marie Kelly, Andrew went to the stables and saddled a horse. It was a long time since he had woken at dawn to go riding in Hyde Park. This was his favourite time of day, when the grass was still dewy and everything appeared untouched. How could he waste such an opportunity? Within minutes, he was galloping through the trees opposite the Harrington mansion, laughing to himself and occasionally letting out a cry of joy, like a soldier celebrating victory, because that was how he felt, remembering the loving look she had given him before they had said goodbye until the following night. It was as though she could see in his eyes that, unwittingly, he had been searching for her for years – and perhaps I should take this opportunity to apologise for my earlier scepticism and confess that there is nothing that cannot be expressed in a look. A look, it seems, is a bottomless well of possibilities.

And so Andrew rode on, seized by a wild impulse, overwhelmed by a burning, pulsating sensation that might reasonably be described as happiness. Prey to the effects of such a violent infatuation, everything he rode past appeared to sparkle, as though each of its elements – the paths strewn with dead leaves, the rocks, the trees, even the squirrels leaping from branch to branch – were lit by an inner glow.

But, have no fear, I shall not become bogged down in lengthy descriptions of practically luminous parkland, because not only do I have no taste for it but it would be untrue. Despite Andrew's altered vision, the landscape clearly did not undergo any transformation, not even the squirrels, which are well known as creatures that pursue their own interests.

After more than an hour of strenuous, exhilarating riding, Andrew remembered he had a whole day to get through before he could return to Marie Kelly's humble bed, and must find some way of distracting himself from the dreadful feeling that would assail him when he realised that the hands of the clock were not turning at their usual speed but were actually slowing down on purpose. He decided to drop in on his cousin Charles, which he usually did when he wanted him to share in his joy, even though this time he had no intention of telling him anything. Perhaps he was simply curious to see what Charles would look like to his feverish gaze, which had the power to enhance everything. Would he glow, like the squirrels in the park?

IV

Breakfast had been laid out in the Winslow dining room for young Charles, who was doubtless still lazing in bed. On a table next to the French windows, the servants had set out a dozen covered platters, bread rolls, jams and marmalades, and several jugs brimming with grapefruit juice and milk. Most of it would be thrown away because, contrary to appearance, they were not expecting a regiment, only Andrew, who, given his famous lack of appetite in the mornings, would almost certainly be content to nibble at a roll, ignoring the extravagant spread displayed in his honour.

Andrew was surprised by the sudden concern he felt at such waste. He had spent years contemplating tables like this, creaking under the weight of food no one would eat. This curious response was the first of many that would result from his forays into Whitechapel, inhabited by people capable of killing one another for a half-eaten roll. Would his experiences there stir his conscience as they had his emotions? He was the type of person whose cultivation of his inner life left little time for worrying about the outside world of the street. He was above all devoted to resolving the mystery that was himself, to studying his feelings and responses: all his time was taken up in attempting to fine-tune the instrument that was his spirit until he felt satisfied with the sound it produced.

There were times, owing to the constantly changing and rather unpredictable nature of his thought patterns, when this task appeared as impossible to him as lining up the goldfish in their bowl, but until he succeeded he sensed he would be unable to worry about what went on in the world, which for him started where his own pleasant, carefully scrutinised private concerns ended. In any case, he thought, it would be interesting to observe in himself how hitherto unknown preoccupations emerged through simple exposure. Who could tell? Perhaps his response to these new worries might hold the key to the mystery of who the real Andrew Harrington was.

He took an apple from the fruit bowl and settled into an armchair to wait yet again for his cousin to return to the land of the living. He had rested his muddy boots on a footstool and was smiling as he remembered Marie Kelly's kisses and how they had both, gently but completely, made up for all the years they had been starved of affection, when his eye alighted on the newspaper lying on the table. It was the morning edition of the *Star*, announcing in bold print the murder of a Whitechapel prostitute called Anne Chapman. It gave details of the horrific mutilation she had suffered: besides her uterus, which he had already learned about from Marie Kelly, her bladder and womb had also been removed. Among other things, the newspaper also mentioned a couple of cheap rings missing from one of her fingers. It appeared the police had no clues as to the murderer's identity although, after questioning other East End whores, the name of a possible suspect had emerged: a Jewish cobbler nicknamed Leather Apron, who was in the habit of robbing prostitutes at knife point. The article came with a macabre illustration of a policeman dangling a lamp over the bloody corpse of a woman sprawled on the pavement.

Andrew shook his head. He had forgotten that his paradise was surrounded by hell itself, and that the woman he loved was an angel trapped in a world full of demons.

He closely read the three-page report on the Whitechapel crimes committed to date, feeling worlds away from it all in this luxurious dining room, where man's capacity for baseness and aberration was kept at bay as surely as the dust tirelessly polished away by servants. He had thought of giving Marie Kelly the money to pay off the gang of blackmailers she thought were responsible for the crimes, but the report did not seem to be pointing in that direction. The precise incisions on the bodies suggested that the killer had surgical knowledge, which implicated the entire medical profession, although the police had not ruled out furriers, cooks and barbers – anyone, in short, whose job brought them into contact with knives.

Queen Victoria's medium was reported to have seen the killer's face in a dream. Andrew sighed. The medium knew more about the killer than he, even though he had bumped into the fellow moments before he had committed the crime.

'Since when did you develop an interest in the affairs of empire, cousin?' asked Charles's voice from behind him. 'Ah, no – I see you are reading the crime pages.'

'Good morning, Charles,' said Andrew, tossing the paper on to the table as though he had been idly leafing through it.

'The coverage given to the murders of those wretched tarts is incredible,' his cousin remarked, plucking a cluster of shiny grapes from the fruit bowl and sitting in the armchair opposite. 'Although I confess to being intrigued by the importance they're attaching to this sordid affair: they've put Scotland Yard's finest detective, Fred Abberline, in charge of the investigation. Clearly the Metropolitan Police are out of their depth in a case like this.'

Andrew pretended to agree, nodding abstractedly as he gazed out of the window, watching the wind scatter an air-balloon-shaped cloud. He did not want to arouse his cousin's attention by showing too much interest in the affair, but the truth was he longed to know every detail of the crimes, apparently confined to the area where his beloved lived. How would his cousin react if he told him he had bumped into that brutal murderer in a murky Whitechapel alleyway? The sad fact was that, even so, he was unable to describe the fellow except to say he was enormous and evil-smelling.

'In any case, regardless of Scotland Yard's involvement, all they have are suspicions, some of them quite preposterous,' his cousin went on, plucking a grape from the bunch and rolling it between his fingers. 'Did you know they suspect one of the Red Indians from that Buffalo Bill show we saw last week, and even the actor Richard Mansfield, who is playing in *Strange Case of Doctor Jekyll and Mr Hyde* at the Lyceum? I recommend it, by the way: Mansfield's transformation on stage is truly chilling.'

Andrew promised he would go, tossing the remains of his apple on to the table.

'Anyway,' Charles concluded rather wearily, 'the poor wretches in Whitechapel have formed vigilante groups and are patrolling the streets. It seems London's population is growing so fast the police force can no longer cope. Everybody wants to live in this accursed city. People come here from all over the country in search of a better life, only to end up being exploited in factories, contracting typhus fever or turning to crime in order to pay an inflated rent for a cellar or some other airless hole. Actually, I'm amazed there aren't more murders and robberies, considering how many go unpunished. Mark my words, Andrew, if the criminals became organised, London would be theirs. It's hardly surprising Queen Victoria fears a popular uprising – a revolution like the one our French neighbours endured, which would end with her and her family's heads on the block. Her empire is a hollow façade that needs progressively shoring up to stop it collapsing. Our cows and sheep graze on Argentinian pastures, our tea is grown in China and India, our gold comes from South Africa and Australia, and the wine we drink from France and Spain. Tell me, cousin, what, apart from crime, do we produce ourselves? If the criminal elements planned a proper rebellion they could take over the country. Fortunately, evil and common sense rarely go hand in hand.'

Andrew liked listening to Charles ramble in this relaxed way, pretending not to take himself seriously. He admired his cousin's contradictory spirit, which reminded him of a house divided into endless chambers all separate from one another, so that what went on in one had no repercussions in the others. This explained why his cousin was able to glimpse, amid his luxurious surroundings, the most suppurating wounds and forget them a moment later, while he found it impossible to copulate successfully after a visit to a slaughterhouse or a hospital for the severely injured. It was as if Andrew had been designed like a seashell: everything disappeared and resonated inside him. That was the basic difference between them: Charles reasoned and he felt.

'The truth is, these sordid crimes are turning Whitechapel into a place where you wouldn't want to spend the night,' Charles declared sententiously, abandoning his nonchalance to lean across the table and stare meaningfully at his cousin. 'Especially with a tart.'

Andrew gaped at him. 'You know about it?'

His cousin smiled. 'Servants talk, Andrew. You ought to know by now our most intimate secrets circulate like underground streams beneath the luxurious ground we walk on,' he said, stamping his feet symbolically on the carpet.

Andrew sighed. His cousin had not left the newspaper there by accident. In fact, he had probably not even been asleep. Charles enjoyed this kind of game. It was easy to imagine him hiding behind one of the many screens that partitioned the vast dining room, waiting patiently for his stunned cousin to fall into the trap he had laid.

'I don't want my father to find out, Charles,' begged Andrew.

'Don't worry, cousin. I'm aware of the scandal it would cause in the family. But tell me, are you in love with the girl or is this just a passing fancy?'

Andrew remained silent. What could he say?

'You needn't reply,' his cousin said, in a resigned voice. 'I'm afraid I wouldn't understand either way. I only hope you know what you're doing.'

Andrew, of course, did not know what he was doing, but could not stop doing it. Each night, like a moth drawn to the flame, he returned to the miserable room in Miller's Court, hurling himself into the relentless blaze of Marie Kelly's passion. They made love all night, driven by frantic desire, as though they had been poisoned during dinner and did not know how long they had left to live, or as though the world around them were being decimated by the plague. Soon Andrew understood that if he left enough coins on her bedside table, their passion could continue gently smouldering beyond the dawn. His money preserved their fantasy, and even banished Joe, Marie Kelly's husband, whom Andrew tried not to think of when, disguised in his modest clothes, he strolled with her through the maze of muddy streets.

Those were peaceful, pleasant walks, full of encounters with the girl's friends and acquaintances, the long-suffering foot-soldiers of a war without trenches; a bunch of poor souls who rose from their beds each morning to face a hostile world, driven on by the sheer animal instinct for survival. Fascinated, Andrew found himself admiring them, as he would a species of exotic flower alien to his world. He became convinced that life in Whitechapel was more real, simpler, easier to understand than it was in the luxuriously carpeted mansions where he spent his days.

Occasionally, he had to pull his cap down over his eyes in order not to be recognised by the bands of wealthy young men who laid siege to the neighbourhood some nights. They arrived in luxurious carriages and mobbed the streets, like rude, arrogant conquistadors, in search of some miserable brothel where they could satisfy their basest instincts for, according to a rumour Andrew had frequently heard in West End smoking clubs, the only limits on what could be done with the wretched Whitechapel tarts were money and imagination. Watching these boisterous incursions, Andrew was assailed by a sudden protective instinct, which could only mean he had unconsciously begun to see Whitechapel as a place he should perhaps watch over. However, there was little he could do, confronted with those barbarous invasions, besides feeling sad and helpless, and trying to forget about them in the arms of his beloved. She appeared more beautiful to him by the day, as though beneath his caresses she had recovered the innate sparkle of which life had robbed her.

But, as everyone knows, no paradise is complete without a serpent, and the sweeter the moments spent with his beloved, the more bitter the taste in Andrew's mouth when he recalled that what he had of Marie Kelly was all he could ever have. Because, although it was never enough and each day he yearned for more, the love that could not exist outside Whitechapel, for all its undeniable intensity, remained arbitrary and illusory. And while outside a crazed mob tried to lynch the Jewish cobbler nicknamed Leather Apron, Andrew quenched his anger and fear in Marie Kelly's body.

He wondered whether his beloved's fervour sprang from her own realisation that they had embarked upon a reckless love affair, and that all they could do was greedily clasp the unexpected rose of happiness as they tried to ignore the painful thorns. Or was it her way of telling him she was prepared to rescue their apparently doomed love even if it meant altering the very course of the universe? And if that was the case, did he possess the same strength? Did he have the necessary conviction to embark upon what he already considered a lost battle?

However hard he tried, Andrew could not imagine Marie Kelly moving in his world of refined young ladies, whose sole purpose in life was to display their fecundity by filling their houses with children, and to entertain their spouses' friends with their pianistic accomplishment. Would Marie Kelly succeed in fulfilling this role while trying to stay afloat amid the waves of social rejection that would doubtless seek to drown her, or would she perish like an exotic bloom removed from its hothouse?

The newspapers' continued coverage of the whores' murders scarcely managed to distract Andrew from the torment of his secret fears. One morning, while breakfasting, he came across a reproduction of a letter the murderer had audaciously sent to the Central News Agency, assuring the police they would not catch him easily and promising he would carry on killing, testing his fine blade on the

Whitechapel tarts. Appropriately enough, the letter was written in red ink and signed 'Jack the Ripper', a name that, however you looked at it, Andrew thought, was far more disturbing and imaginative than the rather dull 'Whitechapel Murderer' by which he had been known until then.

The new name was taken up by all the newspapers, and inevitably conjured up the villain of the penny dreadfuls, Spring Heeled Jack, and his treatment of women. It was rapidly adopted by everyone, as Andrew soon discovered from hearing it uttered everywhere he went. The words were always spoken with sinister excitement, as though for the sad souls of Whitechapel there was something thrilling and even fashionable about a ruthless murderer stalking the neighbourhood with a razor-sharp knife. Furthermore, as a result of this disturbing missive, Scotland Yard was deluged with similar correspondence (in which the alleged killer mocked the police, boasted childishly about his crimes and promised more murders). Andrew had the impression that England was teeming with people desperate to bring excitement into their lives by pretending they were murderers, normal men whose souls were sullied by sadistic impulses and unhealthy desires that fortunately they would never act upon.

Besides hampering the police investigation, the letters also transformed the vulgar individual he had bumped into in Hanbury Street into a monstrous creature apparently destined to personify man's most primitive fears. Perhaps this uncontrolled proliferation of would-be perpetrators of his macabre crimes prompted the real killer to surpass himself. On the night of 30 September, at the timber merchants' in Dutfield Yard, he murdered Elizabeth Stride – the whore who had originally put Andrew on Marie's trail – and a few hours later, in Mitre Square, Catherine Eddowes, whom he had time to rip open from pubis to sternum, remove her left kidney and even cut off her nose.

Thus began the cold month of October, in which a veil of gloomy resignation descended upon the inhabitants of Whitechapel who, despite Scotland Yard's efforts, felt more than ever abandoned to their fate. There was a look of helplessness in the whores' eyes, but also a strange acceptance of their dreadful lot. Life became a long and anxious wait, during which Andrew held Marie Kelly's trembling body tightly in his arms and whispered to her that she need not worry, provided she stayed away from the Ripper's hunting ground, the area of backyards and deserted alleyways where he roamed with his thirsty blade, until the police managed to catch him.

But his words did nothing to calm a shaken Marie, who had even begun sheltering other whores in her tiny room at Miller's Court to keep them off the unsafe streets. It resulted in her having a fight with her husband, Joe, during which he broke a window. The following night, Andrew gave her the money to fix the glass and keep out the piercing cold. However, she simply placed it on her bedside table and lay back dutifully on the bed so that he could take her. Now though all she offered him was a body, a dying flame, and the grief-stricken despair she had been unable to keep from her eyes in recent days, a look in which he thought he glimpsed a desperate cry for help, a silent appeal to him to take her away before it was too late.

Andrew made the mistake of pretending not to notice her distress, as though he had forgotten that everything could be expressed in a look. He felt incapable of altering the very course of the universe, which for him translated into the even more momentous feat of confronting his father. Perhaps that was why, as a silent rebuke for his cowardice, she began to go out looking for clients and spending the nights getting drunk with her fellow whores in the Britannia. There they cursed the uselessness of the police and the power of the monster from hell who continued to mock them, most recently by sending George Lusk, socialist firebrand and self-proclaimed president of the Whitechapel Vigilance Committee, a cardboard box containing a human kidney.

Frustrated by his lack of courage, Andrew watched her return drunk each night to the little room. Then, before she could collapse on the floor or curl up like a dog beside the warm hearth, he would take her in his arms and put her to bed, grateful that no knife had stopped her in her tracks. But he knew she could not keep exposing herself to danger in this way, even if the murderer had not struck for several weeks and more than eighty policemen were patrolling the neighbourhood. He also knew he was the only one able to stop her. For that reason, sitting in the gloom while his beloved spun her drunken nightmares of corpses with their guts ripped out, Andrew would resolve to confront his father the very next day. But when the next day came all he could do was prowl around his father's study, not daring to go in. And when it grew dark, his head bowed in shame, occasionally clutching a bottle, he returned to Marie Kelly's little room, where she received him with her eyes' silent reproach.

Then Andrew remembered all the things he had said to her, the impassioned declarations he had hoped would seal their union. How he had been trying to find her for he did not know how long – eighteen, a hundred, five hundred years – how he knew that if he had undergone reincarnations he had looked for her in every one, because they were twin spirits destined to meet each other in the labyrinth of time, and other such pronouncements. Now he was sure Marie Kelly could only see his avowals as a pathetic attempt to cloak his animal urges in romanticism or, worse, to conceal the thrill he derived from those voyeuristic forays into the wretched side of existence. 'Where is your love now, Andrew?' her eyes seemed to ask, before she trudged off to the Britannia, only to return a few hours later rolling drunk.

Until, on that cold night of 7 November, Andrew watched her leave again for the tavern, and something inside him shifted. Whether it was the alcohol, which, consumed in the right quantity, can clear some people's heads, or simply that enough time had passed for this clarity to occur naturally, it finally dawned on him that without Marie Kelly his life would no longer have any meaning so he had nothing to lose by fighting for a future with her. Filled with resolve, suddenly able to breathe freely once more, he left the room, slamming the door resolutely, and strode off towards the place where Harold Barker waited while his master took his pleasure. The coachman was huddled like an owl on the seat, warming himself with a bottle of brandy.

That night his father was to discover his youngest son was in love with a whore.

V

Yes, I know that when I began this tale I promised there would be a fabulous time machine, and there will be. There will even be intrepid explorers and fierce native tribes – a must in any adventure story. But all in good time. Isn't it necessary at the start of any game to place all the pieces on their respective squares? Of course it is – so let me continue to set up the board, slowly but surely, by returning to young Andrew, who might have taken the opportunity of the long journey back to the Harrington mansion to sober up, but who chose instead to cloud his thoughts further by finishing the bottle he had in his pocket.

Ultimately, there was no point in confronting his father with a sound argument and reasoned thinking: he was sure that any civilised discussion of the matter would be impossible. He needed to dull his senses as much as he could, staying just sober enough not to be completely tongue-tied. There was no point in slipping back into the elegant clothes he always left judiciously in a bundle on the carriage seat.

That night there was no longer any need for secrecy. When they arrived at the mansion, Andrew stepped out of the carriage, asked Harold to stay where he was, and hurried into the house. The coachman watched in dismay as he ran up the steps in his rags, and wondered if he would hear Mr Harrington's shouts from where he sat.

Andrew had forgotten his father had a meeting with businessmen that night until he staggered into the library. A dozen men stood gaping at him in astonishment. This was not the situation he had anticipated, but he had too much alcohol in his blood to be put off. He searched for his father amid the array of dinner jackets, and finally found him by the fireplace, next to his brother Anthony. Glass in one hand, cigar in the other, both men looked him up and down. But his clothing was the least of it, as they would soon discover, thought Andrew, who in the end felt pleased to have an audience. Since he was about to stick his head in the noose, it was better to do so in front of witnesses than alone with his father in his study.

He cleared his throat loudly under the fixed gaze of the gathering, and said: 'Father, I've come here to tell you I'm in love.'

His words were followed by a heavy silence, broken only by an embarrassed cough here and there.

'Andrew, this is hardly a suitable moment to—' his father began, visibly irritated, before Andrew silenced him with a sudden gesture of his hand.

'I assure you, Father, this is as unsuitable a moment as any other,' he said, trying to keep his balance so he would not have to finish his bravura performance flat on his face.

His father bridled, but remained silent.

Andrew took a deep breath. The moment had come for him to destroy his life. 'And the woman who has stolen my heart,' he declared, 'is a Whitechapel whore by the name of Marie Kelly.'

Having unburdened himself, he smiled defiantly at the gathering. Faces fell, heads were clutched in hands, arms flapped in the air, but no one said a word: they all knew they were witnessing a melodrama with two protagonists and, of course, that William Harrington must speak. All eyes were fixed on the host.

Staring at the pattern on the carpet, his father shook his head, let out a low, barely repressed growl, and put down his glass on the mantelpiece, as though it were suddenly encumbering him.

'Contrary to what I've heard you maintain, gentlemen,' Andrew went on, unaware of the rage stirring in his father's breast, 'whores aren't whores because they want to be. I assure you that any one of them would choose to have a respectable job if they could. Believe me, I know what I'm saying.' His father's colleagues continued to demonstrate their ability to express surprise without opening their mouths. 'I've spent a lot of time in their company, these past few weeks. I've watched them washing in horse-troughs in the mornings, seen them sitting down to sleep, held against the wall by a rope if they could not find a bed . . .'

The more he went on speaking in this way about prostitutes, the more Andrew realised his feelings for Marie Kelly were deeper than he had imagined. He gazed round with infinite pity at the men with their orderly lives, their dreary, passionless existences, who would consider it impractical to yield to a near-uncontrollable urge. He could tell them what it was like to lose one's head, to burn up with feverish desire. He could tell them what the inside of love looked like, because he had split it open like a piece of fruit.

But Andrew could not tell them this or anything else because at that moment his father, emitting enraged grunts, strode unsteadily across the room, almost harpooning the carpet with his cane. Without warning, he struck his son hard across the face. Andrew staggered backwards, stunned by the blow. When he finally understood what had happened, he rubbed his stinging cheek, trying to put on the same smile of defiance. For a few moments that seemed like eternity to those present, father and son stared at one another in the middle of the room, until William Harrington said: 'As of tonight I have only one son.'

Andrew tried not to show any emotion. 'As you wish,' he replied coldly. Then, to the guests, he made as if to bow. 'Gentlemen, my apologies, I must leave this place for ever.'

With as much dignity as he could muster, Andrew turned on his heel and left the room. The cold night air had a calming effect on him. In the end, he thought, trying not to trip as he descended the steps, nothing that had happened had come as a surprise. His disgraced father had just disinherited him, in front of half of

London's wealthiest businessmen, giving them a first-hand display of his famous temper, unleashed against his offspring without the slightest compunction. Now Andrew had nothing, except his love for Marie Kelly. If before the disastrous encounter he had entertained the slightest hope that his father might give in, and even let him bring his beloved to the house, to remove her from the monster stalking Whitechapel, it was clear now that they must live by their own means. He climbed into the carriage and ordered Harold to return to Miller's Court.

The coachman, who had been pacing round the vehicle in circles, waiting for the dénouement of the drama, clambered back onto the box and urged the horses on. He was trying to imagine what had taken place inside the house – and to his credit, based on the clues he had been perceptive enough to pick up, we must say that his reconstruction of the scene was remarkably accurate.

When the carriage stopped in the usual place, Andrew got out and hurried towards Dorset Street, anxious to embrace Marie Kelly and tell her how much he loved her. He had sacrificed everything for her. Still he had no regrets, only a vague uncertainty regarding the future. But they would manage. He was sure he could rely on Charles. His cousin would lend him enough money to rent a house in Vauxhall or Warwick Street, at least until they were able to find decent jobs that would allow them to fend for themselves. Marie Kelly could find work at a dressmaker's – but what skills did he possess? It made no difference. He was young, able-bodied and willing. He would find something. The main thing was he had stood up to his father, and what happened next was neither here nor there. Marie Kelly had pleaded with him, silently, to take her away from Whitechapel, and that was what he intended to do, with or without anyone else's help. They would leave that accursed neighbourhood, that outpost of hell.

Andrew glanced at his watch as he paused beneath the stone archway into Miller's Court. It was five o'clock in the morning. Marie Kelly would probably have already returned to the room, probably as drunk as he. Andrew visualised them communicating through a haze of alcohol in gestures and grunts like Darwin's primates. With boyish excitement, he walked into the yard where the flats stood. The door to number thirteen was closed. He banged on it a few times but got no reply. She must be asleep, but that would not be a problem.

Careful not to cut himself on the shards of glass sticking out of the window frame, Andrew reached through the hole and flicked open the door catch, as he had seen Marie do after she had lost her key. 'Marie, it's me,' he said, opening the door. 'Andrew.'

Allow me at this point to break off the story to warn you that what took place next is hard to relate, because the sensations Andrew experienced were apparently too numerous for a scene lasting only a few seconds. That is why I need you to take into account the elasticity of time, its ability to expand or contract like an accordion, regardless of clocks. I am sure this is something you will have experienced frequently in your own life, depending on which side of the bathroom door you have found yourself. In Andrew's case, time expanded in his mind, creating an eternity of a few seconds. I am going to describe the scene from that perspective, and therefore ask you not to blame my inept story-telling for the discrepancies you will no doubt perceive between the events and their correlation in time.

When he first opened the door and stepped into the room, Andrew did not understand what he was seeing or, more precisely, he refused to accept what he was seeing. During that brief but endless moment, he still felt safe, although the certainty was forming in some still-functioning part of his brain that what he saw before him would kill him. Nobody could be faced with a thing like that and go on living, at least not completely. And what he saw before him, let's be blunt about it, was Marie Kelly – but at the same time it wasn't, for it was hard to accept that the object lying on the bed in the middle of all the blood was she.

Andrew could not compare what awaited him in that room with anything he had seen before because, like most other men, he had never been exposed to a carefully mutilated human body. And once Andrew's brain had finally accepted that he was indeed looking at a meticulously destroyed corpse, although nothing in his pleasant life of country-house gatherings and fancy headwear seemed to offer him any clues, he had no time to feel the appropriate revulsion: he could not avoid the terrible line of reasoning that led him to the inevitable conclusion that this human wreckage must be his beloved.

The Ripper, for this could be the work of none other, had stripped the flesh off her face, rendering her unrecognisable, and yet, however great the temptation, Andrew could not deny the corpse belonged to Marie Kelly. It seemed an almost simplistic, not to say improbable, approach, but given its size and appearance and, above all, the place where he had found it, the dismembered corpse could only be that of Marie Kelly.

After this, of course, Andrew was overcome by a devastating pain, which, despite everything, was only a pale expression of what it would later become: it was still tempered by the shock paralysing and, to some extent, protecting him. Once he was convinced he was standing before the corpse of his beloved, he felt compelled by a sort of posthumous loyalty to look tenderly upon that ghastly sight, but he was incapable of contemplating with anything other than revulsion her flayed face, the skull's macabre, caricatured smile peeping through the strips of flesh.

But how could the skull on which he had bestowed his last passionate kisses revolt him now? The same applied to the body he had worshipped for nights on end, and which, ripped open and half skinned, he now found sickening. It was clear to him from his reaction that in some sense, although it was made of the same material, this object had ceased to be Marie Kelly. The Ripper, in his zeal to discover how she was put together inside, had reduced her to a simple casing of flesh, robbing her of her humanity.

After this last reflection, the time came for Andrew to focus, with a mixture of fascination and horror, on specific details, like the darkish brown lump between her feet, possibly her liver, or the breast lying on the bedside table, which, far from its natural habitat, he might have mistaken for a soft bun had it not been topped with a purplish nipple. Everything appeared neatly arranged, betraying the murderer's grisly calm. Even the heat Andrew now noticed suffusing the room, suggested the ghoul had taken the time to light a nice fire in order to work in more comfort.

Andrew closed his eyes: he had seen enough. He did not want to know any more. Besides showing him how cruel and indifferent man could be towards his fellow human beings, the atrocities he could commit, given enough opportunity, imagination and a sharp knife, the murderer had provided him with a shocking and brutal lesson in anatomy. For the very first time Andrew realised that life, real life, had no connection with the way people spent their days, whose lips they kissed, what medals were pinned to their breasts or the shoes they mended. Life, real life, went on soundlessly inside our bodies, flowed like an underwater stream, occurred like a silent miracle of which only surgeons and pathologists were aware – and perhaps that ruthless killer. They alone knew that, ultimately, there was no difference between Queen Victoria and the most wretched beggar in London: both were complex machines made up of bone, organs and tissue, whose fuel was the breath of God.

This is a detailed analysis of what Andrew experienced during those fleeting moments when he stood before Marie Kelly's dead body, although this description makes it seem as if he were gazing at her for hours, which was what it felt like to him. Eventually guilt began to emerge through the haze of pain and disgust for he immediately held himself responsible for her death. It had been in his power to save her, but he had arrived too late. This was the price of his cowardice. He let out a cry of rage and impotence as he imagined his beloved being subjected to this butchery.

Suddenly it dawned on him that unless he wanted to be linked to the murder he must get out before someone saw him. It was even possible the murderer was still lurking outside, admiring his macabre handiwork from some dark corner, and would have no hesitation in adding another corpse to his collection. He gave Marie Kelly a farewell glance, unable to bring himself to touch her, and with a supreme effort of will forced himself to withdraw from the little room, leaving her there.

As though in a trance, he closed the door behind him, leaving everything as he had found it. He walked towards the exit to the flats, but was seized by intense nausea and only just made it to the stone archway. There, half kneeling, he vomited, retching violently. After he had brought up everything, which was little more than the alcohol he had drunk that night, he leaned back against the wall, his body limp, cold and weak. From where he was, he could see the little room, number thirteen, the paradise where he had been so happy, now hiding his beloved's dismembered corpse from the night. He took a few steps and, confident that his dizzy spell had eased sufficiently for him to walk, staggered out into Dorset Street.

Too distressed to get his bearings, he wandered aimlessly, letting out cries and sobs. He did not even attempt to find the carriage: now that he knew he was no longer welcome in his family home there was nowhere for him to tell Harold to go. He trudged along street after street, guided only by the forward movement of his feet. When he calculated he was no longer in Whitechapel, he looked for a lonely alley and collapsed, exhausted and trembling, in the midst of a pile of discarded boxes. There, curled up, he waited for night to pass.

As I predicted above, when the shock began to subside, his pain increased. His sorrow intensified until it became physical torment. Suddenly it was agony to be in his body, as if he lay in a sarcophagus lined with nails. He wanted to flee, unshackle himself from the excruciating substance he was made of, but he was trapped inside that martyred flesh. Terrified, he wondered if he would have to live with the pain for ever. He had read somewhere that the last image people see before they die is engraved on their eyes. Had the Ripper's savage leer been etched on Marie Kelly's pupils? He could not say, but he knew that if the rule were true he would be the exception:

whatever else he might see before he died, his eyes would always reflect Marie Kelly's mutilated face.

Without the desire or strength to do anything, Andrew let the hours slip by. Occasionally, he raised his head from his hands and let out a howl of rage to show the world his bitterness about all that had happened, which he was now powerless to change. He hurled random insults at the Ripper, who had conceivably followed him and was waiting, knife in hand, at the entrance to the alley. Then he laughed at his fear. For the most part, though, he wailed pitifully, oblivious to his surroundings, hopelessly alone with his own horror.

The arrival of dawn, leisurely sweeping away the darkness, restored his sanity somewhat. Sounds of life reached him from the entrance to the alley. He stood up with difficulty, shivering in his servant's threadbare jacket, and walked out into the street, which was surprisingly lively.

Noticing the flags hanging from the fronts of the buildings, Andrew realised it was Lord Mayor's Day. Walking as upright as he could, he joined the crowd. His grubby attire drew no more attention than that of any ordinary tramp. He had no notion of where he was, but that did not matter, since he had nowhere to go and nothing to do. The first tavern he came to seemed as good a destination as any. It was better than being swept along on the human tide making its way to the Law Courts to watch the arrival of the new mayor, James Whitehead. The alcohol would warm his insides, and at the same time blur his thoughts until they were no longer a danger to him.

The seedy public house was half empty. A strong smell of sausages and bacon coming from the kitchen made his stomach churn and he secluded himself in the corner furthest from the stoves and ordered a bottle of wine. He was forced to place a handful of coins on the table in order to persuade the man to serve him. While he waited, he glanced at the other customers, reduced to a couple of regular patrons, drinking in silence, oblivious to the clamour in the streets outside. One of them stared back at him, and Andrew felt a flash of sheer terror. Could he be the Ripper? Had he followed him there? He calmed down when he realised the man was too small to be a threat to anyone, but his hand was still shaking when he reached for the wine bottle. He knew now what man was capable of, any man, even the little fellow peacefully sipping his ale. He probably did not have the talent to paint the Sistine Chapel, but what Andrew could not be sure of was whether he was capable of ripping a person's guts out and arranging their entrails around their body.

He gazed out of the window. People were coming and going, carrying on their lives without the slightest token of respect. Why did they not notice that the world had changed, that it was no longer habitable? Andrew gave a deep sigh. The world had changed only for him. He leaned back in his seat and applied himself to getting drunk. After that he would see. He glanced at the pile of money. He calculated he had enough to purchase every last drop of alcohol in the place, and so, for the time being, any other plan could wait. Sprawled over the bench, trying hard to prevent his mind from elaborating the simplest thought, Andrew let the day go by, his numbness increasing as he drew closer to the edge of oblivion.

But he was not too dazed to respond to the cry of a newspaper vendor. 'Read all about it in the *Star*! Special edition: Jack the Ripper caught!'

Andrew leaped to his feet. The Ripper caught? He could hardly believe his ears. He leaned out of the window and, screwing up his eyes, scoured the street until he glimpsed a boy selling newspapers on a corner. He beckoned him over and bought a copy from him through the window. With trembling hands, he cleared away several bottles and spread the newspaper on the table. He had not misheard. 'Jack the Ripper Caught!' the headline declared. Reading the article proved slow and frustrating, due to his drunken state, but with patience and much blinking, he managed to decipher what was written.

The article began by declaring that Jack the Ripper had committed his last ever crime the previous night. His victim was a prostitute of Welsh origin called Marie Jeanette Kelly, discovered in the room she rented in Miller's Court, at number twenty-six Dorset Street. Andrew skipped the following paragraph, which listed in gory detail the gruesome mutilations the murderer had perpetrated on her, and went straight to the description of his capture.

The newspaper stated that less than an hour after he had committed the heinous crime, the murderer who had terrorised the East End for four months had been caught by George Lusk and his men. Apparently, a witness who preferred to remain anonymous had heard Marie Kelly's screams and alerted the Vigilance Committee. Unhappily, they reached Miller's Court too late, but had managed to corner the Ripper as he fled down Middlesex Street. At first, the murderer tried to deny his guilt, but soon gave up after he was searched and the still warm heart of his victim was found in one of his pockets. The man's name was Bryan Reese, and he worked as a cook on a merchant vessel, the *Slip*, which had docked at the Port of London from Barbados the previous July and would be setting sail for the Caribbean the following week.

During his interrogation by Frederick Abberline, the detective in charge of the investigation, Reese had confessed to the five murders of which he was accused, and had even shown his satisfaction at having been able to execute his final bloody act in the privacy of a room with a nice warm fire. He was tired of always having to kill in the street. 'I knew I was going to follow that whore the moment I saw her,' the murderer had gloated, before going on to claim he had murdered his own mother, a prostitute like his victims, as soon as he was old enough to wield a knife. This detail, which might have explained his behaviour, had yet to be confirmed.

Accompanying the article was a photogravure of the murderer so that Andrew could finally see the face of the man he had bumped into in the gloom of Hanbury Street. His appearance was disappointing. He was an ordinary-looking fellow, rather heavily built, with curly sideburns and a bushy moustache that drooped over his top lip. Despite his rather sinister smirk, which probably owed more to the conditions in which he had been photographed than anything else, Andrew had to admit he might just as well have been an honest baker as a ruthless killer. He certainly had none of the gruesome features Londoners' imaginations had ascribed to him.

The following pages gave other related news items, such as the resignation of Sir Charles Warren following his acknowledgement of police incompetence in the case, or statements from Reese's astonished fellow seamen on the cargo vessel, but Andrew already knew everything he wanted to know and went back to the front page. From what he could work out, he had entered Marie Kelly's little room moments after the murderer had left and shortly before Lusk's mob arrived, as if they were all keeping to a series of dance steps. He hated to think what would have happened had he delayed fleeing any longer and been discovered standing over Marie Kelly's body by the Vigilance Committee. He had been lucky, he told himself.

He tore out the first page, folded it and put it into his jacket pocket, then ordered another bottle to celebrate that, although his heart was irreparably broken, he had escaped being beaten to a pulp by an angry mob.

Eight years later, Andrew took that same cutting from his pocket. Like him, it was yellowed with age. How often had he re-read it, recalling Marie Kelly's horrific mutilations like a self-imposed penance? He had almost no other memories of the intervening years. What had he done during that time? It was difficult to say. He vaguely remembered Harold taking him home after scouring the various pubs in the vicinity and finding him passed out in that den. He had spent several days in bed with a fever, ranting and suffering from nightmares in which Marie Kelly's corpse lay stretched out on her bed, her insides strewn about the room, or in which he was slitting her open with a huge knife while Reese looked on approvingly.

In a brief moment of clarity during his feverish haze, he was able to make out his father sitting stiffly on the edge of his bed, begging forgiveness for his behaviour. But it was easy to apologise now there was nothing to accept. Now all he had to do was join in the theatrical display of grief that the family, even Harold, had decided to put on for him as a mark of respect. Andrew waved his father away, with an impatient gesture that, to his annoyance, the proud William Harrington took to be absolution, judging from his smile of satisfaction as he left the room, as though he had sealed a successful deal. William Harrington had wanted to clear his conscience and that was what he had done, whether his son liked it or not. Now he could forget the matter and get back to business. Andrew did not really care: he and his father had never seen eye to eye and were not likely to do so now.

He recovered from his fever too late to attend Marie Kelly's funeral, but not her killer's execution. The Ripper was hanged at Wandsworth Prison, despite the objections of several doctors, who maintained Reese's brain was worthy of scientific study: its bumps and folds must contain the crimes he had been predestined to commit since birth and should be recorded. Andrew watched as the executioner snuffed out Reese's life but this did not bring back Marie Kelly's or those of her fellow whores. Things did not work like that; the Creator knew nothing of bartering, only of retribution. At most, a child might have been born at the moment when the rope snapped the Ripper's neck, but bringing back the dead to life was another matter. Perhaps that explained why so many had begun to doubt His power and even to question whether it was really He who had created the world.

That same afternoon, a spark from a lamp set alight the portrait of Marie Kelly hanging in the Winslows' library. That, at least, was what Charles said – he had arrived just in time to put out the fire.

Andrew was grateful for Charles's gesture, but the affair could not be ended by removing the cause. No, it was something that was impossible to deny. Thanks to his father's generosity, Andrew got back his old life, but being reinstated as heir to the vast fortune his father and brother continued to amass meant nothing to him now. All that money could not heal the wound inside, although he soon realised that spending it in the opium dens of Poland Street helped. Too much drink had made him immune to alcohol, but opium was a far more effective and gentler aid to forgetting. Not for nothing had the ancient Greeks used it to treat a wide range of afflictions.

Andrew began to spend his days in the opium den, sucking his pipe as he lay on one of the hundreds of mattresses screened off by exotic curtains. In those rooms, lined with fly-blown mirrors that made their dimensions seem uncertain in the dim light cast by the gas lamps, Andrew fled his pain in the labyrinths of a shadowy, never-ending daydream. From time to time a skinny Malay filled his pipe bowl for him, until Harold or his cousin pulled back the curtain and led him out. If Coleridge had resorted to opium to alleviate the trifling pain of toothache, why should Andrew not use it to dull the agony of a broken heart, he replied, when Charles warned him of the dangers of addiction. As always his cousin was right, and although as his suffering abated Andrew stopped visiting the opium den, for a while he was obliged to carry phials of laudanum around with him.

That period lasted two or three years, until the pain finally disappeared, giving way to something far worse: emptiness, lethargy, numbness. Marie Kelly's murder had obliterated his will to live, severed his unique communication with the world, leaving him deaf and dumb, manoeuvring him into a corner of the universe where nothing happened. He had turned into an automaton, a gloomy creature that lived out of habit, without hope, simply because life, real life, had no link to the way he spent his days, but occurred quietly inside him, like a silent miracle, whether he liked it or not. In short, he became a lost soul, shutting himself in his room by day and roaming Hyde Park by night. Even the action of a flower coming into bud seemed rash, futile and pointless.

In the meantime, his cousin Charles had married one of the Keller sisters – Victoria or Madeleine, Andrew could not remember which – and had purchased an elegant house in Elystan Street. This did not stop him visiting Andrew nearly every day, and occasionally dragging him to his favourite brothels on the off-chance that one of the new girls might have the fire between her legs to rekindle his cousin's dulled spirit. But to no avail: Andrew refused to be pulled out of the hole into which he had dug himself.

To Charles – whose point of view I shall adopt at this juncture, if you will consent to this rather obvious switch of perspective within a paragraph – this showed the resignation of someone who has embraced the role of victim. After all, the world needed martyrs as evidence of the Creator's cruelty. It was even conceivable that his cousin had come to view what had happened to him as an opportunity to search his soul, to venture into its darkest, most inhospitable regions.

How many people go through life without experiencing pure pain? Andrew had known complete happiness and utter torment; he had used up his soul, so to speak, exhausted it completely. And now, comfortably installed with his pain, like a fakir on a bed of nails, he seemed to await who knew what: perhaps the applause signalling the end of the performance. Charles was certain that if his cousin was still alive it was because he felt compelled to experience that pain to the hilt. It was irrelevant whether this was a practical study of suffering or to atone for his guilt. Once Andrew felt he had achieved this, he would take a last bow and leave the stage for good.

Thus, each time Charles visited the Harrington mansion and found his cousin prone but still breathing, he heaved a sigh of relief. And when he arrived home empty-handed, convinced that anything he could do for Andrew was useless, he reflected on how strange life could be, how flimsy and unpredictable it was if it could be altered so drastically by the mere purchase of a painting. Was it within his power to change his cousin's life again? Could he alter the path it would take before it was too late? He did not know. The only thing he was certain of was that, given everyone else's indifference, he had to try.

In the little room on Dorset Street, Andrew opened the cutting and read for the last time, as though it were a prayer, the account of

Marie Kelly's mutilations. Then he folded it and replaced it in his coat pocket. He contemplated the bed, which bore no trace of what had happened there eight years before. But that was the only thing that was different: everything else remained unchanged – the grimy mirror, in which the crime had been immortalised, Marie Kelly's little perfume bottles, the cupboard where her clothes still hung, even the ashes in the hearth left from the fire the Ripper had lit to make slitting her open cosier. He could think of no better place to take his own life.

He placed the barrel of the revolver under his jaw and crooked his finger around the trigger. Those walls would be splattered with blood once more, and far away, on the distant moon, his soul would at last take up its place in the little hollow awaiting him in Marie Kelly's bed.

VI

With the revolver barrel digging into the flesh beneath his jaw, and his finger poised on the trigger, Andrew thought how strange it was for him to have come to this. He had chosen to bring about his own death even though most of his life he had, like everyone else, been content merely to fear it, imagine it in every illness, see it lurking treacherously all around him in a world of precipices, sharp objects, thin ice and jumpy horses, mocking the fragility of those who claimed to be kings of Creation. All that worrying about death, he thought, only to embrace it now. But that was how things were: it was enough to find life a sterile, unrewarding exercise to want to end it, and there was only one way to do that. And he had to confess that the vague unease he felt was in no way existential. Dying itself did not worry him in the least, because fear of death, whether it was a bridge to a biblical universe or a plank artfully suspended above the void, always derived from the certainty that the world went on without us, like a dog after its ticks have been removed.

Broadly speaking, then, pulling the trigger meant pulling out of the game, relinquishing any possibility of being dealt a better hand in the next round. Andrew doubted this could happen. He had lost all faith. He did not believe fate had any reward in store for him that would make up for the pain he had suffered. He did not believe such recompense existed. He was afraid of something far more mundane: the pain he would doubtless feel when the bullet shattered his jaw. Naturally, it would not be pleasant, but it was part of his plan, and therefore something he must accept. He felt his finger grow heavy as it rested on the trigger, gritted his teeth and prepared to put an end to his tragic life.

Just then, a knock came on the door. Startled, Andrew opened his eyes. Who could this be? Had McCarthy seen him arrive and come to ask for money to fix the window? The knocking became more insistent. That accursed money-grubber! If the man had the gall to stick his snout through the hole in the window, Andrew would not hesitate to shoot him. What did it matter now if he broke the absurd commandment about not killing your fellow man, especially if that man happened to be McCarthy?

'Andrew, I know you're in there. Open the door.'

With a bitter grimace, Andrew recognised his cousin Charles's voice. Charles, Charles – always following him everywhere, looking out for him. He would have preferred it to be McCarthy. He could not shoot Charles. How had his cousin found him? And why did he go on trying when Andrew himself had long since given up?

'Go away, Charles, I'm busy,' he cried.

'Don't do it, Andrew! I've found a way of saving Marie!'

'Saving Marie?' Andrew laughed grimly. He had to admit his cousin had imagination, although this was verging on bad taste. 'Perhaps I should remind you Marie is dead,' he shouted. 'She was murdered in this miserable room eight years ago. When I could have saved her I didn't. How can we save her now, Charles? By travelling through time?'

'Exactly,' his cousin replied, slipping something beneath the door.

Andrew glanced at it with vague curiosity. It looked like a leaflet.

'Read it, Andrew,' his cousin implored, through the broken window. 'Please read it.'

Andrew felt rather ashamed that his cousin should see him with the revolver pressed ridiculously against his jaw – perhaps not the most suitable place if you wanted to blow your head off. Knowing his cousin would not go away, he lowered the gun with an exasperated sigh, placed it on the bed and rose to fetch the piece of paper.

'All right, Charles, you win,' he muttered. 'Let's see what this is about.'

He picked up the sheet of paper and examined it. It was a faded sky-blue handbill. He read it, unable to believe that what it said could be true. Amazing though it seemed, he was holding the advertisement for a company called Murray's Time Travel, which offered journeys through time. This was what it said:

> Tired of travelling through space?
> Now you can travel through time, into the fourth dimension.
>
> Make the most of our special opening offer and journey to the year 2000. Witness an era only your grandchildren will live to see. Spend three whole hours in the year 2000 for a mere one hundred pounds. See with your own eyes the future war between automatons and humans that will change the fate of the world. Don't be the last to hear about it.

The text was accompanied by an illustration intended to portray a fierce battle between two powerful armies. It showed a landscape of supposedly ruined buildings, a mound of rubble before which were ranged the two opposing sides. One was clearly human; the other consisted of humanoid creatures apparently made of metal. The drawing was too crude to make out anything more.

What on earth was this? Andrew felt he had no choice but to unlock the door. Charles walked in, closing it behind him. He stood breathing into his hands to warm them, but beaming contentedly at having intervened to stop his cousin's suicide. For the time being, at least. The first thing he did was seize the pistol from the bed.

'How did you know I was here?' asked Andrew, while his cousin posed in front of the mirror waving the gun about furiously.

'You disappoint me, cousin,' replied Charles, emptying the bullets from the chamber into his cupped hand and depositing them in his coat pocket. 'Your father's gun cabinet was open, a pistol was missing, and today is the seventh of November. Where else would I have gone to look for you? You may as well have left a trail of breadcrumbs.'

'I suppose so,' conceded Andrew. His cousin was right. He had not gone out of his way to cover his tracks.

Charles held the pistol by its barrel and handed it to Andrew. 'Here you are. You can shoot yourself as many times as you like now.'

Andrew snatched the gun and stuffed it into his pocket, eager to make the embarrassing object disappear. He would just have to kill himself some other time. Charles looked at him with mock-disapproval, waiting for some sort of explanation, but Andrew did not have the energy to convince him that suicide was the only solution he could envisage. Before his cousin had the chance to lecture him, he decided to side-step the issue by enquiring about the leaflet.

'What's this? Some kind of joke?' he asked, waving the piece of paper in the air. 'Where did you have it printed?'

Charles shook his head. 'It's no joke, cousin. Murray's Time Travel is a real company. The main offices are in Greek Street in Soho. And, as the advertisement says, they offer the chance to travel through time.'

'But, is that possible?' stammered Andrew, taken aback.

'It certainly is,' replied Charles, completely straight-faced. 'What's more, I've done it myself.'

They stared at one another for a moment.

'I don't believe you,' said Andrew at last, trying to detect a hint in his cousin's solemn face that would give the game away, but Charles shrugged.

'I'm telling the truth,' he assured him. 'Last week, Madeleine and I travelled to the year 2000.'

Andrew burst out laughing, but his cousin's earnest expression silenced his guffaws. 'You're not joking, are you?'

'No, not at all,' Charles replied. 'Although I can't say I was all that impressed. The year 2000 is a dirty, cold year where man is at war with machines. But not seeing it is like missing a new opera that's all the rage.'

Andrew listened, still stunned.

'It's a unique experience,' his cousin added. 'If you think about it, it's exciting because of all it implies. Madeleine has even recommended it to her friends. She fell in love with the human soldiers' boots. She tried to buy me a pair in Paris, but couldn't find any. I suspect it's too soon yet.'

Andrew reread the leaflet to make sure he was not imagining things. 'I still can't believe . . .' he stammered.

'I know, cousin, I know. But, you see, while you've been roaming Hyde Park like a lost soul the world has moved on. Time goes by even when you're not watching it. And, believe me, strange as it may seem to you, time travel has been the talk of all the salons, the favoured topic of discussion, since the novel that gave rise to it came out last spring.'

'A novel?' asked Andrew, increasingly bewildered.

'Yes. *The Time Machine* by H. G. Wells. It was one of the books I lent you. Didn't you read it?'

Since Andrew had shut himself away in the house, refusing to go along with Charles on those outings to taverns and brothels, his cousin had started bringing him books. They were usually new works by unknown authors, inspired by the century's craze for science to write about machines capable of performing the most elaborate miracles. The stories were known as 'scientific romances' – the English publishers' translation of Jules Verne's 'extraordinary voyages', an expression that had taken hold with amazing rapidity and was used to describe any fantasy novel that tried to explain itself by using science. According to Charles, these novels captured the spirit that had inspired the works of Bergerac and Samosata, and had taken over from the old tales of haunted castles.

Andrew remembered some of the madcap inventions in those tales, such as the anti-nightmare helmet hooked up to a tiny steam engine that sucked out bad dreams and turned them into pleasant ones. But the one he remembered best was the machine that made things grow, invented by a Jewish scientist who used it on insects: the image of London attacked by a swarm of flies the size of airships, crushing towers and flattening buildings as they landed on them, was ridiculously terrifying. There had been a time when Andrew would have devoured such books but, much as he regretted it, the worlds of fiction were not exempt from his steadfast indifference to life: he did not want any type of balm but to stare straight into the gaping abyss, thus making it impossible for Charles to reach him via the secret passage of literature. Andrew assumed that this fellow Wells's book must be buried at the bottom of his chest, under a mound of similar novels he had scarcely glanced at.

When Charles saw the empty look on his cousin's face he gestured to him to sit back down in his chair and drew up the other. Leaning forward slightly, like a priest about to take confession from one of his parishioners, he began summarising the plot of the novel that, according to him, had revolutionised England. Andrew listened sceptically. As he could guess from the title, the main character was a scientist who had invented a time machine that allowed him to journey through the centuries. All he had to do was pull on a little lever and he was propelled at great speed into the future, gazing in awe as snails ran like hares, trees sprouted from the ground like geysers, the stars circled in the sky, which changed from day to night in a second . . . This wild and wonderful journey took him to the year 802,701, where he discovered that society had split into two different races: the beautiful and useless Eloi and the monstrous Morlocks, creatures that lived underground, feeding off their neighbours up above, whom they bred like cattle.

Andrew bridled at this description, making his cousin smile, but Charles quickly added that the plot was unimportant, no more than an excuse to create a flimsy caricature of the society of their time. What had shaken the English imagination was that Wells had envisaged time as a fourth dimension, transforming it into a sort of magic tunnel you could travel through.

'We are all aware that objects possess three dimensions – length, breadth and thickness,' explained Charles. 'But in order for this object to exist,' he went on, picking up his hat and twirling it in his hands like a conjuror, 'in order for it to form part of this reality we find ourselves in, it needs duration in time as well as in space. That is what enables us to see it, and prevents it disappearing before our very eyes. We live, then, in a four-dimensional world. If we accept that time is another dimension, what is to stop us moving through it? In fact, that's what we are doing. Just like our hats, you and I are moving forwards in time, albeit in a tediously linear fashion, without leaving out a single second, towards our inexorable end. What Wells is asking in his novel is why we can't speed up this journey, or even turn around and travel backwards to that place we refer to as the past – which, ultimately, is no more than a loose thread in the skein of our lives. If time is a spatial dimension, what prevents us moving around in it as freely as we do in the other three?'

Pleased with his explanation, Charles replaced his hat on the bed. Then he studied Andrew, allowing him a moment to assimilate what he had just said.

'I must confess when I read the novel I thought it was rather an ingenious way of making what was basically a fantasy believable,' he went on, a moment later, when his cousin said nothing, 'but I never imagined it would be scientifically achievable. The book was a raging success, Andrew, people spoke of nothing else in the clubs, the salons, the universities, during factory breaks. Nobody talked any more about the crisis in the United States and how it might affect England, or Waterhouse's paintings or Oscar Wilde's plays. The only thing people were interested in was whether time travel was possible or not. Even the women's suffrage movement was fascinated by the subject and interrupted their regular meetings to discuss it. Speculating about what tomorrow's world would be like or discussing which past events ought to be changed became England's favourite pastime, the quickest way to liven up conversation during afternoon tea.

'Naturally, such discussions were futile, because nobody could reach any enlightened conclusions, except in scientific circles, where an even more heated debate took place, whose progress was reported almost daily in the national newspapers. But nobody could deny it was Wells's novel that had sparked off people's yearning to journey into the future, to go beyond the bounds imposed on them by their fragile, destructible bodies. Everybody wanted to glimpse the future, and the year 2000 became the most logical objective, the year everyone wanted to see. A century was easily enough time for everything to be invented that could be invented, and for the world to have been transformed into a marvellously unrecognisable, magical, possibly even a better place.

'Ultimately, this all seemed to be no more than a harmless amusement, a naïve desire – that is, until last October, when Murray's Time Travel opened for business. This was announced with great fanfare in the newspapers and on publicity posters. Gilliam Murray could make our dreams come true. He could take us to the year 2000. Despite the cost of the tickets, huge queues formed around his building. I saw people who had always maintained that time travel was impossible waiting like excited children for the doors to open. Nobody wanted to pass up this opportunity. Madeleine and I couldn't get seats for the first expedition, only the second. And we travelled in time, Andrew. Believe it or not, I have been a hundred and five years into the future and returned. This coat still has traces of ash on it. It smells of the war of the future. I even picked up a piece of rubble from the ground when no one was looking, a rock we have displayed in the drawing-room cabinet, a replica of which must still be intact in some building in London.'

Andrew felt like a boat spinning in a whirlpool. It seemed incredible to him that it was possible to travel in time, not to be condemned to see only the era he was born into, the period that lasted as long as his heart and body held out, but to be able to visit other eras, other times where he did not belong, leap-frogging his own death, the tangled web of his descendants, desecrating the sanctuary of the future, journeying to places hitherto only dreamed of or imagined. For the first time in years he felt a flicker of interest in something beyond the wall of indifference with which he had surrounded himself.

He immediately forced himself to snuff out the flame before it became a blaze. He was in mourning, a man with an empty heart and a dormant soul, a creature devoid of emotion, the perfect example of a human being who had felt everything there was for him to feel. He had nothing in the whole wide world to live for. He could not live, not without her.

'That's remarkable, Charles.' He sighed wearily, feigning indifference to these unnatural journeys. 'But what has this to do with Marie?'

'Don't you see, cousin?' Charles replied, in an almost scandalised tone. 'This man Murray can travel into the future. No doubt if you offered him enough money he could organise a private tour for you into the past. Then you'd really have someone to shoot.'

Andrew's jaw dropped. 'The Ripper?' he said, his voice cracking.

'Exactly,' replied Charles. 'If you travel back in time you can save Marie.'

Andrew gripped the chair to stop himself falling off it. Was it possible? Could he really travel back in time to the night of 7 November 1888 and save Marie? The possibility that this might be true made him feel giddy, not just because of the miracle of travelling through time, but because he would be going back to a period when she was still alive: he would be able to hold in his arms the body he had seen cut to ribbons. But what moved him most was that someone should offer him the chance to save her, to put right his mistake, to change a situation it had taken him all these years to learn to accept as irreversible. He had always prayed to the Creator to be able to do that. It seemed he had been calling upon the wrong person. This was the age of science.

'What do you say, Andrew? We have nothing to lose by trying,' he heard his cousin remark.

Andrew stared at the floor, struggling to put some order into the tumult of emotions he felt. He did not really believe it was possible, and yet if it was, how could he refuse to try? This was the chance for which he had waited eight years. He raised his head and gazed at his cousin, shaken. 'All right,' he said in a hoarse whisper.

'Excellent, Andrew,' said Charles, overjoyed, and clapped him on the back. 'Excellent.'

His cousin smiled unconvincingly, then looked down at his shoes again: he was going to travel back to his old haunts, to relive moments already past, back to his own memories.

'Well,' said Charles, glancing at his pocket watch. 'We'd better have something to eat. I don't think travelling back in time on an empty stomach is a good idea.'

They left the little room and made their way to Charles's carriage, which was waiting by the stone archway. They followed the same routine that night as though it were no different from any other. They dined at the Café Royal, which served Charles's favourite steak and kidney pie, let off steam at Madame Norrell's brothel, where Charles liked to try out the new girls while they were still fresh, and ended up drinking until dawn in the bar at Claridge's, where Charles rated the champagne list above any other.

Before their minds became too clouded by drink, Charles explained to Andrew that he had journeyed into the future on a huge tramcar, the Cronotilus, which was propelled through the centuries by an impressive steam engine. But Andrew was incapable of showing any interest in the future: his mind was taken up with imagining what it would be like to travel in the exact opposite direction, into the past. There, his cousin had assured him, he would be able to save Marie by confronting the Ripper.

Over the past eight years, Andrew had built up feelings of intense rage towards that monster. Now he would have the chance to vent them. However, it was one thing to threaten a man who had already been executed, quite another to confront him in the flesh, in the sort of sparring match Murray would set up for him. Andrew gripped the pistol, which he had kept in his pocket, as he recalled the burly man he had bumped into in Hanbury Street, and tried to cheer himself with the thought that, although he had never shot a real person before, he had practised his aim on bottles, pigeons and rabbits. If he remained calm, everything would go well. He would aim at the Ripper's heart or his head, let off a few shots calmly, and watch him die a second time. Yes, that was what he would do. Only this time, as though someone had tightened a bolt in the machinery of the universe to make it function more smoothly, the Ripper's death would bring Marie Kelly back to life.

VII

Although it was early morning, Soho was already teeming with people. Charles and Andrew had to push their way through the crowded streets, full of men in bowlers and women wearing hats adorned with plumes and even the odd dead bird. Couples strolled along the pavements arm in arm, sauntered in and out of shops, or stood waiting to cross the streets, along which moved, as slowly as lava, a torrent of luxurious carriages, cabriolets, trams and carts carrying barrels, fruit, or mysterious shapes covered with tarpaulins, possibly bodies robbed from the graveyard. Scruffy second-rate artists, performers and acrobats displayed their dubious talents on street corners in the hope of attracting the attention of some passing promoter.

Charles had not stopped chattering since breakfast, but Andrew could hardly hear him above the loud clatter of wheels on the cobbles and the piercing cries of vendors. He was content to let his cousin guide him through the grey morning, immersed in a sort of stupor from which he was roused only by the sweet scent of violets as they passed one of many flower-sellers with fragrant baskets.

The moment they entered Greek Street, they spotted the modest building where the offices of Murray's Time Travel were situated. It was an old theatre that had been remodelled by its new owner, who had not hesitated to blight the neo-classical façade with a variety of ornamentation that alluded to time. At the entrance, a flight of steps, flanked by two columns, led up to an elegant, sculpted wooden door crowned by a pediment decorated with a carving of Chronos spinning the wheel of the zodiac. The god of time, depicted as a sinister old man with a flowing beard reaching to his navel, was bordered by a frieze of carved hourglasses, a motif repeated on the arches above the tall windows on the second floor. Between the pediment and the lintel, ostentatious pink marble lettering announced that this picturesque edifice was the head office of Murray's Time Travel.

Charles and Andrew noticed passers-by stepping off the section of pavement outside the unusual building. As they drew closer, they understood why. A nauseating odour made them screw up their faces in disgust and invited them to regurgitate the breakfast they had just eaten. The cause of the stench was a viscous substance, which a couple of workmen, masked with neckerchiefs, were vigorously washing off part of the façade with the aid of brushes and pails of water. As the brushes made contact with the dark substance, it slopped on to the pavement, transformed into a revolting black slime.

'Sorry about the inconvenience, gents,' one of the workmen said, pulling down his neckerchief. 'Some louse smeared cow dung all over the front of the building, but we'll soon have it cleaned off.'

Exchanging puzzled looks, Andrew and Charles pulled out their handkerchiefs and, covering their faces like highwaymen, hurried through the front door. In the hallway, the evil smell was being kept at bay by rows of strategically placed vases of gladioli and roses. Just as on the outside of the building, the interior was filled with a profusion of objects whose theme was time. The central area was taken up by a gigantic mechanical sculpture consisting of an enormous pedestal out of which two articulated spider-like arms stretched towards the shadowy ceiling. They were clutching an hourglass the size of a calf embossed with iron rivets and bands. It contained not sand but a sort of blue sawdust that flowed gracefully from one section to the other and even gave off a faint, evocative sparkle when caught by the light from the nearby lamps. Once the contents had emptied into the lower receptacle, the arms turned the hourglass by means of some complex hidden mechanism, so that the artificial sand never ceased to flow, a reminder of time itself.

Alongside the colossal structure there were many other remarkable objects. Although less spectacular, they were more noteworthy for having been invented many centuries before, like the bracket clocks bristling with levers and cogs that stood silently at the back: according to the plaques on their bases, they were early efforts at mechanical timepieces. The walls were lined with hundreds of clocks, from the traditional Dutch *stoelklok*, adorned with mermaids and cherubs, to Austro-Hungarian examples with seconds pendulums. The air was filled with a relentless ticking, which must have become an endless accompaniment to the lives of those who worked in the building and without whose comforting presence they doubtless felt bereft on Sundays.

A young woman stood up from her desk in the corner and came over to Andrew and Charles. She walked with the grace of a rodent, her steps following the rhythm of the insistent ticking. After greeting them courteously, she informed them excitedly that there were still a few tickets left for the third expedition to the year 2000 and that they could make a reservation if they wished. Charles refused her offer with a dazzling smile, telling her they were there to see Gilliam Murray. The woman hesitated briefly, then informed them that he was in the building and, although he was a very busy man, she would do her best to arrange for them to meet him. Charles showed his appreciation of this with an even more captivating smile. Once she had managed to tear her eyes away from his perfect teeth, she wheeled round and gestured to them to follow her.

At the far end of the vast hall a marble staircase led to the upper floors. She guided the cousins down a long corridor lined with tapestries depicting various scenes from the war of the future. Naturally, the corridor, too, was replete with the obligatory clocks, hanging on the walls and standing on dressers or shelves, filling the air with their ubiquitous ticking. When they reached Murray's ostentatious office door, the woman asked them to wait outside, but Charles ignored her request and followed her in, dragging his cousin behind him.

The gigantic proportions of the room surprised Andrew, as did the clutter of furniture and the numerous maps lining the walls. He was reminded of the campaign tents from which field marshals orchestrated wars. They had to glance around the room several times before they discovered Gilliam Murray, lying stretched out on a rug, playing with a dog.

'Good day, Mr Murray,' said Charles, before the secretary had a chance to speak. 'My name is Charles Winslow and this is my cousin, Andrew Harrington. We would like a word with you, if you are not too busy.'

Gilliam Murray, a strapping fellow in a garish purple suit, accepted the thrust sportingly, but with the enigmatic expression of a man who holds a great many aces up his sleeve, which he has every intention of pulling out at the first opportunity. 'I always have time for two such illustrious gentlemen as yourselves,' he said, picking himself up.

When he had risen to his full height, Andrew and Charles could see that Gilliam Murray seemed to have been magnified by some kind of spell. Everything about him was oversized, from his hands, which appeared capable of wrestling a bull to the ground by its horns, to his head, which looked more suited to a Minotaur. However, he moved with extraordinary, even graceful, agility. His straw-coloured hair was combed carefully back, and the smouldering intensity of his big blue eyes betrayed an ambitious, proud spirit, which he toned down with a friendly smile.

With a wave, he invited to them to follow him to his desk on the far side of the room. He led them along the trail he had forged between globes, tables piled with books, and notebooks strewn all over the floor. Andrew noticed there was no shortage of clocks there either. Besides those hanging from the walls and invading the bookcase, an enormous glass cabinet contained a collection of portable clocks, sundials, intricate water clocks and other artefacts showing the evolution of the display of time. It appeared to Andrew that presenting all these objects was Murray's clever way of showing the absurdity of man's vain attempts to capture an elusive, absolute, mysterious and indomitable force. With his colourful collection, he seemed to be saying that man's only achievement was to strip time of its metaphysical essence, transforming it into a commonplace instrument for ensuring he did not arrive late to meetings.

Charles and Andrew lowered themselves into two plush Jacobean-style armchairs facing the majestic desk at which Murray sat, framed by an enormous window behind him. As the light streamed in through the leaded panes, suffusing the office with rustic cheer, it even occurred to Andrew that the entrepreneur had a sun all of his own, while everyone else was submerged in the dull morning light.

'I hope you'll forgive the unfortunate smell in the entrance,' Murray said, with a grimace. 'This is the second time someone has smeared excrement on the front of the building. Perhaps an organised group is attempting to disrupt the smooth running of our enterprise in this unpleasant way.' He shrugged his shoulders despairingly, as though to emphasise how upset he was about the matter. 'As you can see, not everyone thinks time travel is a good thing for society. And yet society has been clamouring for it ever since Mr Wells's wonderful novel came out. I can think of no other explanation for these acts of vandalism, as the perpetrators have not claimed responsibility or left any clues. They simply foul the front of our building.'

He stared into space for a moment, lost in thought. Then he appeared to rouse himself, sat upright and looked straight at his visitors. 'But, tell me, gentlemen, what can I do for you?'

'I would like you to organise a private journey back to the autumn of 1888, Mr Murray,' replied Andrew, who had been waiting impatiently for the giant to allow them to get a word in edgeways.

'To the Autumn of Terror?' asked Murray, taken aback.

'Yes, to the night of November the seventh, to be precise.'

Murray studied him silently. Finally, without trying to conceal his annoyance, he opened one of the desk drawers and took out a bundle of papers tied with a ribbon. He set them on the desk wearily, as if he were showing them some tiresome burden he was compelled to suffer. 'Do you know what this is, Mr Harrington?' He sighed. 'These are the letters we receive every day from private individuals. Some want to be taken to the hanging gardens of Babylon, others to meet Cleopatra, Galileo or Plato, still more to see with their own eyes the battle of Waterloo, the building of the Pyramids or Christ's crucifixion. Everybody wants to go back to their favourite moment in history, as though it were as simple as giving an address to a coachman. They think the past is at our disposal. I am sure you have your reasons for wanting to travel to 1888, like those who wrote these requests, but I'm afraid I can't help you.'

'I only need to go back eight years, Mr Murray,' replied Andrew. 'And I'll pay anything you ask.'

'This isn't about distances in time or about money,' Murray scoffed. 'If it were, Mr Harrington, I'm sure we could come to some arrangement. Let us say the problem is a technical one. We can't travel anywhere we want in the past or the future.'

'You mean you can only take us to the year 2000?' exclaimed Charles, visibly disappointed.

'I'm afraid so, Mr Winslow. We hope to be able to extend our offer in the future. However, for the moment, as you can see from our advertisement, our only destination is May the twentieth, 2000, the exact day of the final battle between the evil Solomon's automatons and the human army led by the brave Captain Shackleton. Wasn't the trip exciting enough for you, Mr Winslow?' he asked, with a flicker of irony, giving Charles to understand he did not forget easily the faces of those who had been on his expeditions.

'Oh, yes, sir,' Charles replied, after a brief pause. 'Most exciting. Only I assumed—'

'You assumed we could travel in either direction along the time continuum,' Murray interposed. 'But I'm afraid we can't. The past is beyond our competence.' His face bore a look of genuine regret, as though he were weighing up the damage his words had done to his visitors. 'The problem, gentlemen,' he sighed, leaning back in his chair, 'is that, unlike Wells's character, we don't travel through the time continuum. We travel outside it, across the surface of time, as it were.'

He fell silent, staring at them without blinking, with the serenity of a cat.

'I don't understand,' Charles declared.

Gilliam Murray nodded, as though he had expected that reply. 'Let me make a simple comparison: you can move from room to room inside a building, but you can also walk across its roof, can you not?'

Charles and Andrew nodded, somewhat put out by Murray's seeming wish to treat them like a couple of foolish children.

'Contrary to all appearances,' their host went on, 'it was not Wells's novel that made me look into the possibilities of time travel. If you have read the book, you will understand that the author is simply throwing down the gauntlet to the scientific world by suggesting a direction for their research. Unlike Verne, he cleverly avoided any practical explanations of the workings of his invention, choosing instead to describe his machine to us using his formidable imagination – a perfectly valid approach, given the book is a work of fiction. However, until science proves such a contraption is possible, his machine will be nothing but a toy. Will that ever happen?

'I'd like to think so: the achievements of science so far this century give me great cause for optimism. You will agree, gentlemen, we live in remarkable times. Times when man questions God daily. How many marvels has science produced over the past few years? Some, such as the calculating machine, the typewriter or the electric lift, have been invented simply to make our lives easier, but others cause us to feel powerful because they render the impossible possible. Thanks to the steam locomotive, we are now able to travel long distances without taking a single step, and soon we will be able to relay our voices to the other side of the country without having to move, like the Americans, who are already doing so with the so-called telephone.

'There will always be people who oppose progress, who consider it a sacrilege for mankind to transcend his own limitations. Personally I believe science ennobles man, reaffirms his control over nature, in the same way that education or morality helps us overcome our primitive instincts. Take this marine chronometer, for example,' he said, picking up a wooden box lying on the desk. 'Today these are mass-produced and every ship in the world has one, but that wasn't always the case. Although they may appear now always to have formed part of our lives, the Admiralty was obliged to offer a prize of twenty thousand pounds to the person who could invent a way of determining longitude at sea, because no clockmaker was capable of designing a chronometer that could withstand the rolling of a vessel without going wrong. The competition was won by a man called John Harrison, who devoted forty years of his life to solving this thorny scientific problem. He was nearly eighty when he finally received the prize money.

'Fascinating, don't you think? At the heart of each invention lie one man's efforts, an entire life dedicated to solving a problem, to inventing an instrument that will outlast him, will go on forming part of the world after he is dead. So long as there are men who aren't content to eat the fruit off the trees or to summon rain by beating a drum, but who are determined instead to use their brains in order to transcend the role of parasite in God's creation, science will never give up trying.

'That's why I am sure that very soon, as well as being able to fly like birds in winged carriages, anyone will be able to get hold of a machine similar to the one Wells dreamed up, and travel anywhere they choose in time. Men of the future will lead double lives, working during the week in a bank, and on Sundays making love to the beautiful Nefertiti or helping Hannibal conquer Rome. Can you imagine how an invention like that would change society?'

Murray studied the two men for a moment before he replaced

the box on the desk, where it sat, lid open, like an oyster or an engagement ring. Then he added, 'But in the meantime, while science is looking for a way to make these dreams come true, we have another method of travelling in time, although unfortunately this one does not enable us to choose our destination.'

'What method is that?' Andrew enquired.

'Magic,' boomed Murray.

'Magic?' echoed Andrew, taken aback.

'Yes, magic,' repeated his host, waving his fingers in the air mysteriously and making a sound like wind whistling down a chimney, 'but not the conjuring tricks you see in music halls or theatres, or the sort those frauds from the Golden Dawn claim to perform. I'm talking about genuine magic. Do you believe in magic, gentlemen?'

Andrew and Charles paused, a little confused by the direction the conversation was taking, but Murray needed no reply. 'Of course not,' he grumbled. 'That's why I avoid mentioning it. I prefer my clients to believe we are travelling through time by means of science. Everybody believes in science. It has become far more credible than magic. We live in modern times. But, I assure you, magic does exist.'

Then, to Andrew and Charles's surprise, he rose deftly from his seat and gave a shrill whistle. The dog, which had been lying on the carpet all this time, stood up at once and trotted gaily over to its master. 'Gentlemen, I'd like you to meet Eternal,' he said, as the creature circled him excitedly. 'Do you like dogs? It's quite safe to stroke him.'

As though this were some sort of requirement they must fulfil for Gilliam Murray to continue his discourse, Charles and Andrew stood up and ran their hands over the soft, well-brushed coat of the golden retriever.

'Gentlemen,' Murray declared, 'be aware that you are stroking a miracle. For, as I told you, there is such a thing as magic. It is even tangible. How old do you think Eternal is?'

Charles had no difficulty in answering the question: he had several dogs on his country estate and had grown up with them.

He examined the animal's teeth with a knowledgeable air, and replied confidently, 'A year, two at the most.'

'Spot on,' confirmed Gilliam, kneeling and scratching the dog's neck affectionately. 'You look a year old, don't you? That's your age in real time?'

Andrew took this opportunity to catch his cousin's eye, anxious to know what he thought of all this. Charles's tranquil smile put his mind at rest.

'As I said,' Murray went on, rising to his feet, 'I didn't decide to set up my company on account of Wells's novel. It was a complete coincidence, although I won't deny I have greatly benefited from the hidden longing he stirred in people. Do you know why time travel is so attractive? Because we all dream of it. It is one of man's oldest desires. But would you have considered it possible, gentlemen, before Wells wrote his book? I don't think so. And I assure you neither would I. What Mr Wells has done is to make an abstract craving real, to articulate this latent desire ever-present in man.'

Murray paused, giving his summary the opportunity to descend on his visitors, like dust settling on furniture after a carpet has been beaten.

'Before setting up this company, I worked with my father,' he resumed. 'We financed expeditions. We were one of the hundreds of societies sending explorers to the furthest corners of the world with the aim of gathering ethnographic and archaeological data to publish in scientific journals, or finding exotic insects or flowers for the showcases of some science museum eager to display God's wildest creations. But, regardless of the business side of things, we were driven by a desire to get to know as accurately as possible the world we lived in. We were, to coin a phrase, spatially curious. However, we never know what fate has in store for us, do we, gentlemen?'

Again without waiting for a reply, Gilliam Murray gestured for them to follow him. Eternal at his heels, he led them through the obstacle course of tables and globes towards one of the side walls.

Unlike the others, which were lined with shelves crammed with atlases, geographical treatises, books on astronomy and numerous other works on obscure subjects, this wall was covered with maps, arranged according to when the regions on them had been charted.

The collection covered a journey that started with a few reproductions of Renaissance maps inspired by Ptolemy's works, which made the world look alarmingly small, like an insect with its legs chopped off, reduced to little more than a shapeless Europe. Next came the German Martin Waldseemüller's map, where America had broken away from Asia, and finally the works of Abraham Ortelius and Gerhardus Mercator, which showed a much larger world, similar in size to that of the present day. Following this chronological order from left to right, as guided by Murray, the cousins felt as though they were watching the petals of a flower open or a cat stretch itself. The world seemed to unfurl before their eyes, to grow, as navigators and explorers extended its frontiers.

Andrew found it fascinating that only a few centuries earlier people had had no idea that the world went on across the Atlantic, or that its true size depended on the courage and fortunes of explorers, whose dare-devil journeys had filled the medieval void, the dwelling place of sea monsters. On the other hand, he regretted that the world's dimensions were no longer a mystery, that the most recent maps of land and sea constituted an official world in which all that was left to chart were coastlines.

Murray made them pause in front of the last gigantic map in his collection. 'Gentlemen, you have in front of you possibly the most accurate world map in all of England,' he announced, openly gloating. 'I keep it continually updated. Whenever another region of the planet is charted, I have a new version drawn up and I burn the obsolete one. I consider this a symbolic gesture, like erasing my old, imprecise idea. Many of the expeditions you see here were made possible by our funding.'

The map was a blurred mass of multicoloured lines that, Murray explained, represented all the expeditionary voyages hitherto undertaken by man, the vicissitudes of which he had written up, doubtless with morbid enjoyment, in the chart's left-hand margin. However, one glance at the map was enough to see that the precision with which each sinuous voyage had been traced eventually became pointless: it was impossible to follow any single journey owing to the criss-cross of the lines that recorded every expedition. These ranged from the earliest, such as that of Marco Polo (represented by a gold line snaking around India, China, Central Asia and the Malayan archipelago), to the most recent, like that undertaken by Sir Francis Younghusband, who had travelled from Peking to Kashmir, crossing the Karakoram mountains with their soaring glacier-topped peaks.

The squiggles were not confined to land: others left *terra firma*, imitating the foamy wake of legendary ships such as Columbus's caravels as they crossed the Atlantic Ocean, or the *Erebus* and the *Terror* as they tried to find a short-cut to China via the Arctic Ocean. These last two lines vanished suddenly, as had the actual ships when sailing across the Lancaster Strait, the so-called North-west Passage. Andrew decided to follow the blue line that cut across the island of Borneo, that sultry paradise overrun by crocodiles and gibbons to the south-east of Asia. It followed the tortuous journey of Sir James Brooke, nicknamed the Rajah of Sarawak, a name with which Andrew was familiar because the explorer popped up in Salgari's novels as a ruthless pirate slayer.

Then Murray asked them to concentrate on the most intricate part of the map, the African continent. There, all of the expeditions that had attempted to discover the mythical source of the Nile – those of the Dutchwoman Alexandrine Tinné, Mr and Mrs Baker, Burton and Speke and, most famously, Livingstone and Stanley, as well as many more – converged to form a tangled mesh, which, if nothing else, illustrated the fascination Africa had held for the intrepid wearers of pith helmets.

'The account of how we discovered time travel began exactly twenty-two years ago,' Murray announced theatrically.

As he had heard the story many times before, Eternal stretched out at his master's feet. Charles smiled gleefully at this promising beginning, while Andrew's lips twisted in frustration. He realised he would need a lot of patience before he found out whether or not he would be able to save Marie Kelly.

VIII

Permit me, if you will, to perform a little narrative juggling at this point, and recount the story Gilliam Murray told them in the third person instead of the first, as if it were an excerpt from an adventure story, which is the way Murray would ultimately have liked to see it.

Back then, at the beginning of the nineteenth century, the main ambition of most expeditionary societies was to discover the source of the Nile, which Ptolemy had situated in the Mountains of the Moon, the magnificent range rising out of the heart of Africa. However, modern explorers seemed to have had no more luck than Herodotus, Nero or anyone else who had searched in vain for it throughout history. Richard Burton and John Speke's expedition had only succeeded in making enemies of the two explorers, and David Livingstone's had thrown little light on the matter.

When Henry Stanley found Livingstone in Ujiji, he was suffering from dysentery. Nevertheless, he refused to return with Stanley to the metropolis and set off on another expedition, this time to Lake Tanganyika. He had to be brought back from there on a litter, racked with fever and utterly exhausted. The Scottish explorer died at Chitambo, and his final journey was made as a corpse, embalmed and enclosed in a large piece of bark from a myonga tree. It took porters nine months to carry him to the island of Zanzibar, whence he was finally repatriated to Great Britain. He was buried in 1878 in Westminster Abbey with full honours, the source of the Nile remaining a mystery.

Everyone, from the Royal Geographic Society to the most insignificant science museum, wanted to take credit for discovering its elusive location. The Murray family were no exception, and at the same time as the *New York Herald* and the London *Daily Telegraph* sponsored Stanley's new expedition, they, too, sent one of their most experienced explorers to the inhospitable African continent.

His name was Oliver Tremanquai, and he had undertaken several expeditions to the Himalayas. He was also a veteran hunter. Among the creatures he killed with his expert marksmanship were Indian tigers, Balkan bears and Ceylonese elephants. Although never a missionary, he was a deeply religious man, and never missed an opportunity to evangelise any natives he might come across, listing the merits of his God like someone selling a gun.

Excited about his new mission, Tremanquai left for Zanzibar, where he acquired porters and supplies. However, a few days after he had made his way into the continent the Murrays lost all contact with him. The weeks crept by and still they received no message. They began to wonder what had become of the explorer. With great sorrow, they gave him up for lost as they had no Stanley to send after him.

Ten months later, Tremanquai burst into their offices, days after a memorial service had taken place with the permission of his wife – loath to don her widow's weeds. As was only to be expected, his appearance caused the same stir as if he had been a ghost. He was terribly gaunt, his eyes were feverish, and his filthy, malodorous body hardly looked as if he had spent the intervening months washing in rosewater. As was obvious from his deplorable condition, the expedition had been a complete disaster from the outset. No sooner had they penetrated the jungle than they were ambushed by Somali tribesmen. Tremanquai was unable even to take aim at those feline shadows emerging from the undergrowth before he was felled by a cascade of arrows. There, in the stillness of the jungle, far from the eyes of civilisation, the expedition was brutally massacred. The attackers had left him for dead, like his men.

But life had toughened Tremanquai and he had survived. He roamed the jungle for weeks, wounded and feverish, arrows still stuck in his flesh, using his rifle as a crutch, until his pitiful wanderings brought him to a small native village encircled by a palisade. Exhausted, he collapsed before the narrow entrance to the fence, like a piece of flotsam washed up by the sea.

He awoke several days later completely naked, stretched out on an uncomfortable straw mattress with repulsive poultices on his wounds. He was unable to identify the features of the young girl applying the sticky greenish dressings as belonging to any of the tribes he knew. Her body was long and supple, her hips extremely narrow and her chest almost as flat as a board. Her dark skin gave off a faint, dusky glow. He soon discovered that the men possessed the same slender build, their delicate bone structure almost visible beneath their slight musculature. Not knowing what tribe they belonged to, Tremanquai decided to invent a name for them. He called them the Reed People, because they were as slim and supple as reeds.

Tremanquai was an excellent shot, but he had little imagination. The Reed People's otherworldly physique, as well as the big black eyes in their exquisite doll-like faces, was a source of astonishment, but as his convalescence progressed, he discovered further reasons to be amazed: the impossible language they used to communicate with each other, a series of guttural noises he found impossible to reproduce, even though he was accustomed to imitating the most outlandish dialects; the fact that they all looked the same age; and the absence in the village of the most essential everyday implements. It was as though the life of these savages took place elsewhere, or as if they had succeeded in reducing it to a single act: breathing.

But one question above all preyed insistently on Tremanquai's mind: how did the Reed People resist the neighbouring tribes' repeated attacks? They were few in number, they looked neither strong nor fierce, and apparently his rifle was the only weapon in the village.

He soon discovered the answer. One night, a lookout warned that ferocious Masai tribesmen had surrounded the village. From his hut, with his carer, Tremanquai watched his saviours form a group in the centre of the village facing the narrow entrance, which curiously had no door. Standing in a fragile line as though offering themselves up for sacrifice, the Reed People linked hands and began to chant an intricate tune. Recovering from his astonishment, Tremanquai reached for his rifle and dragged himself back to the window with the intention of defending his hosts as best he could. Scarcely any torches were lit in the village, but the moon cast sufficient light for an experienced hunter like himself to take aim. He set his sights on the gap in the stockade, hoping that if he managed to pick off a few Masai the others might think the village was defended by white men and flee.

To his surprise, the girl gently lowered his weapon, indicating to him that his intervention was unnecessary. Tremanquai bridled, but the Reed girl's serene gaze made him think again. From his window, he watched with trepidation and bewilderment as the savage horde of Masai spilled through the entrance and his hosts carried on their discordant incantation while the spears came ever closer. The explorer steeled himself to witness the passive slaughter.

Then something happened, which Tremanquai had described in a quavering, incredulous voice, as though he found it hard to believe the words he himself was uttering. The air had split open. He could think of no better way to describe it. It was like tearing off a strip of wallpaper, he said, leaving the wall bare. Except in this case it was not a wall but another world. A world the explorer was at first unable to see into from where he was standing, but which gave off a pale glow, lighting the surrounding darkness. Astonished, he watched the first of the Masai tumble into the hole that had opened between them and their intended victims and vanish from reality, from the world Tremanquai was in, as though they had dissolved into thin air. On seeing their brothers swallowed up by the night, the rest of the Masai fled in panic. The explorer shook his head slowly, stunned by what he had seen.

He had lurched out of his hut and approached the hole that his hosts had opened in the very fabric of reality with their chanting. As he stood facing the opening, which flapped like a curtain, he realised it was bigger than he had first thought. It rose from the ground, reaching above his head, and was easily wide enough for a carriage to pass through. The edges billowed over the landscape, concealing then exposing it, like waves breaking on the shore. Fascinated, Tremanquai peered through it as if it were a window. On the other side, there was a very different world from ours, a sort of plain of pinkish rock, swept by a harsh wind that blew sand up from the surface: in the distance, blurred by the swirling dust, he was able to make out a range of sinister mountains. Disoriented and unable to see, the Masai floundered in the other world, gibbering and running each other through with their spears. Those left standing fell one by one. Tremanquai watched the macabre dance of death, transfixed: the Masais' bodies were caressed by a wind not of his world, like the strange dust clogging their nostrils.

The Reed People, still lined up in the middle of the village, resumed their ghostly chanting, and the hole began to close, slowly narrowing before Tremanquai's eyes until it had disappeared. The explorer moved his hand stupidly across the space where the air had split open. Suddenly it seemed as if there had never been anything between him and the choir of Reed People, which now broke up, its members wandering to different corners of the village, as though nothing out of the ordinary had occurred.

For Tremanquai, the world as he had known it would never be the same. He realised he now had only two choices. One was to see the world, which he had hitherto believed to be the only world, as one of many, superimposed like the pages of a book, so that all you had to do was thrust a dagger into it to open a pathway through all of them. The other was simpler: he could lose his mind.

That night, understandably, the explorer was unable to sleep. He lay on his straw mattress, eyes wide open, body tense, alert to the slightest noise coming from the darkness. The knowledge that he was surrounded by witches, against whom his rifle and his God were useless, filled him with dread. As soon as he was able to walk more than one step without feeling dizzy, he fled the Reed People's village. It took him several weeks to reach the port of Zanzibar, where he survived as best he could until he was able to stow away on a ship bound for London. He was back ten months after he had set out, but his experiences had changed him utterly.

It had been a disastrous voyage and, naturally enough, Sebastian Murray, Gilliam's father, did not believe a word of his story. He had no idea what had happened to his most experienced explorer during the months he had gone missing, but he was clearly unwilling to accept Tremanquai's tales of Reed People and their ridiculous holes in the air, which he considered the ravings of a lunatic. And his suspicions were borne out as Tremanquai proved incapable of living a normal life with his 'widow' and their two daughters. His wife would doubtless have preferred to carry on taking flowers to his grave than to live with the haunted misfit Africa had returned to her.

Tremanquai veered between apathy and random fits of madness, which swiftly turned the hitherto harmonious family home upside down. His accesses of insanity, which occasionally drove him to run naked through the streets or shoot at the hats of passers-by from his window, were a constant menace to the otherwise peaceful neighbourhood, and he was eventually carted off to the asylum at Guy's Hospital, where he was locked away.

Yet he was not entirely abandoned. Unbeknown to his father, Gilliam Murray went to see him in hospital as often as he could, moved by the grief he felt that one of his family's best men should be reduced to such a wretched state, but also thrilled to hear him narrate that incredible story. The young man of barely twenty, as Murray then was, visited the explorer with the eagerness of a child at a puppet show, and Tremanquai never disappointed him. Sitting on the edge of his camp-bed, his gaze straying towards the damp patches on the walls, he needed no encouragement to retell the tale of the Reed People, embellishing it with new and extraordinary details each time, grateful for the audience and for being given time to inflate his fantasy.

For a while, Murray believed he would regain his sanity, but after four years of incarceration, Tremanquai hanged himself in his cell. He left a note on a grubby piece of paper. In a spidery scrawl that could just as well have been his normal writing as distorted by his inner torment, he stated ironically that he was departing this world for another, which was only one of the many that existed.

By that time Murray had begun working in his father's company. Although Tremanquai's story still seemed to him sheer madness, but perhaps for that very reason, without his father's knowledge he sent two explorers to Africa to search for the apparently non-existent Reed People. Samuel Kaufmann and Forrest Austin were a couple of numbskulls, partial to showing off and drunken sprees, whose every expedition ended in disaster. But they were the only men his father would not miss, and the only two who would nonchalantly set off to the Dark Continent in search of a tribe of singing witches with the power to open doorways to other worlds. They were also the only men to whom, because of their glaring ineptitude, he dared assign a mission so hopeless, which was really only a modest tribute to the memory of the hapless Oliver Tremanquai.

Kaufmann and Austin left England almost in secret. Neither they nor Gilliam Murray could have known that they would become the most famous explorers of their day. Following instructions, as soon as they set foot in Africa they sent telegrams giving news of their progress. Murray read these cursorily before placing them in his desk drawer with a sad smile.

Everything changed when, three months later, he received one telling him they had at last found the Reed People. He could not believe it! Were they playing a joke on him in revenge for his having sent them on a wild-goose chase? he wondered. But the details contained in the telegrams ruled out any possibility of deceit because, as far as he remembered, they tallied entirely with those embellishing Oliver Tremanquai's story. Astonished though he was, he could only conclude that both they and Tremanquai were telling the truth: the Reed People did exist.

From that moment on, the telegrams became Gilliam Murray's reason for getting up in the morning. He awaited their arrival with eager anticipation, reading and rereading them behind the locked door of his office, unwilling for the time being to share the amazing discovery with anyone, not even his father.

According to the telegrams, once they had located the village, Kaufmann and Austin had no difficulty in being accepted as guests. In fact, the Reed People were apparently incapable of putting up any form of resistance. Neither did they seem particularly interested in the explorers' reasons for being there. They simply accepted their presence. The two men asked for no more and, rather than lose heart when faced with the difficulty of carrying out the essential part of their mission (which was to discover whether or not these savages could open passageways to other worlds), they resolved to be patient and treat their stay as a paid holiday. Murray could imagine them lounging around in the sun all day, polishing off the crates of whisky they had sneaked with them on the expedition while he had pretended to be looking the other way.

Amazingly, they could not have thought up a better strategy, for their continual state of alcoholic stupor, and the frequent dancing and fighting they engaged in naked in the grass, drew the attention of the Reed People, who were curious about the amber liquid that generated such jolly antics. Once they began sharing their whisky, a rough camaraderie sprang up between them, which Murray rejoiced in back in his office, for it was without doubt the first step towards a future co-existence. He was not mistaken, although fostering this primitive contact until it grew into a common bond of trust and friendship cost him several consignments of the best Scotch. To this day he wondered whether so many bottles had really been necessary for such a small tribe.

At last, one morning, he received the long-awaited telegram, in which Kaufmann and Austin described how the Reed People had led them to the middle of the village and, in a seemingly beautiful gesture of friendship and gratitude, had opened for them the hole through to the other world. The explorers described the aperture and the pink landscape they had glimpsed through it, using exactly the same words as Tremanquai had employed five years earlier. This time, however, the young Murray no longer saw them as part of a made-up story: now he knew it was for real.

All of a sudden he felt trapped, suffocated, and not because he was locked away in his little office. He felt hemmed in by the walls of a universe he was now convinced was not the only one of its kind. But this constraint would soon end, he thought. He devoted a few moments to the memory of Oliver Tremanquai. He assumed that the man's deep religious beliefs had prevented him from assimilating what he had seen, leaving him no other course than the precarious path of madness. Luckily, that pair of oafs, Kaufmann and Austin, possessed far simpler minds, which should spare them a similar fate.

He reread the telegram hundreds of times. Not only did the Reed People exist, they practised something that Murray, unlike Tremanquai, preferred to call magic, rather than witchcraft. An unknown world had opened itself up to Kaufmann and Austin, and naturally they could not resist exploring it.

As Murray read their subsequent telegrams, he regretted not having accompanied them. With the blessing of the Reed People, who left them to their own devices, the pair made brief incursions into the other world, diligently reporting its peculiarities. It consisted largely of a vast pink plain of faintly luminous rock, stretching out beneath a sky permanently obscured by incredibly dense fog. If there were any sun behind it, its rays were unable to shine through. As a consequence, the only light came from the strange substance on the ground, so that while one's boots were clearly visible, the landscape was plunged into gloom, day and night merging into an eternal dusk, making it very difficult to see long distances. From time to time, a raging wind whipped the plain, producing sand storms that made everything even more difficult to see.

The two men had immediately noticed something strange: the

moment they stepped through the hole their pocket watches stopped. Once back in their own reality the mechanisms mysteriously stirred again. It was as though they had unanimously decided to stop measuring the time their owners spent in the other world. Kaufmann and Austin looked at one another – it is not difficult to imagine them shrugging their shoulders, baffled.

They made a further discovery after spending a night, according to their calculations, in the camp they had set up right beside the opening so that they could keep an eye on the Reed People. There was no need for them to shave, because while they were in the other world their beards stopped growing. In addition, Austin had cut his arm seconds before stepping through the hole, and as soon as he was on the other side it had stopped bleeding, to the point that he had even forgotten to bandage it. He did not remember the wound until the moment they were back in the village and it bled again.

Intrigued, Gilliam Murray wrote down this extraordinary incident in his notebook, as well as what had happened with their watches and beards. Everything pointed to some impossible stoppage of time. While he speculated in his office, Kaufmann and Austin stocked up on ammunition and food and set out towards the only thing that broke the monotony of the plain: the ghostly mountain range, scarcely visible on the horizon.

As their watches continued to be unusable, they decided to measure the time their journey took by the number of nights they slept. This method soon proved ineffective, because at times the wind rose so suddenly and with such force they were obliged to stay awake all night holding the tent down, or their accumulated tiredness crept up on them when they stopped for food or rest. All they could say was that after an indeterminate length of time, which was neither very long nor very short, they reached the mountains. They proved to be made of the same luminous rock as the plain but had a hideous appearance, like a set of rotten, broken teeth, their jagged peaks piercing the thick clouds that blotted out the sky.

The two men spotted a few hollows that looked like caves. Having no other plan, they decided to scale the slopes until they reached the nearest one. This did not take long. Once they had reached the pinnacle of a small mountain, they had a broader view of the plain. Far off in the distance the hole had been reduced to a bright dot on the horizon. They could see their way back, acting as a guiding light. They were not worried that the Reed People might close the hole, because they had taken the precaution of bringing what remained of the whisky with them.

It was then that they noticed other bright dots shining in the distance. It was difficult to see clearly through the mist, but there must have been half a dozen. Were they more holes leading to other worlds?

They found the answer in the very cave they intended to explore. As soon as they entered it they could see it was inhabited. There were signs of life everywhere: burned-out fires, bowls, tools and other basic implements – things Tremanquai had found so conspicuous by their absence in the Reed People's village. At the back of the cave they discovered a narrow enclosure, the walls of which were covered with paintings. Most depicted scenes from everyday life, and from the willowy rag-doll figures, only the Reed People could have painted them. Apparently, that dark world was where they really lived. The village was no more than a temporary location, a provisional settlement, perhaps one of many they had built in other worlds.

Kaufmann and Austin did not consider the drawings particularly significant. But two caught their attention. One of these took up nearly an entire wall. As far as they could tell it was meant to be a map of that world, or at least the part the tribe had succeeded in exploring, which was limited to the area near the mountains. What intrigued them was that this crude map marked the location of some other holes, and, if they were not mistaken, what they contained. The drawings were easy enough to interpret: a yellow star represented a hole, and the painted images next to it, the hole's contents. At least, this was what they deduced from the dot surrounded by huts, apparently representing the hole the explorers had climbed through to get there and the village on the other side. The map showed four other openings, fewer than those the two men had glimpsed on the horizon. Where did they lead?

Whether from idleness or boredom, the Reed People had only painted the contents of the holes nearest their cave. One seemed to depict a battle between two different tribes: one human-shaped, the other square or rectangular. The remainder of the drawings were impossible to make out. Consequently, the only thing Kaufmann and Austin could be clear about was that the world they were in contained dozens of holes like the one they had come through, but they could only find out where any of them led if they passed through them: the Reed People's scrawls were as mystifying as the dreams of a blind man.

The second painting that caught their eye was on the opposite wall and showed a group of Reed People running from what looked like a gigantic four-legged monster with a dragon's tail and spikes on its back. Kaufmann and Austin glanced at one another, alarmed to find themselves in the same world as a wild animal whose mere image was enough to scare the living daylights out of them. What would happen if they came across the real thing? However, this discovery did not make them turn back. They both had rifles and enough ammunition to kill a whole herd of monsters, assuming they existed and were not simply a mythological invention. They also had whisky, which would fire up their courage – or, at least, turn the prospect of being eaten by an elephantine monster into a relatively minor nuisance. What more did they need?

Accordingly, they decided to carry on exploring, and set out for the opening where the battle was going on between the two tribes because it was closest to the mountains. The journey was gruelling, hampered by freak sandstorms that forced them to erect their tent and take refuge inside if they did not want to be scoured like cooking pots. Thankfully, they did not meet any of the giant creatures. Of course, when they finally reached the hole, they had no idea how long it had taken them to get there, only that the journey had been exhausting.

Its size and appearance were identical to the one they had first stepped through into that murky world. The only difference was that, instead of crude huts, inside this one there was a ruined city. Scarcely a single building remained standing, yet there was something oddly familiar about the structures. They stood for a few moments, surveying the ruins from the other side of the hole, as one would peer into a shop window, but no sign of life broke the calm. What kind of war could have wrought such terrible devastation?

Depressed by the dreadful scene, Kaufman and Austin restored their courage with a few slugs of whisky, then donned their pith helmets and leaped valiantly through the opening. Their senses were immediately assailed by an intense familiar odour. Smiling with bewilderment, it dawned on them that they were simply smelling their own world again: they had been unaware of it during their journey across the pink plain.

Rifles at the ready, they scoured their surroundings, moving cautiously through the rubble-filled streets, shocked at the sight of so much devastation, until they stumbled across another obstacle, which stopped them dead in their tracks. Kaufmann and Austin gazed incredulously at the object blocking their path: it was none other than the clock tower of Big Ben. It lay in the middle of the street like a severed fish head, the vast clock face a great eye staring at them with mournful resignation.

The discovery made them glance uneasily about them. Strangely moved, they cast an affectionate eye over each toppled edifice, the desolate ruined landscape where a few plumes of black smoke darkened the sky over a London razed to the ground. Neither could contain their tears. In fact, the two men would have stood there for ever, weeping over the remains of their beloved city, had it not been for a peculiar clanking sound that came from nearby.

Rifles at the ready again, they followed the clatter until they came to a small mound of rubble. They clambered up it noiselessly, crouching low. Unseen in their improvised lookout, they saw what was causing the racket. It was coming from strange, vaguely humanoid metal creatures, powered by what looked like tiny steam engines attached to their backs. The loud clanging noise they had heard was the sound of clumsy iron feet knocking against the metal debris strewn on the ground. The bemused explorers had no idea what these creatures might be, until Austin plucked from the rubble what looked like the crumpled page of a newspaper.

With trembling fingers, he opened it and discovered a photograph of the same creatures as the ones they could see below them. The headline announced the unstoppable advance of the automatons, and went on to encourage readers to rally to the support of the human army led by the brave Captain Derek Shackleton. What most surprised them, however, was the date: this loose page was from a newspaper printed 3 April 2000. As one, Kaufmann and Austin shook their heads, very slowly from left to right, but before they had time to express their amazement in a more sophisticated way, the remains of a rafter in the mound of rubble fell into the street with a loud crash, alerting the automatons.

Kaufmann and Austin exchanged terrified glances, and took to their heels, running full pelt towards the hole they had come through without looking back. They easily slipped through it again, but did not stop running until their legs would carry them no further.

They erected their tent and cowered inside, trying to collect their thoughts, to absorb what they had seen – with the obligatory help of some whisky, of course. It was clearly time for them to return to the village and report back to London everything they had seen. They were certain that Gilliam Murray would be able to explain it.

However, their problems did not end there. On the way back to the village, they were attacked by a gigantic beast with spikes on its back, whose potential existence they had forgotten about. They had great difficulty in killing it. They used up nearly all their ammunition trying to scare it away, because the bullets kept bouncing off the spiked armour without injuring it. Finally, they managed to chase it away by shooting at its eyes, its only weak point as far as they could determine.

Having successfully fought off the beast, they arrived back at the hole without further incident, and immediately sent a message to London relating all their discoveries.

As soon as he received their news, Gilliam Murray set sail for Africa. He joined the two explorers in the Reed People's village where, like doubting Thomas plunging his fingers into Christ's wounds after he had risen from the dead, he made his way to the razed city of London in the year 2000. He spent many months with the Reed People, although he could not be sure exactly how many as he spent extensive periods exploring the pink plain in order to verify Kaufmann and Austin's claims.

Just as they had described in their telegrams, in that sunless world watches stopped ticking, razors became superfluous, and nothing appeared to mark the passage of time. Consequently he concluded that, incredible though it might seem, the moments he spent there were a hiatus in his life, a temporary suspension of his inexorable journey towards death. He realised his imagination had not been playing tricks on him when he returned to the village and the puppy he had taken with him ran to join its siblings: they had all come from the same litter but now the others were grown dogs. Gilliam had not needed to take a single shave during his exploration of the plain, but Eternal, the puppy, was a far more spectacular manifestation of the absence of time in the other world.

He also deduced that the holes did not lead to other universes, as he had first believed, but to different times in a world that was none other than his own. The pink plain was outside the time continuum, outside time, the arena in which man's life took place alongside that of plants and other animals. And the beings inhabiting that world, Tremanquai's Reed People, knew how to break out of the time continuum by creating holes in it that enabled man to travel in time, to cross from one era to another.

This realisation filled Murray with excitement and dread. He had made the greatest discovery in the history of mankind: he had discovered what lay underneath the world, what lay behind reality. He had discovered the fourth dimension.

How strange life was, he thought. He had started out trying to find the source of the Nile, and ended up discovering a secret passage that led to the year 2000. But that was how all the greatest discoveries were made. Had not the voyage of the *Beagle* been prompted by spurious financial and strategic interests? The discoveries resulting from it would have been far less interesting had a young naturalist perceptive enough to notice the variations between finches' beaks not been on board. And yet the story of natural selection would revolutionise the world. His discovery of the fourth dimension had happened in a similarly random way.

But what use was there in discovering something if you could not share it with the rest of the world? Gilliam wanted to take Londoners to the year 2000 so that they could see with their own eyes what the future held for them. The question was: how? He could not possibly take boatloads of city-dwellers to a native village in the heart of Africa, where the Reed People were living. The only answer was to move the hole to London. Was that possible? He did not know, but he would lose nothing by trying.

Leaving Kaufmann and Austin to guard the Reed People, Murray returned to London, where he built a cast-iron box the size of a room. He took it, with a thousand bottles of whisky, to the village, where he planned to strike a bargain that would change people's perception of the known world. Drunk as lords, the Reed People consented to his whim of singing their magic chants inside the sinister box. Once the hole had materialised, he herded them out and closed the heavy doors behind them. The three men waited until the last of the Reed People had succumbed to the effects of the whisky before setting off for home.

It was an arduous journey, and only when the enormous box was on the ship at Zanzibar did Murray begin to breathe more easily. Even so, he barely slept a wink during the passage. He spent almost the entire time on deck, gazing lovingly at the fateful box and wondering whether it was not in fact empty. Could one really steal a hole? His eagerness to know the answer to that question gnawed at him, making the return journey seem interminable. He could hardly believe it when at last they docked at Liverpool.

As soon as he reached his offices, he opened the box in complete secret. The hole was still there! They had successfully stolen it! The next step was to show it to his father.

'What the devil is this?' exclaimed Sebastian Murray, when he saw the hole shimmering inside the box.

'This is what drove Oliver Tremanquai mad, Father,' Gilliam replied, pronouncing the explorer's name with affection. 'So, take care.'

His father turned pale. Nevertheless, he accompanied his son through the hole and travelled into the future, to a demolished London where humans hid in the ruins like rats. Once he had got over the shock, father and son agreed they must make this discovery known to the world. And what better way to do this than to turn the hole into a business? Taking people to see the year 2000 would bring in enough money to cover the cost of the journeys and to fund further exploration of the fourth dimension.

They proceeded to map out a secure route to the hole into the future, eliminating any dangers, setting up lookout posts and smoothing the road so that a tramcar with thirty seats could cross it easily. Sadly, his father did not live long enough to see Murray's Time Travel open its doors to the public, but Murray consoled himself with the thought that at least he had seen the future beyond his own death.

IX

Once he had finished telling his story, Murray fell silent and looked expectantly at his two visitors. Andrew assumed he was hoping for some kind of response, but had no idea what to say. He felt embarrassed. Everything his host had told them was no more believable than an adventure story. That pink plain seemed about as real to him as Lilliput, the South Sea Island inhabited by little people where Lemuel Gulliver had been shipwrecked. From the stupefied smile on Charles's face, however, he assumed his cousin did believe it. After all, he had travelled to the year 2000: what did it matter whether he had got there by crossing a pink plain where time had stopped?

'And now, gentlemen, if you would kindly follow me, I'll show you something only a few trusted people are allowed to see,' Murray declared, resuming the guided tour of his commodious office.

With Eternal continually running round his master, the three men walked across to another wall, where a small collection of photographs awaited them with what was probably another map, although this was concealed behind a red silk curtain. Andrew was surprised to discover that the photographs had been taken in the fourth dimension, although they might easily have depicted any desert, since cameras were unable to record the colour of this or any other world. He had to use his imagination, then, to see the white smear of sand as pink. The majority documented routine moments during the expedition: Murray and two other men, presumably Kaufmann and Austin, putting up tents; drinking coffee during a pause; lighting a fire; posing in front of the phantom mountains, almost entirely obscured by thick fog. It all looked too normal.

Only one of the images made Andrew feel he was contemplating an alien world. In it Kaufmann (who was short and fat) and Austin (who was tall and thin) stood smiling exaggeratedly, hats tilted to the side of their heads, rifles hanging from their shoulders, and one boot resting on the massive head of a fairy-tale dragon, which lay dead on the sand like a hunting trophy. Andrew was about to lean towards it and take a closer look at the amorphous lump, when an awful screeching noise made him start. Beside him, Murray was pulling a gold cord, which drew back the silk curtain, revealing what was behind it.

'Rest assured, gentlemen, you will find no other map like it anywhere in England,' he declared, swelling with pride. 'It is an exact replica of the drawing in the Reed People's cave, expanded, naturally, after our subsequent explorations.'

What the puppet-theatre curtain had uncovered looked more like a drawing by a child with an active imagination than a map. The colour pink predominated, of course, representing the plain, with the mountains in the middle. But the shadowy peaks were not the only geological feature on the map: in the right-hand corner, for example, there was a squiggly line, presumably a river, and close by it a light-green patch, possibly a forest or meadow. Andrew could not help feeling that these everyday symbols, used in maps that charted the world he lived in, were incongruous in what was supposed to be a map of the fourth dimension. But the most striking thing about the drawing was the gold dots peppering the plain, evidently meant to symbolise the holes. Two – the entrance to the year 2000, and the one now in Murray's possession – were linked by a thin red line, which must represent the route taken by the time-travelling tramcar.

'As you can see, there are many holes, but we still have no idea where they lead. Does one of them go back to the autumn of 1888? Who knows? It is certainly possible,' said Murray, staring significantly at Andrew. 'Kaufmann and Austin are trying to reach the one nearest the entrance to the year 2000, but they still haven't found a way to circumnavigate the herd of beasts grazing in the valley right in front of it.'

While Andrew and Charles studied the map, Murray knelt down to stroke the dog. 'Ah, the fourth dimension. What mysteries it holds,' he mused. 'All I know is that our candle never burns out there, to use a poetic turn of phrase. Eternal only looks one, but he was born four years ago. And I suppose that must be his actual age – unless the long periods he has spent on the plain, where time seems to leave no mark, are of no matter. Eternal was with me while I carried out my studies in Africa, and since we came back to London, he sleeps next to me every night inside the hole. I did not name him "Eternal" for nothing, gentlemen, and while I can, I'll do everything in my power to honour his name.'

Andrew felt a shiver run down his spine when his and the dog's eyes met.

'What is that building supposed to be?' asked Charles, pointing to an image of a castle close to the mountains.

'Ah . . . that,' Gilliam said uneasily. 'That's Her Majesty's palace.'

'The Queen has a palace in the fourth dimension?' asked Charles, astonished.

'That's right, Mr Winslow. Let us call it a thank-you present for her generous contribution to our expeditions,' Gilliam paused, unsure whether he should go on. At last he added, 'Ever since we organised a private journey to the year 2000 for the Queen and her entourage, she has shown great interest in the laws governing the fourth dimension and, well . . . She made it known to us that she would like a private residence to be put at her disposal on the plain, where she could spend time when her duties allow, as one does at a spa. She has been going there for some months now, which makes me think her reign will be a long one . . .' he said, with no attempt to conceal his irritation at having been forced to make this concession. He, no doubt, had to be content to spend his nights in a wretched tent with Eternal. 'But that doesn't concern me. All I want is to be left alone. The Empire wishes to conquer the moon. Let it . . . But the future is mine!'

He closed the little curtain and led them back to his desk. He invited them to take a seat, and himself sat in his armchair, while Eternal – the dog who would outlive mankind, excepting Murray, the Queen and the lucky employees at her palace outside the time continuum – slumped at his feet.

'Well, gentlemen, I hope I've answered your question about why we are only able to take you to May the twentieth in the year 2000, where all you will see is the result of the most decisive battle in human history,' he said ironically.

Andrew snorted. None of that interested him in the slightest, at least while he was unable to experience anything other than pain. He was back at square one, it seemed. He would have to go ahead with his suicide plan as soon as Charles's back was turned. The man had to sleep some time.

'So, there's no way of travelling back to the year 1888?' said his cousin, apparently unwilling to give up.

'Not without a time machine,' replied Murray, shrugging his shoulders.

'We'll just have to hope science invents one soon,' Charles said ruefully, patting his cousin's knee and rising from his chair.

'It's just possible that one has already been invented, gentlemen,' Murray blurted out.

Charles swivelled to face him 'What do you mean?'

'Hm, it's just a suspicion . . . but when our company first started, there was someone who vehemently opposed it. He insisted time travel was too dangerous, that it had to be taken slowly. I always suspected he said this because he had a time machine, and wanted to experiment with it before making it public. Or perhaps he wanted to keep it to himself, to become the only master of time.'

'Who are you talking about?' asked Andrew.

Murray sat back in his chair, a smug grin on his face. 'Why, Mr Wells, of course,' he replied.

'But, whatever gave you that idea?' asked Charles. 'In his novel Wells only writes about journeying into the future. He doesn't even envisage the possibility of going back in time.'

'That's exactly my point, Mr Winslow. Just imagine, gentlemen, if somebody were to build a time machine, the most important invention in the history of humanity. Given its incredible potential, they would have no choice but to keep it secret, to prevent it falling into the hands of some unscrupulous individual who might use it for their own ends. But would they be able to resist the temptation to divulge their secret to the world? A novel would be the perfect way of making their invention known without anyone ever suspecting it was anything but pure fiction. Don't you agree? Or if vanity doesn't convince you as a motive, then what if they weren't trying to satisfy their ego at all? What if *The Time Machine* were merely a decoy, a message in a bottle cast into the sea, a cry for help to somebody who might know how to interpret it? Who knows? Anyway, gentlemen, Wells did contemplate the possibility of going back in time, and with the aim of changing it, moreover, which I imagine is what motivates you, Mr Harrington.'

Andrew jumped, as if he had been discovered committing a crime. Murray smiled at him wryly, then rifled through one of his desk drawers. He pulled out a copy of *Science Schools Journal* dating from 1888 and threw it on to the table. The title on the cover of the dog-eared periodical was *The Chronic Argonauts*, by H. G. Wells. He handed it to Andrew, asking him to take good care of it as it was a rare copy.

'Exactly eight years ago, as a young man having recently arrived in London and ready to conquer the world, Wells published a serial novel entitled *The Chronic Argonauts*. The main character was a scientist called Moses Nebogipfel, who travelled back in time to commit a murder. Perhaps Wells considered he had overreached himself, and when he recycled the idea for his novel, he eliminated the journeys into the past, perhaps so as not to give his readers ideas. In any case, he decided to concentrate solely on travelling into the future. He made his protagonist a far more upright character than Nebogipfel, as you know, and never actually mentions his name in the novel. Perhaps Wells could not resist this gesture.'

Andrew and Charles stared at one another, then at Murray, who was scribbling something in a notebook. 'Here is Wells's address,' he said, holding out a scrap of paper to Andrew. 'You have nothing to lose by seeing whether my suspicions are well founded or not.'

X

Drifting through the scent of roses suffusing the lobby, the cousins left the offices of Murray's Time Travel. In the street, they hailed the first hansom cab they saw and gave the driver the address in Woking, Surrey, where the author H. G. Wells lived. The meeting with Gilliam Murray had plunged Andrew into a profound silence where God only knew what dark thoughts he was grappling with. But the journey would take at least three hours, and therefore Charles was in no hurry to draw his cousin into conversation. He preferred to leave him to gather his thoughts. They had experienced enough excitement for one day, and there was still more to come. In any case, he had learned to sit back and enjoy the frequent unexpected bouts of silence that punctuated his relationship with Andrew, so he closed his eyes and let himself be rocked by the cab as it sped out of the city.

Although they were not troubled by the silence, I imagine that you, who are in a sense sharing their journey, might find it a little tiresome. Therefore, rather than lecture you on the nature and quality of this inviolate calm, scarcely broken by the cab's creaks and groans, or describe to you the view of the horses' hindquarters upon which Andrew's gaze was firmly fixed, and, since I am unable even to relate in any exciting way what was going on in Andrew's head (where the prospect of saving Marie Kelly was slowly fading because, although a method of travelling through time had apparently been discovered, it was still impossible to do so with any accuracy), I propose to make use of this lull in proceedings to tell you about something still pending in this story. I alone can narrate this, as it is an episode about which the cab's occupants are completely unaware.

I refer to the spectacular ascent up the social ladder of their respective fathers, William Harrington and Sydney Winslow. William Harrington presided over it, with his typical mixture of good fortune and rough-and-ready abilities, and although both men resolved to keep it secret, they cannot do so from me, as I see everything whether I wish to or not.

I could give you my honest opinion of William Harrington, but what I think is of no consequence. Let us rather stick with Andrew's idea of his father, which is not far from the truth. Andrew saw his father as a warrior of commerce, capable, as you will discover, of the most heroic exploits in the field of business. However, when it came to everyday hand-to-hand combat, in which the struggles that make us human take place, allowing us to show kindness or generosity, he was apparently incapable of anything but the meanest acts, as you have already seen. William Harrington was of the class of person who possesses a self-assurance that is both their strength and their downfall, a cast-iron confidence that can easily turn into excessive, blind arrogance. In the end, he was like someone who stands on his head, then complains that the world is upside down, or, if you prefer, like someone who believes God created the Earth for him to walk upon, with which I have said enough.

William Harrington returned from the Crimea to a world dominated by machines. He realised straight away that this would not supersede the old way of doing things since even the glass in the Crystal Palace, that transparent whale then marooned in Hyde Park, had been made by hand. That was evidently not the way to grow rich, a goal he had set himself, with the typical insouciance of a twenty-year-old, as he lay in bed at night with his new wife, the rather timid daughter of the match manufacturer for whom he worked.

The thought of being trapped in the dreary life already mapped out for him kept him awake, and he wondered whether he ought not to rebel against such a common fate. Why had his mother gone to the trouble of bringing him into the world if the most exciting moment in his life was having been lamed by a bayonet? Was he doomed to be just another anonymous cipher, or would he pass into the annals of history?

His lamentable performance in the Crimea would appear to suggest the former, yet William Harrington had too voracious a nature to be content with that. 'As far as I can tell, I only have one life,' he said to himself, 'and what I don't achieve in this one I won't achieve in the next.'

The following day he called on his brother-in-law Sydney, a bright, capable young man who was wasting his life as an accountant in the family match firm, and assured him that he, too, was destined for greater things. However, in order to achieve the rapid social ascent William envisaged, they must forget the match business and start up their own enterprise, easily done if they made use of Sydney's savings. During the course of a long drinking session, William convinced his brother-in-law to let him play with his money, declaring that a small amount of entrepreneurial risk would inject some excitement into his dull life. They had little to lose and much to gain. It was essential they find a business that would bring in large profits quickly, he concluded.

To his amazement, Sydney agreed, and soon put his imaginative mind to work. He arrived at their next meeting with the plans for what he was convinced would be a revolutionary invention. The Bachelor's Helpmate, as he had called it, consisted of a chair designed for lovers of erotic literature, and was equipped with a lectern that automatically turned the pages, allowing the reader to keep both hands free. William could see from Sydney's detailed drawings that the device came with accessories, such as a small washbasin, and even a sponge, so that the client did not have to interrupt his reading to get up from the chair. Sydney was convinced his product would make their fortune, but William was not so sure: his brother-in-law had clearly confused his own necessities with those of others. However, once William had succeeded in the difficult task of convincing him that his sophisticated seat was not as essential to the Empire as he had imagined, they found themselves without a decent idea to their names.

Desperate, they concentrated on the flow of merchandise coming in from the colonies. What products had not yet been imported? What unfulfilled needs did the British have? They looked around carefully, but it seemed nothing was wanting. Her Majesty, with her tentacular grasp, was already divesting the world of everything her subjects required. Of course, there was one thing they lacked, but this was a necessity no one cared to mention.

They discovered it one day while strolling through the commercial district of New York, where they had gone in search of inspiration. They were preparing to return to the hotel and soak their aching feet in a basin of salt water, when their eye fell on a product displayed in a shop window. Behind the glass was a stack of strange packets containing fifty sheets of moisturised paper. Printed on the back were the words 'Gayetty's Medicated Paper'. What the devil was this for? They soon discovered the answer from the instructions pasted in the window, which, without a hint of embarrassment, depicted a hand applying the product to the most intimate area of a posterior. This fellow Gayetty had obviously decided that corncobs and parish newsletters were a thing of the past.

Once they had recovered from their surprise, William and Sydney looked at each other meaningfully. This was it! It did not take a genius to imagine the warm reception thousands of British backsides, raw from being rubbed with rough newspaper, would give this heaven-sent gift. At fifty cents a packet, they would soon make their fortune. They purchased enough stock to furnish a small shop they acquired in one of London's busiest streets, filled the window with their product, put up a poster illustrating its correct usage, and waited behind the counter for customers to flock in. But not a single soul walked through the door on the day the shop opened, or in the days that followed, which soon turned into weeks.

It took William and Sydney three months to admit defeat. Their dreams of wealth had been cruelly dashed at the outset, although they had enough medicated paper never to need worry about procuring another Sears catalogue. However, at times society obeys its own twisted logic, and the moment they closed their disastrous shop, their business suddenly took off. In the dark corners of inns, in alleyway entrances, in their own homes during the early hours, William and Sydney were assailed by a variety of individuals who, in hushed tones and glancing furtively about them, ordered packets of their miraculous paper before disappearing back into the gloom.

Surprised at first by the cloak-and-dagger aspect they were obliged to adopt, the two young entrepreneurs soon became accustomed to tramping the streets at dead of night, one limping along, the other puffing and panting, to make their clandestine deliveries far from prying eyes. They soon grew used to depositing their embarrassing product in house doorways, or signalling with a tap of their cane on window-panes, or tossing packets off bridges on to barges passing noiselessly below, slipping into deserted parks and retrieving wads of pound notes stashed under a bench, whistling like a couple of songbirds through mansion railings. Everyone in London wanted to use Gayetty's wonderful paper without their neighbour finding out, a fact of which William slyly took advantage, increasing the price of his product to what would eventually become an outrageous sum – which most customers were nevertheless willing to pay.

Within a couple of years they were able to purchase two luxurious dwellings in the Brompton Road area, from where they soon upped sticks for Kensington. In addition to his collection of expensive canes, William measured his success by the ability to acquire ever larger houses.

Amazed that the reckless act of placing his entire savings at his brother-in-law's disposal had provided him with a fine mansion in Queen's Gate from whose balcony he could survey the most elegant side of London, Sydney resolved to enjoy what he had, giving himself to the pleasures of family life, so extolled by the clergy. He filled his house with children, books, paintings by promising artists, took on a couple of servants and, at a safe distance from them now, cultivated the disdain he claimed he had always felt towards the lower classes to the extent that it became contempt. In brief, he quietly adapted to his new affluence even though it was based on the ignoble business of selling toilet paper.

William was different. His proud, inquisitive nature made it impossible for him to be satisfied with that. He needed public recognition, to be respected by society. In other words, he wanted the great and the good of London to invite him foxhunting, to treat him as an equal. But, much as he paraded through London's smoking rooms doling out his card, this did not happen. Faced with a situation he was powerless to change, he built up a bitter resentment of the wealthy élite, who subjected him to the most abysmal ostracism while wiping their distinguished backsides with the paper he provided. During one of the rare gatherings to which the two men were invited, his anger boiled over when some wag bestowed on them the title 'Official Wipers to the Queen'. Before anyone could laugh, William Harrington hurled himself on the insolent dandy, breaking his nose with the pommel of his cane before Sydney managed to drag him away.

The gathering proved a turning point in their lives. William Harrington learned from it a harsh but valuable lesson: the medicinal paper to which he owed everything, and which had generated so much wealth, was a disgrace that would stain his life for ever unless he did something about it. He began to invest part of his earnings in less disreputable businesses, such as the burgeoning railway industry. In a matter of months he had become the majority shareholder in several locomotive repair shops. His next step was to buy a failing shipping company called Fellowship, inject new blood into it, and turn it into the most profitable of ocean-going concerns. Through his tiny empire of successful businesses, which Sydney managed with the easy elegance of an orchestra conductor, in less than two years William had dissociated his name from medicinal paper, cancelling the final shipment and leaving London plunged in silent despair.

In the spring of 1872, Annesley Hall invited him to his first hunt gathering on his Newstead estate, which was attended by all of London society, who eagerly applauded William's extraordinary achievements. It was there that the witty young man who had made a joke at his expense regrettably perished. According to the newspaper account, the ill-fated youth accidentally shot himself in the foot.

It was around that time when William Harrington dusted off his old uniform and commissioned a portrait of himself bursting out of it, smiling as though his unadorned chest were plastered with medals, and greeting all who entered his mansion with the masterful gaze of sole owner of that corner opposite Hyde Park.

This, and no other, was the secret their fathers so jealously guarded and whose air of light entertainment I considered appropriate for this rather wearisome journey. But I am afraid we have reached the end of our story too soon. Total silence still reigns in the cab and is likely to do so for some time because, when he is in the mood, Andrew is capable of daydreaming for hours, unless prodded with a red-hot poker or doused in boiling oil – neither of which Charles is in the habit of carrying around with him. Therefore I have no other choice but to take flight again so that we reach their destination, Mr Wells's house, more quickly than they do. Not only, as you will have gathered from some of my commentaries, am I not subject to the cab's tortuous pace but I can travel at the speed of light, so that – *voilà!* – in the blink of an eye, or faster still, we find ourselves in Woking, floating above the roof of a modest three-storey house with a garden overrun by brambles and silver birch, whose frail façade trembles slightly as the trains to Lynton roar past.

XI

I immediately discover I have picked an inopportune moment to intrude upon Herbert George Wells's life. In order to inconvenience him as little as possible, I could quickly pass over the description of his physical appearance by saying no more than that the celebrated author was a pale, skinny young man who had seen better days. However, of all the characters swimming like fish in this story, Wells is the one who appears most frequently, no doubt to his regret, which compels me to be a little more precise in my depiction of him.

Besides being painfully thin, with a deathly pallor, Wells sported a fashionable moustache, straight with downward-pointed ends that seemed too big and bushy for his childish face. It hung like a dark cloud over an exquisite, rather feminine mouth, which, with his blue eyes, would have lent him an almost angelic air were it not for the roguish smile playing on his lips. In brief, Wells looked like a porcelain doll with twinkling eyes, behind which roamed a lively, penetrating intellect. For lovers of detail, or those lacking in imagination, I shall go on to say that he weighed little more than eight stone, wore a size eight and a half shoe and his hair neatly parted on the left. That day he smelt slightly of stale sweat – his body odour was usually pleasant – as some hours earlier he had been for a ride with his new wife through the surrounding Surrey roads astride their tandem bicycle, the latest invention that had won the couple over because it needed no food or shelter and never strayed from where you left it. There is little more I can add, short of dissecting the man or going into intimate details such as the modest proportions and slight south-easterly curvature of his manhood.

At that very moment, he was seated at the kitchen table, where he usually did his writing, a magazine in his hands. His stiff body, bolt upright in his chair, betrayed his inner turmoil. For while it might have seemed as though Wells were simply letting himself be enveloped by the rippling shadows cast by the afternoon sun shining on the tree in the garden; he was in fact trying to contain his simmering rage. He took a deep breath, then another and another, in a desperate effort to summon a soothing calm. Evidently this did not work, for he ended up hurling the magazine against the kitchen door. It fluttered through the air like a wounded pigeon and landed a yard or two from his feet.

Wells gazed at it with slight regret, then sighed and stood up to retrieve it, scolding himself for this outburst of rage unworthy of a civilised person. He put the magazine back on the table and sat in front of it again, with the resigned expression of one who knows that accepting reversals of fortune with good grace is a sign of courage and intelligence.

The magazine in question was an edition of the *Speaker*, which had published a devastating review of his most recent novel, *The Island of Doctor Moreau*, another popular work of science fiction. Beneath the surface lurked one of his pet themes: the visionary destroyed by his own dreams. The protagonist is a man called Prendick, who is shipwrecked and has the misfortune to be washed up on an uncharted island that turns out to be the domain of a mad scientist exiled from England because of his brutal experiments on animals. On that remote island, the eponymous doctor has become like a primitive god to a tribe made up of the freakish creations of his unhinged imagination, the monstrous spawn of his efforts to turn wild animals into men.

The work was Wells's attempt to go one step further than Darwin by having his deranged doctor attempt to modify life by speeding up the naturally slow process of evolution. It was also a tribute to Jonathan Swift, his favourite author: the scene in which Prendick returns to England to tell the world about the phantasmagorical Eden he has escaped from is almost identical to the chapter in which Gulliver describes the land of the Houyhnhnm. And although Wells had not been satisfied with his book, which had evolved almost in fits and starts from the rather haphazard juxtaposition of more or less powerful images, and had been prepared for a possible slating by the critics, it stung all the same.

The first blow had taken him by surprise, as it had come from his wife, who considered the killing of the doctor by a deformed puma he had tried to transform into a woman a jibe at the women's movement. How could Jane possibly have thought that? The next jab came from the *Saturday Review*, a journal he had hitherto found favourable in its judgements. To his further annoyance, the objectionable article was written by Peter Chalmers Mitchell, a young, talented zoologist who had been Wells's fellow pupil at the Normal School of Science, and who, betraying their once friendly relations, now declared bluntly that Wells's intention was simply to shock. The critic in the *Speaker* went still further, accusing the author of being morally corrupt for insinuating that anyone succeeding through experimentation in giving animals a human appearance would logically go on to engage in sexual relations with them. 'Mr Wells uses his undoubted talent to shameless effect,' declared the reviewer. Wells asked himself whether his or the critic's mind was polluted by immoral thoughts.

Wells was only too aware that unfavourable reviews, while tiresome and bad for morale, were like storms in a teacup that would scarcely affect the book's fortunes. The one before him now, glibly referring to his novel as a depraved fantasy, might even boost sales, smoothing the way for his subsequent books. However, the wounds inflicted on an author's self-esteem could have fatal consequences in the long-term: a writer's most powerful weapon, his true strength, was his intuition and, regardless of whether he had any talent, if the critics combined to discredit it, he would be reduced to a fearful creature who took a mistakenly guarded approach to his work that would eventually stifle his latent genius. Before cruelly vilifying them, mud slingers at newspapers and journals should bear in mind that all artistic endeavours were a mixture of effort and imagination, the embodiment of a solitary endeavour, of a sometimes long-nurtured dream, when they were not a desperate bid to give life meaning.

But they would not get the better of Wells. Certainly not. They would not confound him, for he had the basket.

He contemplated the wicker basket sitting on one of the kitchen shelves, and his spirits lifted, rebellious and defiant. The basket's effect on him was instantaneous. As a result, he was never parted from it, lugging it around from pillar to post, despite the suspicions this aroused in his nearest and dearest. Wells had never believed in lucky charms or magical objects, but the curious way in which it had come into his life, and the string of positive events that had occurred since then, compelled him to make an exception in the case of the basket. He noticed that Jane had filled it with vegetables. Far from irritating him, this amused him. In allocating it that dull domestic function, his wife had at once disguised its magical nature and rendered it doubly useful: not only did the basket bring good fortune and boost his self-confidence, not only did it embody the spirit of personal triumph by evoking the extraordinary person who had made it, it was also just a basket.

Calmer now, Wells closed the magazine. He would not allow anyone to put down his achievements, of which he had reason to feel proud. He was thirty years old and, after a long, painful period of battling against the elements, his life had taken shape. The sword had been tempered and, of all the forms it might have taken, had acquired the appearance it would have for life. All that was needed now was to keep it honed, to learn how to wield it and, if necessary, allow it to taste blood occasionally. Of all the things he could have been, it seemed clear he would be a writer – he was one already. His three published novels testified to this. A writer. It had a pleasant ring to it. And it was an occupation that he was not averse to: since childhood it had been his second choice, after that of becoming a teacher – he had always wanted to stand on a podium and stir people's consciences, but he could do that from a shop window, and perhaps in a simpler and more far-reaching way.

A writer. Yes, it had a pleasant ring. A very pleasant ring indeed.

Wells cast a satisfied eye over his surroundings, the home with which literature had provided him. It was a modest dwelling, but one that would have been far beyond his means a few years before, when he was barely scraping a living from the articles he managed to publish in local newspapers and the exhausting classes he gave, when only the basket kept him going in the face of despair.

He could not help comparing it with the house in Bromley where he had grown up, that miserable hovel reeking of the paraffin with which his father had doused the wooden floors to kill the armies of cockroaches. He recalled with revulsion the dreadful kitchen in the basement, with its awkwardly placed coal stove, and the back garden with the shed containing the foul-smelling outside privy, a hole in the ground at the bottom of a trodden-earth path that his mother was embarrassed to use – she imagined the employees of Mr Cooper, the tailor next door, watched her comings and goings. He remembered the creeper on the back wall, which he used to climb to spy on Mr Covell, the butcher, who was in the habit of strolling around his garden, like an assassin, forearms covered with blood, holding a dripping knife fresh from the slaughter. And in the distance, above the rooftops, the parish church and its graveyard crammed with decaying moss-covered headstones, below one of which lay the tiny body of his baby sister Frances, who, his mother maintained, had been poisoned by their evil neighbour Mr Munday during a macabre tea party.

No one, not even he, would have imagined that the necessary components could come together in that revolting hovel to produce a writer, and yet they had – although the delivery had been long drawn-out and fraught. It had taken him precisely twenty-one years and three months to turn his dreams into reality. According to his calculations, that was, for – as though he were addressing future biographers – Wells usually identified 5 June 1874 as the day upon which his vocation was revealed to him in what was perhaps an unnecessarily brutal fashion. That day he suffered a spectacular accident, and this experience, the enormous significance of which would be revealed over time, also convinced him that it was the whims of Fate and not our own will that shaped our future.

Like someone unfolding an origami bird in order to find out how it is made, Wells was able to dissect his present life and discover the elements that had gone into making it up. In fact, tracing the origins of each moment was a frequent pastime of his. This exercise in metaphysical classification was as comforting to him as reciting the twelve times table to steady the world each time it became a swirling mass. Thus, he had determined that the fateful spark to ignite the events that had turned him into a writer was something that might initially appear puzzling: his father's lethal spin bowling on the cricket pitch. But when he pulled on that thread the carpet quickly unravelled: without his talent for spin bowling his father would not have been invited to join the county cricket team; had he not joined the county cricket team he would not have spent the afternoons drinking with his team-mates in the Bell, the pub near their house; had he not frittered away his afternoons in the Bell, neglecting the tiny china shop he ran with his wife on the ground floor of their dwelling, he would not have become acquainted with the pub landlord's son; had he not forged those friendly ties with the strapping youth, when he and his sons bumped into him at the cricket match they were attending one afternoon, the lad would not have taken the liberty of picking young Bertie up by the arms and tossing him into the air; had he not tossed Bertie into the air, Bertie would not have slipped out of his hands; had he not slipped out of the lad's hands, the eight-year-old Wells would not have fractured his tibia when he fell against one of the pegs holding down the beer tent; had he not fractured his tibia and been forced to spend the entire summer in bed, he would not have had the perfect excuse to devote himself to the only form of entertainment available to him in that situation – reading, a harmful activity, which, under any other circumstances, would have aroused his parents' suspicions, which would have prevented him discovering Dickens, Swift and Washington Irving, the writers who planted the seed inside him that, regardless of the scant nourishment and care he could give it, would eventually come into bloom.

Sometimes, in order to appreciate the value of what he had even more, lest it lose its sparkle, Wells wondered what might have become of him if the miraculous sequence of events that had thrust him into the arms of literature had never occurred. And the answer was always the same. If the curious accident had never taken place, Wells was certain he would now be working in some pharmacy, bored witless and unable to believe that his contribution to life was to be of such little import. What would life be like without any purpose? He could imagine no greater misery than to drift through it aimlessly, frustrated, building an existence interchangeable with that of his neighbour, aspiring only to the brief, fragile and elusive happiness of simple folk. Fortunately, his father's lethal bowling had saved him from mediocrity, turning him into someone with a purpose – turning him into a writer.

The journey had by no means been an easy one. It was as if just as he glimpsed his vocation, just as he knew which path to take, the wind destined to hamper his progress had risen, like an unavoidable accompaniment, a fierce, persistent wind in the form of his mother. For it seemed that, besides being one of the most wretched creatures on the planet, Sarah Wells's sole mission in life was to bring up her sons, Bertie, Fred and Frank, to be hard-working members of society, which for her meant becoming a shop assistant, a draper or some other selfless soul, who, like Atlas, proudly but discreetly carried the world on their shoulders. Wells's determination to amount to more was a disappointment to her, although one should not attach too much importance to that: it had merely added insult to injury.

Little Bertie had been a disappointment to his mother from the very moment he was born: he had had the gall to emerge from her womb a fully equipped male when, nine months earlier, she had only consented to cross the threshold of her despicable husband's bedroom on condition he gave her a little girl to replace the one she had lost.

It was hardly surprising that, after such inauspicious beginnings, Wells's relationship with his mother should continue in the same vein. Once the pleasant respite afforded by his broken leg had ended – after the village doctor had kindly prolonged it by setting the bone badly and being obliged to break it again to correct his mistake – little Bertie was sent to a commercial academy in Bromley, where his two brothers had gone before him. Their teacher, Mr Morley, had been unable to make anything of them. The youngest boy, however, soon proved that all the peas in a pod are not necessarily the same. Mr Morley was so astonished by Wells's dazzling intelligence that he even turned a blind eye to the non-payment of his registration fee. However, such preferential treatment did not stop the mother uprooting her son from the milieu of blackboards and desks where he felt so at home, and sending him to train as an apprentice at the Rodgers and Denyer drapery in Windsor.

After three months of toiling from seven thirty in the morning until eight at night, with a short break for lunch in a windowless cellar, Wells feared his youthful optimism would begin to fade, as it had with his elder brothers – he barely recognised them as the cheerful, determined fellows they had once been. He did everything in his power to prove to all and sundry that he did not have the makings of a draper's assistant, abandoning himself to frequent bouts of daydreaming, to the point at which the owners had no choice but to dismiss the young man who mixed up the orders and spent most of his time wool-gathering in a corner.

Thanks to the intervention of one of his mother's second cousins, he was then sent to assist a relative in running a school in Wookey, where he would also be able to complete his teacher-training. Unfortunately, this employment, far more in keeping with his aspirations, ended almost as soon as it had begun when it was discovered that the headmaster was an impostor: he had obtained his post by falsifying his academic qualifications.

The by-now-not-so-little Bertie once again fell prey to his mother's obsessions. She deflected him from his true destiny by sending him off on another mistaken path. Aged just fourteen, Wells began work in the pharmacy run by Mr Cowap, who was instructed to train him as a chemist. However, the pharmacist soon realised the boy was far too gifted to be wasted on such an occupation, and placed him in the hands of Horace Byatt, headmaster at Midhurst Grammar School, who was on the lookout for exceptional students to imbue his establishment with the academic respectability it needed.

Wells easily excelled over the other boys, who were, on the whole, mediocre students, and was instantly noticed by Byatt, who contrived with the pharmacist to provide the talented boy with the best education they could. Wells's mother soon frustrated the plot hatched by the pair of idle philanthropists, whose intention it had been to lead little Bertie astray, by sending her son to another drapery, this time in Southsea. Wells spent two years there in a state of intense confusion, trying to understand why that fierce wind insisted on blowing him off course each time he found himself on the right path.

Life at the Southsea Drapery Emporium was suspiciously similar to a sojourn in hell. It consisted of thirteen hours' hard work, followed by a night spent shut in the airless hut that passed for a dormitory, where the apprentices slept so close together that even their dreams got muddled up. A few years earlier, convinced that her husband's fecklessness would end by bankrupting the china-shop business, his mother had accepted the post of housekeeper at Uppark Manor, a rundown estate on Harting Down where, as a girl, she had worked as a maid. It was to here that Wells wrote her a series of despairing, accusatory letters – which, out of respect, I will not reproduce here – alternating childish demands with sophisticated arguments in a vain attempt to persuade her to set him free.

As he watched his longed-for future slip through his fingers, Wells did his utmost to weaken his mother's resolve. He asked her how she expected him to help her in her old age on a shop assistant's meagre wage: with the studies he intended to pursue he would obtain a wonderful position. He accused her of being intolerant, stupid, even threatened to commit suicide or other dreadful acts that would stain the family name for ever. None of this had any effect on his mother's resolve to turn him into a respectable draper's boy.

It took his former champion Horace Byatt, overwhelmed by growing numbers of pupils, to come to the rescue: he offered Wells a post at twenty pounds for the first year, and forty thereafter. Wells was quick to wave the figures in front of his mother, who reluctantly allowed him to leave the drapery. Relieved, the grateful Wells placed himself under the orders of his saviour, to whose expectations he was anxious to live up. During the day he taught the younger boys, and at night he studied to finish his teacher-training, eagerly devouring everything he could find about biology, physics, astronomy and other science subjects. The reward for his titanic efforts was a scholarship to the Normal School of Science in South Kensington, where he would study under none other than Professor Thomas Henry Huxley, the famous biologist who had been Darwin's lieutenant during his debates with Bishop Wilberforce.

Despite all this, it could not be said that Wells left for London in high spirits. He did so more with deep unhappiness at not receiving his parents' support in this huge adventure. He was convinced his mother hoped he would fail in his studies, confirming her belief that the Wells boys were only fit to be drapers, that no genius could possibly be produced from a substance as dubious as her husband's seed. For his part, his father was the living proof that failure could be enjoyed as much as prosperity. During the summer they had spent together, Wells had looked on with dismay as his father, whom age had deprived of his sole refuge, cricket, clung to the one thing that had given his life meaning. He wandered around the cricket pitches like a restless ghost, carrying a bag stuffed with batting gloves, pads and cricket balls, while his china shop foundered like a captainless ship, holed in the middle of the ocean. Things being as they were, Wells did not mind having to stay in a rooming house where the guests appeared to compete in producing the most original noises.

He was so accustomed to life revealing its most unpleasant side to him that when his aunt Marie Wells proposed he lodge at her home on Euston Road, his natural response was suspicion, for the house was warm, cosy, suffused with a peaceful, harmonious atmosphere, and bore no resemblance to the squalid dwellings he had lived in up until then. He was so grateful to his aunt for providing him with this long-awaited reprieve in the interminable battle that was his life that he considered it almost his duty to ask for the hand of her daughter Isabel, a gentle, kind girl, who wafted silently around the house.

But Wells soon realised the rashness of his decision: after the wedding, which was settled with the prompt matter-of-factness of a tedious formality, he confirmed what he had already suspected, that his cousin had nothing in common with him. He also discovered that Isabel had been brought up to be a perfect wife, that is to say, to satisfy her husband's every need except, of course, in the marriage bed, where she behaved with the coldness ideal for a procreating machine but entirely unsuited to pleasure. In spite of all this, his wife's frigidity proved a minor problem, easily resolved by visiting other beds. Wells soon discovered an abundance of delightful alternatives to which his hypnotic grandiloquence gained him entry, and dedicated himself to enjoying life now that it seemed to be going his way.

Immersed in the modest pursuit of pleasure that his guinea-a-week scholarship allowed, Wells gave himself over to the joys of the flesh, to making forays into hitherto unexplored subjects, such as literature and art, and to enjoying every second of his hard-earned stay at South Kensington. He also decided the time had come to reveal his innermost dreams to the world by publishing a short story in the *Science Schools Journal*.

He called it *The Chronic Argonauts* and its main character was a mad scientist, Dr Nebogipfel, who had invented a machine he used to travel back in time to commit a murder. Time travel was not an original concept: Dickens had already written about it in *A Christmas Carol* and Edgar Allan Poe in 'A Tale of the Ragged Mountains', but in both of those stories the journeys always took place during a dream or state of trance. By contrast, Wells's scientist travelled of his own free will and by means of a mechanical device. In brief, his idea was brimming with originality. However, this first tentative trial at being a writer did not change his life, which, to his disappointment, carried on exactly as before.

All the same, his first story brought him the most remarkable reader he had ever had, and probably would ever have. A few days after its publication, Wells received a card from an admirer who asked if he would accept to take tea with him. The name on the card sent a shiver down his spine: Joseph Merrick, better known as the Elephant Man.

XII

Wells began to hear about Merrick the moment he set foot in the biology classrooms at South Kensington. For those studying the workings of the human body, Merrick was something akin to Nature's most amazing achievement, its finest-cut diamond, living proof of the scope of its inventiveness. The so-called Elephant Man suffered from a disease that had horribly deformed his body, turning him into a shapeless, almost monstrous creature. This strange affliction, which had the medical profession scratching its heads, had caused the limbs, bones and organs on his right side to grow uncontrollably, leaving his left side practically unaffected. An enormous swelling on the right side of his skull, for example, distorted the shape of his head, squashing his face into a mass of folds and bony protuberances, and even dislodging his ear. Because of this, Merrick was unable to express anything more than the frozen ferocity of a totem. Owing to this lopsidedness, his spinal column curved to the right, where his organs were markedly heavier, lending all his movements a grotesque air. As if this were not enough, the disease had also turned his skin into a coarse, leathery crust, like dried cardboard, covered with hollows and swellings and wart-like growths.

To begin with Wells could scarcely believe that such a creature existed, but the photographs secretly circulating in the classroom soon revealed to him the truth of the rumours. The photographs had been stolen or purchased from staff at the London Hospital, where Merrick now resided, having spent half his life being displayed in side-shows at third-rate fairs and travelling circuses. As they passed from hand to hand, the blurred, shadowy images in which Merrick was scarcely more than a blotch caused a similar thrill to the photographs of scantily clad women they became mixed up with, although for different reasons.

The idea of having been invited to tea with this creature filled Wells with a mixture of awe and apprehension. Even so, he arrived on time at the London Hospital, a solid, forbidding structure located in Whitechapel. In the entrance a steady stream of doctors and nurses went about their mysterious business. Wells looked for a place where he would not be in the way, his head spinning with the synchronised activity in which everyone seemed to be engaged, like dancers in a ballet. Perhaps one of the nurses he saw carrying bandages had just left an operating theatre where some patient was hovering between life and death. If so, she did not quicken her step beyond the brisk but measured pace evolved over years of dealing with emergencies. Amazed, Wells had been watching the non-stop bustle from his vantage-point for some time when Dr Treves, the surgeon responsible for Merrick, finally arrived.

Treves was a small, excitable man of about thirty-five who masked his childlike features behind a bushy beard, clipped neatly like a hedge. 'Mr Wells?' he enquired, trying unsuccessfully to hide the evident dismay he felt at the author's offensive youthfulness.

Wells nodded, and gave an involuntary shrug as if apologising that he did not demonstrate the venerable old age Treves apparently required of those visiting his patient. He instantly regretted his gesture, for he had not requested an audience with the hospital's famous guest.

'Thank you for accepting Mr Merrick's invitation,' said Treves. The surgeon had quickly recovered from his initial shock and reverted to the role of intermediary.

With extreme respect, Wells shook his capable, agile hand, which was accustomed to venturing into places out of bounds to most other mortals. 'How could I refuse to meet the only person who has read my story?' he retorted.

Treves nodded vaguely, as though the vanity of authors and their jokes were of no consequence to him. He had more important things to worry about. Each day, new and ingenious diseases emerged that required his attention, the extraordinary dexterity of his hands, and his vigorous resolve in the operating theatre. He gestured to Wells with an almost military nod that he should follow him up a staircase to the upper floors of the hospital. A relentless throng of nurses descending in the opposite direction hampered their ascent, nearly causing Wells to lose his footing on more than one occasion.

'Not everybody accepts Joseph's invitations, for obvious reasons,' Treves said, raising his voice almost to a shout, 'although, strangely, this does not sadden him. Sometimes I think he is more than satisfied with the little he gets out of life. Deep down, he knows his bizarre deformities are what enable him to meet any bigwig he wishes to in London, something unthinkable for your average commoner from Leicester.'

Wells thought Treves's observation in rather poor taste, but refrained from making any comment because he had immediately realised he was right: Merrick's appearance, which had hitherto condemned him to a life of ostracism and misery, now permitted him to hobnob with the cream of London society, although it remained to be seen whether or not he considered his various deformities too high a price to pay for rubbing shoulders with the aristocracy.

The same hustle and bustle reigned on the upper floor, but with a few sudden turns down dimly lit corridors, Treves had guided his guest away from the persistent clamour. Wells followed as he strode along a series of never-ending, increasingly deserted passageways. As they penetrated the furthest reaches of the hospital, the diminishing numbers of patients and nurses clearly related to the wards and surgeries becoming progressively more specialised. However, Wells could not help comparing this gradual extinction of life to the terrible desolation surrounding the monsters' lairs in children's fables. All that was needed were a few dead birds and some gnawed bones.

While they walked, Treves used the opportunity to tell Wells how he had become acquainted with his extraordinary patient. In a detached, even tone that betrayed the tedium he felt at having to repeat the story yet again, Treves explained he had met Merrick four years earlier, shortly after being appointed head surgeon at the hospital. A circus had pitched its tent on a nearby piece of wasteland, and its main attraction, the Elephant Man, was the talk of all London. If what people said about him was true, he was the most deformed creature on the planet. Treves knew that circus owners were in the habit of creating freaks with the aid of fake limbs and makeup that were impossible to spot in the gloom, but he also acknowledged that this sort of show was the last refuge for those unfortunate enough to be born with a defect that earned them society's contempt.

The surgeon had had few expectations when he visited the fair, motivated purely by unavoidable professional curiosity. But there was nothing fake about the Elephant Man. After a rather sorry excuse for a trapeze act, the lights dimmed and the percussion launched into a poor imitation of tribal drumming in an overlong introduction that nevertheless succeeded in giving the audience a sense of trepidation. Treves watched, astonished, as the fair's main attraction entered, and saw with his own eyes that the rumours circulating fell far short of reality. The appalling deformities afflicting the creature who dragged himself across the ring had transformed him into a misshapen figure resembling a gargoyle. When the performance was over, Treves convinced the circus owner to let him meet the creature in private. Once inside his modest wagon, the surgeon thought he was in the presence of an imbecile, convinced the swellings on his head must inevitably have damaged his brain.

But he was mistaken. A few words with Merrick were enough to show Treves that the hideous exterior concealed a courteous, educated, sensitive being. He explained to the surgeon that he was called the Elephant Man because he had had a fleshy protuberance between his nose and upper lip, a tiny trunk measuring about eight inches. It had made it hard for him to eat and had been unceremoniously removed a few years before. Treves was moved by his gentleness, and because, despite the hardship and humiliation he had suffered, he apparently bore no resentment towards the humanity Treves was so quick to despise when he could not get a cab or a box at the theatre.

When the surgeon left the circus an hour later, he had firmly resolved to do everything in his power to take Merrick away from there and offer him a decent life. His reasons were clear: in no other hospital records in the world was there any evidence of a human being with such severe deformities as Merrick's. Whatever this strange disease was, of all the people in the world, it had chosen to reside in his body alone, transforming the wretched creature into a unique individual, a rare species of butterfly that had to be kept behind glass. Clearly, Merrick must leave the circus in which he was languishing at the earliest opportunity. Little did Treves know that in order to accomplish the admirable goal he had set himself, he would have to begin a long, arduous campaign that would leave him drained.

He started by presenting Merrick to the Pathology Society, but this led only to its distinguished members subjecting the patient to a series of probing examinations and ended in them becoming embroiled in fruitless, heated debates about the nature of the mysterious illness, which invariably turned into slanging matches where someone would always take the opportunity to try to settle old scores. However, his colleagues' disarray, far from discouraging Treves, heartened him: ultimately it underlined the importance of Merrick's life, making it all the more imperative to remove him from the precarious world of show-business.

His next step had been to try to get him admitted to the hospital where he worked so that he could be easily examined. Unfortunately, hospitals did not provide beds for chronic patients, and consequently, although the management applauded Treves's idea, their hands were tied. Faced with the hopelessness of the situation, Merrick himself suggested Treves find him a job as a lighthouse keeper, or some other occupation that would cut him off from the rest of the world.

But Treves would not admit defeat. Out of desperation, he went to the newspapers and, in a few weeks, managed to move the whole country with the wretched predicament of the fellow they called the Elephant Man. Donations poured in, but Treves did not only require money: he wanted to give Merrick a decent home. He decided to turn to the only people who were above society's absurd, hidebound rules: the royal family. He persuaded the Duke of Cambridge and the Princess of Wales to agree to meet the creature. Merrick's refined manners and extraordinarily gentle nature did the rest. That was how Merrick had come to be a permanent guest in the hospital wing where Treves and Wells now found themselves.

'Joseph is happy here,' declared Treves, in a suddenly thoughtful voice. 'The examinations we carry out on him from time to time are fruitless, but that does not seem to worry him. He is convinced his illness was caused by an elephant knocking down his heavily pregnant mother while she was watching a parade. Sadly, Mr Wells, this is a pyrrhic victory. I have found Merrick a home but I am unable to cure his illness. His skull is growing bigger by the day, and I'm afraid that soon his neck will be unable to support the incredible weight of his head.'

Treves's blunt evocation of Merrick's death, with the bleak desolation that seemed to permeate that wing of the hospital, plunged Wells into a state of extreme anxiety.

'I would like his last days to be as peaceful as possible,' the surgeon went on, oblivious to the pallor spreading over his companion's face. 'But apparently this is asking too much. Every night, the locals gather under his window shouting insults at him and calling him names. They even think he is to blame for killing the whores who have been found mutilated in the neighbourhood. Have people gone mad? Merrick couldn't hurt a fly. I have already mentioned his extraordinary sensibility. Do you know that he devours Jane Austen's novels? And, on occasion, I've even surprised him writing poems. Like you, Mr Wells.'

'I don't write poems, I write stories,' Wells murmured hesitantly, his increasing unease apparently making him doubt everything.

Treves scowled at him, annoyed that he would want to split hairs over what he considered such an inconsequential subject as literature.

'That's why I allow these visits,' he said, shaking his head regretfully, before resuming where he had left off, 'because I know they do him a great deal of good. I imagine people come to see him because his appearance makes even the unhappiest souls realise they should thank God. Joseph, on the other hand, views the matter differently. Sometimes I think he derives a sort of twisted amusement from these visits. Every Saturday, he scours the newspapers, then hands me a list of people he would like to invite to tea, and I obligingly forward them his card. They are usually members of the aristocracy, wealthy businessmen, public figures, painters, actors and other more or less well-known artists . . . People who have achieved a measure of social success and who in his estimation have one last test to pass: confronting him in the flesh. Joseph's deformities are so hideous they invariably evoke either pity or disgust in those who see him. I imagine he can judge from his guests' reaction whether they are the kind-hearted type or riddled with fears and anxieties.'

They came to a door at the far end of a long passageway.

'Here we are,' said Treves, plunging for a few moments into a respectful silence. Then he looked Wells in the eye, and added, in a sombre, almost threatening tone: 'Behind this door waits the most horrific-looking creature you have probably ever seen or will ever see; it is up to you whether you consider him a monster or an unfortunate wretch.'

Wells felt a little faint.

'It is not too late to turn back. You may not like what you discover about yourself.'

'You n-need not w-worry about me,' stammered Wells.

'As you wish,' said Treves, with the detachment of one washing his hands of the matter. He took a key from his pocket, opened the door and, gently but resolutely, propelled Wells over the threshold.

Wells held his breath as he ventured inside the room. He had taken a couple of faltering steps when he heard the surgeon close the door behind him. He gulped, glancing about the place Treves had practically hurled him into once he had fulfilled his minor role in the disturbing ceremony. He found himself in a spacious suite of rooms containing various normal pieces of furniture. The ordinariness of the furnishings combined with the soft afternoon light filtering in through the window to create a prosaic, unexpectedly cosy atmosphere that clashed with the image of a monster's lair. Wells stood transfixed for a few seconds, thinking his host would appear at any moment. When this did not happen, and not knowing what was expected of him, he wandered hesitantly through the rooms. He was immediately overcome by the unsettling feeling that Merrick was spying on him from behind one of the screens, but continued weaving in and out of the furniture, sensing this was another part of the ritual. But nothing he saw gave away the uniqueness of the rooms' occupant: there were no half-eaten rats strewn about, or the remains of some brave knight's armour.

In one of the rooms, however, he came across two chairs and a small table laid out for tea. He found this innocent scene still more unsettling, for he could not help comparing it to the gallows awaiting the condemned man in the town square, its joists creaking balefully in the spring breeze.

Then he noticed an intriguing object on a table next to the wall, beneath one of the windows. It was a cardboard model of a church. Wells walked over to marvel at the exquisite craftsmanship. Fascinated by the wealth of detail in the model, he did not at first notice the crooked shadow appearing on the wall: a stiff figure, bent over to the right crowned by an enormous head.

'It's the church opposite. I had to make up the parts I can't see from the window.'

The voice had a laboured, slurred quality.

'It's beautiful,' Wells breathed, addressing the lopsided silhouette projected on the wall.

The shadow shook its head with great difficulty, unintentionally revealing to Wells what a struggle it was for Merrick to produce even this simple gesture to play down the importance of his own work. Having completed the arduous movement, he remained silent, stooped over his cane, and Wells realised he could not go on standing there with his back to him. The moment had arrived when he must turn and look his host in the face. Treves had warned him that Merrick paid special attention to his guests' initial reaction – the one that arose automatically, almost involuntarily, and which he therefore considered more genuine, more revealing than the faces people hurriedly composed to dissimulate their feelings once they had recovered from the shock. For those few brief moments, Merrick was afforded a rare glimpse into his guests' souls, and it made no difference how they pretended to act during the subsequent meeting, since their initial reaction had already condemned or redeemed them. Wells was unsure whether Merrick's appearance would fill him with pity or disgust. Fearing the latter, he clenched his jaw as tightly as he could, tensing his face to prevent it registering any emotion. He did not even want to show surprise, but merely to gain time before his brain could process what he was seeing and reach a logical conclusion about the feelings a creature as apparently deformed as Merrick produced in a person like him. In the end, if he experienced repulsion, he would willingly acknowledge this and reflect on it later, after he had left.

Wells drew a deep breath, planted his feet firmly on the ground, which had dissolved into a soft, quaking mass, and slowly turned to face his host. What he saw made him gasp. Just as Treves had warned, Merrick's deformities gave him a terrifying appearance. The photographs Wells had seen of him at the university, which mercifully veiled his hideousness behind a blurred gauze, had not prepared him for this. He wore a dark grey suit and was propping himself up with a cane. Ironically, these accoutrements, which were intended to humanise him, only made him look more grotesque.

Teeth firmly clenched, Wells stood stiffly before him, struggling to suppress a physical urge to shudder. He felt as if his heart was about to burst out of his chest and beads of cold sweat trickled down his back, but he could not make out whether these symptoms were caused by horror or pity. Despite the unnatural tension of his facial muscles, he could feel his lips quivering, perhaps as they tried to form a grimace of horror, yet at the same time he noticed tears welling in his eyes so did not know what to think. Their mutual scrutiny went on for ever, and Wells wished he could shed at least one tear that would encapsulate his pain and prove to Merrick, and to himself, that he was a sensitive, compassionate being, but those pricking his eyes refused to brim over.

'Would you prefer me to wear my hood, Mr Wells?' asked Merrick, softly.

The strange voice, which gave his words a liquid quality as if they were floating in a muddy brook, struck renewed fear into Wells. Had the time limit Merrick usually put on his guests' response expired? 'No . . . that won't be necessary,' he murmured.

His host moved his gigantic head laboriously in what Wells assumed was a nod of agreement.

'Then let us have our tea before it goes cold,' he said, shuffling to the table in the centre of the room.

Wells did not respond immediately, horrified by the way Merrick was obliged to walk. Everything was an effort for him, he realised, observing the complicated manoeuvres he had to make to sit down. Wells had to suppress an urge to rush over and help him, afraid this gesture usually reserved for the elderly or infirm might upset him. Hoping he was doing the right thing, he sat down as casually as possible in the chair opposite his host. Again, he had to force himself to sit still as he watched Merrick serve the tea. He mostly tried to fulfil this role using his left hand, which was unaffected by the disease, although he still employed the right to carry out minor tasks within the ceremony. Wells could not help but silently admire the extraordinary dexterity with which Merrick was able to take the lid off the sugar bowl or offer him a biscuit with a hand as big and rough as a lump of rock.

'I'm so glad you were able to come, Mr Wells,' said Merrick, after he had succeeded in the arduous task of serving the tea without spilling a single drop, 'because it allows me to tell you in person how much I enjoyed your story.'

'You are very kind, Mr Merrick,' replied Wells.

Once it had been published, curious about how little impact it had made, Wells had read and reread it at least a dozen times to try to discover why it had been so completely overlooked. Imbued with a spirit of uncompromising criticism, he had weighed up the plot's solidity, appraised its dramatic pace, considered the order, appropriateness, and even the number of words he had used, only to regard his first and quite possibly his last work of fiction with the unforgiving, almost contemptuous, eye with which the Almighty might contemplate the tiresome antics of a capuchin monkey. It was clear to him now that the story was a worthless piece of excrement: his writing a shameless imitation of Nathaniel Hawthorne's pseudo-Germanic style, and his main character, Dr Nebogipfel, a poor, unrealistic copy of the exaggerated depictions of mad scientists already to be found in Gothic novels. Nevertheless, he thanked Merrick for his words of praise, smiling with false modesty and fearing they would be the only ones his writings ever received.

'A time machine . . .' said Merrick, delighting in the juxtaposition of words he found so evocative. 'You have a prophetic imagination, Mr Wells.'

Wells thanked him again for this new and rather embarrassing compliment. How many more eulogies would he have to endure before he asked him to change the subject?

'If I had a time machine like Dr Nebogipfel's,' Merrick went on dreamily, 'I would travel back to ancient Egypt.'

Wells found the remark touching. Like any other person, this creature had a favourite period in history, as he must have a favourite fruit, season or song. 'Why is that?' he asked, with a friendly smile, providing his host with the opportunity to expound on his tastes.

'Because the Egyptians worshipped gods with animals' heads,' replied Merrick, slightly shamefaced.

Wells stared at him stupidly. He was unsure what surprised him more: the naïve yearning in Merrick's reply or the awkward bashfulness that accompanied it, as though he were chiding himself for wanting such a thing, for preferring to be a god worshipped by men instead of the despised monster he was. If anyone had a right to feel hatred and bitterness towards the world, surely he did. And yet Merrick reproached himself for his sorrow, as though the sunlight through the window-pane warming his back or the clouds scudding across the sky ought to supply reason enough for him to be happy. Lost for words, Wells took a biscuit from the plate and nibbled it with intense concentration, as though he were making sure his teeth still worked.

'Why do you think Dr Nebogipfel didn't use his machine to travel into the future as well?' Merrick then asked, in that unguent voice, which sounded as if it were smeared with butter. 'Wasn't he curious? I sometimes wonder what the world will be like in a hundred years.'

'Indeed . . .' murmured Wells, at a loss to respond to this remark, too.

Merrick belonged to that class of reader who was able to forget with amazing ease the hand moving the characters behind the scenes of a novel. As a child Wells had also been able to read in that way. But one day he had decided he would be a writer, and from that moment on he had found it impossible to immerse himself in stories with the same innocent abandon: he was aware that characters' thoughts and actions were not his. They answered to the dictates of a higher being, to someone who, alone in his room, moved the pieces he himself had placed on the board, more often than not with an overwhelming feeling of indifference that bore no relation to the emotions he intended to arouse in his readers. Novels were not slices of life but more or less controlled creations reproducing slices of imaginary, polished lives, where boredom and the futile, useless acts that make up any existence were replaced with exciting, meaningful episodes. At times, Wells longed to be able to read in that carefree, childlike way again but, having glimpsed behind the scenes, he could only do this with an enormous leap of his imagin-ation. Once you had written your first story there was no turning back. You were a deceiver and you could not help treating other deceivers with suspicion.

It occurred to Wells briefly to suggest that Merrick ask Nebogipfel himself, but he changed his mind, unsure whether his host would take his riposte as the gentle mockery he intended. What if Merrick really was too naïve to tell the difference between reality and a simple work of fiction? What if this sad inability and not his sensitivity allowed him to experience the stories he read so intensely? If so, Well's rejoinder would sound like a cruel jibe, aimed at wounding his ingenuousness. Fortunately, Merrick fired another question at him, which was easier to answer: 'Do you think somebody will one day invent a time machine?'

'I doubt such a thing could exist,' replied Wells, bluntly.

'And yet you've written about it!' his host exclaimed, horrified.

'That's precisely why, Mr Merrick,' he explained, trying to think of a simple way to bring together the various ideas underlying his conception of literature. 'I assure you that if it were possible to build a time machine I would never have written about it. I am only interested in writing about what is impossible.'

At this, he recalled a quote from Lucian of Samosata's *True Histories*, which he could not help memorising because it perfectly summed up his thoughts on literature: 'I write about things I have neither seen nor verified nor heard about from others and, in addition, about things that have never existed and could have no possible basis for existing.' Yes, as he had told his host, he was only interested in writing about things that were impossible. Dickens was there to take care of the rest, he thought of adding, but did not. Treves had told him Merrick was an avid reader. He did not want to risk offending him if Dickens happened to be one of his favourite authors.

'Then I'm sorry that because of me you'll never be able to write about a man who is half human, half elephant,' murmured Merrick.

Once more, Wells was disarmed. After he had spoken, Merrick's gaze wandered to the window. Wells was unsure whether the gesture was meant to express regret or to give him the opportunity to study Merrick's appearance as freely as he wished. In any case, Wells's eyes were unconsciously, irresistibly, almost hypnotically drawn to him, confirming what he already knew full well – that Merrick was right: if he had not seen him with his own eyes, he would never have believed such a creature could exist. Except, perhaps, in the fictional world of books.

'You will be a great writer, Mr Wells,' his host declared, continuing to stare out of the window.

'I wish I could agree,' replied Wells, who, following his first failed attempt, was entertaining serious doubts about his abilities.

Merrick turned to face him. 'Look at my hands, Mr Wells,' he said, holding them out. 'Would you believe that these hands could make a church out of cardboard?'

Wells gazed at his host's mismatched hands. The right was enormous and grotesque while the left looked like that of a ten-year-old girl. 'I suppose not,' he admitted.

Merrick nodded slowly. 'It is a question of will, Mr Wells,' he said, striving for a tone of authority. 'That's all.'

Coming from anyone else's mouth these words might have struck Wells as trite, but uttered by the man in front of him they became an irrefutable truth. This creature was living proof that man's will could move mountains and part seas. In that hospital wing, a refuge from the world, the distance between the attainable and the unattainable was more than ever a question of will. If Merrick had built that cardboard church with his deformed hands, what might not he, Wells, be capable of? He was only prevented from doing whatever he wanted by his lack of self-belief.

He could not help agreeing, which seemed to please Merrick, judging from the way he fidgeted in his seat. In an embarrassed voice, Merrick went on to confess that the model was to be a gift for a stage actress with whom he had been corresponding for several months. He referred to her as Mrs Kendall, and from what Wells could gather she was one of his most generous benefactors. He had no difficulty in picturing her as woman of good social standing, sympathetic to the suffering of the world, so long as they were not on her doorstep. She had discovered in the Elephant Man a novel way of spending the money she usually donated to charity. When Merrick explained that he was looking forward to meeting her in person when she returned from her tour in America, Wells could not help smiling, touched by the amorous note that, consciously or not, had slipped into his voice. But at the same time he felt a pang of sorrow, and hoped Mrs Kendall's work would delay her in America so that Merrick could go on believing in the illusion of her letters and not be faced with the discovery that impossible love was only possible in books.

After they had finished their tea, Merrick offered Wells a cigarette, which he courteously accepted. They rose from their seats and went to the window to watch the sunset. For a few moments, the two men stood staring down at the street and at the façade of the church opposite, every inch of which Merrick must have been familiar with. People came and went, a pedlar with a handcart hawked his wares, and carriages trundled over the uneven cobblestones strewn with foul-smelling dung from the hundreds of horses going by each day. Wells watched Merrick gazing at the frantic bustle with almost reverential awe. He appeared to be lost in thought.

'You know something, Mr Wells?' he said finally. 'I can't help feeling sometimes that life is like a play in which I've been given no part. If you only knew how much I envy all those people . . .'

'I can assure you, you have no reason to envy them, Mr Merrick,' Wells replied abruptly. 'Those people you see are specks of dust. Nobody will remember who they were or what they did after they die. You, however, will go down in history.'

Merrick appeared to mull over his words, as he studied his misshapen reflection in the window-pane.

'Do you think that gives me any comfort?' he asked mournfully.

'It ought to,' replied Wells, 'for the time of the ancient Egyptians has long since passed, Mr Merrick.'

His host did not reply. He continued staring down at the street, but Wells found it impossible to judge from his expression, frozen by the disease into a look of permanent rage, what effect his words, a little blunt perhaps but necessary, had had on him. He could not stand by while the other wallowed in his own tragedy. He was convinced Merrick's only comfort could come from his deformity, which, although it had marginalised him, had also made him a singular being.

'No doubt you are right, Mr Wells,' Merrick said, continuing to gaze at his reflection. 'One should probably resign oneself to not expecting too much of this world we live in, where people fear anyone who is different. Sometimes I think that if an angel were to appear before a priest he would probably shoot it.'

'I suppose that is true,' observed Wells, the writer in him excited by the image his host had just evoked. And, seeing Merrick still caught up in his reflections, he decided to take his leave. 'Thank you so much for the tea, Mr Merrick.'

'Wait,' replied Merrick. 'There's something I want to give you.' He shuffled over to a small cupboard and rummaged around inside it for a few moments until he found what he had been looking for. Wells was puzzled to see him pull out a wicker basket. 'When I told Mrs Kendall I had always dreamed of being a basket-maker, she employed a man to come and teach me,' Merrick explained, cradling the object in his hands as though it were a new-born infant, or a bird's nest. 'He was a kindly, mild-mannered fellow, who had a workshop on Pennington Street, near the London docks. From the very beginning he treated me as though my looks were no different from his. But when he saw my hands, he told me I could never manage delicate work like basket-weaving. He was very sorry, but we would evidently be wasting our time. Yet striving to achieve a dream is never a waste of time, is it, Mr Wells? "Show me," I told him. "Only then will we know whether you are right or not."'

Wells contemplated the perfect piece of wickerwork Merrick was cupping in his deformed hands.

'I've made many more since then, and have given some away to my guests. But this one is special, because it is the first I ever made. I would like you to have it, Mr Wells,' he said, presenting him with the basket, 'to remind you that everything is a question of will.'

'Thank you,' stammered Wells, touched. 'I am honoured, Mr Merrick, truly honoured.'

He smiled warmly as he said goodbye, and walked towards the door.

'One more question, Mr Wells,' he heard Merrick say behind him.

Wells turned to look at him, hoping he was not going to ask for the accursed Nebogipfel's address so that he could send him a basket, too.

'Do you believe that the same God made us both?' Merrick asked, with more frustration than regret.

Wells repressed a sigh of despair. What could he say to this? He was weighing up various possible replies when, all of a sudden, Merrick emitted a strange sound, as if a cough or grunt had convulsed his body from head to foot, threatening to shake him apart at the seams. Wells listened, alarmed, as the loud, hacking sound continued to rise uncontrollably from his throat, until he realised what was happening. There was nothing seriously wrong with Merrick: he was laughing.

'It was a joke, Mr Wells, only a joke,' he explained, cutting short his rasping chortle as he became aware of his guest's startled response. 'Whatever would become of me if I was unable to laugh at my own appearance?'

Without waiting for Wells to reply, he walked towards his work table, and sat in front of the model of the church.

'Whatever would become of me?' Wells heard him mutter, in a tone of profound melancholy. 'Whatever would become of me?'

Wells watched him concentrate on his clumsy hands sculpting the cardboard and was seized by a feeling of deep sympathy. He found it impossible to believe Treves's theory that this remarkably innocent, gentle creature invited public figures to tea to submit them to some sinister test. On the contrary, he was convinced that all Merrick wanted from this limited intimacy was a few meagre crumbs of warmth and sympathy. It was far more likely that Treves had attributed him with those motives to unnerve guests to whom he took a dislike, or possibly to make allowances for Merrick's extreme naïvety by crediting him with a guile he did not possess. Or perhaps, thought Wells, who had no illusions about the sincerity of man's motives, the surgeon's intentions were still more selfish and ambitious: perhaps he wanted to show people that he was the only one who understood the soul of the creature to whom he clung desperately in the knowledge that he would be guaranteed a place beside him in history.

Wells was irritated by the idea of Treves taking advantage of Merrick's face being a terrifying mask he could never take off, a mask that could never express his true emotions, in order to attribute to him whatever motives he wished, in the knowledge that no one but Merrick could ever refute them. And now that Wells had heard him laugh, he wondered whether the so-called Elephant Man had not in fact been smiling at him from the moment he stepped into the room, a warm, friendly smile intended to soothe the discomfort his appearance produced in his guests, a smile no one would ever see.

As he left the room, he felt a tear roll down his cheek.

XIII

That was how the wicker basket had come into Wells's life, and with it he found that the winds of good fortune soon began to blow off the years of accumulated dust. Shortly after the basket's arrival, he obtained his degree in zoology with distinction, began giving courses in biology for the University of London External Programme, took up the post of editor-in-chief of the *University Correspondent* and began writing the odd short article for the *Educational Times.* Thus, in a relatively short period of time, he earned a large sum of money, which helped him recover from his disappointment over the lack of interest in his story, and boosted his self-confidence. He got into the habit of venerating the basket every night, giving it long, loving looks, running his fingers over the tightly woven wicker. He carried out this simple ritual behind Jane's back, and found it encouraged him so much he felt invincible, strong enough to swim the Atlantic or wrestle a tiger to the ground with his bare hands.

But Wells scarcely had time to enjoy his achievements before the members of his tattered family discovered that little Bertie was on his way to becoming a man of means, and entrusted him with the task of maintaining their fragile and threatened cohesion. Without protest, Wells resigned himself to taking on the mantle of clan defender, knowing that none of its other members was up to the task. His father, having finally freed himself from the burden of the china shop, had moved to a cottage in Nyewood, a tiny village south of Rogate, where he had a view of Harting Down and the elms at Uppark. Life had gradually washed up the rest of the family in the tiny house.

The first to arrive was Frank. He had left the drapery a few years earlier to become a travelling watch salesman, an occupation in which he had not been very successful – a fact borne out by the two enormous trunks of unsold watches he brought with him. They gave off a loud, incessant whirring sound and rattled like a colony of mechanical spiders. Then came Fred, his trusting brother, who had been unceremoniously dismissed from the company where he worked as soon as the boss's son was old enough to occupy the seat he had unknowingly kept warm for him. Finding themselves together again, and with a roof over their heads, Bertie's brothers devoted themselves to licking each other's wounds and, infected by their father's relaxed attitude to life, soon accepted this latest downturn with good cheer.

The last to arrive was their mother, dismissed from her beloved paradise at Uppark because the onset of deafness had rendered her useless and irritable. The only one who did not return to the fold was Frances, perhaps because she felt there would not be enough room for her infant coffin. Even so, there were too many of them, and Wells had to make a superhuman effort to keep up his endless hours of teaching to protect that nest, buzzing with the sound of Frank's watches, that pesthouse of happy walking-wounded reeking of snuff and stale beer, to the point at which he ended up vomiting blood and collapsing on the steps of Charing Cross station.

The diagnosis was clear: tuberculosis. And although he made a swift recovery, this attack was a warning to Wells to stop burning the midnight oil or the next onslaught would be more serious. He accepted this in a practical spirit. He knew that, when the wind was favourable, he had plenty of ways to make a living, so had no difficulty in drawing up a new life plan. He abandoned teaching and resolved to live solely from his writings. This would allow him to work at home, with no timetables and pressures than those he chose to impose on himself. He would finally be able to live the peaceful life his fragile health required.

Thus he set about swamping the local newspapers with articles, penning the odd essay for the *Fortnightly Review* and, after much persistence, managed to persuade the *Pall Mall Gazette* to offer him a column. Overjoyed by his success, and seeking the fresh air indispensable to his sick lungs, the whole family moved to a country house in Sutton, near the North Downs, one of the few areas that had as yet escaped becoming a suburb of London. For a while, Wells believed his quiet seclusion was to be his life, but once again he was mistaken: this was an imaginary truce. Apparently chance considered him a most amusing toy, for it decided to change the course of his life again, although this time the twist involved the pleasant, popular veneer of fated love.

In the classroom Wells had established friendly relations with a pupil of his, Amy Catherine Robbins, whom he nicknamed Jane, and during the walk they happened to share to Charing Cross station to catch their respective trains, he could not help mesmerising the girl with his eloquent banter. He indulged in it with no other purpose than to allow himself to swell with pride at being able to impress such a beautiful, adorable girl with his words. However, those innocent conversations bore unexpected fruit. His wife, Isabel, alerted him to it on their return from a weekend in Putney, where they had been invited by Jane and her mother. She it was who assured him that, whether or not he had intended it, the girl had fallen head over heels in love with him. Wells could only raise an eyebrow when his wife demanded he stop seeing his former pupil if he wished their marriage to survive.

It was not difficult to choose between the woman who refused his caresses and the cheerful, apparently uninhibited Jane. Wells packed up his books, his furniture and the wicker basket, and moved into a miserable hovel in Mornington Place in a rundown area of north London between Euston and Camden Town. He wished he could have abandoned the marital home spurred on by a violent passion, but he had to leave that to Jane. His real reasons for leaving were the playful curiosity he felt when he glimpsed her little body beneath her dress and, above all, the chance to escape monotony and discover a new life, given that he could predict how the old one would turn out.

However, his first impression was that love had caused him to make a serious mistake: not only had he moved to the worst possible place for his tormented lungs – a neighbourhood in which the air was polluted by soot borne on the wind and mixed with smoke from the locomotives passing through on their way north – but Jane's mother, convinced her poor daughter had fallen into the clutches of a degenerate because Wells was still married to Isabel, had moved in with the couple. She seemed determined to undermine their patience with her endless, vociferous reproaches.

These unforeseen events, with the additional worrying certainty that it would be impossible for him to run no less than three homes on the proceeds of his articles, compelled Wells to take the basket and shut himself into a cupboard, the only place safe from Mrs Robbins's intrusive presence. Hidden among the coats and hats, he stroked the wicker for hours on end, like Aladdin trying to bring back the power of his magic lamp.

This may have seemed an absurd, desperate, or even pathetic strategy, but the day after he performed this rubbing of the basket, Lewis Hind, the literary editor of the *Gazette*'s weekly supplement sent for him. He needed someone capable of writing stories with a scientific slant, short stories reflecting on and even predicting where the relentless onslaught of inventions bent on changing the face of that century would lead. Hind was convinced Wells was the ideal man for the job. What he was proposing, in fact, was that he resurrect his childhood dream, and have another stab at becoming a writer.

Wells accepted, and in a few days drafted a story entitled 'The Stolen Bacillus', which delighted Hind and earned Wells five guineas. The story also drew the attention of William Ernest Henley, editor of the *National Observer*, who promptly invited him to contribute to the pages of his journal, convinced the young man would produce far more ambitious stories if he had room to experiment. Wells was delighted and terrified in equal measure at being given the chance to write for such a prestigious magazine, which at that time was publishing a serialised version of *The Nigger of the Narcissus* by his idol Joseph Conrad. This was no longer writing news items, articles or short stories. He was being offered the space for his imagination to run wild, the freedom to be a real writer of fiction.

Wells awaited his meeting with Henley in a state of nervous tension bordering on collapse. Since the editor of the *National Observer* had asked to see him, Wells had been rummaging through his large mental stockpile of ideas in search of a story original and striking enough to impress the veteran publisher. None seemed to live up to his offer. The rendezvous was drawing near, and Wells still did not have a good story to show Henley. It was then that he turned to the basket and saw that, although it looked empty, it was actually brimming with novels, a cornucopia that needed only a gentle nudge to pour forth its torrent of ideas. This extravagant image was, of course, Wells's way of expressing in poetic language what really happened when he saw the basket: inevitably he remembered his conversation with Merrick and, to his amazement, each time he recalled it he discovered, like a nugget of gold hidden on the bed of a stream, another idea that could be made into a novel. Whether deliberately or by accident, it was as though Merrick had supplied him with enough plots to last several years while he and Wells had pretended they were having tea. He recalled Merrick's disappointment at Dr Nebogipfel being so uninterested in venturing into the unknown world of tomorrow, and this omission appeared worth rectifying now that he had the experience of writing all those articles.

Without a second thought, he got rid of the unsavoury Nebogipfel, replacing him with a respectable, anonymous scientist in whom any inventor could see himself portrayed, and who even embodied the archetypal scientist of the dawning new century. Endeavouring to create something more than just a naïve fantasy from his idea of time travel, Wells gave it the same scientific veneer he had given the stories he wrote for Hind, making use of a theory he had developed in his earlier essays published in the *Fortnightly Review*: the idea that time was the fourth dimension in a universe that appeared to be three-dimensional. The idea would be far more impressive if he used it to explain the workings of the contraption his character would use to travel through the time continuum.

A few years earlier, an American medium called Henry Slade had been tried for criminal deception. Besides bragging of his ability to communicate with the spirits of the dead, he would drop knots, conches and snails' shells into his magician's hat, then pull out identical versions, but with the spirals going in the other direction. Slade maintained that a secret passageway to the fourth dimension was hidden in his hat, which explained the reversal the objects underwent. To many people's astonishment, the magician was defended by a handful of eminent physicists, including Johann Zöllner, professor of physics and astronomy, all of whom argued that what might appear to be a fraud from a three-dimensional point of view was perfectly feasible in a four-dimensional universe. The whole of London was on tenterhooks during the trial.

This, with the work of Charles Hinton, a mathematician who had come up with the hypercube, a cube out of phase with time that contained every single instant of its existence, all occurring at the same time – which man's current three-dimensional vision prevented him seeing – made Wells realise that the idea of the fourth dimension was in the air. No one was sure what it involved, but the words sounded so mysterious and evocative that society longed for, positively demanded it to be real.

For most people, the known world was a tiresome, hostile place, but that was because they could see only part of it. Now they were consoled by the notion that, just as bland roast meat is made tastier with seasoning, the universe improved if they imagined it was no longer reduced to what they could see, but contained a hidden component that could somehow make it bigger. The fourth dimension gave their dull planet a magical feel; it conjured up the existence of a different world in which desires that were impossible in the three-dimensional one might be realised. These suspicions were backed up by concrete actions, such as the recent founding of the Society for Psychic Research in London.

Wells was also forced to endure becoming embroiled almost every day in tiresome debates on the nature of time with his colleagues at the Faculty of Science. One thing led to another, as they say, and as every thinker was turning the fourth dimension into his private playground, Wells had no difficulty combining both ideas to develop his theory of time as another spatial dimension through which it was possible to travel in exactly the same way as it was through the other three.

By the time he entered Henley's office he could visualise his novel with startling clarity, enabling him to relay it with a preacher's conviction and zeal. The time traveller's story would be divided into two parts. In the first he would explain the workings of his machine to a gathering of sceptical guests, to whom he had chosen to present his invention and whom he must try to convince. This group would consist of a doctor, a mayor, a psychologist and some other representative of the middle classes. Unlike Jules Verne, who took up whole chapters with detailed explanations of how his contraptions worked – as though he himself doubted their credibility – Wells's explanations would be straightforward and concise, using simple examples that would enable the reader to assimilate an idea that might otherwise seem too abstract. 'As you are aware,' his inventor would observe, 'the three spatial dimensions (length, breadth, and thickness) are defined in reference to three planes, each of which is at right angles to the other.'

However, under normal circumstances, man's movement through his three-dimensional universe was incomplete. He had no difficulty in moving along its length and breadth, but was unable to overcome the laws of gravity in order to move up and down freely, except by using a hot-air balloon. Man was similarly trapped in the time line, and could only move in time mentally – summoning up the past through memory, or visualising the future by means of his imagination. He could free himself from this constraint if he had a machine that, like the hot-air balloon, enabled him to triumph over the impossible, that is to say, to project himself physically into the future by speeding up time, or going back into the past by slowing it down. In order to help his guests understand the idea of this fourth dimension, the inventor referred to the mercury in a barometer: it moved up and down over a period of days, yet the line represented by its movement was drawn not in any recognised spatial dimension but in that of time.

The second part of the novel would describe the journey that his main character would undertake to put his machine to the test once his guests had left. As a tribute to Merrick's memory, he would set off towards the unfathomable oceans of the future, a future that Wells outlined briefly but eloquently to the editor of the *National Observer*.

Henley, an enormous fellow, virtually a giant, condemned to walk with a crutch because of a botched childhood operation, and on whom Stevenson claimed to have based his idea for Long John Silver, pulled an incredulous face. Talking about the future was dangerous. It was rumoured in literary circles that Verne had portrayed tomorrow's world in a novel called *Paris in the Twentieth Century*, but that his editor, Pierre-Jules Hetzel, had refused to publish it, considering naïve and pessimistic his vision of 1960, when criminals were executed by electric shock, and a system of 'photographic telegraphs' made it possible to send copies of documents anywhere in the world. And it seemed Verne had not been the only author to envisage the future. Many others had tried and failed in the same way.

But Wells did not let Henley's words discourage him. Leaning forwards in his seat, he stood up for himself, assuring Henley that people were eager to read about the future, and that someone should take the risk and publish the first novel about it.

And so it was that, in 1893, *The Time Machine* came out in serial form in the prestigious *National Observer*. However, to Wells's understandable despair, before the novel could be published in its entirety, the owners of the magazine sold it. The new board of directors carried out the usual purges, putting an end to Henley and his publishing projects. Happily, Wells scarcely had time to wallow in his misfortune for Henley, like his Stevensonian alter ego, was a hard nut to crack. He immediately took over at the helm of the *New Review*, where he offered to continue serialising the story of the time traveller, and even convinced the stubborn William Heinemann to publish the novel.

Encouraged by Henley's doggedness, Wells resolved to complete his unfinished novel. However, as was becoming the custom, this turned out to be a difficult undertaking, hampered by the usual impediments, although this time of a far more humiliating nature. At the insistence of his doctors, Wells had once again moved to the country with Jane, to a modest boarding-house in Sevenoaks. But along with the wicker basket and a stream of boxes and trunks came Mrs Robbins, like a piece of junk no one dared throw out. By this time, Jane's mother had gone to unspeakable lengths in her role of leech, reducing her daughter to little more than a pale, worn-out shell with her constant complaints. Mrs Robbins had no need of reinforcements in her war of attrition against Wells. She found an ally in the boarding-house landlady, once she had discovered that it was not a marriage being consummated each night in her house but the sinful cohabitation of a shy young girl and a depraved defendant in a divorce suit.

Battling on two fronts, Wells was scarcely able to concentrate sufficiently to make any headway with his novel. His only consolation was that the section of the plot – the time traveller's journey – to which he was giving shape interested him far more than the part he had already written: it enabled him to steer the novel towards the domain of social allegory, where he could deal with the political questions simmering inside him.

Convinced that in the distant future mankind would have succeeded in evolving fully on a scientific as well as a spiritual level, the time traveller rode across the plains of time on his machine until he reached the year 802,701, a date chosen at random, and sufficiently far off in the future for Wells to be able to verify his predictions *in situ*. By the flickering light of a paraffin lamp, terrorised by the landlady's threats, Wells related, in fits and starts, his inventor's foray into a world that resembled a huge enchanted garden. To complete the enchantment, this Garden of Eden was inhabited by the beautiful slender Eloi, the exquisite result of a human evolution that had not only corrected the weaknesses of the species, but had rid it of ugliness, coarseness and other unprepossessing features. From what the traveller was able to observe, the delicate Eloi lived a peaceful life, in harmony with nature, without laws or government, free from ill-health, financial troubles, or any other kind of difficulty that would make survival a struggle. Neither did they appear to have any notion of private property: everything was shared in that almost Utopian society, which personified the Enlightenment's most hopeful predictions about the future of civilisation.

Like a benevolent, somewhat romantic creator, Wells even had his inventor establish a friendly relationship with a female Eloi named Weena, who insisted on following him around after he had saved her from drowning in a river, captivated like a child by the charm the stranger exuded. Whenever the inventor's back was turned Weena, fragile and slender as a porcelain doll, would garland him with flowers or fill his pockets with blossoms, gestures that conveyed the gratitude she was unable to express through her language, which, although mellow and sweet, remained dishearteningly impenetrable to his ear.

Once Wells had painted this idyllic picture, he proceeded to destroy it with merciless, satirical precision. A couple of hours with the Eloi was enough for the traveller to understand that things were not as perfect as they seemed: these were indolent creatures, with no cultural interests or any drive towards self-improvement, incapable of higher feelings, a bunch of idlers imbued with a hedonism bordering on simple-mindedness. Freed from the dangers that stir courage in men's hearts, the human race had culminated in these lazy, sensual creatures, because intelligence could not thrive where there was no change, and no necessity for it. As if that were not enough, the sudden disappearance of his time machine aroused the inventor's suspicions that the Eloi were not alone in that world. Clearly they shared it with other inhabitants who had the strength to move the machine from where he had left it and hide it inside a gigantic sphinx dominating the landscape.

He was not mistaken: beneath the make-believe paradise dwelled the Morlocks, a simian race afraid of daylight, who, he would soon discover to his horror, had regressed to a state of savage cannibalism. It was the Morlocks who fed the Eloi, fattening their neighbours who lived above ground before gorging on them in their subterranean world.

Their reprehensible eating habits notwithstanding, the traveller was forced to acknowledge that the last vestiges of human intelligence and reason survived in that brutal race, which their need to operate the network of machinery in their underground tunnels had helped preserve.

Afraid of remaining trapped in the future, with no means of travelling back to his own time, the inventor had no alternative but to follow in the footsteps of Aeneas, Orpheus and Hercules and descend into the underworld, into the realm of the Morlocks, to retrieve his machine. Having done so, he made a frenzied escape through time, travelling deep into the future, until he arrived at a strange beach stretching out beneath a shadowy sky. He could see from a swift glance at this new future, whose rarefied air made his lungs smart, that life had divided into two species: a variety of giant screeching white butterfly, and a terrifying crab with enormous pincers, which he was glad to get away from.

No longer curious about what had befallen mankind, which had apparently become extinct, but about the Earth itself, the inventor continued his journey in great strides of a thousand years. At his next stop, more than thirty million years from his own time, he discovered a desolate planet, an orb that had almost stopped rotating, feebly illuminated by a dying sun. A scant snowfall struggled to spread its white veil over a place where there was no sound. The twitter of birds, the bleating of sheep, the buzz of insects and the barking of dogs that made up the music of life were no more than a flicker in the traveller's memory.

Then he noticed a bizarre creature with tentacles splashing around in the reddish sea before him, and his profound grief gave way to a nameless dread that compelled him to clamber back onto his machine. Back in the seat, at the helm of time, he felt a dreadful emptiness. He felt no curiosity about the ominous landscapes awaiting him further into the future. Neither did he wish to go back in time, now he knew that all men's achievements had been futile. He decided the moment had come for him to go back to his own time, to where he truly belonged. On the way back he ended by closing his eyes, for now that the journey in reverse made extinction into a false resurrection, he could not bear to see the world around him grow verdant, the sun recover its stifled splendour, the houses and buildings spring up again, testaments to the progress and trends in human architecture. He only opened his eyes when he felt himself surrounded by the familiar four walls of his laboratory. Then he pulled the lever and the world stopped being a nebulous cloud and took on its old consistency.

Once he had arrived back in his own time, he heard voices and the noise of plates in the dining room, and discovered he had stopped his machine on the Thursday after his departure. After pausing for a few moments to catch his breath, the inventor appeared before his guests, not so much out of a desire to share his experiences with them but because he was attracted by the delicious smell of roast meat, which, after the diet of fruit he had been forced to live on in the future, was an irresistible temptation. After sating his appetite voraciously – in front of his astonished guests, who gaped in awe at his ghastly pallor, his scratched face and the peculiar stains on his jacket – the traveller finally recounted his adventure. Naturally, no one believed in his fantastic voyage, even though he showed them the strange blossoms from his pockets and the sorry state of his time machine.

In the novel's epilogue, Wells had the narrator, who was one of the traveller's guests, finger the exotic flowers, reflecting with optimism that even when physical strength and intelligence has died out, gratitude will live on in men's hearts.

When the novel finally came out under the title *The Time Machine*, it caused a sensation. By August, Heinemann had already printed six thousand paperbacks and fifteen hundred hardbacks. Everyone was talking about it, though not because of its shocking content. Wells had been at pains to present a metaphorical but devastating vision of the ultimate price of a rigidly capitalistic society. Who would not see in the Morlocks the evolutionary result of the working class, brutalised by appalling conditions and exhausting hours, working from dawn until dusk, a class that society had slowly and discreetly begun to move below ground, while the surface of the Earth was reserved for the wealthy classes? With the aim of stirring his readers' consciences, Wells had even inverted the social roles: the Eloi – futile and decorative as the Carolingian kings – were fodder for the Morlocks, who, despite their ugliness and barbarism, were at the top of the food chain.

However, to Wells's astonishment, all his attempts to raise society's awareness paled before the excitement his notion of time travel stirred. One thing was clear: whatever the reasons, this novel, written under such adverse conditions, and which, at little more than forty thousand words, had even required padding with a publicity booklet, had secured him a place in the hall of fame, or had at least brought him to its threshold. And this was far more than he had ever expected when he had penned the first of those forty thousand words.

Like a murderer removing all trace of his crime, the first thing Wells did on becoming a successful author was to burn as many copies as he could find of that childish drivel *The Chronic Argonauts*. He did not want anyone to discover that the excellence they attributed to *The Time Machine* was the end result of such lengthy fumbling and had not emerged in its finished state from his apparently brilliant mind. After that, he tried to enjoy his fame, although this did not prove easy.

There was no doubting he was a successful author, but one with an extended family to support. And while Jane and he had married and moved to a house with a garden in Woking (the basket sticking out like a sore thumb among Jane's hat boxes), Wells had to take care not to let down his guard. There was no question of him stopping for a rest. He must carry on writing – it did not matter what: anything to take advantage of his popularity in the bookshops.

This was not a problem for Wells, of course. He had only to turn to the basket. Like a magician rummaging in his hat, Wells pulled out another novel called *The Wonderful Visit*. This told the story of how one balmy August night an angel fell out of the sky and landed in the marshes of a little village called Sidderford. When the local vicar, an amateur ornithologist, heard about the arrival of this exotic bird, he went out to hunt it with his shotgun and succeeded in destroying the angel's beautiful plumage before taking pity on it and carrying it to the vicarage where he nursed it back to health. Through this close contact, the vicar realised that, although different, the angel was an admirable and gentle creature from which he had much to learn.

The idea for the novel, like the plot of *The Island of Doctor Moreau*, which he would write some months later, was not his, but Wells tried not to see this as stealing, rather as his own special tribute to the memory of a remarkable man, Joseph Merrick, who had died in the horrible way Treves had predicted two years after the unforgettable invitation to tea. And as tributes went, he considered his far more respectful than the surgeon's own: according to what he had heard, Treves was exhibiting Merrick's deformed skeleton in a museum he had opened in the London Hospital. As Wells had said to Merrick, he had gone down in history.

And – who could say? – perhaps that convoluted tale *The Time Machine*, which owed so much to Merrick, would do the same for Wells. In the meantime, it had brought him more than one surprise, he said to himself, remembering the time machine, identical to the one he had written about in his novel, that was hidden in his attic.

Dusk had begun to submerge the world in a coppery light that lent an air of distinction to everything, including Wells who, sitting quietly in his kitchen, looked like a sculpture of himself in flour. He shook his head, banishing the doubts stirred up by the harsh review in the *Speaker*, and picked up the envelope that had appeared in his letterbox that afternoon. He hoped it was not from yet another newspaper asking him to predict the future. Ever since *The Time Machine* had been published, the press had held him up as an official oracle, and kept encouraging him to display his supposed powers of divination in their pages.

But when he tore the envelope open he discovered he was not being asked to predict anything. Instead, he found himself holding a publicity leaflet from Murray's Time Travel, with a card in which Gilliam Murray invited him to take part in the third expedition to the year 2000. Wells clenched his teeth to stop himself unleashing a stream of oaths, crumpled the leaflet and hurled it across the room, as he had the magazine moments before.

The ball of paper flew precariously through the air until it hit the face of a young man who should not have been there. Wells stared with alarm at the intruder who had just walked into his kitchen. He was a well-dressed young man, now rubbing his cheek where the ball of paper had made a direct hit, and shaking his head with a sigh, as though chastising a mischievous child. Just behind him was a second man, whose features so resembled those of the first that they must be related. The author studied the man nearest to him, unable to decide whether he ought to apologise for having hit him with the ball of paper or ask what the devil he was doing in his kitchen. But he had no time to do either, for the man spoke first.

'Mr Wells, I presume,' he said, raising his arm and pointing a gun at him.

XIV

A young man with a bird-like face. This was what Andrew thought when he saw the author of *The Time Machine*, the book that had transformed all England while he was wandering like a ghost amid the trees in Hyde Park. On finding the front door locked, Charles had led him silently round the back of the house. After crossing a rather overgrown garden, they had burst into the small, narrow kitchen whose cramped space the two of them seemed to fill.

'Who are you and what are you doing in my house?' the author demanded, remaining seated at the table, perhaps because in that way less of his body was exposed to the pistol aimed at him – which was also undoubtedly the reason why he had asked the question in such an incongruously polite manner.

Without lowering the gun, Charles turned to his cousin and nodded. It was Andrew's turn to take part in the performance. He suppressed a sigh of displeasure. He deemed it unnecessary to have burst into the author's house brandishing a gun, and he regretted not having given some thought during the journey to what they would do once they reached the house. Instead he had left everything up to his cousin, whose impetuosity had put them in a very awkward situation. But there was no turning back now, so Andrew approached Wells, determined also to improvise. He had no idea how to do so, only that he must mimic his cousin's severe, resolute manner. He reached into his jacket pocket for the cutting and, with the abrupt gesture appropriate to the situation, placed it on the table between the author's hands.

'I want you to stop this happening,' he said, trying his best to sound commanding.

Wells stared blankly at the cutting, then contemplated the intruders, his eyes moving from one to the other like a pendulum. Finally he consented to read it. As he did so, his face remained impassive.

'I regret to tell you that this tragic event has already occurred, and as such belongs to the past. And as you are fully aware, the past is unchangeable,' he concluded disdainfully, returning the cutting to Andrew.

Andrew paused for a moment. Then, a little flustered, he took the yellowing piece of paper and put it back into his pocket. Clearly uncomfortable at being forced into such close proximity – the kitchen did not seem big enough to accommodate another person – the three men gawped at one another, like actors who have suddenly forgotten their lines. However, there was room for another slim person, and even for one of those new-fangled bicycles that were all the rage, with their aluminium spokes, tubular frames and modern pneumatic tyres.

'You're wrong,' said Charles, brightening. 'The past isn't unalterable, not if we have a machine capable of travelling in time.'

Wells gazed at him with a mixture of pity and weariness. 'I see,' he murmured, as though it had suddenly dawned on him what this business was all about. 'But you're mistaken if you imagine I have one at my disposal. I'm only a writer, gentlemen.' He shrugged apologetically. 'I have no time machine. I simply made one up.'

'I don't believe you,' replied Charles.

'It's the truth.' Wells sighed.

Charles tried to catch Andrew's eye, as though his cousin would know what to do next in their madcap adventure. But they had come to a dead end. Andrew was about to tell him to lower the gun, when a young woman walked into the kitchen. She was a slim, small, amazingly beautiful creature, who looked as though she had been delicately wrought by a god tired of churning out inferior specimens. But what really grabbed Andrew's attention was the contraption she had with her, one of those so-called bicycles that were replacing horses because they allowed people to ride peacefully on country roads without exerting themselves too much. Charles, on the other hand, did not let himself be distracted by it and, having instantly identified the girl as Wells's wife, he swiftly grabbed her arm and placed the barrel of the gun against her temple. Andrew was amazed by his speed and agility, as though he had spent his whole life making this kind of movement.

'I'll give you one more chance,' Charles said to the author, who had turned pale.

The exchange that followed was as inconsequential as it was idiotic, but I will reproduce it word for word, even though it is scarcely worth mentioning, simply because I am not trying to make any one episode in this story stand out.

'Jane,' said Wells, in a faint, almost inaudible voice.

'Bertie,' replied Jane, alarmed.

'Charles—' Andrew began.

'Andrew,' Charles interrupted him.

Then there was silence. The afternoon light threw their shadows into relief. The curtain at the window billowed slightly. Out in the garden, the branches of the tree that rose from the ground like a crooked pikestaff rustled eerily as they shook in the breeze. A group of pale shadows nodded, embarrassed by the clumsy melodrama of the scene, as if this were a novel by Henry James (who, incidentally, will also make an appearance in this story).

'Very well, gentlemen,' declared Wells at last, in a good-natured voice, rising from his chair. 'I think we can solve this in a civilised way without anyone getting hurt.'

Andrew looked beseechingly at his cousin.

'It's up to you, Bertie.' Charles gave a sardonic smile.

'Let go of her and I'll show you my time machine.'

Andrew stared at him in amazement. Were Gilliam Murray's suspicions true? Did Wells really have a time machine?

Obviously pleased, Charles released Jane, who crossed the very short distance separating her from her beloved Bertie and threw her arms around him.

'Don't worry, Jane,' the author calmed her. 'Everything will be all right.'

'Well, then,' said Charles, impatiently.

Wells gently extricated himself from Jane's embrace and contemplated Charles with visible distaste. 'Follow me to the attic.'

Forming a sort of funeral procession, with Wells leading the way, they climbed a creaking staircase that seemed as though it might give way beneath their feet at any moment. The attic had been built in the roof space above the second floor, and had an unpleasantly claustrophobic feel to it, due to the low, sloping ceiling and the extravagant collection of assorted bric-à-brac. In a corner under the window, through which the last rays of sunlight were filtering, stood the strange contraption. Judging from his cousin's awed expression and the way he practically bowed before it, Andrew assumed this must be the time machine. He approached the object, examining it with a mixture of curiosity and suspicion.

At first sight, the machine capable of breaking down the barriers confining man to the present looked like some sort of sophisticated sleigh. However, the rectangular wooden pedestal to which it was fixed suggested it was not designed to travel through space, but would need to be dragged along, which would be difficult owing to its size. The apparatus was surrounded by a waist-high brass rail, a flimsy barrier that had to be stepped over to gain access to the sturdy seat in the middle. The seat vaguely resembled a barber's chair, to which had been attached two exquisitely carved wooden arms, and was upholstered in rather lurid red velvet. In front of it, supported by two elegant bars, also made of brass, was a medium-sized dial, the control panel with three monitors showing the day, the month and the year. A delicate glass lever protruded from a wheel to the right of the dial. The machine seemed to have no other handles, and Andrew deduced that the whole thing worked by pulling on this single lever.

Behind the seat there was a complicated mechanism resembling a spirit still. A shaft stuck out of it, supporting a huge round disc covered with strange symbols. It looked as if it might spin round. Apparently designed to protect the machine, it was bigger than a Spartan shield, and was undoubtedly the most spectacular part of the contraption. Finally, a little plaque screwed to the control panel read: 'Made by H. G. Wells'.

'Are you an inventor, too?' Andrew asked, taken aback.

'Of course not – don't be absurd,' replied Wells, pretending to be annoyed. 'As I already told you, I'm only a writer.'

'Well, if you didn't build it, where did you get it from?'

Wells sighed, apparently annoyed at having to explain himself to these strangers. Charles pressed the revolver into Jane's temple once more, harder this time. 'My cousin asked you a question, Mr Wells.'

The author shot him a black look. 'Soon after my novel was published,' he said, realising he had no choice but to comply with the intruders, 'I received a letter from a scientist who told me that for years he had been secretly working on a time machine very similar to the one I described in my book. He said it was almost finished, and he wanted to show it to somebody, but he didn't know whom. He considered, not without good reason, that it was a dangerous invention, capable of arousing unhealthy interest. My novel had convinced him I was the right man to confide in. We met a couple of times, with the aim of getting to know one another, of finding out whether we could really trust each other. We realised we could, not least because we had very similar ideas about the many inherent dangers of time travel. He built the machine here in this very attic. And the little plaque was his affectionate way of showing his gratitude for my collaboration. I don't know if you remember my book, but this amazing machine is nothing like the hulking great thing illustrated on the cover. It doesn't work in the same way, either, of course, but don't ask me how it does, because I'm not a man of science.

'When the time came to try it out, we decided he should have the honour. I would oversee the operation from the present. As we had no way of knowing whether the machine would withstand more than one journey, we decided to travel far into the past, but to a time that was peaceful. We chose a period prior to the Roman invasion, when this area was inhabited by witches and druids, a period that should not have entailed much danger, unless the druids wanted to sacrifice us to some deity. My friend boarded the machine, set it to the agreed date and pulled on the lever. I watched him disappear before my very eyes. Two hours later, the machine came back without him. It was perfectly intact, although there were a few worrying fresh bloodstains on the seat. I haven't seen him since.'

There was a deathly silence.

Charles lowered his pistol and asked: 'Have you tried it?'

'Yes,' confessed Wells, a little shamefaced. 'But only a few brief exploratory journeys into the past, no more than four or five years. And I was careful to change nothing, because I was afraid of the consequences that that might have on the fabric of time. I didn't have the courage to venture into the future. I don't share the same spirit of adventure as the inventor in my novel. This is all too much for me. In fact, I was thinking of destroying the thing.'

'Destroying it?' Charles exclaimed in horror. 'But why?'

Wells shrugged, giving them to understand he was not quite sure of the answer to that question.

'I don't know what became of my friend,' he replied. 'Perhaps there is a guardian of time, who fires indiscriminately at anyone trying to change events in the past to their own advantage. In any case, I don't know what to do with his extraordinary legacy.'

He frowned at the machine, as though he were contemplating a cross he had to bear every time he went for a walk. 'I dare not tell anyone about it, because I cannot even begin to imagine how it would change the world, for better or worse. Have you ever wondered what makes men act responsibly? I'll tell you: they only have one go at things. If we had machines that allowed us to correct all our mistakes, even the most foolish ones, we would live in a world of irresponsible people. Given its potential, all I can really use it for is my own rather futile purposes. But what if one day I yield to temptation and decide to use it for personal gain – for example, to change something in my past, or to travel into the future in order to steal some incredible invention with which I could improve my present circumstances? I would be betraying my friend's dream . . .' He gave a despondent sigh. 'As you can see, this amazing machine has become a burden to me.'

With these words, he looked Andrew up and down intimidatingly, as though he were sizing him up for an imaginary coffin.

'However, you wish to use it to save a life,' he almost whispered. 'What nobler cause could there be? If I let you do it and you succeed, it will justify the machine's existence.'

'Quite so. What nobler cause could there be than to save a life?' Charles reaffirmed hurriedly – Wells's unexpected consent had apparently left his cousin speechless. 'And I assure you Andrew will succeed,' he said, going over to his cousin and clapping him heartily on the shoulder. 'My cousin will kill the Ripper and save Marie Kelly.'

Wells glanced at his wife, seeking her approval.

'Oh, Bertie, you must help him,' declared Jane, full of excitement. 'It's so romantic.'

Wells looked again at Andrew, trying to conceal the flash of envy his wife's remark had triggered in him. But deep down he knew Jane had used the right adjective to describe what the young man intended to do. There was no place in his own ordered life for love like that, the sort that caused tragedies, or started wars requiring the construction of giant wooden horses: love that could easily end in death. No, he would never know what that kind of love was. He would never know what it meant to lose control, to be consumed, to give in to his instincts. And yet, despite his inability to abandon himself to these passions, as ardent as they were destructive, despite his pragmatic, cautious nature, which only allowed him to pursue harmless amorous liaisons that could not possibly degenerate into unhealthy obsessions, Jane loved him. All of a sudden this seemed an inexplicable miracle for which he ought to be thankful.

'All right,' he declared, now in good spirits. 'Let's do it. Let's kill the monster and save the girl!'

Infected by his burst of enthusiasm, Charles took the cutting about Marie Kelly's murder out of his bemused cousin's pocket, and approached Wells so that they could study it together.

'The crime took place on the seventh of November 1888, at about five in the morning,' he pointed out. 'Andrew needs to arrive a few minutes earlier, lie in wait for the Ripper near Marie Kelly's room, then shoot the ogre when he appears.'

'It sounds like a good plan,' Wells agreed. 'But we must bear in mind that the machine only travels through time, not space, which means it won't move from here. Your cousin will need several hours' leeway to reach London.'

Like an excited child, Wells leaped over to the machine and began adjusting the monitors on the control panel. 'There we are,' he declared. 'I've programmed it to take your cousin back to that date. Now all we have to do is wait until two in the morning to begin the journey. That way he'll arrive in Whitechapel in time to prevent the crime being committed.'

'Perfect,' exclaimed Charles.

The four looked at one another in silence, not knowing how to fill the time before the journey began. Luckily, one of them was a woman.

'Have you had supper yet, gentlemen?' asked Jane, showing the practical nature of her sex.

Less than an hour later, Charles and Andrew discovered that Wells had married an excellent cook. They were squeezed around the table in the narrow kitchen, tucking into one of the most delicious roasts they had ever eaten, a most agreeable way of passing the time until the early hours. During supper, Wells showed an interest in the voyages to the year 2000, and Charles spared no detail. Feeling as if he were recounting the plot of one of the fantasy novels he was so fond of, Charles described how he and the other tourists had travelled across the fourth dimension in a tramcar called the

Cronotilus, until they reached the ruined London of the future. There, hidden behind a pile of rocks, they had witnessed the final battle between the evil Solomon and the brave Captain Derek Shackleton.

Wells bombarded him with so many questions that after he had finished his story, Charles asked the author why he had not gone on one of the expeditions, if he was so interested in the outcome of that future war. Wells went quiet, and Charles realised during the ensuing silence that he had unwittingly offended the author.

'Forgive my inquisitiveness, Mr Wells,' he apologised hurriedly. 'Of course not everyone can afford a hundred pounds.'

'Oh, it isn't the money,' Jane broke in. 'Mr Murray has invited Bertie to take part in his voyages on several occasions, but he always refuses.'

As she said this, she glanced at her husband, perhaps in the hope that he might feel encouraged to explain himself. But Wells stared at the joint of lamb with a mournful smile.

'Who would want to travel in a crowded tramcar when they can make the same journey in a luxurious carriage?' Andrew interposed.

The three others looked at the young man, exchanged puzzled glances, then nodded slowly in agreement.

Wells wiped the grease from his lips with a napkin. 'But let's get back to the matter in hand,' he declared, with renewed enthusiasm. 'On one of my exploratory trips in the machine, I travelled back six years, arriving in the same attic when the house was occupied by the previous tenants. If I remember correctly, they had a horse tethered in the garden. I propose that you climb down the creeper quietly, so as not to wake them, then jump on the horse and ride to London as fast as you can. Once you have killed the Ripper, come straight back here. Climb onto the machine, set the date for today and pull the lever. Do you understand?'

'Y-yes,' Andrew stammered.

Charles leaned back in his seat and gazed at him affectionately. 'You're about to change the past, cousin,' he mused. 'I still can't believe it.'

Jane brought in a bottle of port and poured a glass for the guests. They sipped slowly, glancing at their watches occasionally, visibly impatient, until the author said, 'Well, the time has come to make history.'

He set down his glass on the table and solemnly steered them once more to the attic.

'Here, cousin,' Charles said, handing Andrew the pistol. 'It's already loaded. When you shoot the swine, make sure you aim at his chest.'

'At his chest,' echoed Andrew, his hand shaking as he took it, quickly slipping it into his pocket so that neither Wells nor his cousin would see how terrified he was.

Both men took an arm and guided him ceremoniously towards the machine. Andrew climbed over the brass rail and sat in the seat. Despite his feeling of unreality, he could not help noticing the dark splatter of blood on the upholstery.

'Now listen to me,' said Wells, in a commanding tone. 'Try to avoid making contact with anyone, even with your beloved, no matter how much you want to see her alive again. Just shoot the Ripper and come straight back the same way you went before you meet your past self. I don't know what the consequences of such an unnatural encounter might be, but I suspect it would wreak havoc in the fabric of time, and bring about a catastrophe that might destroy the world. Now, tell me, have I made myself clear?'

'Yes, don't worry,' murmured Andrew, more intimidated by the harshness in Wells's voice than by the possibly fatal consequences of his desire to save Marie Kelly if he made a mistake.

'Another thing,' said Wells, returning to the fray, although this time in a less menacing voice, 'your journey won't be anything like you read in my novel. You won't see any snails walking backwards. I confess to having used a certain amount of poetic licence. The effects of time travel are far less exhilarating. The moment you pull on the lever, you'll notice a surge of energy, followed almost immediately by a blinding flash. That's all. Then, quite simply, you'll be in 1888. You might feel dizzy or sick after the journey – I hope that won't affect your aim,' he added sarcastically.

'I'll bear it in mind,' Andrew muttered, absolutely terrified.

Wells nodded, reassured. Apparently, he had no other advice to give because he began to hunt for something on a shelf full of knick-knacks. The others watched him without saying a word.

When at last Wells found what he had been looking for, he declared: 'If you don't mind, we'll keep the cutting in this little box. When you come back we'll open it and find out whether you managed to change the past. I imagine that if your mission has been successful, the headline will announce the death of Jack the Ripper.'

Andrew nodded feebly, and handed Wells the cutting. Then Charles went to his cousin, placed a hand solemnly on his shoulder and gave him an encouraging smile, in which Andrew thought he glimpsed a hint of anxiety. When his cousin stepped aside, Jane approached the machine, wished Andrew good luck, and gave him a little peck on the cheek. Wells beamed as he watched the ritual.

'Andrew, you're a pioneer,' he observed, once these displays of encouragement were over, as though he felt he must close the ceremony with a lofty remark of the sort carved in stone. 'Enjoy the journey. If in the next few decades time travel becomes commonplace, changing the past will doubtless be considered a crime.'

Then, adding to Andrew's unease, he asked the others to take a few steps back to avoid being singed by the burst of energy the machine would give off when its occupant pulled the lever. Andrew watched them step back, trying to conceal his anxiety. He took a deep breath, struggling to control the panic and confusion that were almost overwhelming him. He was going to save Marie, he told himself. He was travelling back in time, to the night of her death, to shoot her killer before he had a chance to rip her guts out, thus changing history and erasing the eight years of suffering he had endured. He looked at the date on the panel – the accursed date that had ruined his life. He could not believe it was in his power to save her, yet all he had to do to overcome his disbelief was to pull that lever. Nothing more. Then whether or not he believed in time travel would become irrelevant.

His trembling hand glistened with sweat as he grasped the lever.

The coolness of the glass in his palm seemed absurd because it was such a commonplace sensation. He glanced at the three figures waiting expectantly by the attic door.

'Go on, cousin,' prompted Charles.

Andrew pulled the lever.

To begin with, nothing happened. Then he became aware of a faint persistent purring, and the air seemed to quiver, as though he were hearing the world's insides rumble. All of a sudden, the hypnotic drone was broken by an eerie crack, and a bright flash of blue light pierced the attic's gloom. A second deafening crack was followed by another flash of light, then another, with sparks flying in all directions as though they were trying to light up every corner of the room. Suddenly Andrew found himself at the centre of a continuous burst of blue lightning bolts. On the far side stood Charles, Jane and Wells, who had stretched his arms out in front of the other two, whether to protect them from the shower of sparks or to prevent them rushing to his aid, Andrew could not tell. The air, perhaps the world, possibly time, or everything at once, disintegrated before his eyes. Reality fragmented.

Then, just as the author had described, an intense light blinded him and the attic disappeared. He gritted his teeth to stifle a scream, as he felt himself fall through the air.

XV

Andrew had to blink at least a dozen times before he could see properly again. As the attic went back to apparent normality, his wildly racing heart began to slow down. He was relieved not to feel dizzy or sick. Even his panic had begun to subside once he realised he had not been burned to a crisp by the lightning, which had left a smell of singed butterflies in the air. His only discomfort was that his whole body felt tense as a result of his anxiety, but in the end he was even glad of that. This was no picnic he was going on. He was about to change the past, to alter events that had already taken place. He, Andrew Harrington, was going to shake up time. Was it not better to be on the alert, to be on his guard?

When the effects of the flash had finally died away and he was able to see properly, he plucked up the courage to step down off the machine, as quietly as possible. The solidity of the floor surprised him, as if he had been expecting the past to be made of mist or fog or some other equally ethereal or malleable substance, simply because the time that corresponded to it had already been used up.

However, as he discovered when he placed his foot tentatively on the ground, that reality was as solid and real as the one he had left. But was he in 1888? He glanced suspiciously around the attic, still plunged into darkness, even savouring a few mouthfuls of air, looking for some detail to prove he was in the past, that he had indeed travelled in time. He discovered it when he peered out of the window: the road looked the same as he remembered it, but there was no sign of the cab that had brought them, and in the garden he saw a horse that had not been there before. Was a simple nag tied to a fence enough to distinguish one year from another? As evidence it seemed rather flimsy and unromantic.

Disappointed, he carefully surveyed the peaceful backdrop of the night sky studded with stars, like rice grains randomly scattered. He saw nothing strange there either. After a few moments of fruitless search, he told himself there was no reason why he should notice any significant differences since he had only travelled back eight years.

Then he shook his head. He could not waste time collecting evidence like an entomologist. He had a mission to fulfil, in which time was very much of the essence. He opened the window and, after testing the creeper's resistance, followed Wells's instructions and began to climb down it as quietly as possible so as not to alert the occupants of the house. This proved easy, and once he reached the ground, he crept towards the horse, which had been watching him impassively, and stroked its mane. The horse had no saddle, but Andrew found one hanging on the fence. He could not believe his luck. He put it on the horse's back and secured the girth, avoiding any sudden gestures that might make the animal nervous, keeping an eye on the darkened house. Then he took the reins, and coaxed it out into the road with affectionate whispers. He was amazed at his own calm. He mounted, glanced back one last time to ensure that everything was still as disappointingly quiet, then set off towards London.

Only when he was on his way, a fast-moving splodge in the darkness, did it dawn on Andrew that soon he was going to see Marie Kelly. He felt a pang, and became tense again. Yes, incredible though it might seem to him, in the year he was in now, at this time in the morning, she was still alive: she had not been murdered. She would probably be in the Britannia at that very moment, drinking to forget her spineless lover before stumbling home into the arms of death.

But then he remembered he was not allowed to see her, not allowed to embrace her, to nestle his head on her shoulder and breathe in her longed-for odour. No, Wells had forbidden it, because that simple gesture could alter the fabric of time, bring about the end of the world. He must limit himself to killing the Ripper and returning the way he had come, as the author had ordered. His action must be swift and precise, like a surgical intervention whose consequences would only be visible when the patient came to – that was to say, once he had travelled back to his own time.

Whitechapel was immersed in a deathly silence. He was surprised at the absence of the usual hurly-burly, until he remembered that during those weeks Whitechapel was a feared neighbourhood in whose alleyways the monster known as Jack the Ripper roamed, doling out death with his knife. He slowed his mount as he entered Dorset Street, aware that, in the intense silence, its hoofs on the cobblestones must produce a din like that of a smithy in his forge.

He dismounted a few yards from the entrance to Miller's Court, and tethered the animal to an iron railing, away from any streetlamps so that it was less likely to be noticed. Then, after making sure the street was empty, he darted through the stone archway leading to the flats. The tenants were all asleep, so he had no light to guide him through the pitch darkness, but Andrew could have found his way blindfold. The further he ventured into that powerfully familiar place, the more overwhelmed he was by a sadness that culminated when he reached Marie Kelly's room, which was also in darkness.

Nostalgia gave way to profound shock when he remembered that while he was standing before the modest abode that had been both heaven and hell to him his father was slapping his face in the Harrington mansion. That night, thanks to a miracle of science, there were two Andrews in the world. He wondered whether his other self might be aware of his existence, too, in the form of goose pimples or a sharp pain in his stomach, as he had heard sometimes happened with twins.

The echo of footsteps interrupted his reverie. His heart beat faster and he ran to hide round the corner of one of the neighbouring dwellings. He had thought of hiding there from the very beginning because, besides seeming to be the safest place, it was scarcely a dozen yards from Marie's door, the perfect distance to be able to see clearly enough to shoot the Ripper, in case he was too afraid to get any closer to him.

Once safely out of sight, back against the wall, Andrew drew the pistol out of his pocket, listening to the footsteps as they drew nearer. The steps that had alerted him had an uncontrolled, irregular quality, typical of a drunk or wounded person. He instantly understood that they could only be those of his beloved, and his heart now fluttered like a leaf in a sudden gust of wind. That night, as on so many others, Marie Kelly was staggering home from the Britannia, but this time his other self was not there to undress her, put her to bed, tuck in her alcoholic dreams.

He poked his head slowly round the corner. His eyes were accustomed enough to the dark for him to be able to make out the reeling figure of Marie pausing outside the door to her tiny room. He had to stop himself running towards her. He felt his eyes moisten as he watched her straighten in a drunken effort to regain her balance, adjust her hat, which was in danger of toppling off with the swaying of her body. She thrust her arm through the hole in the window, forcing the lock for what seemed like an eternity, until finally she managed to open the door. Then she disappeared inside the room, slamming the door behind her. A moment later the faint glow from a lamp cleared part of the swirling gloom in front of her door.

Andrew leaned back against the wall. He had scarcely dried his tears when the sound of more footsteps startled him. Someone else was coming through the entrance into the yard. It took him a few moments to realise this must be the Ripper. His heart froze as he heard the man's boots crossing the cobblestones with cold deliberation. These were the movements of a practised, ruthless predator, who knew there was no escape for his quarry.

Andrew poked his head out again and, with a shudder of terror, saw a huge man calmly approaching Marie's room, surveying the place with a penetrating gaze. He felt strangely queasy: he had already read in the newspapers what was happening now before his eyes. It was like watching a play he knew by heart, and all that remained was for him to judge the quality of the performance. The man paused in front of the door, peering surreptitiously through the hole in the window, as though he intended to reproduce faithfully every detail of the article Andrew had carried in his pocket for eight years – even though it had not yet been written. Now, because of his leapfrogging through time, it seemed more a prediction than a description of events. Except that, unlike then, he was there, ready to change it. Viewed in this light, what he was about to do felt like touching up an already completed painting, like adding a brushstroke to *The Three Graces* or *The Girl with the Pearl Earring*.

After gleefully establishing that his victim was alone, the Ripper cast a final glance around him. He seemed pleased, overjoyed even, at the entrenched calm of the place that would allow him to commit his crime in unexpected seclusion. His attitude incensed Andrew, and he stepped out of his hiding place without considering the possibility of shooting him from there. Suddenly the prospect of finishing off the Ripper from a distance, thanks to the sanitised intervention of a weapon, seemed too cold, impersonal and unsatisfying. His intense rage required him to take the man's life in a more intimate way – possibly by strangling him with his bare hands, smashing his skull with the butt of his pistol – that would allow him to feel the Ripper's contemptible life ebbing away at a rhythm he himself imposed. But as he strode resolutely towards the monster, Andrew realised that, however keen he was to engage in hand-to-hand combat, his opponent's colossal stature and his own inexperience of that kind of fighting made inadvisable any strategy that did not involve the weapon he was clutching.

In front of the door to the little room, the Ripper watched him approach with calm curiosity, wondering perhaps where on earth this fellow had sprung from. Andrew stopped prudently about five yards away from him, like a child who fears being mauled by the lion if he gets too close to the cage. He was unable to make out the man's face in the dark, but perhaps that was as well. He raised the revolver, and, as Charles had suggested, aimed at the man's chest. Had he fired straight away, in cold blood, giving no thought to what he was doing – as if it were just another step in the wild sequence of events he appeared to be caught up in – everything would have gone according to plan. His action would have been as swift and precise as a surgical intervention. But, unfortunately, he did stop to think about what he was doing: it dawned on him that he was about to shoot a man, not a deer or even a bottle. His finger froze on the trigger.

The Ripper tilted his head to one side, half surprised, half mocking, and Andrew watched as his hand clutching the revolver started to shake. This weakened his already feeble resolve, while the Ripper, emboldened by his hesitation, swiftly pulled a knife from inside his coat and hurled himself at Andrew in search of his jugular. Ironically, his frenzied charge released Andrew's trigger finger. A sudden, quick, almost abrupt explosion pierced the silence of the night. The bullet hit the man right in the middle of the chest. Still aiming at him, Andrew watched him stagger backwards. He lowered the warm, smoking gun, no less astonished at having used it than he was to find himself in one piece having fended off that surprise attack. This, though, was not strictly true, as he soon discovered from the sharp pain in his left shoulder.

Without taking his eyes off the Ripper, who was swaying before him like a bear on its hind legs, he felt for the source of the pain, and discovered that the knife, although it had missed his main artery, had ripped through the shoulder of his jacket and sliced into his flesh. Although blood was flowing merrily from the wound, it did not appear very deep. Meanwhile, the Ripper was taking his time to prove whether or not Andrew's shot had been fatal. After bobbing around clumsily, he doubled over, letting go of the knife, which ricocheted over the cobblestones and disappeared into the shadows. Then, with a hoarse bellow, he bent down on one knee, as though to acknowledge in his murderer the traits of nobility, and moaned. Finally, when Andrew was beginning to tire of the display of dying and was toying with the idea of kicking the man to the ground, he collapsed in a heap on to the cobblestones and lay there, stretched out at his feet.

Andrew was about to kneel down and check the man's pulse when Marie Kelly, no doubt alarmed by the skirmish, opened the door to her little room. Before she could recognise him, and resisting the temptation to look at her after eight years of her being dead, Andrew turned on his heel. No longer worried about the corpse, he ran towards the exit as he heard her scream: 'Murder, murder!' Only when he had reached the stone archway did he glance back over his shoulder. He saw his beloved kneeling in a shimmering halo of light, closing the eyes of the man who, in a far-off time, in a world that had taken on the consistency of a dream, had mutilated her to the point at which she was unrecognisable.

The horse was standing where he had left it. Out of breath from running, Andrew mounted and rode off as fast as he could. Despite his agitation, he managed to find his way out of the maze of alleyways and on to the main road that would take him back to Woking. It was only when he had left London that he could acknowledge what he had done. He had killed a man, but at least he had done so in self-defence. And, besides, it had not been any man. He had killed Jack the Ripper, saved Marie Kelly, changed events that had already taken place. He urged the horse on violently, anxious to travel back to his own time and discover the results of his action. If things had gone well, Marie would not only be alive but would probably be his wife. Would they have had a child, possibly two or three?

He drove the horse to the limit, as though afraid the idyllic present would dissolve like a mirage if he took too long to reach it.

Woking was still bathed in the serenity that had aroused suspicion in him a few hours earlier. Now, though, he was grateful for the tranquillity that would allow him to end his mission without further incident. He leaped off the horse and opened the gate. He stopped dead in his tracks: a figure was waiting for him beside the door to the house. Andrew remembered what had happened to Wells's friend: this must be some guardian of time with orders to kill him for having meddled with the past. Trying hard not to give way to panic, he pulled the gun from his pocket as fast as he could and aimed it at the man's chest, just as his cousin had suggested he do with the Ripper.

The figure dived to one side and rolled across the lawn until he was swallowed up by darkness. Andrew tried to follow the man's cat-like movements with his revolver, not knowing what else to do, until he saw him nimbly scale the fence and jump into the road.

Only when he heard feet running away did he lower his weapon, calming himself with slow, deep breaths. Could that man have killed Wells's friend? He did not know, but now that he had escaped it did not matter very much. Andrew gave him no more thought and began to climb back up the creeper. This he was obliged to do using only one arm, as his wounded left shoulder throbbed painfully at the slightest effort. Even so, he managed to reach the attic, where the time machine stood waiting for him.

Exhausted and a little faint from loss of blood, he collapsed on to the seat, set the return date on the contraption's control panel and, after bidding 1888 farewell with a longing gaze, pulled on the glass lever without delay.

This time he felt no fear when the flashing lights engulfed him, only the pleasant sensation of going home.

XVI

Once the sparks had stopped flying, leaving wisps of smoke swirling in the air like feathers after a pillow fight, Andrew was surprised to see Charles, Wells and his wife huddled by the door exactly as he had left them. He attempted a triumphant smile but only managed a weak grimace due to light-headedness and his increasingly painful wound. As he prepared to climb down from the machine, the others glimpsed his blood-soaked sleeve.

'Good God, Andrew!' shouted his cousin, leaping towards him. 'What happened to you?'

'It's nothing,' replied Andrew, leaning on Charles to steady himself. 'Only a scratch.'

Wells took his other arm, and between them the two men helped him down the stairs. Andrew tried to walk on his own, but they ignored his efforts so he meekly allowed himself to be guided into a small sitting room – at that moment he would have let himself be carried off by a horde of demons to the depths of hell itself. There was nothing else he could do: the build-up of nervous tension, the loss of blood and the arduous ride had drained his energy. They sat him down on the armchair nearest the hearth, where a roaring fire was blazing.

After examining his wound with what looked to Andrew like an annoyed twist of the lips, Wells ordered his wife to fetch bandages and everything else necessary to stem the bleeding. He all but told her to hurry up before the gushing flow permanently ruined the carpet. Almost at once the fire's healing warmth calmed Andrew's shivering, but it also threatened to send him to sleep. Luckily it occurred to Charles to give him a glass of brandy, which took the edge off his giddiness and the crushing fatigue he felt.

Jane soon returned and saw to his wound with the neat competence of a war nurse. She cut away his jacket sleeve with a pair of scissors, then applied a series of stinging potions and dressings to the torn flesh. To finish off she bandaged it tightly, then stepped back to contemplate her handiwork.

It was only when the most pressing issue had been resolved that the motley rescue team gathered eagerly around the chair where Andrew lay in a state of semi-collapse. They waited for him to recount what had happened. As though he had dreamed it, Andrew remembered the Ripper lying on the ground, and Marie closing his eyes. That could only mean he had succeeded.

'I did it,' he announced, trying to sound enthusiastic despite his fatigue. 'I killed Jack the Ripper.'

His words triggered an outburst of joy, which he observed with amused surprise. After pelting him with pats on his back, they flung their arms around one another, crying out their praise and abandoning themselves to wild excitement more suited to New Year celebrations or pagan rituals. On realising how unrestrained their reaction was, the three calmed themselves, and gazed at him with a mixture of tenderness and curiosity. Andrew grinned back at them, slightly embarrassed, and when it seemed no one had anything else to say, he looked around for any telltale signs that his brushstroke had altered the present. His gaze fell on the cigar box lying on the table, which contained the cutting. Their eyes followed his.

'So,' said Wells, reading his thoughts, 'you threw a pebble into a still pond and now you are itching to see the ripples it made. Let's not put it off any longer. It's time to see whether you really have changed the past.'

Adopting the role of master of ceremonies once more, he walked over to the table, solemnly picked up the box and presented it to Andrew with the lid open, like one of the Three Wise Men. Andrew took the cutting, trying to stop his hand shaking, and felt his heart miss several beats as he began to unfold it. No sooner had he done so than he found himself contemplating the exact headline he had been reading for years. Scanning the article, he realised the contents were also unchanged: as if nothing had happened, the news item related the brutal murder of Marie Kelly at the hands of Jack the Ripper, and his subsequent capture by the Whitechapel Vigilance Committee. Andrew looked at Wells, bewildered. How could this be?

'But I killed him,' he protested feebly. 'This can't be right . . .'

Wells examined the cutting thoughtfully. Everyone in the room gazed at him, waiting for his verdict. After a few moments, he gave a murmur of comprehension. He straightened and, without looking at anyone, began to pace silently around the room. Owing to its narrow dimensions, he had to be content to circle the table a few times, hands thrust in his pockets, nodding now and then as if to reassure the others that his grasp of the matter was growing. Finally, he paused before Andrew, and smiled at him dolefully.

'You saved the girl, Mr Harrington,' he observed, with quiet conviction, 'there is no doubt in my mind about that.'

'B-but in that c-case,' stammered Andrew, 'why is she still dead?'

'Because she must continue being dead in order for you to travel back in time to save her,' the author declared, as though stating the obvious.

Andrew blinked, unable to fathom what Wells was trying to say.

'Think about it: if she had still been alive would you have come to my house? Don't you see that by killing her murderer and preventing her being ripped to shreds you have eliminated your reason for travelling back in time? And if there's no journey, there's no change. As you can see, the two events are inseparable,' explained Wells, flourishing the cutting, which, with its original heading, corroborated his theory.

Andrew nodded slowly, glancing at the others, who looked as bewildered as he.

'It isn't all that complicated,' scoffed Wells, amused by his audience's confusion. 'I'll explain it in a different way. Imagine what must have happened after Andrew travelled back to this spot in the time machine: his other self must have arrived at Marie Kelly's room, but instead of finding his beloved with her entrails exposed to the elements, he found her alive, kneeling by the body of the man whom police would soon identify as Jack the Ripper. An unforeseen avenger had stepped out of nowhere and murdered the Ripper before he could add Marie Kelly to his list of victims. And, thanks to this stranger, Andrew will be able to live with her happily ever after, although the irony is that he will never know he has you – I mean himself – to thank for it,' the author concluded, gazing at him excitedly, with the eagerness of a child expecting to see a tree spring up moments after he has planted a seed. As Andrew was clearly still nonplussed, he added: 'It is as though your action has caused a split in time, created a sort of alternative universe, a parallel world, if you like. And in that world Marie Kelly is alive and happy with your other self. Unfortunately you are in the wrong universe.'

Charles nodded, increasingly persuaded by Wells's explanation, then turned to Andrew, hoping to find his cousin equally convinced. But Andrew needed a few more moments to mull over the writer's words. He lowered his head, trying to ignore the others' enquiring faces in order to consider the matter calmly. Given that nothing in his reality seemed to have changed, his journey in the time machine could not only be considered useless, but it was debatable whether it had even taken place. Yet he knew it had. He could not forget the image of Marie, the gun going off, the jolt it had sent up his arm and, above all, the nasty gash to his shoulder – irrefutable proof that his experience had not been a dream. Yes, those events had really occurred, and the fact that he could not see their effects did not mean there weren't any, as Wells had quickly grasped. Just as a tree's roots grow around a rock, so the consequences of his action, which could not simply vanish into thin air, had created another reality, a parallel world in which he and Marie Kelly were living happily together, a world that would not have existed if he had not travelled back in time.

This meant he had saved his beloved, even though he was not able to enjoy her. All he had was the comforting satisfaction of knowing that he had prevented her death, that he had done everything in his power to make amends. At least his other self would have her, he thought, with a degree of resignation. That other Andrew – who, after all, was him, his own flesh and blood – would be able to fulfil all his dreams. He would be able to make her his wife, to love her regardless of his father's opposition and their neighbours' malicious gossip. He only wished the other Andrew could know what a miracle that was, how during the past eight years while he had been tormenting himself, his luckier self had never stopped loving her, populating the world with the fruit of that love.

'I understand,' he murmured, smiling wanly at his friends.

Wells was unable to suppress a cry of triumph. 'That's wonderful,' he exclaimed, while Charles and Jane resumed patting Andrew on the back.

'Do you know why during my journeys into the past I always avoided seeing myself?' Wells asked, without caring whether anyone was listening. 'Because if I had, it would mean that at some point in my life I would have been obliged to walk through the door and greet myself, which – thankfully for my sanity – has never happened.'

After embracing his cousin repeatedly in a renewed display of euphoria, Charles helped him up out of his chair, while Jane straightened his jacket in a motherly gesture.

'Perhaps those troubling sounds we hear in the night, the creaking noises we assume are the furniture, are simply the footsteps of a future self watching over us as we sleep, without daring to disturb us,' Wells mused, oblivious to the general rejoicing.

It was only when Charles went to shake his hand that he appeared to emerge from his reverie.

'Thanks awfully for everything, Mr Wells,' said Charles. 'I

apologise for having burst into your house like that. I hope you can forgive me.'

'Don't worry, don't worry. All is forgotten,' replied the writer, with a vague wave, as though he had discovered something salutary, even revivifying, in having a gun aimed at him.

'What will you do with the machine? Will you destroy it?' Andrew ventured timidly.

Wells gazed at him, smiling benevolently. 'I suppose so,' he replied, 'now it has fulfilled the mission for which it was quite possibly invented.'

Andrew was moved by his solemn words. He did not consider his personal tragedy the only one that warranted the use of the machine, but was grateful that the author, who scarcely knew him, had sympathised enough with his misfortune to consider it a good enough reason to flout the laws of time and perhaps endanger the world.

'I also think it's for the best, Mr Wells,' said Andrew, having recovered from his emotion, 'because you were right. There is a guardian of time, someone who watches over the past. I bumped into him when I came back, in the doorway to your house.'

'Really?' said Wells, taken aback.

'Yes. Luckily I managed to frighten him off,' replied Andrew. With this, he clasped the author in a heartfelt embrace. Beaming, Charles and Jane contemplated the scene, which would have been touching, were it not for the awkward stiffness with which Wells greeted Andrew's affectionate gesture. When Andrew had finally let go of him, Charles said goodbye to the couple, steering his cousin out of the house lest he throw himself once more at the alarmed author.

Andrew crossed the garden vigilantly, right hand in his pocket on the pistol, afraid the guardian of time might have followed him back to the present and be lying in wait for him. But there was no sign of him. Outside the gate they found the cab that had brought them there only a few hours before, a few hours that to Andrew seemed like centuries.

'Blast, I've forgotten my hat,' said Charles, after Andrew had clambered in. 'I'll be back in a jiffy, cousin.'

Andrew nodded absently, and settled into his seat, utterly exhausted. Through the tiny window he surveyed the encircling darkness as day began to dawn. Like a coat wearing thin at the elbows, night was unravelling at one of the furthest edges of the sky, its opaqueness gradually diluting into an ever paler blue, until a hazy light slowly began to reveal the contours of the world. With the exception of the driver, apparently asleep on his seat, it was as if this stunning display of golden and purple hues was being performed solely for his benefit. Many times over the past few years when Andrew had witnessed the majestic unveiling of dawn he had wondered whether that day he would die, whether that day his increasing torment would compel him to shoot himself with a pistol like the one he was now carrying in his pocket, the one he had removed from its glass cabinet the previous evening without knowing he would use it to kill Jack the Ripper. But now he could not watch the dawn and wonder whether he would be alive to see it tomorrow because he knew the answer: he would see the dawn tomorrow and the day after and the day after that, because he had no reason to kill himself now that he had saved Marie. Should he go ahead with his plan out of sheer inertia, or simply because, as Wells had pointed out, he was in the wrong universe? This did not seem to justify the deed. In any event it felt less noble – and might even imply a fundamentally absurd jealousy of his time twin. After all, he was the other Andrew, and he ought to rejoice in his good fortune as he would his own or, failing that, that of his brother or his cousin Charles. Besides, if the grass in next door's garden was always greener, how much more luxuriantly verdant must it be in the neighbouring universe? He should feel pleased to be happy in another world, to have achieved bliss in it.

Reaching this conclusion threw up another unexpected question: did knowing that you had achieved the life you wanted in another world absolve you from having to try to achieve it in this one? At first, Andrew did not know how to answer this question, but after a few moments' thought he decided it did: he was absolved from being happy; he could be content to lead a peaceful life, enjoying its small pleasures without the slightest feeling of inner frustration. For, however trite it might seem, he could always console himself with the happy thought that he was living a full life in another place, which was both nearby and far away, a place that was inaccessible, uncharted, because it was on the reverse of any map.

Suddenly, he experienced an incredible sense of relief, as though a burden he had been carrying since birth had been lifted from his shoulders. He felt unfettered, reckless and wild. He had an overwhelming desire to reconnect with the world, to tread the common path of life with the rest of humanity, to send a note to Victoria Keller, or to her sister Madeleine, if Victoria was the one Charles had married, inviting her to dinner or to the theatre or for a walk in a park where he could ambush her, brush his lips against hers – simply because he was aware that at the same time he would also *not* be doing that. It seemed that this was the way the universe worked: excluding nothing, allowing everything to happen that could happen. Even if he did decide to kiss her, another Andrew would refrain from doing so, and would carry on rolling down the hill of time until he came to another pair of lips and split into another twin who, after dividing a few more times, would finally plunge over a cliff into the abyss of solitude.

Andrew leaned back in his seat, amazed that each of life's twists and turns should give rise to a new existence vying with the old one to discover which was most authentic, instead of falling like sawdust and being swept away by the carpenter's broom. It made him giddy to think that at each crossroads, clutches of other Andrews were born, and their lives went on at the same time as his, beyond the moment when his own ended, without him being aware of it. Ultimately it was man's limited senses that established the boundaries of the world. But what if, like a magician's box, the world had a false bottom and continued beyond the point where his senses told him it stopped? This was the same as asking whether roses kept their colour when no one was there to admire them. Was he right or was he losing his mind?

This was obviously a rhetorical question, yet the world took the trouble to respond. A soft breeze sprang up, lifting a leaf from among the many carpeting the pavement and making it dance on the surface of a puddle, like a magic trick performed for a single onlooker. Mesmerised, Andrew watched it spin until his cousin's shoe halted its delicate movement.

'All right, we can go now,' said Charles, waving his hat triumphantly, like a hunter showing off a bloodstained duck.

Inside the cab, he raised an eyebrow, surprised at the dreamy smile on his cousin's face. 'Are you feeling all right, Andrew?'

Andrew gazed at his cousin fondly. Charles had moved heaven and earth to help him save Marie Kelly, and he was going to repay him in the best way he could: by staying alive, at least until his moment arrived. He would pay Charles back three-fold for all the affection he had shown him over these past years, years he now felt ashamed to have wasted out of apathy and indifference. He would embrace life – yes, embrace it as he would a wondrous gift, and devote himself to living it to the best of his ability, the way everyone else did, the way Charles did. He would transform life into a long, peaceful Sunday afternoon in which he would wile away the time until nightfall. It could not be that difficult: he might even learn to enjoy the simple miracle of being alive.

'Better than ever, Charles,' he replied, perking up. 'So good, in fact, that I would gladly accept an invitation to dine at your house, provided your charming wife also invites her equally charming sister.'

XVII

This part of the story could end here, and for Andrew it does, except that this is not only Andrew's story. If it were, there would be no need for my involvement: he could have told his own story, as each man recounts the tale of his own life to himself on his deathbed. Yet that tale is always incomplete, for only a man shipwrecked on a desert island from birth, growing up and dying there with no more than a few monkeys for company, can claim without a shadow of doubt that his life is exactly what he thinks it has been – provided, of course, that the macaques have not stashed away in some cave his trunk of books, clothes and photographs, washed up by the tide.

However – with the exception of shipwrecked babies and other extreme cases – each man's life forms part of a vast tapestry, woven together with those of countless other souls keen to judge his actions not only to his face but behind his back. Only if he considers the world around him a backdrop, with puppets that stop moving when he goes to sleep, can he accept that his life has been exactly as he tells it. Otherwise, moments before he breathes his last, he will have to accept that the idea he has of his own life must of necessity be vague, fanciful and uncertain, that there were things that affected him, for good or bad, that he will never know about. They may range from his wife having had an affair with the pastry cook, to his neighbours' dog urinating on his azaleas every time he went out.

So, just as Charles did not witness the charming dance the leaf performed on the puddle, Andrew did not witness what happened when Charles got his beloved hat back. He could have pictured him entering Wells's house, apologising for the fresh intrusion, joking about not being armed this time, and the three of them crawling about on their hands and knees hunting for the elusive hat, except that we know he had no time to wonder about what his cousin was doing because he was too busy with his heart-warming deliberations about other worlds and magicians' boxes.

I, on the other hand, see and hear everything whether I want to or not, and it is my task to separate the seed from the chaff, to decide which events I consider most important in the tale I have chosen to tell. I must therefore go back to the point at which Charles realises he has forgotten his hat and returns to the author's house. You may be wondering what bearing such an insignificant act as the fetching of a hat could possibly have on this story. None whatsoever, I would say, if Charles really had forgotten his hat by accident. But things are not always as they seem, which saves me the trouble of burdening you with a list of examples you could easily find by rummaging around a little in your own life, regardless of whether you live near a pastry shop or have a garden full of azaleas. Let us return to Charles without further ado.

'Blast, I've forgotten my hat,' said Charles, after Andrew had clambered into the cab. 'I'll be back in a jiffy, cousin.'

Charles strode hurriedly across the tiny front garden, and entered the author's house, looking for the tiny sitting room where they had taken Andrew. There was his hat, waiting for him on a peg on the coat-stand exactly where he had left it. He seized it, smiling, and went out into the passageway, but instead of going back the way he had come, as would appear logical, he turned round and mounted the stairs to the attic. There he found the author and his wife hovering around the time machine in the dim glow of a candle placed on the floor. Charles made his presence known, clearing his throat loudly before declaring triumphantly: 'Everything turned out perfectly. My cousin was completely taken in!'

Wells and Jane were collecting the Ruhmkorff coils they had hidden earlier among the shelves of knick-knacks. Charles took care to avoid treading on the switch that activated them from the door, setting off the series of deafening electrical charges that had so terrified his cousin. After asking for Wells's help and telling him about his plan, Charles had been sceptical when the author had come up with the idea of using those diabolical coils; he had confessed rather sheepishly to being one of the many spectators who had fled like frightened rabbits from the museum where their inventor, a pale, lanky Croat named Nikola Tesla, had introduced to the public his devilish device and the hair-raising blue flashes that caused the air in the room to quiver.

However, Wells had assured him that these harmless contraptions would be the least of his worries. Besides, he ought to start getting used to the invention that would revolutionise the world. He went on to tell him, with a tremor of respect in his voice, how Tesla had set up a hydroelectric power station at Niagara Falls, which had bathed the town of Buffalo in electric light. It was the first step in a project that signalled the end of night on Earth, Wells had affirmed. Evidently, the author considered the Croat a genius, and was eager for him to invent a voice-activated typewriter that would free him from the burden of tapping the keys with his fingers while his imagination raced ahead.

In view of the plan's success, Charles had to agree in hindsight that Wells had been brilliant: the journey back in time would never have been as believable without the lightning flashes, which in the end had provided the perfect build-up, before the magnesium powder concealed behind the false control panel blinded whoever pulled the lever.

'Magnificently,' Wells rejoiced, getting rid of the coils he was holding and going to greet Charles. 'I confess I had my doubts: there were too many things that might have gone wrong.'

'True,' admitted Charles, 'but we had nothing to lose and much to gain. I already told you that if we succeeded my cousin might give up the idea of killing himself.' He looked at Wells with genuine admiration. 'And I must say that your theory about parallel universes to explain why the Ripper's death did not change anything in the present was so convincing even I believed it.'

'I'm so glad. But I don't deserve all the credit. You had the most difficult task of hiring the actors, replacing the bullets with blanks, and most of all getting this thing built,' said Wells, pointing to the time machine.

The two men gazed at it fondly for a few moments.

'Yes, and the end result is truly splendid,' Charles agreed. Then he joked: 'What a pity it doesn't work.'

After a brief pause, Wells hastened to chortle politely, emitting a sound like a walnut being cracked.

'What do you intend doing with it?' Wells asked abruptly, as though he wanted to smother the sickly laugh that had shown the world he possessed a sense of humour.

'Nothing, really,' the other man replied. 'I'd like you to keep it.'

'Me?'

'Of course. Where better than at your house? Consider it a thank-you present for your invaluable help.'

'You needn't thank me for anything,' protested Wells. 'I found the whole thing hugely enjoyable.'

Charles smiled to himself: how fortunate that the author had agreed to help him. Also that Gilliam Murray had been willing to join in the charade – which he had even helped to plan – after he had seen how devastated Charles was when he informed him the company did not provide journeys into the past. The wealthy entrepreneur's agreement to play a role had made everything that much easier. Taking Andrew straight to the author's house without calling in at Murray's offices first, in the hope that he would believe Charles's suspicion that Wells had a time machine, would not have been nearly as convincing.

'I'd like to thank you again from the bottom of my heart,' said

Charles, genuinely moved. 'You, too, Jane, for persuading the cab driver to hide down a side street and to tether the horse to the gate while we pretended to intimidate your husband.'

'You've nothing to thank me for either, Mr Winslow. It was a pleasure. Although I'll never forgive you for having instructed the actor to stab your cousin . . .' she chided, with the amused smile of someone gently scolding a naughty child.

'But everything was under control!' protested Charles, pretending to be shocked. 'The actor is an expert with a knife. Besides, I can assure you that without the added encouragement, Andrew would never have shot him. Not to mention that the scar on my cousin's shoulder will be a constant reminder that he saved his beloved Marie's life. Incidentally, I liked the idea of employing someone to play a guardian of time.'

'Wasn't that your doing?' declared Wells, taken aback.

'No,' said Charles. 'I thought you'd arranged it . . .'

'It wasn't me,' replied Wells, perplexed.

'In that case, I think my cousin scared off a burglar. Or perhaps he was a real time traveller,' joked Charles.

'Perhaps.' Wells laughed uneasily.

'Well, the main thing is it all turned out well,' concluded Charles. He congratulated them once again on their successful performances and gave a little bow as he said goodbye. 'And now I really must go or my cousin will start to suspect something. It has been a pleasure meeting you. And remember, Mr Wells, I shall always be one of your most devoted readers.'

Wells thanked him with a modest smile that lingered on his face as Charles's footsteps faded down the stairs. Then he heaved a deep sigh of satisfaction. Hands on hips, he gazed at the time machine, with the fierce affection of a father contemplating his first-born child, and stroked the control panel. Jane watched him, aware that at that very moment her husband was being assailed by an emotion as intense as it was disturbing: he was embracing a dream, a product of his own imagination that had stepped miraculously out of the pages of his book and become a reality.

'We might find some use for the seat, don't you think?' Wells commented, turning towards her.

His wife shook her head – she might have been asking herself what the devil she was doing with such an insensitive fellow – and walked over to the window. The author went and stood beside her, consternation on his face. He placed his arm round her shoulders, and she laid her head against him. Her husband did not lavish her with so much affection that she would pass up this spontaneous gesture, which had taken her as much by surprise as if he had hurled himself from the window, arms akimbo, to confirm once and for all that he was unable to fly. Thus entwined, they watched Charles climb into the cab, which pulled away. They watched it disappear down the street beneath the orange-tinted dawn.

'Do you realise what you did tonight, Bertie?' Jane asked him.

'I nearly set fire to the attic.'

She laughed. 'No, tonight you did something that will always make me feel proud of you,' she said, looking up at him with infinite tenderness. 'You saved a man's life using your imagination.'

PART TWO

IF YOU ENJOYED OUR JOURNEY
INTO THE PAST,
DEAR READER, IN THE
FOLLOWING INSTALMENT OF THIS
EXCITING ADVENTURE
YOU WILL BE TREATED TO AN
EXPEDITION INTO THE FUTURE,
TO THE YEAR 2000,
WHERE YOU WILL WITNESS THE
LEGENDARY BATTLE BETWEEN
HUMANS AND AUTOMATONS.

BE WARNED,
HOWEVER:

THIS EPISODE CONTAINS SCENES OF AN EXTREMELY
VIOLENT NATURE – ONLY TO BE EXPECTED OF
A BATTLE OF SUCH ENORMOUS CONSEQUENCES
FOR THE FUTURE OF THE HUMAN RACE.

Mothers of sensitive children may wish to examine the contents
and expurgate certain passages before entrusting the remainder
to their little ones.

XVIII

Claire Haggerty would gladly have been born into another era if that meant she did not have to take piano lessons or wear insufferably tight dresses, or choose a husband from among an assortment of willing suitors, or carry round one of those silly little parasols she always ended up leaving in the most unexpected places. She had just celebrated her twenty-first birthday, and yet, if anyone had taken the trouble to ask her what she wanted from life they would have heard her reply: 'Nothing, simply to die.'

Naturally, this was not what you would expect to hear from the lips of a charming young lady who had scarcely embarked upon life, but I can assure you it is what Claire would have told you because, as I have previously explained, I possess the ability to see everything, including what no one else can see, and I have witnessed the endless self-questioning she puts herself through in her room before going to bed. While everyone imagines she is brushing her hair in front of the mirror like any normal girl, Claire is lost in contemplation of the dark night outside her window, wondering why she would sooner die than see another dawn. She had no suicidal tendencies. Neither was she irresistibly drawn to the other side by the call of a siren. Nor was the mere fact of being alive so unbearably distressing that she felt she must end it all forthwith. No.

What it boiled down to was something far simpler: the world into which she had been born was not exciting enough for her, and it never would be – or, at least, that was the conclusion she reached during her nightly reflections. Hard as she tried, she was unable to discover anything about her life that was pleasurable, interesting or stimulating. Even more tiresome, she was compelled to pretend she was content with what she had. The time she lived in was dreary and uninspiring; it bored her to tears. And the fact that she could find no one around her who seemed to share her disenchantment made her feel out of place and out of sorts. This profound inner unease, which inevitably isolated her socially, often made her irritable and sharp-tongued, and from time to time, regardless of whether the moon was full or not, she would lose control and turn into a mischievous creature who delighted in wreaking havoc at family gatherings.

Claire knew perfectly well that these fits of frustration, besides being self-indulgent and futile, did her no good at all, especially at such a crucial time in her life. Her main concern ought to have been finding a husband to support and provide her with half a dozen offspring to show the world she was of good breeding stock. Her friend Lucy used to warn her she was gaining a reputation among her suitors for being unsociable, and some had abandoned their courtship after realising that her offhand manner made her an impregnable fortress. Nevertheless, Claire could not help reacting as she did. Or could she?

Sometimes she wondered whether she did everything in her power to overcome her gnawing sense of dissatisfaction, or whether, on the contrary, she derived a morbid pleasure from giving in to it. Why could she not accept the world as it was? Lucy stoically endured the torments of the corset as though they were some sort of atonement aimed at purifying her soul. She did not mind being barred from study at Oxford and put up with being visited by her suitors in scrupulous succession, in the knowledge that sooner or later she must marry one of them. But Claire was not like Lucy: she loathed those corsets, apparently designed by the devil himself;

she longed to be able to use her brain as any man could; and she was not the slightest bit interested in marrying any of the young men hovering around her.

It was the idea of marriage she found most distressing – despite the great progress that had been made since her mother's day. Then when a woman married she was immediately stripped of all her possessions, even the money she earned from paid employment. The law, like an ill-fated wind, blew everything straight into her husband's grasping hands. At least if Claire were to marry now she would keep her possessions, and might even win custody of her children in the event of a divorce. Even so, she continued to consider marriage a form of legal prostitution, as Mary Wollstonecraft had stated in her book *A Vindication of the Rights of Women* – a work that to Claire was as sacred as the Bible. She admired the author's determined struggle to restore women's dignity, her insistence that women should stop being considered the handmaidens of men, whom science deemed more intelligent because their skulls – and therefore their brains – were bigger: she had more than enough evidence to suggest that such enhanced proportions were only good for filling a larger hat.

On the other hand, Claire knew that if she refused to place herself under a man's tutelage, she would have no choice but to make her own living, to try to find employment in one of the few openings available to someone of her position: as a stenographer or nurse. Both occupations appealed to her even less than being buried alive with one of the elegant dandies who took it in turns to worship her.

But what could she do if marriage seemed such an unacceptable alternative? She felt she only could go through with it if she were truly to fall in love with a man – which she considered virtually impossible: her indifference towards men was not confined to her dull crowd of admirers, but extended to every man on the planet, young or old, rich or poor, handsome or ugly. The niceties were unimportant: she was firmly convinced she could never fall in love with any man from her own time, whoever he might be, for the simple reason that his idea of love would pale beside the romantic passion to which she longed to surrender herself.

Claire yearned to be overwhelmed by an uncontrollable, violent fervour that would scorch her very soul; she longed for a furious happiness to compel her to take fateful decisions that would allow her to gauge the strength of her feelings. Yet she longed without hope, for she knew that this type of love had gone out with frilly blouses. What else could she do? Resign herself to living without the one thing she imagined gave meaning to life? No, of course not.

And yet, a few days earlier, something had happened that, to her amazement, had roused her sleeping curiosity, encouraging her to believe that, despite first appearances, life was not devoid of surprises. Lucy had summoned her to her house with her usual urgency and, somewhat reluctantly, Claire had obeyed, fearing her friend had organised yet another of the tedious séances to which she was so partial. Lucy had joined in the latest craze to come out of America with the same zeal she applied to following the latest Paris fashions. Claire was not so much bothered by having to make believe she was conversing with spirits as she was by Eric Sanders, a skinny, arrogant young man, who had set himself up as the official neighbourhood medium. Sanders maintained he had special powers that allowed him to communicate with the dead. Claire knew this was simply a ruse to gather together half a dozen unmarried, impressionable girls, plunge them into an intimidating gloom, terrify them with a preposterously cavernous voice, and take advantage of their proximity to stroke their hands and even their shoulders with impunity. The crafty Sanders had read enough of *The Spirits Book* by Allan Kardec to be able to interrogate the dead with apparent ease and confidence, although he was evidently far too interested in the living to pay much attention to their responses.

After the last séance when Claire had slapped him after she felt a spirit's all too real hand caressing her ankles, Sanders had banned her from any further gatherings, insisting that her sceptical nature was too upsetting to the dead and hampered his communication with them. At first, her exclusion from Sanders's supernatural gatherings had come as a relief, but she ended up feeling disheartened:

she was twenty-one and had fallen out not only with this world but with the world beyond.

However, Lucy had not arranged any séances that evening. She had a far more thrilling proposal, she explained to her friend, smiling excitedly and leading her by the hand to her room. There, she told her to sit down on a small armchair and be patient. Then she began rifling through her desk drawer. Open on a lectern on the desk lay a copy of Darwin's *The Voyage of the Beagle*. The page showed an illustration of a kiwi bird, an extraordinary-looking creature that her friend was copying on to a piece of paper – tracing its simple, rounded form required no artistic ability. Claire could not help wondering whether, besides looking at the pictures, her friend had troubled to read the book that had become a favourite among the middle classes.

Once she had found what she was looking for, Lucy shut the drawer and turned to her friend with an ecstatic smile. What could Lucy possibly find more exciting than communicating with dead people? Claire wondered. She discovered the answer on reading the leaflet her friend thrust into her hand: communicating with people who had not yet been born. The flyer advertised a company called Murray's Time Travel, which offered journeys through time, to the year 2000, to witness the battle between automatons and humans that would decide the fate of humanity. Stunned, Claire re-read the leaflet then studied the crude illustrations that apparently depicted the aforementioned battle. Amid ruined buildings, automatons and humans battled for the future of the world with strange weapons. The figure leading the human army caught her eye – the artist had drawn him in a more heroic pose than the others. According to the caption below, he was the brave Captain Derek Shackleton.

Without giving Claire time to collect herself, Lucy explained she had visited the premises of Murray's Time Travel that very morning. They had informed her that seats were still available for the second expedition, arranged after the success of the first, and she had not hesitated to sign them up for it. Claire looked a little put out, but Lucy did not apologise for having failed to ask her friend's permission. She went on to explain how they would go about travelling to the future without their respective parents finding out: she knew that if they did they would doubtless forbid them to go or, worse, insist on going with them. Lucy wanted to enjoy the year 2000 without the bore of being chaperoned. She had it all worked out: money would be no object, as she had persuaded her wealthy grandmother, Margaret, to give her the amount they needed to cover the cost of both tickets – naturally without telling her what it was for. She had even enlisted her friend Florence Burnett's help. For 'a small fee', the greedy Florence was willing to send them a false invitation to spend the following Thursday at her country house at Kirkby. And so, if Claire was in agreement, on that day the two of them would travel to the year 2000 and be back in time for tea without anybody being the wiser.

After Lucy had finished her gabbled speech, she looked at her friend expectantly. 'Well?' she said. 'Will you go with me?'

And Claire could not, would not – did not know how to – refuse.

The next four days had sped by in a whirl of excitement about the impending trip and the enjoyment of having to prepare for it in secret. Now Claire and Lucy found themselves outside the picturesque premises of Murray's Time Travel, wrinkling their noses at the stench exuding from the entrance. On noticing them, one of the employees, who was cleaning off what looked like excrement on the front of the building, hastened to apologise for the unpleasant smell and assured them that if they ventured across the threshold with a handkerchief or scarf for protection, or holding their breath, they would be attended to in a manner befitting two such lovely ladies. Lucy dismissed the man with a desultory wave, annoyed that anyone should draw attention to an inconvenience she preferred to ignore so that nothing would detract from the thrill of the moment. She seized her friend's arm – Claire was unsure whether this was to bolster her courage or infect her with enthusiasm – and propelled her through the doors to the future.

As they entered the building, Claire glimpsed Lucy's rapt expression and smiled to herself. She knew the reason for her friend's nervous impatience: Lucy was already anxious to come back and describe the future to her friends and family who, whether out of fear, indifference or because they had been unable to secure a seat, had stayed behind in the insipid present. Yes, for Lucy this was simply another adventure with which to regale people – like a picnic ruined by a cloudburst, or an unexpectedly eventful crossing in a boat.

Claire had agreed to accompany her, but for very different reasons. Lucy planned to visit the year 2000 in the same way she would go to a new shop and be home in time for tea. Claire, on the other hand, had no intention of coming back.

A snooty assistant guided them to a hall in which the thirty other privileged travellers to the year 2000 were chattering excitedly. There, she told them that a glass of punch would be served before Mr Murray welcomed them, explained the itinerary of their trip to the future, and the historic moment they were about to witness. When she had finished, she curtsied abruptly and left them to their own devices in the spacious room, which, from the boxes at the sides and the stage at one end, had been the stalls of a theatre. Without the rows of seats and with only a few uncomfortable couches, the space looked over-large. This impression was strengthened by the high ceilings, suspended from which were dozens of oil lamps. Seen from below, they resembled a colony of sinister spiders living oblivious to the world beneath them.

Apart from a few octogenarians, who had difficulty standing because of their brittle bones, no one appeared to want to sit on the couches, perhaps because they found it easier to contain their excitement in an upright position. The only other pieces of furniture were a few tables, from which a couple of diligent maids had begun doling out punch, a wooden pulpit on the stage and, of course, an imposing statue of Captain Shackleton beside the doorway, welcoming them as they walked in.

While Lucy scanned their fellow passengers, listing the names of those present in a way that revealed her likes and dislikes, Claire gazed in awe at the marble figure of a man not yet born. The twice life-size statue of Derek Shackleton on its pedestal recalled some strange descendant of the Greek gods, fixed in a similarly heroic and gallant pose, except that the casual nudity usually flaunted by the Greeks was concealed by something more substantial than a fig leaf. The captain wore a suit of elaborately riveted armour, apparently designed to protect as much of his body as possible from the enemy. It included a sophisticated helmet that left only his jutting chin visible. Claire was disappointed by the headdress: she would have liked to see what the saviour of the human race looked like.

She was convinced the iron-clad visage could not possibly resemble anyone she knew. It had to be a face that only the future could produce. She imagined a noble expression, the eyes radiating confidence – not for nothing was he commanding an army – revealing, almost like a natural secretion, his proud, indomitable spirit. Now and then the dark desolation surrounding him would cloud those handsome eyes with tears, for a vestige of sensitivity survived in his warrior's soul. Claire also imagined a glimmer of yearning in his gaze, especially during the moments of intense loneliness that would assail him between battles.

And what was the cause of his sorrow? Naturally, it could be none other than the absence of a beloved face to contemplate, a smile that would give him courage in moments of weakness, a name he could whisper in his sleep like a comforting prayer, an embrace to return to when the war was over. Briefly, Claire pictured that brave, indestructible man, so tough on the battlefield, murmuring her name at night, like a boy: 'Claire, darling Claire . . .'

She smiled to herself. It was only a silly fantasy, yet she was surprised at the thrill she felt when she imagined being loved by that warrior of the future. How was it possible that a man who had not yet been born could stir her more than any of the young dandies courting her? The answer was simple: she was projecting on to that faceless statue everything she yearned for and could not have. Shackleton was probably completely different from Claire's imagined portrait. Furthermore, his way of thinking, acting, even of loving would be utterly incomprehensible and alien to her. In the century that lay between them, man's values and concerns might have become unrecognisable to anyone viewing them from the past. This was one of life's laws.

If only she could glimpse his face, she thought, she might find out whether she was right if Shackleton's soul was made of opaque glass through which she would never be able to see, or whether the years between them were merely anecdotal. Perhaps there was something inside man, an essence rooted in his very being, which remained unchanged over the centuries – perhaps the very air God had breathed into his creatures to give them life. But there was no way of knowing this because of that blasted helmet. She must be content with the parts of him she was able to see, which were impressive enough: his warrior-like posture, his raised sword, his right leg flexed to reveal sculpted muscles, the left foot firmly planted on the ground, with the heel slightly raised, as though he had been immortalised in the act of charging the enemy.

Only when she followed the direction of his charge did Claire realise that his statue faced another to the left of the door. Shackleton's defiant gesture was aimed at a startling figure almost twice his size. According to the inscription on the base, this was an effigy of Solomon, king of the automatons and the captain's arch enemy, whom he defeated on 20 May 2000, following an endless war that had razed London to the ground. Claire gazed at it, shocked at the terrifying evolution of the automaton. When she was a little girl, her father had taken her to see the Writer, an animated doll invented by Pierre Jacquet Droz, the famous Swiss watchmaker. She still recalled the smartly dressed boy with the sad, chubby face sitting at a desk, dipping his quill into the inkwell and drawing it across a piece of paper. The doll had traced each letter with the alarming slowness of someone living outside time, even pausing occasionally to stare into space, as though waiting for another wave of inspiration. The memory of the doll's staring eyes had always caused a shiver to go down the young Claire's spine when she imagined the monstrous thoughts it might be harbouring. She had been unable to rid herself of this uncomfortable sensation, even after her father had shown her the interlocking rods and cogs in the phantasmagorical child's back, with the lever that turned, bringing the parody to life. Now she could see how that grotesque if harmless child had transformed into the figure towering above her.

Struggling to overcome her fear, she examined it closely. Solomon's creator, unlike Pierre Jacquet Droz, had apparently been uninterested in reproducing something realistically human, limiting himself to a rough copy of the two-legged model. For Solomon had more in common with a medieval suit of armour than with a man: his body was a series of joined-up metal plates crowned by a solid cylindrical head, like a bell, with two square holes for eyes and a slit for a mouth, like a letterbox.

It almost made Claire's head spin to think that the two statues facing one another commemorated an event that had not yet happened. These characters were not only not dead, they had not even been born. Although, in the end, she reflected, no one there could be blamed if they mistook them for memorials because, like the dead, neither the captain nor his nemesis was among the living paying tribute to their memory. It made no difference whether they had already left or had not yet arrived: the main thing was they were not there.

Lucy interrupted Claire's reverie by tugging at her arm and dragging her towards a couple waving from across the room. A short, prissy-looking man in his fifties, crammed into a light blue suit with a flowery waistcoat – its buttons looked as though they might pop under the strain of his girth – was waiting for her with open arms and a grotesquely welcoming smile.

'My dear girl,' he declared, in a fatherly tone. 'What a surprise to see you here. I had no idea your family were going on this little trip. I thought that rascal Nelson suffered from seasickness!'

'My father isn't coming, Mr Ferguson,' Lucy confessed, smiling apologetically. 'Actually, he doesn't know my friend and I are here, and I'm hoping he won't find out.'

'Have no fear, my dear child,' Ferguson hastened to reassure her, delighted by this display of disobedience for which he would not have hesitated to hang his own daughter up by her thumbs. 'Your secret is safe with us, isn't it, Grace?'

His wife nodded with the same syrupy smile, rattling the strings of pearls draped around her neck like a luxurious bandage. Lucy showed her gratitude with a charming little pout, then introduced them to Claire, who tried to hide her revulsion as she felt the man's greasy lips on her hand.

'Well, well,' said Ferguson, after the introductions were over, beaming affectionately at one girl then the other. 'Isn't this exciting? We'll be on our way to the year 2000 in a few minutes, and on top of that, we're going to see a real battle.'

'Do you think it might be dangerous?' asked Lucy, a little uneasily.

'Oh, no, not in the slightest.' Ferguson dismissed her fears with a wave of his hand. 'A good friend of mine, Ted Fletcher, who went on the first expedition, assured me there's absolutely nothing to be afraid of. We'll be viewing the battle from a perfectly safe distance – although that also has its drawbacks. Unfortunately we won't see a lot of the details. Fletcher warned us not to forget our opera glasses. Have you brought yours?'

'No,' replied Lucy, dismayed.

'In that case, stay close to us and you can share ours,' Ferguson advised her. 'You don't want to miss a thing if you can possibly help it. Fletcher told us the battle we're going to see is worth every penny of the small fortune we paid.'

Claire frowned at the repulsive little man who had blatantly reduced to the vulgar level of a variety show the battle that would decide the fate of the planet. She could not help smiling with relief when Lucy greeted another couple walking by, and beckoned them to join the group.

'This is my friend Madeleine,' Lucy declared excitedly, 'and her husband, Mr Charles Winslow.'

Claire's smile froze. She had heard a lot about Charles Winslow – one of the richest and most handsome young men in London – although they had never been introduced. She had lost no sleep over this, as the admiration he inspired in her friends had been enough to make her dislike him. She had pictured him as an arrogant, self-satisfied young man whose main interest in life was to seduce any young girl who crossed his path with his sweet talk. Claire was not in the habit of going to parties, but she had met quite a few young men cut from the same cloth: conceited, spoiled fellows who, thanks to their father's fortunes, led reckless youthful lives they went to great lengths to prolong. Although, apparently, Winslow had decided to settle down – the last she had heard he had married one of the wealthy young Keller sisters, much to the distress of many a young lady in London, among whom she did not include herself. Now that she finally had him in front of her, she had to confess he was indeed a handsome fellow, which, at any rate, would make his exasperating company less insufferable.

'We were just remarking on how exciting this is,' declared the irrepressible Ferguson, once more taking the lead. 'We are about to see London reduced to rubble, yet when we get back it will still be intact, as though nothing had happened – which it hasn't, if we regard time as a linear succession of events. And I have no doubt that after such a terrible sight we will only appreciate this noisy city all the more, don't you agree?'

'Well, that's a very simple way of looking at it,' observed Charles, nonchalantly, avoiding looking at Ferguson.

There was a moment's silence. Ferguson glowered at him, unsure whether or not to be insulted. 'What are you insinuating, Mr Winslow?' he asked.

Charles carried on staring at the ceiling. Perhaps he was wondering whether the air up there, as in the mountains, might be purer. 'Travelling to the year 2000 isn't like going to see the Niagara Falls,' he replied casually, as though unaware that he had upset Ferguson. 'We are travelling into the future, to a world run by automatons. You may be able to forget all about it after you come back from your sightseeing trip, imagining it has nothing to do with you, but that is the world our grandchildren will be living in.'

Ferguson was clearly aghast. 'Are you suggesting we take part in this war?' he asked, as though Charles had suggested they play at moving bodies around in a graveyard.

For the first time, Charles deigned to glance at the man he was talking to, a sarcastic smile playing on his lips. 'You should look at the bigger picture, Mr Ferguson,' he said reprovingly. 'There's no need for us to take part in this war. It would be enough to prevent it.'

'Prevent it?'

'Yes, prevent it. Isn't the future always a result of the past?'

'I'm still not with you, Mr Winslow,' replied Ferguson, coldly.

'The seed of this war is here,' Charles explained, gesturing at their surroundings with a vague nod. 'It is in our hands to stop what is going to happen, to change the future. Ultimately, the war that will end up razing London to the ground is our responsibility – although I'm afraid that even if mankind knew this, he would not consider it a good enough reason to stop producing automatons.'

'But that's absurd. Fate is fate,' objected Ferguson. 'It can't be changed.'

'Fate is fate . . .' repeated Charles, sardonically. 'Is that what you really believe? Do you honestly prefer to hand over responsibility for your actions to the alleged author of some play we are compelled to take part in from birth?' Claire tensed as Charles glanced questioningly at the other members of the group. 'Well, I don't. What's more, I firmly believe we are the authors of our own fate – we write it each day with every one of our actions. If we really had a mind to, we could prevent this future war. Although I imagine, Mr Ferguson, that you would lose a great deal of money if you stopped producing mechanical toys.'

Ferguson was taken aback by the last jibe whereby the insolent young man, besides blaming him for something that had not yet happened, revealed he knew perfectly well who Ferguson was. He gazed at Charles open-mouthed, not knowing what to say, astonished rather than upset by the jaunty bonhomie with which the fellow delivered his barbed comments.

Claire admired Winslow's way of disguising his observations as frivolous, protecting himself from angry ripostes as well as relegating his sharp remarks to the category of impromptu asides, spontaneous reflections, which even he did not appear to take seriously. Ferguson went on opening and closing his mouth while the others looked shocked and Charles smiled elusively.

All of a sudden, Ferguson appeared to recognise a young man wandering lost in the crowd. This gave him the perfect excuse to leave the group and rush to the fellow's aid, thus avoiding the need to respond to Winslow, who did not appear to be expecting a reply anyway. Ferguson returned with an impecunious-looking youth, whom he pushed into the centre of the group and introduced as Colin Garrett, a new inspector at Scotland Yard.

While the others greeted the newcomer, Ferguson beamed contentedly, as though he were showing off the latest rare bird in his collection of acquaintances. He waited for the round of greetings to finish, then spoke to the young inspector, as though hoping to make the others forget his discussion with Charles Winslow. 'I'm surprised to see you here, Mr Garrett. I didn't know an inspector's salary stretched this far.'

'My father left me a little money,' stuttered the inspector, needlessly attempting to justify himself.

'Ah, for a moment there I thought you might be travelling at the expense of Her Majesty's government to bring order to the future. After all, even if it is in the year 2000, the war will still destroy London, the city you're meant to be protecting. Or does the time difference absolve you of your responsibilities? Is your job confined to watching over London in the present? A fascinating question, wouldn't you agree?' Ferguson said to his audience, proud of his own ingenuity. 'The inspector's responsibilities cover space but not time. Tell me, Mr Garrett, does your authority extend to arresting a criminal in the future – assuming his crime is committed within the city?'

The young Garrett stirred uneasily. Had he been given time to reflect calmly, he might have come up with a satisfactory answer, but at that precise moment he had been overwhelmed by an avalanche of sheer beauty, if you will forgive the purple prose – which, on the other hand, is perfectly suited to the occasion: the young girl they had introduced to him as Lucy Nelson had troubled him considerably, so much so that he was scarcely able to concentrate on anything else.

'Well, Inspector?' said Ferguson, growing impatient.

Garrett tried unsuccessfully to drag his eyes away from the girl, who seemed as beautiful as she was unattainable to a poor, dull fellow like him. He suffered also from a crippling shyness that prevented him achieving any success when it came to women. He, of course, had not the remotest idea that three weeks later he would find himself lying on top of her, his lips within kissing distance of hers.

'I have a better question, Mr Ferguson,' said Charles, rallying to the young man's aid. 'What if a criminal from the future travelled in time and committed a crime here in the present? Would the inspector be authorised to arrest a man who, chronologically speaking, had not yet been born?'

Ferguson did not attempt to conceal his irritation at Charles's intrusion. 'Your idea doesn't bear scrutiny, Mr Winslow,' he retorted. 'Why, it's absurd to imagine that a man from the future could visit our own time.'

'In heaven's name, why not?' enquired Charles, amused. 'If we're able to journey into the future, what's to stop men from the future travelling back to the past, especially if you bear in mind that their science will be more advanced than ours?'

'Simply because if that were the case they would already be here,' replied Ferguson, as though the explanation were obvious.

Charles laughed. 'And what makes you think they aren't? Perhaps they're here incognito.'

'Why, that's preposterous!' cried the outraged Ferguson, the veins on his neck beginning to bulge. 'Men from the future would have no need to hide. They could help us in a thousand different ways, bringing us medicines, for example, or improving our inventions.'

'They may prefer to help us surreptitiously. How can you be

sure that Leonardo da Vinci wasn't under orders from a time traveller to leave in his notebooks plans for building a flying machine or a submersible boat, or that he himself wasn't a man from the future whose mission was to travel to the fifteenth century in order to help the advancement of science? A fascinating question, wouldn't you agree?' asked Charles, mimicking Ferguson. 'Or perhaps the time travellers' intentions are quite different. Perhaps they simply want to prevent the war we are going to witness in a few minutes.'

Ferguson shook his head indignantly, as though Charles were trying to argue that Christ had been crucified upside down.

'Maybe I'm one of them,' Charles went on, in a sinister voice. He stepped towards Ferguson and, reaching into his pocket, added: 'Maybe Captain Shackleton himself sent me here to plunge a dagger into the stomach of Nathan Ferguson, owner of the biggest toyshop in London, to stop him producing automatons.'

Ferguson gave a start as Charles prodded his stomach with a forefinger. 'But I only make pianolas . . .' he spluttered, the blood draining from his face.

Charles let out a guffaw, for which Madeleine hurriedly chided him, not without a measure of affection.

'Come now, my darling,' said Charles, apparently deriving a childlike enjoyment from shocking everyone. 'Mr Ferguson knows perfectly well I'm only joking. I don't think we have anything to fear from a pianola. Or do we?'

'Of course not,' burbled Ferguson, trying to regain his composure.

Claire stifled a giggle, but this did not go unnoticed by Charles, who winked at her, before taking his wife's arm and leaving the little gathering – in order, he said, to test the excellent qualities of the punch.

Ferguson heaved a sigh of relief. 'I hope you'll forgive this little incident, my dears,' he said, attempting to recover his smug grin. 'As I'm sure you're aware, Charles Winslow is known all over London for his insolence. If it weren't for his father's money . . .'

A murmur spread through the crowd, drowning his words. Everyone turned to face the back of the room where Gilliam Murray was making his way on to the stage.

XIX

He was without doubt one of the biggest men Claire had ever seen. From the way the boards creaked under his feet, he must have weighed more than twenty stone, yet his movements were graceful, almost sensual. He was dressed in a smart pale purple suit that shimmered in the light. His wore his wavy hair combed back, and an impeccably tasteful bow tie struggled to fit around his broad neck. His enormous hands, which seemed capable of pulling trees up by the roots, rested on the lectern as he waited – with a patient smile – for the murmur to subside. Once silence had settled over the gathering, draped over it like the dust sheets placed on furniture in houses closed for the season, he cleared his throat loudly and unleashed his smooth baritone voice on his audience.

'Ladies and gentlemen, there is no need for me to tell you that you are about to take part in the most astonishing event of the century, the second journey through time in history. Today you will break the chains that bind you to the present, avoid the continuity of the hours, confound the laws governing time. Yes, ladies and gentleman, today you will travel through time – something that, until yesterday, man could only dream about. It is my great pleasure to welcome you on behalf of Murray's Time Travel and to thank you for choosing to take part in our second expedition to the year 2000, which we decided to arrange following the overwhelming success of the first. I guarantee you will not leave here disappointed. As I already mentioned, you will be travelling across the centuries, beyond your lifetime. If this were all Murray's Time Travel had to offer it would still be worthwhile but, thanks to our efforts, you will also have the chance to witness possibly the most important moment in the history of mankind: the battle between the brave Captain Derek Shackleton and the evil automaton Solomon, whose dreams of conquest you will see perish beneath the captain's sword.'

Some timid applause broke out in the first row, but Claire felt this owed more to the emphasis the speaker had laid on his last words than to their implication for the gathering, to whom the outcome of this distant war was surely a matter of indifference.

'Now, if I may, I shall explain in a few simple words the method of travel to the year 2000. We will be journeying in the Cronotilus, a steam tram specially built by our engineers. The vehicle will leave our own time in the present and arrive at midday on the twentieth of May in the year 2000. Naturally, the journey will not take the one hundred and four years separating that date from the present for we shall be travelling outside time – that is to say, through the famous fourth dimension. Although I'm afraid to say, ladies and gentlemen, that you will not see it. When you climb aboard the time-tram, you will notice the windows have been blacked out. This is not because we wish to deny you a glimpse of the fourth dimension, which is nothing more than a vast plain of pink rock, swept by fierce winds where time does not exist. We have covered the windows in your best interests, for the fourth dimension is inhabited by monstrous creatures resembling miniature dragons. They are not friendly. By and large, they keep away from us, but there is always a possibility one may stray too close to the tram for comfort, and we would not wish any ladies to fall into a faint at the sight of so hideous a beast. But have no fear: such an event is very unlikely to occur because these creatures feed exclusively on time. Yes, time is an exquisite delicacy for them, which is why before boarding the tram you are requested to remove your timepieces. This minimises the possibility of their scent attracting any creatures to the vehicle.

Moreover, as you will soon see, the Cronotilus has a turret on its roof, where two expert marksmen will ward off any creature that tries to approach. Put this out of your minds, then, and enjoy the trip.

'In spite of the dangers, the fourth dimension also has some advantages. One of these is that, while you are there, none of you will age for you will be outside time. It is quite possible, dear ladies,' he said, forcing a smile as he addressed a group of matronly women at the front, 'that when you return your friends may even say you look younger.'

The women giggled nervously.

'Now allow me to introduce you to Igor Mazursky,' he went on, beckoning a short, stout fellow on to the stage. 'He will be your guide to the year 2000. Once the Cronotilus reaches its destination, Mr Mazursky will lead you through the ruins of London to the promontory where you will witness the battle to decide the fate of the world. Let me reiterate that there is no risk involved in the expedition. Even so, you must obey Mr Mazursky's instructions at all times to avoid any cause for regret before the journey is over.'

With these words, he flashed a warning look at the crowd and let out a long sigh. Then he adopted a more relaxed, almost dreamy pose at the lectern.

'I imagine most of you think of the future as an idyllic place, where the skies are filled with flying carriages, and tiny winged cabriolets glide like birds in the wind, where floating cities sail the oceans pulled by mechanical dolphins, where shops sell clothes made of special dirt-repellent fabric, luminous umbrellas and hats that play music while we walk along the street. I don't blame you. I also envisaged the year 2000 as a technological paradise in which man would have built a secure, just world in which he lived harmoniously with his fellow man and with Mother Nature. After all, it is a fairly logical assumption to make, given the unstoppable advances of science, the endless miraculous inventions that emerge every day to simplify our lives. Unfortunately we now know this isn't true. The year 2000 is no paradise, I'm afraid. Quite the contrary, as you will presently witness with your own eyes. Rest assured, when you return most of you will feel relieved to be living in our time, however tiresome you may find it. For, as you will know from reading our brochure, in the year 2000 the world is ruled by automatons and the human race is, to put it mildly, considered dispensable. The truth is that the human population has been decimated, and those left are struggling against total extinction. This and no other is the discouraging future awaiting us.'

Gilliam Murray made a dramatic pause to allow the audience to stew in the doom-laden silence.

'I imagine you must find it hard to believe the planet could be taken over by automatons. We have all seen examples of these harmless replicas of men and animals at exhibitions and fairs, and no doubt some of your own children can boast the odd mechanical doll among their toys, as can mine. But has it ever occurred to you that these ingenious artefacts might one day take on a life of their own and pose a threat to the human race? No, of course not. And yet I regret to say that they will. Now, I don't know about you, but I can't help seeing in this a sort of poetic justice meted out by God to teach man a lesson for having attempted to emulate him by creating life.'

He paused again, taking the opportunity to cast a sorrowful eye over the hall, satisfied with the spine-tingling effect his words were having on the assembly.

'Thanks to our research we have been able to reconstruct the disastrous events that led the world into this terrible situation. Allow me, ladies and gentlemen, to take a few moments of your time to relate to you in the past tense something that has not yet happened.'

With these words, Gilliam Murray fell silent once more. Then he cleared his throat and began the story of how the automatons had conquered the planet. Although sadly true, it could easily have been the plot of one of the voguish so-called science-fiction novels, and that is the way I will tell it, provided you have no objections.

In the years leading up to the mid-twentieth century, the production of automatons had risen steeply, and their number and sophistication had reached unprecedented levels. Automatons were everywhere, and performed the most varied tasks. They operated most of the machinery in the factories, where they also did the cleaning and even some secretarial work. Most homes boasted at least two, which carried out household and other tasks hitherto assigned to servants – such as looking after children or stocking the larder. Thus their presence among men became as natural as it was indispensable. In time, their owners, who were incapable of perceiving them as anything but obedient mechanical slaves, stopped noticing them. They even fomented their subtle takeover, happily acquiring the latest models in the belief that they were simply freeing themselves from still more of the numerous tasks they now considered beneath them.

One of the effects of making the automatons part of their household was to turn man into the arrogant ruler of his tiny domain, which usually consisted of a two-storey house and garden. Ousted from the factories by tireless mechanical workers, man grew flabbier and weaker as his activities were reduced to winding up his automatons in the morning, like someone starting the world, which had learned to function without him.

Things being thus, it was hardly strange that man, blinkered by tedium and complacency, failed to notice that his automatons were surreptitiously taking on a life of their own. To begin with their actions were harmless enough: an automaton butler dropping the Bohemian glassware; an automaton tailor sticking a pin into his customer; an automaton gravedigger garlanding a coffin with stinging nettles. These were petty acts of rebellion by which the automatons tested their freedom, the stirrings of awareness fluttering inside their metal skulls, like butterflies trapped in a jar. And yet, as we already mentioned, such acts of mutiny scarcely bothered man, who attributed them to a manufacturing defect, and either sent the automatons back to the factory or had them recalibrated. And we cannot really blame them for their lack of concern because the automatons were not designed to cause harm and could not go beyond these feeble outbursts.

However, this changed when the government ordered the most eminent engineer in England to design an automaton soldier that would free man from the burden of war just as he had been exempted from doing the dusting or pruning hedges. Expanding the Empire would doubtless be far easier if such tasks as invading and plundering neighbouring countries, torturing and ill-treating prisoners were left to the efficient automatons. The engineer did as he was told, and produced a wrought-iron automaton with articulated limbs, as big as a bear standing on its hind legs. In its chest, behind a little shutter, he placed a loaded miniature cannon. But his real innovation was the little steam-powered engine he attached to its back. This made it autonomous: it no longer depended on anyone to wind it up.

Once the prototype was ready, it was tested in secret. The automaton was placed on a cart, covered with a tarpaulin and taken to the village of Slough, home to the observatory that had belonged to William Herschel, the astronomer musician who, many years earlier, had added Uranus to the list of known planets. At intervals along the three-mile stretch between the village and the neighbouring town of Windsor, scarecrows were placed, with watermelons, cauliflowers and cabbages for heads. Then they made the automaton walk along the road testing his hidden weapon on the motionless vegetable-men. The automaton reached its destination amid a swarm of flies attracted by the watermelon flesh splattered over its armour, but not a single puppet's head remained in its wake. An army of these invincible creatures would cut through enemy lines like a knife through butter.

The next step was to present it to the king as the decisive weapon with which to conquer the world, if he so wished. However, owing to the monarch's many obligations, the unveiling was delayed. The automaton was kept in storage for several weeks, which led to disastrous consequences: during its prolonged isolation, the automaton not only came to life without anyone realising it but developed something akin to a soul, with desires, fears and even firm convictions.

By the time it was presented to the king, it had already reflected enough to know what it wanted from life. Or if it had any doubts, they were dispelled upon seeing the little man sprawled on his throne, looking down his nose at it and continually straightening his crown. While the engineer paced back and forth, praising the automaton's attributes and describing the different stages of its construction, the automaton made the little doors on its chest open like those of a cuckoo clock. The monarch, tired of the engineer's exposition, perked up, eyes bright with curiosity, waiting for the birdie to pop out. Instead the shadow of death emerged in the form of a perfectly aimed bullet that made a hole right through the king's forehead, hurling him back on his throne. The accompanying sound of splintering bone interrupted the engineer's monologue: he was aghast at what his creation had done, until the automaton grabbed him by the throat and snapped his neck like a dry twig. Having assured himself that the man draped over his arm was no more than a corpse, the automaton flung him to the ground, apparently pleased by the creativity his nascent mind had shown, at least in the art of killing.

Once he was sure he was the only living thing left in the throne room, he approached the king, with his arthropodal movements, relieved him of the crown and placed it solemnly on his own iron head. Then he studied his reflection – front and side – in the wall mirrors and, since he was unable to smile, nodded. In this rather bloodthirsty manner his life began, for although he was not made of flesh and bone, there was no doubt in his mind that he was also a living being. And in order to feel even more alive what he needed next was a name; the name of a king. After a few moments' reflection, he decided on Solomon. The name was doubly pleasing to him: not only had Solomon been a legendary king, but he was the first man ever endowed with mechanical genius.

According to the Bible, as well as some Arabic texts, Solomon's throne was a magical piece of furniture that lent a theatrical air to his displays of power. Perched at the top of a small flight of steps, flanked by a pair of solid gold lions with swishing tails, and shaded by palm trees and vines where mechanical birds exhaled musky breath, the elaborate revolving chair raised the new king aloft, rocking him gently in mid-air as he pronounced his celebrated judgments.

Now Solomon wondered what he should do next, what goal to pursue. The ease and indifference with which he had snuffed out the lives of those two humans made him think he could do the same to a third, a fourth, a fifth, to a whole choir of singing children, if need be. The increasing number of victims would never compel him to question the morality of taking a human being's life, however dear it was to him or her. Those two dead bodies were his first steps on a path of destruction, but did he have to take it? Was it his destiny, or could he choose a different path, employ his time in something more edifying than slaughter? Solomon saw his doubt duplicated in the dozens of mirrors lining the throne room. Yet he liked the uncertainty because it gave another interesting facet to the soul that had sprouted within his iron chest.

However, for all his doubts about his destiny, it was clear he must flee, disappear, leave at once. And so Solomon slipped out of the palace unnoticed, and wandered through the forests, for how long he did not know. There he perfected his aim with the help of some squirrels, stopping from time to time in a cave or shack to disentangle the weeds from his leg joints or take a break from his meanderings to study the star-studded sky and see whether the fate of automatons as well as that of men was written there.

In the meantime, news of his exploits spread like wildfire through the city, especially among the mechanical creatures, who gazed in reverential awe at the 'Wanted' posters, picturing his face, that papered many walls. Oblivious to all of this, Solomon roamed the hills, plagued with doubt and endlessly tormented about what his mission in life would be

One morning he emerged from the tumbledown shack where he had spent the night to find himself surrounded by dozens of automatons, who broke into excited applause when they saw him. He realised that others had taken it upon themselves to forge his destiny.

The crowd of admirers included every kind of automaton, from rough factory workers and well-dressed nannies to dull office clerks. Those in close contact with man, like butlers, cooks and maids, had been carefully designed to look human, while those destined to work in factories, or in the basements of government buildings surrounded by files, were little more than metal scarecrows, yet they all applauded him with equal fervour for having killed the king. Some even dared touch his armour, treating him like a long-awaited Messiah.

Moved and repelled in equal measure, Solomon decided to call them 'the little ones'. As they had come so far to worship him, he invited them into his shack – and the First Council of Automatons in the Free World was formed. During the meeting Solomon realised that the little ones' hearts were seething with hatred towards the human race. Apparently the insults man had inflicted on the automatons' dignity throughout history were as varied as they were unforgivable: the philosopher Alberto Magno's automaton had been ruthlessly destroyed by his disciple St Thomas Aquinas, who considered it the work of the Devil; but far more flagrant was the case of the Frenchman René Descartes, who, in order to exorcise his grief over the death of his daughter Francine, had constructed a mechanical doll in her likeness. When the captain of a ship he was travelling on had discovered it, he had thrown it overboard. The poignant image of the mechanical girl rusting among the coral enraged the little ones. Other equally dreadful cases kept alive the desire for revenge that had rankled for years in the hearts of these creatures, who now recognised in Solomon the brother who could finally carry it out.

The fate of man was put to the vote. With no abstentions and one against, the result was resoundingly in favour of extermination. In ancient Egypt the statues of the gods were equipped with mechanical arms operated from behind the scenes that spread terror among the acolytes. The time had come to follow their example and unleash the ancient terror upon humans once more. The time had come for them to repay their debts. Man's reign had come to an end. He was no longer the most powerful creature on the planet, if indeed he ever had been. The time of the automatons had come, and under the leadership of their new king they would conquer the planet. Solomon shrugged his shoulders. Why not? he thought. Why not lead my people where they want to go? He readily embraced his fate.

In reality, on further consideration, this was not such a foolish venture, and was even achievable with a little organisation. The little ones were already strategically placed in the enemy camp: they had free access to every home, factory and ministry, and could count on the element of surprise.

Just like someone leaving his body to science, Solomon allowed the builder automatons to see how he was made inside so they could produce an army of automaton soldiers in his image. They worked in secret, in sheds and abandoned factories, while the little ones returned to their posts and patiently awaited their king's command to pounce on the enemy. When it finally came, their synchronised attack was unbelievably brutal and devastating. The human population was decimated in the blink of an eye. That midnight, mankind's dream ended abruptly and fatally: scissors plunged into throats, hammers crushed skulls, and pillows stifled last gasps in a symphony of splintering bones and death rattles orchestrated by the Grim Reaper's baton. And while this panoply of sudden death was occurring in homes, factories blazed, plumes of black smoke spewing from their windows, and an army of automaton soldiers, led by Solomon, swarmed through the streets of the capital like a tidal wave of metal, meeting little or no resistance. Within minutes the invasion had become a calm procession.

Early the next day, the total extermination of the human race began. It lasted a few decades, until all that was left of the world was a pile of rubble, where the few remaining humans, their numbers rapidly diminishing, cowered like frightened rats.

At nightfall, Solomon would look out over the balcony of his palace and cast a proud eye over the remains of the planet they had destroyed. He was a good king: he had done everything expected of him and he had done it well. He was irreproachable. The humans had been defeated, and it was only a matter of time before they became extinct. Suddenly he realised that if humans were wiped off the face of the planet, there would be nothing to prove the automatons had conquered them to take control of it. They needed a specimen to continue to embody the enemy. A specimen of man, the creature who dreamed, aspired, yearned for immortality while wondering why he had been put on the Earth. Taking Noah and the ark as his inspiration, Solomon ordered the capture of a pair of healthy young specimens from among the group of sorry survivors skulking in the ruins – a male and a female, whose only function would be to procreate in captivity so that the vanquished race would not die out.

Reduced to the status of mementoes, the chosen pair was kept in a cage of solid gold, generously fed and pampered, and above all encouraged to reproduce. Solomon told himself that keeping alive with his right hand the race that his left hand had destroyed was an intelligent thing to do.

However, he did not know it yet, but he had chosen the wrong male. He was a proud, healthy youth who pretended to obey orders without protest, apparently grateful for having been spared certain death, but shrewd enough to know his luck would run out as soon as the girl had brought his successor into the world. However, this did not seem to worry him unduly, as he had at least nine months to achieve his goal, which was none other than to study his enemies from the comfort of his cage, observe their customs, learn their movements and discover how to destroy them. When he was not doing this, he was busy preparing his body for death. The day his concubine gave birth to a baby boy, he knew his time had come.

With astonishing calm, he allowed himself to be led to the place of execution. Solomon himself was going to shoot him. As he stood in front of the youth and opened the little doors in his chest so that the hidden cannon could take aim, the boy smiled at him and spoke for the first time: 'Go ahead and kill me, then I'll kill you.'

Solomon tilted his head, wondering if the youth's words contained some hidden message he needed to decipher or were simply a meaningless phrase. He decided it did not matter either way. Without further ado, and feeling an almost jaded disgust, he fired at the insolent boy. The bullet hit him in the stomach, knocking him to the ground.

'I've killed you, now kill me,' he challenged.

He waited a few moments to see if the boy stirred, and when he did not, he ordered his flunkeys to get rid of the body and return to their chores. The guards obeyed. They carried it outside the palace, then threw it down a slope as if it were a piece of refuse.

The body came to rest next to a pile of rubble, where it lay face up, covered with blood. A beautiful pale yellow full moon lit the night sky. The youth smiled at it as though it were a death's head. He had succeeded in escaping from the palace, but the boy he had been when he entered it had been left behind. He had emerged from there a man with a clear destiny: to gather together the few survivors and train them to fight the automatons. To achieve this he would only have to stop the bullet in his stomach killing him, but that would be no problem. His will to live was stronger than the bullet's desire to kill him, stronger than the piece of metal embedded in his intestines. He had prepared for this moment during his captivity, preparing to endure the searing pain, to understand it, subdue and diminish it until he had worn down the bullet's patience. It was a long duel, a dramatic struggle that lasted three days and three moonlit nights, until finally the bullet surrendered. It had realised it was not dealing with a body like the others: the youth's deep hatred of the automatons had made him cling to life.

And yet his hatred was not a result of the automaton uprising, or the horrific murder of his parents and siblings or the wanton destruction of the planet. It did not even relate to Solomon's sickening indifference when he had shot him. No, his hatred was rooted even further in the past. His was an old, unresolved hatred dating back centuries, to the time of his paternal great-grandfather, the first Shackleton to lose his life because of an automaton.

You may have heard of the Turk Mephisto, and other automaton chess players who were in fashion decades ago. Like them, Dr Phibes was a mechanical doll who understood the secrets of chess as if he had invented the game. Dressed in an orange suit, a green bow tie and a blue top hat, Dr Phibes invited visitors to come into his fairground tent and challenge him to a game of chess for four shillings. The contemptuous manner in which he inflicted defeat on his male opponents and the chivalry with which he allowed the ladies to beat him made him a celebrity, and people clamoured to challenge him. His creator, the inventor Alan Tyrell, boasted that his doll had even beaten the world chess champion, Mikhail Chigorin.

However, his profitable appearances at travelling fairs ended abruptly when one opponent became incensed when the insolent doll trounced him in less than five moves and then, adding insult to injury, amicably offered him his wooden hand to shake. Seized with rage, the fellow rose from his seat and, before the fairground barker could stop him, pulled a revolver from his pocket and shot the doll straight through the chest, showering orange splinters everywhere. The loud report alarmed the crowd, and the assailant managed to flee during the commotion before the barker had a chance to demand damages. Within minutes he found himself alone with Dr Phibes, who was leaning slightly to one side in his seat.

The barker was wondering how he would explain all this to Mr Tyrell, when he saw something that startled him. Dr Phibes was wearing his usual smile, but a trickle of blood was oozing from the bullet hole in his chest. Horrified, the barker hurriedly pulled the curtain across, and walked over to the automaton. After examining the doll with some trepidation, he discovered a small bolt on its left side. Drawing it back, he was able to open Dr Phibes as if he were a sarcophagus. Inside, covered with blood and dead as a doornail, was the man with whom, unbeknown to him, he had been working all these months. His name was Miles Shackleton: a miserable wretch who, having no other means of supporting his family, had accepted the trickery Tyrell had offered him after discovering his talent for chess.

When the inventor arrived at the tent and discovered the calamity, he refrained from informing the police about what had happened, fearing he would be arrested for fraud. He silenced the barker with a generous sum and simply reinforced Dr Phibes with an iron plate to protect his new occupant from the wrath of future opponents. But Miles's substitute was nowhere near as skilled at chess as his predecessor: Dr Phibes's reputation began to wane and eventually vanished altogether, rather like Miles Shackleton, who disappeared off the face of the earth. More than likely, he was buried in a ditch between fairgrounds.

When at last his family learned from the fairground man what had become of him, they decided to honour him in the only way they could: by relaying his sad tale through the generations, like a torch whose flame, more than a century later, lit the pupils of the executed youth who, after lifting himself off the ground, glanced back at Solomon's palace with hatred, and murmured to himself, although in fact he was speaking to history: 'Now it's my turn to kill you.'

At first with faltering, then resolute steps, he disappeared into the ruins, determined to fulfil his destiny, which was none other than to become Captain Derek Shackleton, the man who would defeat the king of the automatons.

XX

Gilliam Murray's words evaporated like a spell, leaving his listeners plunged in a profound silence. Casting her eyes quickly around the hall, Claire saw that the moving tale Murray had told – doubtless in the form of an allegory, perhaps to mitigate the crude reality of such frightful events – had succeeded in awakening the interest of the gathering, as well as creating a certain sympathy for Captain Shackleton and even his enemy, Solomon, whom she suspected Murray had deliberately made more human. In any case, she could tell from Ferguson's, Lucy's and even Charles Winslow's awed expression that they were anxious to arrive in the future, to be part of these momentous events, if only as witnesses, and to see how Murray's story unravelled. Claire thought that her face undoubtedly bore a similar look, although for quite different reasons: what had impressed her about the story was not so much the automaton conspiracy, the destruction of London or the ruthless slaughter the dolls had perpetrated against her species, but Shackleton's determination, his personality, his bravery. This man had built an army out of nothing and restored the world's hope, not to mention surviving his own death. How would a man like him love?

After the welcoming speech, the group, led by Murray, headed off through a maze of galleries lined with clocks to the vast warehouse where the Cronotilus was awaiting them. An appreciative murmur rose from the crowd at the sight of the vehicle standing polished and ready. It differed in every way from an ordinary tram except in shape and size; its numerous additions made it look more like a gypsy caravan. Its everyday appearance was buried beneath a riot of shiny chrome pipes studded with rivets and valves that ran along its sides like the tendons in a neck. The only part left exposed were two exquisitely carved mahogany doors. One was the entrance to the passenger compartment, while the other, slightly narrower, led to the driver's cabin, which, Claire deduced, must be partitioned off from the rest of the vehicle since it had the only windows that were not blacked out. She felt relieved that at least the driver would be able to see where he was going. The porthole-shaped windows in their carriage were darkened, as Murray had said they would be. No one would be able to see the fourth dimension and the monsters that lived there would not glimpse their terrified faces, framed in the windows like cameo portraits.

Attached to the front of the vehicle was a sort of battering ram, like those on ice-breakers, no doubt with the alarming function of ploughing through any obstacle in its path, clearing the way at all costs. A complicated steam engine had been attached to the rear, bristling with rods, propellers and cogwheels. This puffed and blew from time to time. like some sea creature, and let out a gasp of steam that playfully lifted the ladies' skirts. However, what made it impossible for the vehicle to be described as a tram was the turret built on its roof, where at that very moment, having clambered up a small ladder bolted to the side, two gruff-looking fellows armed with rifles and a box of ammunition were taking their positions. Claire was amused to see there was also a periscope between the gun turret and the driver's cabin.

The driver, a gangling youth with an idiotic grin, opened the door of the passenger compartment and stood to attention beside it, next to the guide. Like a colonel inspecting his troops, Gilliam Murray walked slowly past the passengers, casting a severe but compassionate eye over them. Claire watched him pause in front of a lady clutching a poodle.

'I'm afraid your little dog will have to stay behind, Mrs Jacobs,' he said, smiling affably.

'But I won't let go of Buffy for a moment,' the woman demurred.

Murray shook his head kindly, yanked the dog away from her with a swift gesture, as if he were pulling out a rotten tooth, and deposited it in the arms of a female assistant. 'Eliza, will you please see to it that Buffy is cared for until Mrs Jacobs's return?'

Murray resumed his inspection, ignoring Mrs Jacobs's feeble protests. Grimacing theatrically, he stopped in front of two men carrying suitcases. 'You won't be needing these either, gentlemen,' he said, relieving them of their luggage.

He then asked everyone to place their timepieces on the tray Eliza was about to pass round, reaffirming that this would diminish the risk of being attacked by the monsters. When everything was to his liking, he planted himself in front of the group, smiling at them with almost tearful pride, like a marshal about to send his troops on a suicide mission. 'Well, ladies and gentlemen, I do hope you enjoy the year 2000. Remember what I said: obey Mr Mazursky at all times. I shall await your return, champagne at the ready.'

After this fatherly farewell, he stepped aside to make way for Mazursky, who politely asked them to climb on board the time-tram.

The passengers formed a straggly line and filed excitedly into the luxurious vehicle. Lined with patterned cloth, the carriage contained two rows of wooden benches separated by a narrow aisle. Several candelabra screwed to the ceiling and walls cast a gloomy, flickering light, which gave it the air of a chapel. Lucy and Claire sat on a bench approximately in the middle of the carriage, between Mr Ferguson and his wife and two nervous young dandies, whose parents, having sent them to Paris and Florence to expose them to art, were now shipping them off to the future in the hope of broadening their horizons. While the other passengers were taking their places, Ferguson, twisting his head round, bored them with a series of observations about the décor. Lucy listened politely, while Claire struggled to blot them out in order to be able to savour the importance of the moment.

When they had all settled, the guide closed the carriage door and sat facing them on a tiny chair, like an overseer on a galley ship. Almost at once, a violent jolt caused some of the passengers to cry out in alarm. Mazursky hurriedly put their minds at rest, explaining that this was simply the engine starting. And, sure enough, the unpleasant juddering soon gave way to a gentle tremor, almost a purr, propelling the vehicle from the rear. Mazursky then looked through the periscope and smiled with satisfaction.

'Ladies and gentlemen, it is my pleasure to inform you that our journey to the future is under way. This very moment we are crossing the fourth dimension.'

As if to confirm this, the vehicle was suddenly swaying from side to side, giving rise to further consternation among the passengers. The guide reassured them once more, apologising for the state of the road and adding that, despite their sustained efforts to keep the path clear, the terrain in the fourth dimension was naturally rough and dotted with bumps and crevices. Claire glanced at her face, reflected in the darkened window, wondering what the landscape looked like behind the black paint blocking their view. However, she scarcely had time to wonder about anything else, for at that very moment, to the passengers' horror, they heard a loud roar outside, followed by a burst of gunfire and a heartrending bellow.

Startled, Lucy clutched Claire's hand.

This time Mazursky limited himself to smiling serenely at the passengers' alarmed faces, as if to say that the roars and gunfire would be a recurring feature of their journey, and the best thing they could do was to ignore them.

'Well,' he declared, rising from his seat and strolling down the aisle, once everyone had recovered a little, 'we shall soon be in the year 2000. Please pay attention while I explain what will happen when we arrive in the future. As Mr Murray mentioned, we will climb out of the tram and I will take you to the promontory where we will watch the battle between humans and automatons. Although they can't see us from below, it is imperative you stay together and keep quiet so as not to give our position away. There is no telling what effect it might have on the fabric of time, although I assume it would not be a positive one.'

Further bellows came from outside, followed by the alarming shots, which Mazursky scarcely appeared to notice. He carried on pacing between the benches, thumbs in his waistcoat pockets, a pensive crease on his brow, like a professor weary of repeating the same old lecture time and again.

'The battle will last approximately twenty minutes,' he went on, 'and will resemble a short three-act play: the evil Solomon will appear with his entourage and be ambushed by the brave Captain Shackleton and his men. A brief but thrilling skirmish will follow, and finally a duel between the automaton known as Solomon and Derek Shackleton, which, as you already know, will end in victory for the humans. Please refrain from applauding when the duel is over: this is not a music-hall act, but an actual event, which we are not supposed to witness. Simply form a line and follow me to the vehicle as quietly as possible. Then we will travel back across the fourth dimension and return home safe and sound. Is that clear?'

The passengers nodded. Lucy pressed Claire's hand again, and beamed at her, full of anticipation. Claire returned the smile, yet hers had nothing in common with her friend's: Claire's was a farewell gesture, her only way of telling Lucy she had been her best friend and would never forget her, but that she must follow her destiny. Likewise, the kisses she had planted on her mother's cheek and her father's wrinkled brow, it had been an affectionate but far more solemn farewell than was appropriate before leaving for the Burnetts' country mansion, but her parents had not noticed. Claire stared again at the blacked-out glass, and wondered whether she was prepared for life in the world of the future, the devastated planet Gilliam Murray had described to them. She was gripped by a pang of fear, which she forced herself to suppress. She could not weaken now that she was so close. She must go ahead with her plan.

Just then, the tram came to a grinding halt. Mazursky took a long look through the periscope, until he was satisfied that everything outside was as it should be. Then, with a mysterious smile, he opened the carriage door. Screwing up his eyes, he scanned the surrounding area one last time, before announcing: 'Ladies and gentlemen, if you would kindly follow me, I will show you the year 2000.'

XXI

While her fellow travellers clambered down from the tram without further ado, Claire paused on the running-board, her right foot poised above the ground of the future, as solemn as when she had ventured into the sea for the very first time. Aged six, she had stepped with infinite care, almost reverentially, into the waves, as though this would determine how the dark enormity of the water responded to her intrusion. In the same way she now ventured into the year in which she had decided to stay, hoping it would treat her with equal respect.

As her heel touched the ground, she was surprised at how hard it felt, as though she had expected the future to be like a partially baked cake simply because it had not yet happened. However, a few steps sufficed to demonstrate that this was not the case. The future was a solid place, and unquestionably real – although it was utterly devastated. Was that heap of rubble really London?

The tram had stopped in a clearing amid the remains of what had probably been a small square, the only reminder of which was a few charred, twisted trees. The surrounding houses had been destroyed. Only the odd wall remained intact – still papered and incongruously adorned with an occasional picture or lamp-fitting – the remnants of a broken staircase, elegant railings now enclosing nothing more than piles of rubble. Dotted along the pavements were grim mounds of ash, probably the remains of fires built by humans from sticks of furniture to ward off the cold night air.

Claire could find no clue in the surrounding ruins as to what part of London they were in, not least because, although it was midday, it was very dark. A gloomy light filtered down from the sky, veiled by the greyish smoke that billowed from dozens of fires, their flames flickering like votive candles between the gaping ruins, obscuring the outlines of that shattered world – a world seemingly abandoned to its fate, like a ship stricken with malaria condemned to drift until time brings it to rest on a coral reef.

When Mazursky considered sufficient time had passed for the passengers to appreciate the depressing face of the future, he asked them to form a group. With him leading the way and one of the marksmen bringing up the rear, they moved off. The time travellers marched out of the square and into an avenue where the devastation struck them as even greater, for there was scarcely anything left standing to suggest that the piles of rubble had once been buildings. The avenue had no doubt once been lined with luxurious town houses, but the prolonged war had turned London into an enormous refuse tip. Magnificent churches had become indistinguishable from foul-smelling boarding-houses in the jumbled mass of bricks and masonry – where occasionally the horrified Claire thought she could make out a skull.

Mazursky led them through mounds that resembled funeral pyres, busily picked over by scavenging crows. The noise of the procession startled the birds, which flew off in all directions, darkening the sky still further. After they had vanished, one remained circling above their heads, tracing a mournful message with its flight, as though the Creator were regretfully signing over the patent of His beleaguered invention to someone else. Mazursky strode ahead, choosing the easiest pathways, or perhaps those with fewer bones, stopping once in a while to chide someone, invariably Ferguson, who was joking about the pervading stench of rotting flesh (or anything else that happened to catch his attention), wringing the odd titter out of the ladies strolling beside him on their husbands' arms, as though they were meandering through the botanical gardens at Kew.

As they ventured deeper into the ruins, Claire began to worry about how she would separate from the group without anyone noticing. It would be difficult with Mazursky listening out for any suspicious sounds, and the marksman at the rear, pointing his rifle into the gloom, and when the excited Lucy gripped her arm, the possibility of escape felt even more remote.

After they had walked for about ten minutes, during which Claire began to suspect they were going round in circles, they reached the promontory: a mound of debris a little taller than the others. Climbing it did not look difficult, as the rubble appeared to form a makeshift flight of steps to the top. At Mazursky's command, they began the ascent, giggling and losing their footing, a band of merry-makers on a country outing, whom the guide no longer tried to silence – he had probably concluded it was impossible. Only when they reached the top of the mound did he order them to be quiet and crouch behind the outcrop of rocks that formed a parapet at the summit. When they had done this, he walked along, pushing down any protruding heads and telling the ladies to close their parasols unless they wanted the automatons to notice a sudden flowering of sunshades on the crest of the hill.

Flanked by Lucy and the exasperating Ferguson, Claire gazed from behind her rock at the deserted street below. It was strewn with rubble, like the ones they had walked through to get to the makeshift viewpoint of where the battle was supposed to take place.

'Allow me to ask you a question, Mr Mazursky,' she heard Ferguson say.

The guide, with the marksman, was squatting a few yards to his left and swivelled to peer at him. 'What is it, Mr Ferguson?' He sighed.

'Given that we've turned up in the future in time to witness the battle that will decide the fate of the planet, just like the first expedition, why haven't we bumped into them?' Ferguson looked round at the others, clearly hoping they would back him up.

Having thought over what he had said, a few of the group nodded, and looked askance at their guide, waiting for an explanation. Mazursky studied Ferguson for a moment in silence, perhaps considering whether or not the impudent man deserved a reply. 'Of course, Mr Ferguson. You're absolutely right,' he finally declared. 'And not only would we bump into the first expedition, but into the third, fourth and all the other future expeditions, don't you think? That is why I take each expedition to a different place, not simply to avoid jams, but so that Terry and I' – he broke off and gestured to the marksman, who gave a timid wave – 'are not constantly bumping into ourselves. If you really must know, at this very moment the first expedition is crouched behind that mound over there.'

Everyone's eyes followed Mazursky's finger as he pointed to one of the neighbouring hillocks from which the battleground of the future was also visible.

'I see,' muttered Ferguson. Then his face lit up and he cried out: 'In that case I could go and say hello to my friend Fletcher!'

'I'm afraid I can't allow that, Mr Ferguson.'

'Why not? The battle hasn't even started yet. I'll be back in no time.'

Mazursky let out a sigh of despair. 'I've told you I can't allow you to—'

'But it'll only take a moment, Mr Mazursky,' pleaded Ferguson. 'Mr Fletcher and I have known each other since—'

'Answer me one thing, Mr Ferguson,' Charles Winslow interrupted him.

Ferguson turned towards him, his hackles up.

'When your friend described his trip to you, did he by any chance tell you that you had appeared out of nowhere to say hello?'

'No,' replied Ferguson.

Charles smiled. 'In that case, stay where you are. You never went to greet your friend, Mr Fletcher, so you can't go now. As you yourself said, fate is fate: it can't be altered.'

Ferguson opened his mouth, but no words came out.

'Now, if you don't mind,' Charles added, turning to face the street, 'I think we'd all like to witness the battle in silence.'

Claire observed with relief that this shut Ferguson up once and for all. The others ignored him too, concentrating their gaze on the street. Claire turned to Lucy, hoping to exchange knowing glances with her friend, but apparently she was already bored with the whole thing: she had picked up a twig and was scratching a kiwi bird in the sand with it.

On her right, Inspector Garrett was watching Lucy draw, an awed expression on his face, as though he were witnessing a small miracle. 'Did you know kiwis only exist in New Zealand, Miss Nelson?' the young man asked, after clearing his throat.

Lucy looked at him, astonished that he, too, should know about this bird, and Claire could not help grinning. Where, if not between two kiwi-lovers, could a stronger love blossom?

Just then a clank of metal, scarcely audible in the distance, startled the group. Everyone, including Ferguson, fixed their eyes expectantly on the end of the street, terrified by the sinister noise that could only herald the arrival of the evil automatons.

They soon emerged, moving slowly through the ruins as though they were the lords of the planet. They looked identical to the statue back in the big hall: huge, angular and threatening, with tiny engines on their backs that let out occasional plumes of steam. Much to everyone's surprise, they were carrying their king aloft on a throne, as in days of yore. Claire sighed, regretting being so far from the scene.

'Take these, my dear,' Ferguson said, handing her his opera glasses. 'You seem more interested than I am.'

Claire thanked him and hurriedly studied the group through Ferguson's glasses. She counted eight automatons altogether: the four bearers, plus two more at front and rear, escorting the throne upon which sat the inscrutable Solomon, ferocious king of the automatons, distinguishable from his replicas only by the crown perched on his iron head. The procession moved forward with excruciating slowness, lurching ridiculously from side to side like toddlers taking their first steps. And in fact, Claire reflected, the automatons had indeed learned to walk by conquering the world. Humans were undoubtedly quicker, but clearly far more fragile than these creatures, who had slowly but surely taken over the planet, perhaps because they had the whole of eternity to do so.

Then, when the cortège was halfway down the street, they heard a loud report. Solomon's crown flew into the air. Everyone gazed in astonishment as the glittering object spun round several times, then fell to the ground and rolled over the rubble until it came to a halt a few yards away. Recovering from their surprise, Solomon and his guards raised their eyes to the top of a small crag blocking their way. The time travellers followed their gaze – and saw him. Standing in an almost identical pose to the statue in the hall, the brave Captain Shackleton was feline and imposing, his sinewy body swathed in shining armour, his deadly sword hanging indolently from his belt. He held an ornate gun bristling with levers. The leader of the humans had no need of a crown to bestow splendour on an already majestic physique, which, unbeknown to him, elevated the outcrop he was perched on to the status of pedestal.

He and Solomon looked each other up and down, their deep-seated hostility making the air crackle with electricity as if in the lead-up to a storm. Then the king of the automatons began to speak: 'I've always admired your courage, Captain,' he said, in his tinny voice, which he tried to imbue with a casual, almost playful tone, 'but this time you've overestimated your chances. How could it occur to you to attack me without your army? Are you really so desperate, or have your men abandoned you?'

Captain Shackleton shook his head, as though he was disappointed by his enemy's words. 'The one positive thing about this war,' he said, with quiet assurance, 'is the way it has united the human race as never before.'

Shackleton's voice was soft and clear, and reminded Claire of how some stage actors delivered their lines. Solomon tilted his head to one side, wondering what his enemy meant. He did not have to wait long to find out. The captain slowly raised his left hand, like someone calling down a falcon, and various shadows emerged from beneath the rubble, debris and stones scattering as they stood up. In a matter of seconds, the unsuspecting automatons found themselves surrounded by Shackleton's men.

Claire's heart raced. The humans had been hiding in the ruins all along, knowing Solomon would take that path. The king of the automatons had walked straight into the trap that would end his reign. The soldiers, whose actions seemed speeded up compared to those of the lumbering automatons, retrieved their rifles from the sand, dusted them off and took aim at their respective targets with the calm solemnity of someone performing a sacrament. The problem was there were only four of them. Claire was shocked that Shackleton's famous army should be reduced to such a paltry number. Perhaps no one else had volunteered to take part in the suicidal attack, or perhaps by this stage of the war, the frequent daily skirmishes had reduced his troops to the point at which these were the only men left. At least they had the advantage of surprise, she thought, impressed by their tactical positioning: two soldiers had appeared out of nowhere in front of the procession, another to the left of the throne and a fourth had popped up at the rear.

The four opened fire as one.

Of the two automatons leading the cortège, one took a direct hit in the chest. Although he was made of iron, his armour ripped open, and he spurted a cascade of cogs and rods on to the ground before falling over with a loud crash. The other was luckier: the bullet aimed at disabling him only grazed his shoulder, barely causing him to totter. The soldier who had appeared behind the procession was cleverer. His bullet shattered the little steam engine on the back of one of the guards bringing up the rear; it keeled over backwards. A moment later, one of the throne-bearers suffered the same fate, felled by a volley of bullets fired by the soldier who had appeared at the side. Losing one of its supports, the throne keeled over dangerously, and sank to the ground, bringing the mighty Solomon with it.

Things seemed to be going splendidly for the humans, but once the automatons had regrouped, the situation changed. The automaton next to the one that had toppled over backwards snatched the weapon of his attacker and smashed it to smithereens. At the same time, no longer encumbered by the throne, a bearer opened the little doors in his chest and fired a direct hit at one of the two soldiers attacking from the front. His fall distracted his comrade, a fatal error that gave the nearest automaton, whose shoulder had been grazed, time to charge him and deliver a direct blow with his fist. The punch threw the soldier into the air; he landed a few yards away.

Panther-like, Shackleton leaped from his rock, and bounded over to them, downing the automaton with a well-aimed bullet before it could finish off his companion. The two remaining soldiers, one now unarmed, stepped back from the fray, and fell in beside their captain, while the four surviving automatons closed ranks around their king.

Although Claire knew nothing about military strategy, you did not need to be a genius to see that once the humans had used the advantage of a surprise, which had perhaps blinded them with the illusion of an easy victory, the automatons' superior strength had turned the battle around with humiliating ease. Outnumbered as they were, it seemed logical to Claire that Shackleton, whose duty as a good captain was to protect his men, would order a retreat. However, the future had already been written, and she was not surprised when she heard Solomon's voice intervene to stop them as they were preparing to flee.

'Wait, Captain,' he declared, in his tinny voice. 'Go, if you want, and plan another ambush. Perhaps you will be more successful next time, but I fear you will only prolong a war that has already gone on far too long. But you could also stay and end it once and for all, here and now.'

Shackleton looked at him suspiciously.

'If you allow me, I'd like to make you a proposition, Captain,' Solomon went on, while his guard broke ranks, opening like a metal cocoon at the centre of which stood their king. 'I propose we fight a duel.'

One of the automatons had rescued a wooden box from the toppled throne, which it now presented to Solomon. The automaton ceremoniously pulled out a magnificent iron sword, the tip of whose blade glinted in the faint light from the sky.

'As you see, Captain, I have had made a broadsword identical to yours so that we could fight with the same weapon humans have used for centuries. I've been practising these last few months, waiting for the moment when I would be able to challenge you.' He sliced through the air with a two-handed thrust. 'Unlike the ignoble pistol, the sword requires skill, deftness and knowledge of your enemy, which makes me think that if I succeed in piercing your entrails with its razor-sharp blade, you will acknowledge my expertise and consent to die.'

Captain Shackleton mulled over Solomon's proposal for a few moments, looking wearier and more disgusted than ever by the war of attrition. Now he had his chance to end it by laying all his bets on a single card.

'I accept your challenge, Solomon. Let's decide the outcome of this war here and now,' he replied.

'So be it,' Solomon declared gravely, scarcely able to contain his joy.

The automatons and human soldiers stepped back a few paces, forming a circle around the duellists. The third and final act was about to begin.

Shackleton unsheathed his sword with a graceful movement and made several feints in the air, aware perhaps that he might never again perform the gesture. After this brief demonstration, he coolly studied Solomon, who was trying to strike a gallant swordsman's pose, but was hindered by his rigid limbs.

Circling the automaton slowly and nimbly, like a wild animal stalking its prey, Shackleton tried to work out where to strike first, while Solomon watched his assailant, sword clumsily raised. Naturally he had given his rival the honour of commencing the duel. With a swift, agile movement, Shackleton traced an arc in the air with his sword, which came crashing down on Solomon's left side. But the two-handed blow only produced a loud metallic clang, like a pealing bell, that hung in the air for a few moments. Following the pathetic outcome of his first strike, he stepped back a few paces, visibly dismayed: the brutal blow had scarcely made Solomon teeter, while it had almost snapped his wrists. As though seeking to confirm his weak position, Shackleton struck again, this time aiming for the automaton's right side. The result was the same, but this time he could not afford to brood over it – he had to avoid Solomon's counter-attack.

After dodging the tip of his sword, which sliced through the air almost grazing his helmet, Shackleton once more put distance between them and, momentarily safe from attack, studied his enemy again, shaking his head slowly in a gesture that betrayed his despair.

Solomon's blows were slow and thus easy to evade, but the captain was aware that if one struck home, his armour would not offer much protection. He had to discover his opponent's weak point. Continuing to aim two-handed blows at the automaton's iron-clad armour would only make his arms stiff, and the effort would exhaust him, slowing him and making him careless: it would leave him, in short, at the automaton's mercy. Shackleton dodged another blow, and ended up behind his enemy's back. Before Solomon had time to turn around, he thrust his sword as hard as he could into the steam engine that gave the automaton life.

There was a great clatter as cogs and rods flew out of the opening in all directions, but also an unexpected burst of steam, which hit Shackleton full in the face, blinding him. Solomon wheeled round with astonishing agility and landed a blow on his dazed enemy. The sword struck the captain's side with such force that it shattered his armour and sent him spinning across the ground like a top.

Claire raised her hand to her mouth to stop herself screaming. She heard the stifled cries of the others around her. Once he had stopped spinning, Shackleton tried to get to his feet, clutching his wounded side, blood streaming over his hip and down his leg, but his strength failed him. He remained on his knees, as though prostrating himself before the king of the automatons, who approached him slowly, savouring his victory.

Solomon shook his head, showing his disappointment at the poor fight his opponent had put up – Shackleton dared not even raise his head to look at him. Then he lifted his sword with both hands, preparing to bring it down on the captain's helmet and split his skull asunder. He could think of no better way to end the cruel war that had established the automatons' supremacy over the human race. He brought the sword down on his victim with all his might but – to his astonishment – Captain Shackleton leaped out of the way at the very last moment. Robbed of its target, the automaton's sword embedded itself in the stony ground with a loud clang. In vain, Solomon tried to pull it out while Shackleton rose up beside him, like a majestic cobra, oblivious to the wound in his side. Slowly, as though taking pleasure from the movement, he raised his sword and brought it down, with one swift surgical blow, on the joint between Solomon's head and his body.

There was an almighty crunch, and the automaton's head rolled across the ground with a series of clangs as it bounced against the rocks. It came to a halt next to the crown it had worn during its reign.

There was a sudden silence. The headless, motionless automaton stood in a grotesque posture, bowed over the sword, the blade still embedded in the rubble. As a final gesture, the brave Captain Shackleton placed his foot on his lifeless enemy's flank and tipped him over. The deafening sound, like that of scrap metal being loaded on to a cart, put an end to the long war that had devastated the planet.

XXII

At the top of the promontory, Mazursky tried in vain to silence the applause unleashed by Captain Shackleton's victory. Fortunately it was drowned in the cheers down in the street, a few yards below, where the men were fervently acclaiming their brave captain. Oblivious to the surrounding clamour, Claire remained crouched behind her rock. She was bemused by the overwhelming storm of emotion that caused her soul to flutter like a flag in the breeze. She had known how the duel would end, yet she had been unable to avoid jumping each time Shackleton was in danger, each time Solomon's blade greedily sought out his flesh, or when Shackleton had attempted in vain to chop down the automaton with his sword, as one fells an oak. She knew this was not so much because she feared the human race might lose the duel, but because of what might happen to the captain himself. She longed to carry on watching events below, even to make sure that, as part of his strategy, Shackleton had exaggerated the severity of the wound inflicted on him by the automaton, but Mazursky had ordered them to line up for the return journey to their own time, and she had no choice but to obey.

The time travellers began their descent of the tiny hillock like an unruly herd of goats, discussing among themselves the exciting highlights of the battle.

'Is that all?' asked Ferguson, apparently the only dissatisfied passenger. 'That poor excuse for a battle is what decided the fate of the planet?'

Mazursky did not deign to reply, taken up as he was with making sure the matrons did not trip and roll down the slope, their skirts flying up with unintended coquettishness.

Claire followed them in silence, ignoring the insufferable Ferguson's comments, and Lucy, who had taken her arm again. One thought hammered persistently in her mind: she had to separate from the group. And she had to do it now, not only because it would no longer be possible once they reached the tram but because the group was in such high spirits that they had still not managed to form an orderly column thus facilitating her escape. Furthermore, she must not stray too far from Shackleton and his men: it would be pointless to get away only to become lost in a maze of ruins. If she was going to act, the time to do it was now: the further they went, the less chance she had. But she must break away from Lucy first.

As though in answer to her prayers, Madeleine Winslow came up to them excitedly, to ask whether they had seen the elegant boots the soldiers were wearing. This was something Claire would never have taken into account, although she seemed to be the only person not to have noticed such an important aspect of the future. Lucy said she had, and immediately went on to discuss the amazing originality of the footwear. Claire shook her head in disbelief at her friend's frivolity, and when Lucy let go of her arm, she took the opportunity to dawdle. She dropped behind the marksman, who had not yet received the order to take up the rear and was strolling along leisurely, no longer bothering to keep an eye on the shadows. Behind him came Charles Winslow and Inspector Garrett, immersed in a lively conversation while they walked. Finally, when she found herself at the back of the group, she hitched up her skirts and made a clumsy dash for it, ducking behind a conveniently placed remnant of wall.

Claire Haggerty stood still, her back against the wall, her heart pounding, listening to the murmur of the group growing fainter and fainter, without anyone apparently having noticed she was missing. When at last they were out of earshot, dry-throated, parasol clasped between her sweaty palms, she poked her head out cautiously and saw that the procession had disappeared round a bend. She had done it! At once she felt a rush of panic as it dawned on her she was alone in that dreadful place, but she quickly told herself this was what she had wanted. Events were unfolding exactly as she had planned when she climbed aboard the Cronotilus. Unless something went horribly wrong, she could stay in the year 2000. Wasn't that what she had wished for?

She drew a deep breath and stepped out from behind the wall. All being well, they would only discover her absence when they reached the time-tram, but even so she must hurry to join Shackleton and his men before the guide found out. After that there would be nothing Mazursky could do and she would be safe. As he had told them himself during the journey, they were in the year 2000 as simple spectators: they must not let themselves be seen by people from the future, still less make contact with them. Finding the captain, then, was her primary objective.

Claire marched off in the opposite direction to her companions, trying not to think of the consequences her unexpected act might have on the fabric of time. She only hoped she would not destroy the universe in her bid to be happy.

Now that she found herself alone, the surrounding devastation seemed even more disturbing. What if she could not find Shackleton? And what if the captain snubbed her, refusing to admit her into his ranks? She could not believe that a true gentleman would abandon a woman to her fate in that terrible world. Besides, she had some knowledge of first aid, which might prove useful, judging from how easy it was to get wounded there, and she was courageous and hard-working enough to help them rebuild the world. And, of course, she was in love with the captain. Although she preferred not to let that show until she was completely sure. In the meantime it was simply a notion, as outrageous as it was exhilarating. She had to admit, however, that she had not given enough thought to what she would do when she met the captain, because she had not really believed her escape plan would work. She would just have to improvise, she told herself, walking round the promontory, before hiking up her skirts in readiness to climb down the steep path, which, if her sense of direction had not failed her, would lead to the street where the ambush had taken place.

She paused when she heard footsteps coming up the path towards her. They were unmistakably human, but Claire followed her instinct and jumped behind the nearest rock. She waited in silence, her heart beating furiously in her chest. The owner of the footsteps stopped near to where she was hiding. Claire was afraid he had seen her and would order her to come out with her hands up or, worse, that he would point his gun at the rock and wait for her to make the first move. Instead the stranger began singing: 'Jack the Ripper's dead/And lying on his bed/He cut his throat/With Sunlight Soap/ Jack the Ripper's dead.'

Claire raised her eyebrows. She knew that song. Her father had learned it from East End children and used to sing it softly to himself as he shaved before going to church. She suddenly imagined herself immersed in the aroma of the new-fangled soap made from pine oil rather than animal fat. She wished she could travel back to her own time simply to tell her father that the song which had so tickled him had survived over the years. Except that she would never go back, come what may. She tried not to think of this, but to concentrate on the present moment, the moment that would mark the start of her new life.

The stranger carried on singing with even greater gusto. Had he come to that secluded place simply to try out his voice? Whatever the case, it was time she made contact with the inhabitants of the year 2000. She gritted her teeth, plucked up all her courage and stepped out of her hiding-place, ready to introduce herself to the stranger who was so casually destroying one of her favourite songs.

Claire Haggerty and the brave Captain Shackleton stared at one another in silence, each reflecting the other's surprise, like two mirrors facing one another. The captain had removed his helmet, which was resting on a nearby stone, and Claire did not need to look twice to realise that the reason he had strayed from the others was not to practise his singing, but to perform a far less noble act to which the ditty he was singing was a simple adjunct. She could not prevent her jaw dropping, and her fingers letting go of the parasol, which made a crunching sound, like a shell breaking, as it hit the ground. After all, this was the first time her delicate eyes had glimpsed the part of a man she was apparently not meant to see until the day her marriage was consummated, and even then probably not quite in such a plain and naked fashion.

As soon as he had recovered from his surprise, Captain Shackleton hastened to tuck away the unseemly part of his anatomy beneath his armour. Then he stared at her, again without a word, embarrassment giving way to curiosity. Claire had not had time to speculate about other details, but Captain Derek Shackleton's face was certainly as she had imagined it would be. Either the Creator had fashioned it according to her precise instructions, or the ape this man was descended from had had a superior pedigree.

But, for whatever reason, Captain Shackleton's face unquestionably belonged to a different era. He had the same graceful chin as the statue and the same serene expression around his mouth, and his eyes, now that she could see them, were in perfect harmony with the rest of his features. Those beautiful grey-green eyes, like a forest immersed in mist where all who ventured were destined to be lost, set the world alight with a gaze so intense, so profound that Claire knew she was in the presence of the most alive man she had ever seen. Yes, beneath that armour plate, that bronzed skin, those sculpted muscles, was a heart that beat with extraordinary force, pumping through the network of veins a stubborn impulsive life that death itself had been unable to conquer.

'I'm Claire Haggerty, Captain,' she introduced herself, trying to stop her voice quaking, 'and I've come from the nineteenth century to help you rebuild the world.'

Captain Shackleton went on staring at her, ashen-faced, through eyes that had seen the destruction of London, raging fires and piles of dead bodies, eyes that had seen the most atrocious side of life but had no idea how to cope with the delicate, exquisite creature in front of him.

'There you are, Miss Haggerty!' she heard someone cry out behind her.

Taken aback, Claire wheeled round and saw the guide coming down the steep path towards her. Mazursky was clearly relieved to have found her.

'I thought I told you all to stay together!' he cried shrilly, as he walked up to her and seized her roughly by the arm. 'You could have stayed behind for ever!'

Claire turned towards Shackleton to implore his aid, but to her astonishment the captain had vanished as though he had been nothing but a figment of her imagination. Indeed, his departure had been so abrupt that, as Mazursky dragged her towards where the others were waiting for them, Claire wondered in all seriousness whether she had really seen him or if he had been a product of her inflamed imagination.

They rejoined the group, and before they headed back to the Cronotilus, the guide made them get into a line with the marksmen at the rear and, irritated, ordered them not to wander off again.

'It's a good thing I noticed you were missing,' Lucy told her, taking Claire's arm. 'Were you dreadfully afraid?'

Claire sighed, and let herself be guided by Lucy like a convalescent patient, unable to think of anything except Captain Shackleton's gentle eyes. But had they looked at her with love? His speechlessness and bewilderment were definite symptoms of infatuation and suggested that he had. In any era they were the typical signs of someone smitten. But even if it were true, what good was it to her if Captain Shackleton had fallen in love with her since she was never going to see him again? She let herself be helped on to the time-tram, as if she had no will of her own.

Dejected, she leaned back in her seat, and when she felt the violent judder of the steam engine starting up, she had to stop herself dissolving into a puddle of tears. As the vehicle shunted through the fourth dimension, Claire wondered how she would endure having to go back and live in her own dull time, especially now she was sure that the only man with whom she could be happy would be born long after she was dead.

'We're on our way home, ladies and gentlemen,' announced Mazursky, unable to conceal his contentment at nearing the end of that eventful journey.

Claire looked at him with annoyance. Yes, they were on their way home to the dreary nineteenth century, and they had not jeopardised the fabric of time. Of course Mazursky was pleased: he had prevented a silly young girl from destroying the universe and avoided the telling-off he would have received from Gilliam Murray had he failed. What did it matter if the price had been her happiness? Claire was so infuriated she could have slapped the guide there and then, even though she knew Mazursky had only been doing his duty. The universe was more important than the fate of any one person, even if she was that person. She tried to curb her irritation at the guide's beaming face. Fortunately, part of her rage evaporated when she looked down and saw that her hands were empty. Mazursky had not done such a perfect job after all – how far could a mere parasol affect the fabric of time?

XXIII

When the girl and the guide vanished along the steep path, Captain Derek Shackleton left his hiding-place and paused to look at where the woman had been standing, as though expecting to discover a trace of her perfume or her voice lingering in the empty space, some sign of her presence that would prove she had not been a figment of his imagination. He was still reeling from the meeting. He could scarcely believe it had happened. He remembered her words: 'I'm Claire Haggerty, Captain, and I've come from the nineteenth century to help you rebuild the world,' she had said, with a charming curtsy. But this was not all he remembered. He was surprised by how clearly the image of her face was etched in his mind. He could conjure, clear as day, her pale visage, her slightly wild features, her smooth, shapely mouth, her jet black hair, her graceful bearing, her voice. And he remembered the look in her eyes. Above all he remembered the way she had gazed at him, enraptured, almost in awe, with mesmerised joy. No woman had ever looked at him like that before.

Then he noticed the parasol and flushed with shame as he remembered why she had dropped it. He went over and carefully picked it up, as though it were an iron bird fallen from some metallic nest. It was a dainty, elegant parasol that betrayed the moneyed status of its owner. What was he supposed to do with it? One thing was clear: he could not leave it there.

Parasol in hand, he set off to where the others were waiting for him, taking the opportunity to collect himself as he walked. To avoid arousing their suspicions, he must hide his agitation at his encounter with the girl.

Just then, Solomon leaped from behind a rock, brandishing his sword. Although he had been daydreaming, the brave Captain Shackleton reacted in a flash, striking the automaton with the parasol as it bore down on him, baying for his blood in his booming metallic voice. The blow glanced off Solomon, but it took him by surprise, and he teetered for a few seconds before toppling backwards down a small incline. Clutching the by now rather dented parasol, Shackleton watched his enemy rattle down the hill. The clattering sound came to an abrupt halt as the automaton hit a pile of rocks. For a few moments, Solomon lay stretched out on his back covered with a thick layer of dust thrown up by his fall. Then he tried laboriously to pick himself up, cursing and hurling insults, which the metallic timbre of his voice made sound even more vulgar. Loud guffaws rang out from the group of soldiers and automatons who were looking on.

'Stop laughing, you swine! I might have broken something!' groaned Solomon, amid further guffaws.

'It serves you right for playing pranks,' Shackleton chided him, walking down the incline and offering him a helping hand. 'Won't you ever tire of your silly ambushes?'

'You were taking too long, my friend,' the automaton complained, allowing Shackleton and two others to pull him to his feet. 'What the hell were you doing up there anyway?'

'I was urinating,' the captain replied. 'By the way, congratulations. That was a great duel. I think we did it better than ever before.'

'True,' a soldier agreed. 'You were both superb. I don't think you performed so well even for Her Majesty.'

'Good. The fact is, it's much easier to perform when you know the Queen of England isn't watching you. In any case, it's exhausting running around in this armour,' said Solomon. After he had freed himself, he gulped air like a fish. His red hair was stuck to his head, his broad face covered with beads of sweat.

'Stop complaining, Martin,' said the automaton with the gash in his chest, who was also removing his head. 'At least you've got one of the main roles. I don't even have time to finish off a soldier before I kick the bucket. And on top of that I have to blow myself up.'

'You know it's harmless, Mike. But if you insist, we can ask Murray to switch some of the roles round next time,' suggested the young man who played the part of Captain Shackleton, in an attempt to keep tempers from fraying.

'Yes, Tom. I can play Jeff's role and he can play mine,' agreed the man playing the first automaton to fall, pointing to the soldier whose task it was to slay him.

'Not on your life, Mike. I've been waiting all week to be able to shoot you. Anyway, after that Bradley kills me,' said Jeff, pointing in turn to the lad concealed inside one of the throne-bearing automatons, who had an S-shaped scar on his left cheek reaching almost to his eye.

'What's that?' he asked, referring to what was in Tom's hand.

'This? A parasol,' Tom replied, holding it up to show the group. 'One of the passengers must have left it behind.'

Jeff whistled in amazement. 'It must have cost a fortune,' he said, scrutinising it with interest. 'A lot more that we get for doing this, at any rate.'

'Believe me, Jeff, we're better off working for Murray than down a mine, or breaking our backs on the Manchester Ship Canal,' said Martin.

'Oh, now I feel a lot better!' the other man retorted.

'Are we going to stay here all day prattling?' asked Tom, slyly concealing the parasol once more, in the hope the others would forget it. 'Let me remind you that the present awaits us outside.'

'You're right, Tom.' Jeff laughed. 'Let's get back to our own time!'

'Without having to cross the fourth dimension!' echoed Martin, roaring with laughter.

The fifteen men made their way through the ruins, walking almost as if in a procession out of respect for those wearing the automatons' heavy garb. As they advanced, Jeff noticed a little uneasily how absent-minded Captain Shackleton looked. (From now on, as I no longer have to keep any secrets, I will refer to him by his real name, Tom Blunt.)

'I still don't understand how people are taken in by this fake rubble,' Jeff remarked, trying to draw his friend out of his brooding silence.

'Remember, they're seeing it from the other side,' Tom responded distractedly.

Jeff feigned incomprehension, determined to keep him talking so that he would forget whatever was bothering him.

'It's like when we go to see a conjuror,' Tom felt obliged to add, although he had never seen one himself. The closest he had come to the world of magic had been when he lodged in the same boarding-house as an amateur magician. Perhaps that was what gave him the authority to go on: 'Conjuring tricks dazzle us, they even make us think magic might exist, but if we only saw how they did it, we'd ask ourselves how we could have been so easily fooled. None of the passengers see through Mr Murray's trickery,' he said, pointing with the parasol at the machine they were walking past, which was responsible for producing enough smoke to hide the roof and beams of the vast shed that housed the set. 'In fact, they're not even suspicious. They only see the end result. They see what they want to see. You'd also believe this pile of ruins was London in the year 2000 if what you wanted to see was London in the year 2000.'

Exactly as Claire Haggerty had believed, he thought, with bitter regret, remembering how the girl had offered to help him rebuild the world.

'Yes, you must admit, the boss has arranged it brilliantly,' his companion acknowledged, following the flight of a crow with his eyes. 'If people found out this was only a set, he'd end up in jail – if they didn't string him up first.'

'That's why it's so important no one sees our faces, right, Tom?' said Bradley.

Tom nodded, trying to suppress a shudder.

'Yes, Bradley,' Jeff reiterated, given his companion's terse response. 'We're obliged to wear these uncomfortable helmets so the passengers won't recognise us if they bump into us somewhere in London. It's another of Murray's safety measures. Have you forgotten what he said to us on our first day?'

'Not likely!' Bradley declared. Then, mimicking his boss's melodious, educated voice, he added: '"Your helmet is your safe-conduct, gentlemen. Anyone who takes it off during the show will live to regret it, believe me."'

'Yes, and I'm not going to be the one to run the risk. Remember what happened to poor Perkins.'

Bradley whistled with fear at the thought, and Tom shuddered again. The group came to a halt in front of a fragmented skyline of burning rooftops. Jeff stepped forward, found the handle hidden in the mural, and opened a door among the clouds. As though plunging into their fluffy interior, the procession left the set, and walked down a passageway to a cramped dressing room. Upon entering, they were surprised by the sound of furious clapping. Gilliam Murray was sprawled on a chair applauding with theatrical enthusiasm.

'*Magnifique*!' he exclaimed. 'Bravo!'

The group was speechless. Gilliam stood up and walked towards them with open arms. 'Congratulations on a wonderful job, gentlemen. Our customers were so thrilled by your performance that some of them even want to come back.'

After acknowledging his clap on the back, Tom moved discreetly away from the others. In the munitions store he left the piece of painted wood covered with bolts and knobs, which, with the aid of the blank charges under the automatons' armour, Murray was able to pass off as a lethal weapon of the future, and started to get changed. He needed to leave there as soon as possible, he told himself, thinking of Claire Haggerty and the problem caused by his blasted bladder. He took off Captain Shackleton's armour, hung it on its hanger and pulled his own clothes out of a box marked 'Tom'. He rolled the parasol up in his jacket, and glanced round to make sure no one had seen him. Murray was giving orders to a couple of waitresses who had entered wheeling trolleys laden with steak and kidney pie, grilled sausages and tankards of beer, while the rest of his fellow workers had also begun to change.

He gazed warmly at the men with whom chance had obliged him to work: Jeff, lean but strong, cheerful and talkative; young Bradley, still an adolescent whose youthful face gave the S-shaped scar on his cheek an even more disturbing air; burly Mike, with his look of perpetual bewilderment; and Martin, the joker, a strapping redhead of uncertain age, whose leathery skin reflected the ravages of a life spent working out in all weathers. It felt strange to Tom that, while in Murray's fictional world they would all have laid down their lives for him, in the real world they might slit his throat for a promise of food or money. After all, what did he know about them except that, like him, they were penniless?

They had gone out drinking together several times; first to celebrate their more than satisfactory début performance, then to mark the success of the one given in honour of Her Majesty the Queen, for which they had received double wages. Last, they had caroused to celebrate their third triumphant performance in advance. That riotous spree had ended like the others in Mrs Dawson's bawdy-house. But, if anything, the revelry had made Tom realise he should avoid keeping company with these fellows or they would land him in trouble.

With the exception of Martin Tucker – who, despite his fondness for pranks, seemed the most decent – he saw them as a bunch of untrustworthy delinquents. Like him, they lived from hand to mouth, doing odd jobs – although it was clear they were not above breaking the law if there was money to be earned. Only a few days before, Jeff Wayne and Bradley Holloway had asked him to play a part in one of their shady dealings – a house in Kensington Gore that looked easy to break into. He had refused to go along, not so much because he had promised himself to make every effort to earn an honest living, but because when it came to breaking the law he preferred to act alone: he knew from experience that he had more chance of survival if he watched his own back. If you depended only on yourself, no one could betray you.

He had slipped into his shirt and was doing up the buttons when, out of the corner of his eye, he saw Gilliam Murray coming over.

'I wanted to thank you personally, Tom,' he said, beaming and stretching out his hand. Tom shook it, forcing a smile. 'None of this would be possible without you. Nobody could play Captain Shackleton better.'

Tom tried to look pleased. Was Murray making a veiled reference to Perkins? From what he had heard, Perkins had been hired to play Shackleton before him. When he had discovered what Murray was up to, he had realised his silence was worth more than the salary Murray intended paying him, and had gone to his office to tell him as much. His attempt at blackmail had not ruffled Murray, who simply told him that if he did not agree with the pay he was free to go, adding in a tone of wounded pride that his Captain Shackleton would never have stooped so low. Perkins smiled ominously and left his office, announcing his intention to go directly to Scotland Yard. He was never seen again. Following his crude effort at extortion, Perkins had vanished into thin air, but Tom and the others suspected Murray's thugs had taken care of him before he got anywhere near Scotland Yard. They could not prove it, but they had no desire to put Murray to the test.

This was why Tom had to keep secret his meeting with Claire Haggerty. If anyone found out that a passenger had seen his face, it was the end for him. He knew Murray would not be content to dismiss him. He would take drastic measures, as he had done with poor Perkins. The fact that he was not to blame was irrelevant: his mere existence would be a constant threat to Murray's scheme, a threat he would have to deal with urgently. If Murray ever found out, Tom would end up like Perkins, however big and strong he might be.

'You know, Tom,' said Murray, 'when I look at you I see a true hero.'

'I just try to play the part of Captain Shackleton as best I can,

Mr Murray,' Tom replied, trying to stop his hands shaking as he pulled on his trousers.

Murray gave what sounded like a growl of pleasure. 'Well, just keep it up, lad, keep it up,' he urged.

Tom nodded. 'Now, if you'll excuse me,' he said, pulling on his cap, 'I'm in a bit of a hurry.'

'You're leaving?' said Murray, disappointed. 'Won't you stay for the jollities?'

'I'm sorry, Mr Murray, I really have to go,' replied Tom. He snatched his bundled-up jacket, taking care not to let Murray see the parasol, and headed for the door that led from the dressing room into the alley at the back of the building. He had to get out of there before Murray noticed the beads of sweat on his brow.

'Tom, wait!' cried Murray.

He swivelled round, his heart knocking in his chest. Murray stared at him solemnly. 'Is she pretty?' he finally asked.

'I beg your pardon?' Tom stammered.

'The reason you're in such a hurry. Is there a pretty lady waiting to enjoy the company of the saviour of the human race?'

'I – I—' Tom stuttered, suddenly aware of the sweat trickling down his cheeks.

Gilliam Murray laughed heartily. 'I understand, Tom,' he said, patting him on the back. 'You don't like people sniffing around in your private life, do you? Don't worry, you're not obliged to reply. Run along now. And don't forget to make sure no one sees you leave.'

Tom nodded mechanically, and moved towards the door, half-heartedly waving to the others. He stepped out into the alley and hurried as fast as he could towards the main street, where he hid at the corner and paused, trying to collect his thoughts. He watched the entrance to the alleyway for a few minutes, in case Murray had sent someone after him, but when no one appeared, he felt reassured. That meant Murray did not suspect anything – at least, not yet. Tom heaved a sigh of relief. Now he must put his trust in the stars to guide him as far away as possible from the girl called Claire Haggerty. It was then he noticed that, in his panic, he had forgotten to change his shoes: he was still wearing the brave Captain Shackleton's boots.

XXIV

The boarding-house on Buckeridge Street was a ramshackle building with a peeling façade, wedged between two taverns that were so noisy it was hard for anyone to sleep on the other side of the partition walls. However, compared to some of the other fleapits Tom had lodged in, the filthy hovel was the nearest thing to a palace he had known. At that time of day, after twelve, the street was filled with the pungent aroma of grilled sausages from the taverns, a constant source of torment for most of the lodgers, whose pockets contained nothing but fluff. Tom crossed the street to the boarding-house, trying his best to ignore the smell and regretting that he had passed up the spread Murray had laid on in their honour – it would have filled his belly for days. In the street he saw the stall belonging to Mrs Ritter, a mournful widow who made a few pence reading people's palms.

'Good afternoon, Mrs Ritter,' he said, with a friendly smile. 'How's business?'

'Your smile's the best thing that's happened to me today, Tom,' the woman replied, cheering up noticeably when she saw him. 'No one seems bothered about the future. Have you managed to convince the whole neighbourhood not to be curious about what fate has in store for them?'

Tom liked Mrs Ritter, and from the moment she had set up her miserable little stand there, he had taken it upon himself to be her champion. From scraps of neighbourhood gossip, Tom had pieced together her tragic story, which might have been the template the Creator had used to reproduce unhappy lives: Mrs Ritter had apparently been spared no misfortune. Tom had decided she had undergone more than her fair share of suffering and resolved to help her as best he could. Unfortunately this stretched little further than stealing apples in Covent Garden or stopping to give her the time of day whenever he went in or out of the boarding-house, and trying to cheer her if she was having a bad day. He had never let her read his palm, and always gave the same explanation: knowing what fate had in store for him would destroy his curiosity, which was the only thing that got him out of bed every morning.

'I would never try to sabotage your business, Mrs Ritter,' he replied, amused. 'I'm sure things will pick up this afternoon.'

'I hope you're right, Tom . . . I hope you're right.'

He bade her farewell, and climbed the rickety staircase that led to his room on the top floor. He opened the door, and examined the room he had been living in for almost two years as though he were seeing it for the first time. When the landlady had first shown him the room, he had eyed critically the dilapidated bed, the worm-eaten chest of drawers, the fly-blown mirror and the tiny window overlooking the waterlogged back alley filled with refuse. Now Tom stared at the wretched space he could scarcely pay for, which represented everything he had been able to make of life. He was struck by the overwhelming certainty that nothing would ever change, that his present existence was so irreversible it would continue into the future, without anything happening to mark the passage of time. Only at moments of remarkable lucidity like this would he realise that life was slipping away from him, like water trickling through his fingers.

But how else could he play the hand he had been dealt? His father had been a miserable wretch who believed he had landed the best job of his life when he was hired to collect the excrement in the cesspools at the back of people's houses. Each night he had ventured forth to unburden the city of its waste, as though Her Majesty in person would one day thank him for his labours. He was utterly convinced that this loathsome task was the cornerstone upon which the British Empire was founded: how could a country stay on top if it was drowning in its own filth? he would say. His greatest aspiration – to his friends' amusement – was to buy a bigger cart that would allow him to shovel more shit than anyone else. If there was one childhood memory etched in Tom's mind it was the unbearable stench his father exuded when he climbed into bed. Tom had tried to fend it off by nestling against his mother and breathing in her sweet smell, which was barely perceptible beneath the sweat from her toil at the cotton mill. But the smell of excrement was preferable by far to the stink of the cheap alcohol his father brought home with him when the blossoming of the city's sewage system put an end to his absurd dreams. And now Tom could no longer fend it off with his mother's fragrance, because an outbreak of cholera had torn her from him.

After her death, there was more room in the communal bed, but Tom slept with one eye open, for he never knew when his father might wake him up with his belt, unleashing his anger at the world on his son's tiny back.

When Tom turned six, his father forced him to go out begging to pay for liquor. Arousing people's sympathy was a thankless but undemanding task, and he did not know how much he would miss it until his father demanded he help him in the new job he had obtained, thanks to his cart and his ability with a shovel. In this way Tom learned that death could cease to be abstract and take on form and substance, leaving a chill in his fingers that no fire would ever warm. But more than anything, he understood that those whose lives were worth nothing became valuable in death, for their bodies contained a wealth of precious organs. He helped his father rob graves and crypts for a retired boxer named Crouch, who sold the corpses to surgeons, until during one of his frequent drunken binges his father fell into the Thames and drowned.

Overnight, Tom found himself alone in the world, but at least now his life was his own. He was no longer forced to disturb the sleep of the dead. Now he would be the one to decide which path he took.

Stealing corpses had turned him into a strong, alert lad who had no difficulty in finding more honest employment. He had found work as a street sweeper, a pest exterminator, a doorman. He even swept chimneys, until the lad he worked with was caught stealing from a customer's house, and the pair were thrown out by the servants after a thrashing. But he put all that behind him the day he met Megan, a beautiful girl with whom he lived for a few years in a stuffy cellar in Hague Street, Bethnal Green. Megan was not only a pleasant respite from his daily struggle, she taught him to read, using old newspapers they fished out of the rubbish. Thanks to her, Tom discovered the hidden meaning behind the symbols that were letters, and learned that life beyond his own little world could be just as awful. Unfortunately in some neighbourhoods happiness is always doomed, and Megan ran off with a chair-maker who did not know the meaning of hunger.

When she returned two months later, her face covered with bruises and blind in one eye, Tom accepted her back as though she had never left. Although her betrayal had dealt the final blow to a love already strained by circumstance, he cared for her day and night, feeding her opium syrup to keep the pain at bay, and reading aloud from old newspapers as though he were reciting poetry. He would have gone on caring for her for the rest of his life, bound to her by pity, which might have changed back into affection, if the infection in her eye had not caused his bed to widen once more.

They buried her one rainy morning in a small church near the lunatic asylum. He alone wept over her grave. He felt he was burying much more than Megan's body. With her went his faith in life, his naïve belief that he would be able to live honourably, and his innocence. That day, in the shoddy coffin of the only woman whom he had dared to love, they were also burying Tom Blunt because, suddenly, he did not know who he was. He did not recognise himself in the young man who, that very night, crouched in the dark waiting for the chair-maker to come home; in the frenzied creature who hurled himself at the man, throwing him against a wall; in the wild animal who set upon him, beating him into the ground with angry fists.

The death cries of this man he had never known were also the cries that heralded the birth of a new Tom: a Tom who seemed capable of anything, a Tom who could perform deeds such as this without a flicker of conscience, perhaps because someone had extracted it and sold it to the surgeons. He had tried to make an honest living, and life had crushed him as if he were a loathsome insect. It was time he looked for other ways to survive, Tom told himself, gazing at the bloody pulp to which he had reduced the chair-maker.

By the time he was twenty, life had instilled a savage harshness in his eyes. Combined with his physical strength, this gave him a disconcerting, even intimidating air, as he loped along the streets. He had no difficulty in being hired by a money-lender in Bethnal Green, who paid him to bully a list of debtors by day, and who he had no qualms about stealing from at night. It was as though the morality that had guided his actions in the past had become no more than a useless obstacle preventing him reaping the benefits of life. There was no longer room for anything but self-interest. Life became a simple routine that consisted of perpetrating violence on anyone he was told to in exchange for enough money to rent a filthy, dank room and the services of a whore when he needed to relax. He was governed by a single emotion, hatred, which he nurtured daily with his fists, as though it were a rare bloom, vague but intense, aggravated by a trifle and often responsible for him arriving at the boarding-house, face black and blue, barred from yet another tavern.

During this period, Tom was aware of the icy indifference with which he snapped people's fingers and whispered threats in his victims' ears, but he justified his actions by telling himself he had no choice: it was pointless to fight against the current dragging him to where he probably belonged. Like a snake shedding its skin, he could only look away as he relinquished God's mercy on his downward spiral to hell. Perhaps, in the end, that was all he was fit for. Perhaps he had been born to break people's fingers, to occupy a place of honour among thieves and wastrels. And he would have reconciled himself to being dragged deeper into the ugly side of life, knowing it was only a matter of time before he committed his next murder, had it not been for someone who believed the role of hero suited him better.

Tom had turned up at Gilliam Murray's offices without knowing anything about the job on offer. He could still remember the astonishment on the big man's face when he walked in, how he had stood up and paced round him, uttering ecstatic cries, pinching his arm muscles and sizing up his jawbone, arms flailing like some demented tailor.

'I don't believe it. You're exactly as I described you,' he declared, to the bewildered Tom. 'You are Derek Shackleton.'

With this he led him down to an enormous cellar where a group of men in strange costumes seemed to be rehearsing a play. That was the first time he had met Martin, Jeff and the others.

'Gentlemen, I'd like to introduce you to your captain,' Murray announced, 'the man for whom you must sacrifice your lives.'

And that was how Tom Blunt, hired thug, crook and troublemaker, became the saviour of mankind. The job did far more than fill his pockets: it saved his soul from the hellfire where it had been roasting. Because, for some reason, it seemed inappropriate to Tom to go round breaking people's bones now that his mission was to save the world. It sounded absurd, as the two things were perfectly compatible, yet the noble spirit of Derek Shackleton was now glowing inside him, filling the gap from which the original Tom Blunt's soul had been extracted, taking him over serenely, naturally, painlessly.

After the first rehearsal, Tom left Captain Shackleton's armour behind but decided to take his character home, or perhaps this was an unconscious act beyond his control. The truth was, he liked looking at the world as though he really were its saviour, seeing it through the eyes of a hero whose heart was as courageous as it was generous. That same day he decided to look for honest work, as though the words of the giant named Gilliam Murray had rekindled the tiny flame of humanity that was still flickering in his depths.

But now all his plans for redemption had been destroyed by that stupid girl. He sat on the edge of the bed and unwrapped the parasol bundled in his jacket. It was doubtless the most expensive thing in his room; selling it would pay his rent for two or three months, he reflected, rubbing the bruise on his side where the bag of tomato juice had been strapped before Martin burst it during their duel. Some good had come out of his meeting with the girl, although it was hard to ignore the tight spot she had put him in. He dreaded to think what would happen if he ever bumped into her in the street. His boss's worst nightmare would come true, for the girl would immediately discover Murray's Time Travel was a fraud. And while that might be the worst consequence, it was not the only one. She would also discover he was no hero from the future, just a miserable wretch who owned nothing but the clothes on his back. Then Tom would be forced to witness her devotion turn to disappointment, possibly even outright disgust, as though she were watching a butterfly change back into a caterpillar. This, of course, was nothing compared to the discovery of the fraud, but he knew he would regret it far more.

Deep down, it gave him immense pleasure to remember the woman's entranced gaze, even though he knew it was not directed at him but at the hero he was impersonating, the brave Captain Shackleton. Yes, he wanted Claire to imagine him in the year 2000, rebuilding the world, not sitting in this gloomy hovel, wondering how much a pawnbroker would give for her parasol.

Anyone who has been to Billingsgate fish market in the early hours knows that smells travel faster than light. Long before the night receives the first flush of dawn, the pungent aroma of shellfish and the overpowering stench of eel filling the fishermen's carts have already mingled with the cold night air. Zigzagging through the oyster stalls and squid sellers hawking their merchandise at three for a penny, Tom Blunt reached the railings at the river entrance, where a crowd of other miserable wretches were flexing their muscles and trying to look enthusiastic in the hope that some kindly skipper would pick them to unload his boat from overseas.

Tom hugged his jacket to him, trying to ward off the cold, and joined the group of men. He immediately spotted Patrick, a tall youth who was as strapping as he was, with whom he had struck up a sort of friendship. They greeted one another with a nod and, like a couple of pigeons puffing their chests, tried to stand out from the crowd and catch the skippers' eyes. Ordinarily, thanks to their glowing physiques, they were both hired straight away, and that morning was no exception. They congratulated one another with a sly grin, and walked towards the designated cargo boat with the dozen other chosen stevedores.

Tom liked this simple, honest work, which required no more than strong arms and a degree of agility: not only did it enable him to see the dawn in all its glory above the Thames, but as he felt the calming yet vivifying fatigue of physical effort steal over him, he could allow his thoughts to drift down unexpected pathways – rather like when he was at Harrow-on-the-Hill, a small rise in the suburbs of London that he had discovered during one of his walks. On top of the hill grew a centuries' old oak surrounded by a dozen graves, as though the dead buried there wanted nothing to do with the others in the tiny adjoining cemetery. He thought of the grassy knoll as his private sanctuary, a sort of outdoor chapel where he could close his ears to the din of the world.

Sometimes when he was up there, he found to his amazement that he was even able to string together a few positive thoughts, which gave him a measure of insight into the usually elusive meaning of his life. As he sat wondering what sort of life John Peachey, the man buried nearest to the oak, must have led, he began to reflect on his own, as though it belonged to someone else, and to judge it with the same objectivity as that of the deceased stranger.

Once their day was done, he and Patrick sat on a pile of boxes waiting to be paid. The two men usually passed the time chatting about this or that, but Tom's thoughts had been elsewhere all week. That was how long it had been since his unfortunate meeting with Claire Haggerty, and still nothing had happened. Apparently, Murray knew nothing about it and possibly never would. Even so, Tom's life would never be the same again. It had already changed. Tom knew London was too big a place for him to run into the girl again, yet he walked around with his eyes wide open, afraid of bumping into her round every corner. Thanks to her, he would always be uneasy, always on the alert: he had even considered growing a beard. He shook his head as he reflected how the most trivial act can change your life: why the devil had he not taken the precaution of emptying his bladder before the performance?

When Patrick finally plucked up the courage to chide him for his morose silence, Tom stared at him in surprise. It was true he had not tried to hide his anxiety from his friend, and now he did not know what to say to him. He merely reassured him with a mysterious, doleful smile, and his companion shrugged his shoulders.

Once they had been paid, the two men strolled away from the market with the leisurely gait of those who have nothing much else to do for the rest of the day. As they walked, Tom gazed at Patrick, afraid his unwillingness to confide in him might have hurt the lad's feelings. Patrick was only a couple of years younger than him, but his baby face made him look even younger, and Tom could not help instinctively taking him under his wing, like the little brother he had never had, even though he knew Patrick could take care of himself. Whether out of apathy or shyness, neither man had shown any interest in developing their friendship outside the port.

'Today's earnings bring me a little closer, Tom,' declared Patrick, in a faintly wistful voice.

'Closer to what?' asked Tom, intrigued, for Patrick had never mentioned any plans to start a business or get married.

The lad looked at him mysteriously. 'To achieving my dream,' he replied solemnly.

Tom was pleased the lad had a dream to drive him on: something lacking in his own life of late. 'And what dream might that be, Patrick?' he asked, knowing he was longing to tell him.

Almost reverentially, Patrick pulled a crumpled piece of paper from his pocket and presented it to him. 'To travel to the year 2000 and see the brave Captain Shackleton triumph over the evil automatons.'

Tom did not take the leaflet he knew by heart. He just stared at Patrick glumly.

'Wouldn't you like to know about the year 2000, Tom?' said Patrick, astonished.

Tom sighed. 'There's nothing for me in the future, Patrick,' he said. 'This is my present, and it's the only thing I want to know about.'

'I see,' murmured Patrick, too polite to criticise his narrow-minded friend.

'Have you had breakfast yet?' Tom asked.

'Of course not!' He groaned. 'I told you, I'm saving up. Breakfast is a luxury I can't afford.'

'In that case allow me to treat you,' Tom offered, putting a fatherly arm round his shoulders. 'I know a place near here where they serve the best sausages in town.'

XXV

After Tom and Patrick had enjoyed a hearty breakfast that would take the edge off their appetites for a week, Tom's pockets were once again empty. He tried not to reproach himself for his extravagant gesture, but next time he must be more careful: although these altruistic deeds made him feel good, they would only be detrimental to him in the long run. He said goodbye to Patrick and, having nothing better to do for the rest of the day, made his way towards Covent Garden, intending to carry on with his charitable works by stealing a few apples for Mrs Ritter.

It was late morning by the time he arrived, and the freshest, crispest produce had been snapped up by the early birds, who came from all over London at the crack of dawn to stock up their larders. But by the same token, daylight had removed the eerie atmosphere cast by the candles perched on mounds of melted wax that the traders stuck on their carts. By now, the market had taken on the air of a country fair; the visitors no longer looked like furtive ghosts, but like people strolling about with all the time in the world to make their purchases while, like Tom, they let themselves be captivated by the heady scent of roses, eglantines and fuchsias wafting from the flower baskets on the western side of the square.

Floating along with the crowds filing dreamily between carts laden with potatoes, carrots and cabbages, a patchwork of colour that went all the way down Bow Street to Maiden Lane, Tom tried to locate some of the Cockney girls milling around the stalls with their baskets of apples. Craning his neck, he thought he spotted one on the other side of a mass of people. He tried to get to her before she disappeared into the crowd, swerving to pass the human wall blocking his way. But this type of abrupt movement, which might have saved Captain Shackleton's life during a skirmish, was unwise in a packed market like Covent Garden.

He realised this when he walked headlong into a young woman crossing his path. Reeling from the collision, she had to steady herself in order not to end up on the ground. Tom stopped and swung round, with the intention of apologising – and found himself face to face with the only person in London he had never wanted to see again. The world suddenly felt like a magician's hat, which could hold everything.

'Captain Shackleton, what are you doing in my time?' asked Claire Haggerty, bewildered.

Only inches away from her, Tom received the full impact of the devotion his mere presence triggered in her. He could even admire the blue of her eyes, a deep, intense blue he knew he would never find anywhere else in the world, however many oceans or skies he saw – a fierce, pure blue, which had probably been on the Creator's palette when He coloured heaven, and of which her eyes were now the sole custodians. Only when he had broken free of her enchanted gaze did Tom realise that this chance encounter might cost him his life. He glanced around to make sure no one was eyeing them suspiciously, but was too dazed to take in what he saw. He fixed his eyes once more on the girl, who was still staring at him, overwhelmed with disbelief and emotion, waiting for him to explain his presence. But what could he tell her without giving away the truth, which was tantamount to signing his own death warrant?

'I travelled back in time to bring you your parasol,' he blurted out – and bit his lip. It sounded absurd, but it was the first thing that had occurred to him. He watched Claire's eyes widen, and prepared for the worst.

'Oh, thank you, you're so kind,' she replied, scarcely able to disguise her joy. 'But you shouldn't have taken the trouble. As you can see, I have another.' She showed him a parasol almost identical to the one he had hidden in his chest of drawers. 'However, as you've journeyed through time to bring it to me, I'll gladly take it back, and I promise I'll get rid of this one.'

Now it was Tom's turn to conceal his astonishment: she had swallowed his lie completely! Yet wasn't it logical? Murray's pantomime was too convincing for a girl as young as her to question it. Claire believed she had travelled to the year 2000, and her certainty gave him legitimacy as a time traveller. It was that simple. When he had recovered from his surprise, he realised she was staring at his empty hands, wondering perhaps why they were not clasping the parasol that had compelled him to journey across an entire century with the sole aim of returning it to her.

'I don't have it with me,' he apologised foolishly.

She waited expectantly for him to come up with a solution to this, and in the sudden silence that enclosed them amid the hustle and bustle, Tom glimpsed the girl's slim, graceful body beneath her robe, and felt painfully aware of how long it had been since he was with a woman. After burying Megan, he had received only the fake tenderness of whores, and had recently forgone even that, considering himself tough enough to do without bartered caresses. Or so he had thought. Now he had in front of him a beautiful, elegant woman, a woman a fellow such as he could never hope to possess, and yet she was staring at him like no other woman ever had. Would her gaze be the tunnel that led him to storm the impregnable fortress? Men had risked their lives for much less since the beginning of time. And so, responding to the atavistic desire of his species, Tom did what reason least advised: 'But I can give it to you this afternoon,' he ventured, 'if you'd be kind enough to take tea with me at the Aerated Bread Company near Charing Cross Underground station.'

Claire's face lit up. 'Of course, Captain,' she replied, excited. 'I'll be there.'

Tom gave her a smile purged of all lust, and tried hard to mask his shock – at her for accepting his invitation and at himself for having proposed a meeting with the very woman he should flee if he valued his life. Clearly it did not mean that much to him if he was prepared to risk it for a roll in the hay with this vision of loveliness. Just then, someone called Claire's name and they turned as one. A fair-haired girl was making her way towards them through the crowd.

'It's my friend Lucy,' said Claire, with amused irritation. 'She won't let me out of her sight for a second.'

'Please, don't tell her I've come here from the future,' Tom warned quickly, regaining some of his composure, 'I'm travelling incognito. If anyone found out, I'd get into a lot of trouble.'

Claire looked at him a little uneasily.

'I'll be waiting for you in the tea rooms at four o'clock,' Tom said brusquely, taking his leave. 'But, please, promise me you'll come alone.'

As he had thought she would, Claire promised without demur. Owing to his circumstances, Tom had never been to the ABC tea rooms, but he was aware that they had been all the rage since the day they opened. They were the only place two young people could meet without the bothersome presence of a chaperone. He had heard they were airy, pleasant and warm, and offered tea and buns at an affordable price. Thus, they were the perfect alternative to walks in the cold or meetings in family reception rooms, spied upon by the young lady's mother, to which young suitors had hitherto been condemned. True, they would be seen, but Tom could think of no better place to meet her – or not one to which she would have agreed to go unaccompanied.

By the time Lucy reached Claire, Tom had vanished into the throng, but Lucy asked her dazed friend who the stranger was she had seen her talking to. Claire simply shook her head mysteriously. As she expected, Lucy soon forgot the matter, and dragged her to a flower stall where they could stock up with heliotropes, bringing the aroma of distant jungles into their bedrooms.

While Claire Haggerty was letting herself be led by the arm and thinking that travelling through time was the most gentlemanly thing anyone had ever done for her, Tom Blunt left Covent Garden Market by the opposite exit, elbowing his way through the crowd and trying not to think of poor Perkins.

He slumped onto his bed in the hovel as if he had been shot at point-blank range. Lying there, he cursed his foolhardy behaviour out loud, as he had been doing in the garbled manner of a drunkard all the way home. Had he taken leave of his senses? What did he think he was doing, asking the girl to meet him again? Well, the answer was easy enough. What he wanted was obvious, and it did not involve marvelling at Claire's beauty for a couple of hours, tortured by the idea that he would never have her. Not on his life: he was going to take advantage of the girl being in love with his other self, the brave Captain Shackleton, to achieve an even greater goal. And he was amazed that for this fleeting pleasure he was prepared to suffer the consequences that such an irresponsible course of action would bring, including his probable demise. Did he really value his life so little? It was sad but true: possessing that beautiful woman was more meaningful to him than anything that might be waiting for him round the corner in his miserable future.

Thinking about it objectively, he had to admit that the logical thing to do was not to turn up at the meeting, and thereby avoid trouble. But this was no guarantee against him bumping into the girl somewhere else, having to explain what he was still doing in the nineteenth century and even invent some excuse for not having come to the tea room. Failure to appear at the appointed hour was not the answer. The only solution he could think of was to go there and find a way to avoid having to explain himself if they bumped into each other again. Some reason why she must not go near him, or even speak to him, he thought excitedly. All things considered, this meeting might even prove beneficial to him in the long run. Yes, this might be a way of solving the problem once and for all.

It was clear that this must be their first and only encounter. He had no choice: he must indulge his desire for the girl on condition that he succeeded in ruling out any possibility of them ever meeting again, nipping in the bud any relationship that might grow up between them. He could not see how they would conceal it from the multitude of spies Murray had posted all over the city, which would put not only him in danger but her, too. This meeting, then, felt like the last meal of the condemned man, and he resolved to enjoy every minute of it.

When it was time to go, he took the parasol, straightened his cap and left the boarding-house. Down in the street, he gave way to an impulse and stopped in front of Mrs Ritter's stall.

'Good afternoon, Tom,' said the old lady.

'Mrs Ritter,' he replied, stretching out his hand, 'I think the time has come for us both to see my future.'

The old woman glanced up at him in surprise, but at once she gripped Tom's hand and, with a wizened finger, slowly traced the lines on his palm, like someone reading a book.

'My God, Tom!' she gasped, gazing up at him with mournful dismay. 'I see . . . death!'

Grimacing, Tom accepted the terrible prediction with resigned fortitude, and withdrew his hand from the old woman's clasp. His worst fears had been confirmed. Getting under Claire Haggerty's skirts would mean death: that was the reward for lust. He said goodbye to the alarmed Mrs Ritter, who doubtless had assumed fate would be kinder to him, then walked down the street towards the tea room where Claire Haggerty would be waiting for him. Yes, there was no doubt about it: he was going to die, but could he call what he had now a life? He quickened his pace.

He had never felt so alive.

XXVI

When he arrived, Claire was sitting at one of the small tables at the back of the tea room, next to a picture window through which the afternoon light filtered on to her hair. Tom gazed at her with awe from the doorway, savouring the knowledge that it was him who this beautiful young girl was waiting for. Once more, he was struck by her fragile demeanour, which contrasted so delightfully with her lively gestures and fervent gaze, and he felt a pleasant stirring in the barren place where he had thought nothing would ever grow again. At least he was not completely dead inside.

Clutching the parasol in his sweaty palm, he made his way towards her through the tables, determined to do everything in his power to have her in his arms by the end of the afternoon.

'Excuse me, sir,' a young woman on her way out waylaid him, 'might I ask where you acquired those boots?'

Taken aback, Tom followed the woman's eyes to his feet. He almost jumped out of his skin when he saw he was still sporting Captain Shackleton's exotic footwear. He stared at the girl, at a loss for what to say. 'In Paris,' he replied.

The young woman appeared content with his reply. She nodded, as if to say such footwear could only come from the birthplace of fashion. She thanked him for the information with a friendly smile, and left the tea room. Tom shook his head and continued across the room towards Claire, who had not yet noticed him and was gazing dreamily out of the window.

'Good afternoon, Miss Haggerty,' he said.

Claire smiled.

'I believe this is yours,' he said, holding out the parasol as if it were a bunch of roses.

'Oh, thank you, Captain,' she responded, 'but, please, take a seat.'

Tom sat on the empty chair, while Claire assessed the sorry state of her parasol with slight dismay, then relegated it to the side of the table, as though its role in the story were over. Then she studied Tom with the strange yearning in her eyes he had noticed during their first meeting, and which had flattered him even though he knew it was not directed at him but at the character he was playing.

'I must compliment you on your disguise, Captain,' she said. 'It's truly amazing. You could be an East End barrow-boy.'

'Er, thanks.' Tom forced a smile to cover his pique.

What was he so surprised about? Her comment only confirmed what he already knew: if he was able to enjoy her company for an afternoon it was precisely because she believed he was an intrepid hero of the future. And it was thanks to this misunderstanding that he would be able to teach her a lesson, by obtaining from her something that, under other circumstances, she would never have conceded. He disguised the joy the thought gave him by glancing around the room, taking the opportunity to try to spot one of Gilliam Murray's possible spies among the chattering customers. He saw no one who struck him as suspicious.

'I can't be too careful,' he remarked, turning back to face her. 'As I said, I mustn't draw attention to myself, and that would be impossible if I wore my armour. It's why I must also ask you not to call me "Captain".'

'Very well,' said the girl, and then, unable to control her excitement at being privy to a secret no one else knew, added: 'I can't believe you're really Captain Derek Shackleton!'

Startled, Tom begged her to be quiet.

'Oh, forgive me,' she apologised, flushing, 'only I'm so excited. I still can't believe I'm having tea with the saviour of—'

Luckily she broke off when she saw the waitress coming over. They ordered tea for two and an assortment of cakes and buns. When she had left to fetch their order, they stared at each other for a few moments, grinning foolishly. Tom watched her attempt to regain her composure, while he wondered how to steer the conversation on to a more personal footing that would assist him in his plan. He had chosen the tea room because there was an inexpensive but clean-looking boarding-house opposite that had seemed the perfect venue for their union. Now all he needed to do was employ his powers of seduction, if he had any, to get her there. He knew this would be no easy feat: evidently a young lady like Claire, who probably still had her virtue intact, would not agree to go to bed with a man she had only just met, even if she did think he was Capitan Shackleton.

'How did you get here?' asked Claire, oblivious to his machinations. 'Did you stow away on the Cronotilus?'

Tom had to stifle his annoyance at her question: the last thing he wanted was to justify his earlier fabrication while he was attempting to spin a credible yarn that would enable him to have his way with her. However, he could scarcely tell her he had travelled back in time to return her parasol and expect her to accept it, as though it were the most natural thing in the world for people to run back and forth between centuries on unimportant errands. The sudden appearance of the waitress with their order gave him time to think up an answer that would satisfy Claire.

'The Cronotilus?' he asked, pretending he knew nothing of the time-tram's existence: if he had used it to travel back to this century he would have had no choice but to stay there until the next expedition to the year 2000. That was almost a month away, which meant this meeting need not be their last.

'It's the steam tram in which we travelled to your century across that dreadful place called the fourth dimension,' Claire explained. Then she paused. 'But if you didn't come on the Cronotilus then how *did* you get here? Is there some other means of time travel?'

'Of course there is,' Tom assured her, assuming that if the girl was taken in by Murray's hoax – if she believed time travel was possible – then the chances were that he could make up any method he liked and she would believe it. 'Our scientists have invented a machine that travels through time instantly, without the need for tiresome journeys through the fourth dimension.'

'And can this machine travel to any era?' she demanded, mesmerised.

'Any time at all,' replied Tom, carelessly, as though he had had enough of travelling across the centuries.

He reached for a bun and munched it cheerfully, as if to show her that, despite all he had seen, he could still enjoy the simplest pleasures of life, such as English baking.

Claire asked: 'Do you have it with you? Can you show it me?'

'Show you what?'

'The time machine you used to travel here.'

Tom almost choked on his bun. 'No, no,' he said hastily. 'That's out of the question.'

She responded in a manner that took Tom by surprise, pouting rather childishly and folding her arms stiffly.

'I can't show it to you because . . . it's not something you can see,' he improvised, trying to mollify her anger before it set in.

'You mean it's invisible?' She looked at him suspiciously.

'I mean it's not a carriage with wings that flies through time,' he explained.

'What is it, then?'

Tom stifled a sigh of despair. What was it, indeed, and why could he not show it to her?'

'It's an object that doesn't move physically through the time continuum. It's fixed in the future and from there it . . . well, it makes holes we can travel through to other eras. Like a drill, only instead of making holes in rocks, it digs tunnels through the fabric of time. That's why I can't show it to you, although I'd like nothing better.'

For a few moments she was silent, clearly intrigued. Then she murmured, 'A machine that makes holes in the fabric of time. And you went through one of those tunnels and came out today?'

'That's right,' replied Tom.

'And how will you get back to the future?'

'Through the same hole.'

'Are you telling me that, at this very moment, somewhere in London, there's a tunnel leading to the year 2000?'

Tom took a sip of tea. He was beginning to tire of this conversation. 'Opening it in the city would have been too obvious, as I'm sure you understand,' he said cautiously. 'The tunnel always opens outside London, at Harrow-on-the-Hill, a tiny knoll with an old oak surrounded by headstones. But the machine can't keep it open for very long. It will close in a few hours' time, and I have to go back through it before that happens.'

With these words, he gazed at her solemnly, hoping she would stop plying him with questions if she knew they had so little time together.

'You may think me reckless for asking, Captain,' he heard her say, after a few moments' reflection, 'but would you take me back with you to the year 2000?'

'I'm afraid that's impossible, Miss Haggerty.' Tom sighed.

'Why not? I promise I—'

'Because I can't go ferrying people back and forth through time.'

'But what's the point of inventing a time machine if you don't use it for—'

'Because it was invented for a specific purpose!' Tom cut across her, exasperated by her stubbornness. Was she really that interested in time travel?

He instantly regretted his abruptness, but the harm was done. She looked at him, shocked by his irate tone. 'And what purpose might that be, if you don't mind me asking?' she retorted, echoing his angry voice.

Tom sat back in his seat and watched her struggling to suppress her mounting fury. There was no point in carrying on with this. The way the conversation was going, he would never be able to coax her to the boarding-house. In fact, he would be lucky if she didn't walk out on him there and then, tired of his filibustering. What had he expected? He was no Gilliam Murray. He was a miserable wretch with no imagination. He was out of his depth in the role of time traveller. He might as well give up, forget the whole thing, take his leave of the girl graciously while he still could and go back to his life as a nobody – unless, of course, Murray's thugs had other ideas.

'Miss Haggerty,' he began, resolved to end the meeting politely on some pretext, but just then she placed her hand on his.

Taken aback, Tom forgot what he had been about to say. He gazed at her slender hand resting on his among the crockery, like a sculpture whose meaning he was unable to fathom. When he raised his eyes, he found her gazing at him with infinite sweetness.

'Forgive my awkward questions, which no doubt you are not allowed to answer.' She leaned delightfully towards him across the table. 'It was a very rude way of thanking you for bringing back my parasol. In any case, you needn't tell me what the machine is for, as I already know.'

'You do?' said Tom, flabbergasted.

'Yes,' she assured him, with an enchantingly conceited grin.

'And are you going to tell me?'

Claire looked first to one side, then to the other. 'It's for assassinating Mr Ferguson.'

Tom raised his eyebrows. Mr Ferguson? Who the devil was Mr Ferguson, and why did he have to be assassinated?

'Don't try to pretend, Captain.' Claire chuckled. 'There really is no need. Not with me.'

Tom laughed heartily with her, letting out a few loud guffaws to release the tension accumulated during her interrogation. He had no idea who Mr Ferguson was, but he sensed that his best bet was to pretend he knew everything about the man down to his shoe size and the type of shaving lotion he used, and pray she would not ask anything about him. 'I can't hide anything from you, Miss Haggerty,' he said. 'You're far too intelligent.'

Claire's face glowed with pleasure. 'Thank you, Captain. But it really wasn't difficult to guess that your scientists invented the machine to travel back to this point in time in order to assassinate the inventor of the automatons before he could create them, thus preventing the destruction of London and the death of so many people.'

Was it really possible to travel back in time to change events? Tom wondered. 'You're quite right, Miss Haggerty. I was sent to kill Ferguson and save the world from destruction.'

The girl thought about this, then said: 'Only you didn't succeed, because we witnessed the war of the future with our own eyes.'

'Right again,' Tom acknowledged.

'Your mission was a failure,' she whispered, with a hint of dismay. Then she fixed her eyes on him, and murmured: 'But why? Because the tunnels don't stay open long enough?'

Tom spread his arms, pretending to be awed by her astuteness. 'Yes,' he confessed, and with a sudden flash of inspiration, he added: 'I made several exploratory journeys to try to find Ferguson, but I failed. There wasn't enough time. That's why you might bump into me again in the future, only if you do you mustn't come up to me because I won't know you yet.'

She blinked, trying to grasp his meaning. 'I understand,' she said finally. 'You made those journeys prior to this one and arrived here days afterwards.'

'Exactly!' he exclaimed, and encouraged by how much sense this gibberish was apparently making to her, he added: 'Although from your point of view this would seem to be my first visit, it isn't. I've made at least half a dozen other forays into your time before this one. What's more, this journey, which for you is my first, is also my last, because use of the machine has been prohibited.'

'Prohibited?' asked Claire, her fascination growing.

Tom cleared his throat with a gulp of tea, and, emboldened by the effect his words were having on her, went on: 'Yes, indeed. The machine was built halfway through the war, but when the mission failed, the inventors forgot their Utopian idea of preventing the war before it broke out and concentrated their efforts instead on trying to win it. They invented weapons that could cut through the automatons' reinforced armour.' Claire Haggerty nodded, probably recalling the soldiers' impressive guns. 'The machine was left to rot, though it was placed under guard to prevent anyone travelling illegally into the past and tampering with anything. Still, I was able to use it secretly, but I only managed to open the tunnel for ten hours, and I have three left before it closes. That's all the time I have. After that I have to go back to my own world. If I stay here, hero or no, they'll find me and execute me for travelling illegally in time. That means, in three hours from now, I'll be gone for ever.'

With these words, he pressed her hand tenderly, while inwardly applauding his own performance. To his amazement, not only had he solved the problem of chance meetings in the future but had managed to tell her they had a short time together before they must say goodbye for ever. Only three hours. No more.

'You risked your life to bring me my parasol,' she said slowly, as though she had suddenly understood the real dangers Tom had braved.

'Well, the parasol was only an excuse,' he replied, gazing passionately into her eyes. The moment had come. It was now or never. 'I risked my life to see you again because I love you, Claire,' he lied, in the softest voice he could muster.

He had said it. Now she must say the same thing to him. Now she must confess she loved him, too – that she loved the brave Captain Shackleton.

'How can you love me? You don't even know me,' she teased, smiling sweetly.

That was not the response Tom had been hoping for. He disguised his dismay with another gulp of tea. Did she not realise they had no time for anything except giving themselves to one another? He only had three hours! Had he not been clear enough? He replaced the cup in its saucer and glanced out of the window at the boarding-house opposite, its beds waiting with their clean sheets, ever further out of reach. The girl was right: he did not know her, and she did not know him. And as long as they remained strangers there was no possibility of them ever becoming lovers. He was fighting a losing battle . . .

But what if they did know each other? Did he not come from the future? What was there to stop him claiming that, from his point of view, they already knew each other? Between this meeting and their encounter in the year 2000, he could make up any number of events it would be impossible for her to refute, he told himself. He had discovered the perfect strategy for leading her to the boarding-house, meek as a lamb.

'This time you're wrong, Claire. I know you far better than you think,' he confessed, clasping her hand in both of his. 'I know who you are, your dreams, your desires, the way you see the world. I know everything about you and you know everything about me. And I love you, Claire. I fell in love with you in a time that doesn't exist yet.'

She was astonished. 'But if we're never to meet again,' she mused, 'how will we get to know each other? How will you fall in love with me?'

Tom realised he had fallen into his own trap. He stifled a curse and, playing for time, gazed at the street outside. What could he say now? He watched the carriages go by, indifferent to his distress, making their way among the vendors' barrows. Then his eye fell on the red pillar box on the corner, solid and steadfast, sporting the insignia VR on the front.

'I fell in love with you through your letters,' he blurted out.

'What letters? What are you talking about?' exclaimed Claire, startled.

'The love letters we've been sending one another all these years.'

She stared at him, aghast. And Tom understood that what he said next had to be credible, for it would determine whether she surrendered to him or slapped his face. He closed his eyes and smiled faintly, pretending he was evoking some memory, while he tried desperately to think.

'It happened during my first exploratory journey to your time,' he said. 'I came out on the hill I told you about. From there I walked to London, where I was able to verify that the machine was reliable when it came to opening the hole at the specified date: I had travelled from the year 2000 to the eighth of November 1896.'

'The eighth of November?'

'Yes – that is to say, the day after tomorrow,' Tom confirmed. 'That was my first trip into your century. But I scarcely had time to do anything else, because I had to get back to the hill before the hole closed. I hurried as fast as I could, and I was about to enter the tunnel when I saw something I hadn't noticed before.'

'What?' she asked, burning with curiosity.

'Under a stone next to the grave marked John Peachey, I found a letter. I picked it up and discovered to my amazement that it was addressed to me. I stuffed it into the pocket of my disguise, and opened it in the year 2000. It was a letter from a woman I'd never met, living in the nineteenth century.' Tom paused for dramatic effect. 'Her name was Claire Haggerty and she said she loved me.'

Claire gasped. Tom watched, a tender smile on his face, as she attempted to digest what she had heard, struggling to understand that she was responsible for their situation, or would be responsible for it in the future. For if he loved her now it was because she had loved him in the past. She stared into her cup, as though she were able to see him in the tea leaves in the year 2000, reading with bewilderment the letter in which a strange woman from another century, a woman who was already dead, declared her undying love for him. A letter she had written.

Tom persisted, like a lumberjack who sees the tree he has been hacking begin to teeter and swings his axe harder: 'In your letter, you told me we would meet in the future – or, more precisely, I would meet you because you had already met me,' he said. 'You implored me to write back, insisting you needed to hear from me. Although it seemed very strange to me, I replied to your letter, and on my next visit to the nineteenth century, two days later, I left it beside the same tombstone. On my third visit I found your reply, and that was how our correspondence through time began.'

'Good God,' the girl gasped.

'I had no idea who you were,' Tom continued, not wanting to give her any respite, 'but I fell in love with you all the same, with the woman who wrote those letters. I imagined your face when I closed my eyes. I whispered your name in my sleep, amid the ruins of my devastated world.'

Claire fidgeted in her seat. 'How many letters did we write to each other?' she managed to ask.

'Seven, in all,' Tom replied randomly, because it sounded a good number: not too many and not too few. 'We hadn't time to write more before they prohibited the use of the machine, but it was enough, my love.'

Upon hearing the captain utter those words, Claire heaved a sigh.

'In your last letter, you named the day we would finally meet. The twentieth of May in the year 2000, the day I defeated Solomon and ended the war. That day I did as you instructed in your letter, and after the duel I looked for a secluded spot among the ruins. Then I saw you and, as you had described, you dropped the parasol, which I was to return to you using the time machine. Once I reached your era I was to go to Covent Garden market, where we would meet, and then I was supposed to invite you to tea and tell you everything,' Tom added wistfully: 'And now I understand why. It was so these events would take place in the future. Do you see, Claire? You will write those letters to me in the future because I am telling you now that you will.'

'Good God,' she repeated, almost out of breath.

'But there's something else you need to know,' announced Tom, determined to fell the tree with one final blow. 'In one of your letters you spoke of how we would love one another this afternoon.'

'*What?*'

'Yes, Claire, this afternoon we will love one another in the boarding-house over the road, and in your own words it will be the most magical experience of your life.'

Claire's cheeks flushed bright pink.

'I can understand why you're surprised, but imagine how I felt. I was astonished when I read the letter in which you described our lovemaking, because for you it was something we'd already done, but as far as I was concerned it hadn't happened.' Tom smiled sweetly. 'I've come from the future to fulfil my destiny, Claire, which is to love you.'

'But, I—' she tried to protest.

'You still don't understand, do you? We've got to make love, Claire,' said Tom, 'because in reality we already have.'

It was the final axe blow. And, like the oak, Claire teetered on her chair and crashed to the floor.

XXVII

If she had wanted draw everyone's attention, thought Tom, she couldn't have found a better way to do so. Claire's sudden fainting fit, and the din of the shattering china, dragged with the tablecloth on to the floor, had brought to an abrupt standstill the conversations in the tea room, plunging it into stunned silence. From the back of the room, where he had been relegated during the ensuing commotion, Tom watched the bevy of ladies rallying round the girl. Like a rescue team with years of practice, they stretched her out on a couch, placed a pile of cushions under her feet, loosened her corset (that diabolical item of clothing entirely to blame for her fainting fit – it had prevented her breathing in the amount of air necessary for such a charged conversation) and went to fetch smelling salts to bring her round.

Tom watched her come to with a loud gasp. The female staff and customers had formed a sort of matriarchal screen around her to prevent the gentlemen in the room from glimpsing more of her flesh than was seemly. A few minutes later he saw Claire stumble through the human wall, pale as a ghost, and peer confusedly around her. He waved at her awkwardly with the parasol. After a few moments' hesitation, she staggered towards him through the onlookers. At least she seemed to recognise him as the person with whom she had been taking tea before she had passed out.

'Are you all right, Miss Haggerty?' he asked, when she reached him. 'Perhaps a little fresh air would do you good . . .'

She nodded and settled her hand on Tom's arm, like a tame falcon landing on its owner's glove, as though going outside to get some air and escape from all those prying eyes was the best idea he had ever had. Tom led her out, spluttering an apology for having upset her. Once outside, they paused on the pavement, unable to stop themselves glancing up at the boarding-house looming across the road. With a mixture of unease and resignation, Claire, whose cheeks had recovered some of their colour, peered at the place where that afternoon she was fated to give herself to the brave Captain Shackleton, the saviour of the human race, a man not yet born, who was standing next to her, trying to avoid her eyes.

'And what if I refuse, Captain?' She spoke as though addressing the air. 'What if I don't go up there with you?'

It would be fair to say that the question took Tom by surprise for, in view of the disastrous conclusion to their meeting, he had given up all hope of accomplishing his wicked aim. However, despite her impressive fainting fit, the girl had forgotten nothing of what he had told her, and was clearly still convinced by his story. Tom had improvised on the blank page of the future a chance encounter, a romance that would explain what was going to happen, and even encourage the girl to yield to it without fear or regret, and to her, this was the only possible outcome. A momentary pang of remorse made him consider the possibility of helping her out of her predicament, which she seemed ready to face as though it were an act of contrition. He could tell her the future was not written in stone, that she could choose. But he had invested too much energy in the venture to abandon his prey now she was almost within reach. He remembered one of Gilliam Murray's pet phrases, and repeated it in a suitably doom-laden voice: 'I've no idea what effect it would have on the fabric of time.'

Claire looked at him rather uneasily as he shrugged his shoulders, absolving himself of responsibility. After all, she could not blame him for anything: he was there because she had asked him to come in her letters. He had travelled through time to perform an act she had told him they had already performed – and with a wealth of detail. He had journeyed across time to set their romance in motion, to trigger off what had already happened but had not yet taken place. She seemed to have reached the same conclusion: what choice did she have – to walk away and carry on with her life, marry one of her admirers? This was her opportunity to experience something she had always dreamed of: a great love that spanned the centuries. Not seizing it would be like having deceived herself all her life.

'The most magical experience of my life.' She smiled. 'Did I really write that?'

'Yes,' replied Tom, emphatically. 'Those were your exact words.'

Claire hesitated. She could not go to bed with a stranger just like that. Except that this was a unique case: she had to give herself to him or the universe would suffer the consequences. She must sacrifice herself to protect the world. But was it really a sacrifice? Did she not love him? Was the flurry of emotions that overwhelmed her whenever she looked at him not love? It had to be. The feeling that made her light up inside and go weak at the knees had to be love, because if that was not, then what was it? Captain Shackleton had told her they would make love that afternoon and then she would write him beautiful letters. Why resist if that was what she really wanted? Ought she to refuse because she was retracing the steps of another Claire, who was, after all, herself? Ought she to refuse because it felt more like an obligation than a genuine desire, a spontaneous gesture? Try as she might, she could find no good reason for not doing what she longed to do with all her heart. Neither Lucy nor any of her other friends would approve of her going to bed with a stranger.

In the end, that was what decided the matter for her. Yes, she would go to bed with him, and she would spend the rest of her life pining for him, writing him long, beautiful letters soaked with her perfume and her tears. She knew she was both passionate and stubborn enough to keep alive the flame of her love, even though she would never again see the person who had set it ablaze. It was her fate, apparently. An exceptional fate, not without a hint of tragedy – far more pleasant to bear than the dreary marriage she might enter into with one of her dull suitors. She set her lips in a determined line.

'I hope you aren't exaggerating to avoid a blow to your pride, Captain,' she joked.

'I'm afraid there's only one way to find out,' Tom parried.

Her determination to deal with the situation in such a good-natured way was a huge relief to him: he no longer felt so bad about having his way with her. He was preparing to enjoy her body by means of a despicable ploy before vanishing from her life for ever. But although he considered the conceited young woman was only getting what she deserved, his own underhand behaviour made him feel surprisingly uneasy. He deduced from his sense of disquiet that he still had some scruples, after all. However, he felt decidedly less guilty now that the girl also seemed set on deriving unequivocal enjoyment from offering her body to Captain Shackleton, the courageous hero who had whispered her name amid the ruins of the future.

Compared to some of the places Tom was used to sleeping in, the boarding-house was clean, even cosy. The girl might think it unfit for someone of her social class, but there was nothing to make her flee in horror. While he was asking about a room, he watched her out of the corner of his eye as she casually surveyed the pictures that decorated the modest hallway. He admired the way she tried to appear blasé, as though spending her afternoons in bed with men from the future in London boarding-houses was second nature to her.

They climbed the stairs leading to the first floor and went along the narrow corridor. As he watched her walking in front of him, with a mixture of boldness and submission, Tom became aware for the first time of what was about to happen. There was no turning back: he was going to make love to this girl. He was going to hold her naked, eager, even passionate body in his arms. He suddenly burned with lust that sent a shudder from his head to his toes. He tried to contain his excitement as they paused before the door.

All at once Claire tensed. 'I know it will be wonderful,' she said, half closing her eyes as if to bolster her courage.

'It will,' Tom echoed, trying to conceal his eagerness to undress her. 'You told me so yourself.'

She gave a sigh of resignation. Without further ado, Tom pushed open the door and gestured politely for her to go in, then closed it behind them.

When they had vanished inside, the narrow corridor was once more deserted. The last rays of the evening sun filtered through the grimy window at the far end. It was a fading light with coppery tones, a soft, pale, almost melancholy glow that shone on the floating dust particles turning them into tiny glittering insects. Although, given the leisurely, hypnotic way they swirled at random, a spray of pollen might be a more suitable metaphor, do you not agree?

From behind a few of the closed doors came the unmistakable sounds of amorous engagement: grunts, stifled cries, and even the occasional hearty slap of a hand on a tender buttock – noises that added to the rhythmical creaking of bed frames, suggested that the lovemaking going on there was not of a conjugal nature. Mingled with a few of the guests' carnal exploits, other sounds of a less lustful nature, like snippets of conversation or a child crying, gave the finishing touches to the chaotic symphony of the world.

The corridor in the boarding-house was some thirty yards long and decorated with prints of misty landscapes; several oil lamps were attached to the walls. As was his custom, the landlord, Mr Pickard (I feel it would be churlish not to introduce him by name even though he will not be appearing again in this tale), was at that very moment preparing to light the lamps, in order not to leave it in darkness, which might have led to all sorts of mishaps when his guests later left the establishment.

Those were his footsteps echoing on the stairs. Each night he found them more difficult to climb, for the years had taken their toll, and recently he could not help giving a triumphant sigh when he reached the top. Mr Pickard took the box of matches out of his trouser pocket and began lighting the half-dozen lamps. He did so very slowly, slipping the match under each shade, like a skilled swordsman performing a final thrust, and holding it there until the oil-soaked wick caught light. Time had transformed this gesture into an almost mechanical ceremony. None of the guests would have been able to tell what he was thinking as he performed his daily lamp-lighting ritual, but I am not one of the guests and, as with all the other characters in this novel, his innermost thoughts are not off limits to me.

Mr Pickard was thinking about his little granddaughter Wendy, who had died of scarlet fever more than ten years earlier: he could not help comparing the lighting of the lamps with the manner in which the Creator behaved towards all His creatures, allowing them to burn, then snuffing them out when He felt like it, without any explanation or consideration for those He left plunged into darkness. When Mr Pickard had lit the last lamp, he walked back down the corridor and descended the stairs, exiting this tale as discreetly as he had entered it.

After he had gone, the corridor was once more deserted, although brightly lit. You are probably hoping I will not describe it to you again, but I am afraid I will, as I have no intention of crossing the threshold into the room Tom and Claire are in and rudely intruding on their privacy. Take pleasure in the flickering shadows on the flowery wallpaper, and play at seeing bunnies, bears and puppies in their shifting shapes as evening turns to night, as – oblivious of man's concerns – minutes turn inexorably into hours, like a snowball rolling down a hill.

I will not ask how many little animal shapes you managed to see before the door to the room finally opened and Tom stepped out. A smile of satisfaction playing on his lips, he tucked his shirt into his trousers and pulled on his cap. Gently extricating himself from Claire's embrace, he had told her he must go before the hole in time closed. She had kissed him with the solemnity of one who knows she is kissing the man she loves for the very last time, and with her kiss still imprinted on his lips, Tom Blunt descended the stairs, wondering how it was possible to feel like the happiest man in the world and at the same time the most despicable creature in the universe.

XXVIII

Two days had gone by since their meeting and, to his surprise, Tom was still alive. No one had shot him in the head as he sat up with a start in his bed, or followed him through the streets waiting to thrust a thirsty blade into his side, or tried to run him down in a carriage or push him in front of a train. Tom could only presume that this agonising calm, this excruciating slowness in finishing him off, was either their way of tormenting him or that no one was going to make him pay for what he had done. More than once, unable to bear the strain, he had been on the point of ending it all himself, slitting his throat or throwing himself off a bridge into the Thames, in the family tradition. Either method seemed a good way of escaping from the apprehension that had even infiltrated his dreams, transforming them into nightmares in which Solomon roamed the streets of London with his metal-insect gait, making his way through the crowds thronging the pavements, and clambering with difficulty up the stairs to his room.

Tom awoke when the automaton broke down his door and, for a few bewildered moments, believed he really was the brave Captain Shackleton, who had escaped from the year 2000 and was hiding in 1896. He was powerless to dispel those dreams, but if at night he was at the mercy of his fears, in daytime he was able to overcome them; by keeping a level head, he had managed to compose himself and was even prepared to accept his fate with calm resignation. He would not take his own life. It was far more dignified to die looking his killers straight in the eye, whether they were made of flesh and blood or of cast iron.

Convinced he had not long to live, Tom saw no point in going to the docks to look for work: he could just as well die with empty pockets. He spent his days wandering aimlessly around London, like a leaf blown by the wind. Occasionally he would stretch out in some park, like a drunk or a vagrant, while in his mind he went over every detail of his encounter with the girl, her ardent caresses, her intoxicating kisses, the passion and ease with which she had given herself to him. He told himself again that it had all been worth it, and that he had no intention of putting up any resistance when they came to make him pay for those moments of happiness. Part of him could not help considering the bullet that was so long in coming as just punishment for his despicable behaviour.

On the third day, his wanderings took him to Harrow-on-the-Hill, the place he usually went to in search of peace. He could think of no better place to wait for his killers, as he tried to understand the random sequence of events that made up his life, to try to give it some meaning. There, he sat in the shade of the old oak and breathed in deeply as he cast a dispassionate eye over the city. Seen from the hill, the capital of empire always looked disappointing to him, like a sinister barge with pointed spires and smoking factory chimneys for masts. He exhaled slowly, trying to forget how famished he was. He hoped they would come for him today, or he would have to steal some food before nightfall to stop his stomach rumbling.

Where were Murray's thugs? he wondered, for the hundredth time. If they came now he would see them from his vantage-point, greet them with his most dazzling smile, unbutton his shirt and point to his heart to make it easier for them. 'Go ahead and kill me,' he would say. 'Don't worry, I won't really kill you later. I'm no hero. I'm just Tom, the despicable wretch Tom Blunt. You can bury me here, next to my friend John Peachey, another wretch like me.'

It was at this point that, looking towards the headstone, he noticed the letter tucked under a stone beside it. For a moment he thought he was imagining things. Intrigued, he picked it up and, with an odd sensation of remembering a dream, he saw it was addressed to Captain Derek Shackleton. He hesitated for a moment, not knowing what to do – but, of course, there was only one thing he could do. As he opened the envelope he could not help feeling he was trespassing, reading someone else's correspondence.

He unfolded the sheet of paper inside and discovered Claire Haggerty's neat, elegant handwriting. He began to read slowly, straining to recall the meaning of each letter, declaiming aloud, as though he wanted to explain to the squirrels the travails of men.

From Claire Haggerty to Captain Shackleton

Dear Derek,
I was obliged to start writing this letter at least a dozen times before realising there was only one possible way to begin, and that is to avoid all preliminary explanations and obey the dictates of my heart: I love you, Derek. I love you as I have never loved anyone. I love you now and I will love you for ever. And my love for you is the only thing that keeps me alive.

I can see the surprise on your face as you read these words written to you by an unknown woman, because I assure you I know that face well. But believe me, my sweet: I love you. Or, rather, we love each other. For, although it might seem even stranger to you, as you do not know who I am, you love me too – or you will do in a few hours, or possibly a few moments, from now. However reluctant you are, however incredible all this seems, you will love me. You simply have no choice. You will love me because you already do.

If I allow myself to address you so affectionately it is because of what we have already shared, and because you must know that I can still feel the warmth of your touch on my skin, the taste of you on my lips. I can feel you inside me. Despite my initial doubts, despite my young girl's foolish fears, I am overwhelmed by the love you foresaw, or maybe it is an even greater love than that, a love so great nothing will contain it.

Shake your head as much as you like as you try to understand these ravings, but the explanation is quite simple. It boils down to this: what has not yet happened to you has already happened to me. It is one of the strange anomalies that occur in time travel, when journeying back and forth across the centuries. But you know all about that, don't you? For, if I am not mistaken, you found this letter next to the big oak tree when you stepped out of a time tunnel, so you will not find it so difficult to believe everything I am telling you.

Yes, I know the place where you come out and your reason for travelling to my time, and my knowing this can mean only one thing: that what I am saying is true, it is not a hoax. Trust me, then, without reservation. And trust me above all when I tell you we love each other. Start loving me now by replying to this letter and reciprocating my feelings, please.

Write me a letter and leave it beside John Peachey's headstone on your next visit: that will be our way of communicating from now on, my love, for we still have six more letters to write to each other. Are your eyes wide with surprise? I do not blame you, and yet I am only repeating what you told me yesterday. Please write to me, my love, for your letters are all I have left of you.

Yes, that is the bad news: I will never see you again, Derek, which is why I cherish your letters. I shall go directly to the point: the love we are going to profess to one another is the result of a single encounter, for we shall meet only once. Well, twice actually, but the first time (or the last time if we follow the chronology our love has turned on its head) will last only a few minutes. Our second meeting, in my time, will last longer and be more meaningful, for it will feed the love that will rage in our hearts for ever, a love our letters will keep alive for me and will initiate for you. And yet, if we respect time, I will never see you again. You, on the other hand, do not yet know me, even though we made love together less than a few hours ago.

Now I understand your nervousness yesterday when we met at the tea room: I had already stirred you with my words.

We will meet on 20 May in the year 2000, but I will tell you all about that first meeting in my last letter. Everything will begin with that meeting, although, now I think about it, I realise that cannot be true because you will already know me through my letters. Where does our love story begin, then? Here, with this letter? No, this is not the beginning either. We are trapped in a circle, Derek, and no one knows where a circle begins. We can only follow the circle until it closes, as I am doing now, trying to stop my hand trembling. This is my role, the only thing I have to do, because I already know what you will do: I know you will reply to my letter, I know you will fall in love with me, I know you will look for me when the time comes. Only the details will come as a surprise to me.

I suppose I should end this letter by telling you what I look like, my way of thinking and seeing the world, as during our meeting in the tea room when I asked you how you could possibly love me without knowing me, and you assured me you knew me better than I could ever imagine. And you knew me, of course, through my letters, so let us begin. I was born on 15 March 1875 in West London. I am slim, of medium height, I have blue eyes and black shoulder-length hair, which, contrary to the norm, I wear loose.

Forgive my brevity, but describing myself physically feels like an undignified exercise in vanity. Besides, I would rather tell you more about my inner soul. I have two older sisters, Rebecca and Evelyn. They are both married and live in Chelsea, and it is by comparing myself to them that I can best give you an idea of what I am like. I have always felt different. Unlike them, I have found it impossible to adapt to the time I live in. I do not know how to explain this to you, Derek, but my time bores me. I feel as though I am watching a comedy at the theatre and everybody else is laughing. Only I am impervious to the supposed hilarity of the characters' remarks. And this dissatisfaction has turned me into a problem child, someone it is best not to invite to parties, and who must be kept an eye on during family get-togethers, for I have ruined more than one by breaking the norms that dictate the behaviour of the society I live in, to the astonishment of the guests.

Something else that makes me feel very different from the other young women I know is my lack of interest in getting married. I loathe the role women are supposed to fulfil in marriage, and for which my mother tries so hard to groom me. I can think of no better way to destroy my free spirit than to become a sensible housewife who spends her days drilling the moral values she has learned into her children and ordering servants around, while her husband goes out into the world of work, that dangerous arena from which women, universally deemed too sensitive and delicate, have been quietly banished.

As you can see, I am independent and adventurous and, although this might strike you as incongruous, I do not fall easily in love. To be honest, I never thought I would be able to fall in love with anyone the way I have fallen in love with you. I had honestly begun to feel like a dusty bottle in a wine cellar waiting to be uncorked at a special occasion that never arrived. And yet I suppose it is owing to my very nature that this is happening.

I will come here to fetch your letter the day after tomorrow, my love, just as you told me I would. I am longing to hear from you, to read your words of love, to know you are mine even though we are separated by an ocean of time.

Yours ever more,

C

Despite the effort involved in reading, Tom re-read Claire's letter three times, with the exact look of surprise the girl had predicted, though for quite different reasons, of course. After the third reading, he replaced it carefully in the envelope and leaned back against the tree, trying to understand the contradictory feelings the pages stirred in him. The girl had swallowed every word, and had come all that way to leave him a letter! He realised that while for him it was all over, for her it was just beginning.

He saw now how far his adventure had gone. He had played

with the girl without stopping to think of the consequences, and now he 'knew' what they were. Yes, this letter unintentionally revealed to him the effect his misbehaviour had had on his victim, and he would rather not have known. Not only had Claire believed his cock-and-bull story to the point of obediently following the next step in the sequence of events, but their physical encounter had been the breath of life her nascent love had needed to catch fire, apparently taking on the proportions of an inferno. And now the blaze was consuming her. Tom marvelled not only that one brief encounter could produce so much love but that the girl was prepared to devote her life to keeping it alive, like someone stoking a fire in the forest to keep wolves at bay. What amazed him most of all, though, was that Claire was doing this for him because she loved him. No one had ever expressed such love for him before, he thought uneasily, and it no longer mattered that it was directed towards Captain Shackleton: the man who had bedded her, undressed her tenderly, taken her gently was Tom Blunt. Shackleton was a mere act, an idea, but Claire had fallen in love with Tom's way of acting him.

And how did that make him feel? he asked himself. Should being loved so unreservedly and passionately produce the same feelings in him, just as his reflection appeared when he leaned over a pond? He was unable to answer that question. And, besides, there was little point in speculating about it – he would probably be dead by the end of the day.

He glanced again at the letter he was holding. What was he supposed to do with it? Suddenly he realised there was only one thing he could do: he must reply to it, not because he intended to take on the role of star-crossed lover in the story he had unthinkingly set in motion, but because the girl had insinuated she would be unable to live without his letters. Tom imagined her travelling there in her carriage, walking to the top of the little hill and finding no reply from Captain Shackleton. He was convinced Claire would be unable to cope with this sudden twist in the plot, his unexpected, mysterious silence. After weeks of going to Harrow and leaving empty-handed, he could imagine her taking her own life in the same passionate way she had decided to love him, perhaps by plunging a sharp dagger through her heart, or downing a flask of laudanum.

Tom could not let that happen. Whether he liked it or not, as a result of his little game Claire Haggerty's life was in his hands. He had no choice.

As he walked back to London across country, keeping away from the roads, tensing at the slightest sound, he realised something had changed: he no longer wanted to die. And not because his life seemed more worth living than before but because he had to reply to the girl's letter. He had to keep himself alive in order to keep Claire alive.

Once in the city, he stole some writing paper from a stationer's shop and, satisfied that Gilliam Murray's thugs had not followed him nor were posted round his lodgings, he locked himself into his room in Buckeridge Street. Everything seemed quiet. The usual afternoon noises wafted up to his window, a harmonious melody in which no discordant notes were struck. He pushed the chair up to the bed to make an improvised desk, and spread the paper out on the seat, with the pen and ink he had also purloined. He took a deep breath.

After half an hour of grappling with the page, deeply frustrated, he had discovered that writing was not as easy as he had imagined. It was far more arduous than reading. He was appalled to find it was impossible for him to transfer to paper the thoughts in his head. He knew what he wanted to say, but each time he started a sentence his original idea seemed to drift away and become something entirely different. He still remembered the rudiments of writing that Megan had taught him, but he did not know enough grammar to be able to form proper sentences and, more importantly, he did not know how to express his ideas with the clarity Claire had.

He gazed down at the indecipherable jumble of letters and

crossings-out that defiled the pristine page. The only legible words were 'Dear Claire', with which he had so optimistically begun his missive. The rest was a pitiful demonstration of a semi-illiterate man's first attempt at writing a letter. He screwed up the sheet of paper, bowing to the inevitable. If Claire received a letter like this she would take her own life anyway, incapable of understanding why the saviour of mankind wrote like a chimpanzee. He wanted to reply, yet was unable to. But Claire had to find a letter at the foot of the oak tree in two days' time or . . .

Tom lay back on the bed, trying to gather his thoughts. Clearly he needed help. He needed someone to write the letter for him – but who? He did not know anyone who could write. And it couldn't be just anyone – for example, a schoolteacher whose fingers he would threaten to break if he refused. The chosen person not only had to be able to write properly, he had to have enough imagination to play a spirited part in the charade. On top of that, he needed to be capable of corresponding with the girl in the same passionate tone. Who could he find who possessed all those qualities?

It came to him in a flash. He leaped to his feet, thrust aside the chair and pulled open the bottom drawer of his chest. There it was, like a fish gasping out of water: the novel. He had purchased it when he first started working for Murray, because his boss had told him it was thanks to this book that his business had been such a success. And Tom, who had never owned a book in his life, had gone out and bought it straight away. Actually reading it, however, had been too exacting a task for him, and he had given up after the third page, yet he had held on to it, not wanting to resell it because in some sense he owed who he was now to that author.

He opened the book and studied the photograph of the writer on the inside flap. The caption below said he lived in Woking, Surrey. Yes, if anyone could help him it had to be the fellow in the photograph, a young man with bird-like features named H. G. Wells.

* * *

With no money to hire a carriage and reluctant to risk hiding on a train bound for Surrey, Tom concluded that the only way for him to reach the author's house was on foot. The three-hour coach ride to Woking would take him three times as long on foot, so if he left straight away he would reach his destination in the early hours of the morning. Obviously this was not the best time to arrive unexpectedly at someone's house – unless in case of an emergency, which this was. He put Claire's letter into his pocket, pulled on his cap and left the boarding-house for Woking without a second thought. He had no choice, and was not in the least daunted by the walk. He knew he could count on his sturdy legs and stamina to complete the marathon journey without weakening.

During his long trudge to the author's house, while he watched night spread itself lazily over the landscape, and glanced over his shoulder every now and then to make sure neither Murray's thugs nor Solomon were following him, Tom Blunt toyed with different ways of introducing himself to Wells. In the end, the one he decided was the cleverest also sounded the most far-fetched: he would introduce himself as Captain Derek Shackleton. He was sure the saviour of mankind would be far better received at any time of day than plain old Tom Blunt, and there was nothing to stop him successfully playing the role offstage as he had already done with Claire.

As Shackleton, he could tell the author the same tale he had told the girl, and show him the letter he had found when he came through the time hole on his first visit to their time. How could this Wells fellow not be taken in if he himself had written a novel about time travel? If, though, he were to make his story believable, Tom would need to think up a good reason why neither he nor anyone else from the future was able to write the letter. Perhaps he could explain that by the year 2000 man had fallen out of the habit of writing, because the task had been given to automaton scribes. In any event, introducing himself as Captain Shackleton still seemed like the best plan: it seemed preferable for the famous hero of the future, rather than a nobody, to beg the famous author's help in getting out of the predicament into which lust had got him.

When he arrived in Woking in the early hours, the place was immersed in an idyllic calm. It was a cold but beautiful night. Tom spent almost an hour reading letterboxes before he came to the one marked 'Wells'. He was standing in front of a darkened three-storey house enclosed by a not-too-high fence. He took a deep breath and climbed over it. There was no point in waiting.

He crossed the garden reverentially, as though he were walking into a chapel, climbed the steps to the front door, and was about to ring when his hand stopped short of the bell. The echo of a horse's hoofs, shattering the nocturnal silence, made him freeze. He turned slowly as he heard the animal draw near, and almost immediately saw it stop outside the fence. A shiver ran down his spine as he watched the rider, barely more than a shadow, dismount and open the gate. Was it one of Murray's thugs?

The fellow made a swift gesture that left him in no doubt: he pulled a gun from his pocket and pointed it straight at him. Tom instantly dived to one side, rolling across the lawn and disappearing into the darkness. Out of the corner of his eye he watched the stranger try to follow his sudden movement with the gun. Tom had no intention of making himself an easy target. He leaped to his feet and, in two strides, had reached the fence. He was convinced he would feel the warm sting of the bullet entering his back at any moment, but apparently he was moving too quickly, and it did not happen. He clambered over the fence and pelted down the street until he reached the fields. He ran for at least five minutes.

Only then, panting, did he allow himself to stop and look behind him to see whether Murray's thug was following him. All he could see was black night enfolding everything. He had managed to lose the man. He was safe, at least for the moment, for he doubted that his killer would bother looking for him in that pitch blackness. He would go back to London to report to Murray. Feeling calmer,

Tom found a place behind some bushes and settled down for the night. The next morning, after making sure the thug had really gone, he would return to the author's house and ask for his help, as planned.

XXIX

'You saved a man's life using your imagination,' Jane had said to him, only a few hours earlier, and her words were still echoing in his head as he watched the dawn light flood in through the tiny attic window, revealing the contours of the furniture and their two figures intertwined on the seat of the time machine. When he had suggested to his wife they might find a use for the seat, this was not exactly what he had had in mind, but he had thought it best not to upset her, and especially not now.

Wells gazed at her tenderly. Jane was breathing evenly, asleep in his arms, having given herself to him with renewed enthusiasm, reviving the almost violent fervour of their first months together. Wells had watched this passion ebb with the resigned sorrow of one who knows only too well that passionate love does not last for ever, merely transfers to other bodies. But there was no law, apparently, against its embers being rekindled by a timely breeze. This discovery had left a rather foolish grin on the author's face, which he had not seen reflected in his mirror for a long time. And it was all due to the words floating in his head – 'You saved a man's life using your imagination' – words that had made him shine once more in Jane's eyes, and which I trust you have also remembered, because they link this scene and Wells's first appearance in our tale, which I informed you would not be his last.

When his wife went down to make breakfast, he decided to remain sitting on the machine a while longer. He took a deep breath, contented and extraordinarily at ease with himself. There were times in his life when Wells considered himself an exceptionally ridiculous human being, but he seemed now to be going through a phase where he was able to see himself in a different, more charitable and – why not say it? – a more admiring light. He had enjoyed saving a life, as much because of Jane's unexpected offering as for the fantastic gift he had been given as a result: this machine that had arisen from his imagination, the ornate sleigh that could travel through time – or that was what they had made Andrew Harrington believe. Contemplating it now by daylight, Wells had to admit that when he had given it that cursory description in his novel, he never imagined it might turn out to be such a beautiful object if someone decided to build it.

Feeling like a naughty child, he sat up ceremoniously, placed his hand with exaggerated solemnity on the glass lever to the right of the control panel and smiled wistfully. If only the thing worked. If only he could hop from era to era, travel through time at his whim until he reached its furthest frontier – if such a thing existed – go to the place where time began or ended. But the machine could not be used for that. In fact, the machine had no use at all. And now he had removed the gadget that lit the magnesium, it could not even blind its occupant.

'Bertie,' Jane called from downstairs.

Wells started. He stood up, straightened his clothes, rumpled from their earlier passionate embraces, and hurried downstairs.

'There's a young man to see you,' she said, a little uneasily. 'He says his name is Captain Derek Shackleton.'

Wells paused at the foot of the stairs. Derek Shackleton? Why did that name ring a bell?

'He's waiting in the sitting room. But he said something else, Bertie . . .' Jane went on hesitantly, unsure what tone she should adopt to express what she was about to say. 'He says he's from . . . the year 2000.'

From the year 2000? Now Wells knew where he had heard that name before.

'Ah, in that case it must be very urgent,' he said, grinning mysteriously. 'Let's hurry and find out what the gentleman wants.'

With these words, he strode towards the tiny sitting room. Next to the chimneypiece, too nervous to sit down, Wells discovered a young man dressed in modest clothing. Before saying anything he looked him up and down, amazed. He was a magnificent specimen of the human race, with his statuesque muscles, noble face and eyes brimming with ferocity, like those of a cornered panther.

'I'm George Wells,' he introduced himself, once he had finished his examination. 'What can I do for you?'

'How do you do, Mr Wells?' the man from the future greeted him. 'Forgive me for barging in so early in the morning, but it's a matter of life or death.'

Wells smiled inwardly at the rehearsed introduction.

'I'm Captain Derek Shackleton and I've come from the future. From the year 2000, to be precise.' The young man stared at him expectantly, waiting for him to respond. 'Does my name mean something to you?' he asked, on seeing the author was not overly surprised.

'Naturally, Captain,' Wells replied, as he rifled through a wastepaper basket next to a set of book-lined shelves. A moment later, he extracted a ball of scrunched-up paper, which he unfolded and handed to his visitor, who cautiously took it from him. 'How could it not? I receive one of these leaflets every week without fail. You are the saviour of the human race, the man who in the year 2000 will free our planet from the yoke of the evil automatons.'

'That's right,' the young man ventured, unnerved by the author's mocking tone.

A tense silence followed, during which Wells stood with his hands in his pockets contemplating his visitor with a disdainful air.

'You must be wondering how I travelled to your time,' the young man said finally, like an actor obliged to prompt himself in order to carry on with his performance.

'Now you mention it, yes,' said Wells, without curiosity.

'Then I'll explain,' said the young man, trying to ignore Wells's manifest indifference. 'When the war started, our scientists invented a machine capable of making holes in time, with the aim of tunnelling from the year 2000 to your era. They wanted to send someone to kill the man who made automatons and prevent the war happening. That someone is me.'

Wells let out a guffaw that took his visitor aback. 'I'll grant you have an impressive imagination, young man,' he said.

'You don't believe me?' the other man asked, although the tinge of regret in his voice gave his question the air of bitter acknowledgement.

'Of course not,' the author declared cheerily. 'But don't be alarmed. It's not because you failed to make your ingenious lie sound convincing.'

'B-but, then . . .' the youth stammered, bewildered.

'I don't believe it's possible to travel to the year 2000, or that man will be at war with automatons then. The whole thing is just a silly invention. Gilliam Murray may be able to fool the whole of England, but he can't fool me.'

'So . . . you know the whole thing is a fraud?' murmured the young man, clearly flabbergasted.

Wells nodded solemnly, glancing at Jane, who looked bewildered.

'And you're not going to denounce him?' the lad asked finally.

'No, I haven't the slightest intention of doing so,' he replied. 'If people are prepared to part with good money to watch you defeat a lot of fake automatons, then maybe they deserve to be swindled. And, besides, who am I to deprive them of the illusion of having travelled to the future? Must I destroy their fantasy because someone is getting rich from it?'

'I see,' murmured the visitor, still mystified, and then, with a hint of admiration, he added: 'You're the only person I know who thinks it's a hoax.'

'Well, I suppose I have a certain advantage over the rest of humanity,' replied Wells.

He smiled at the youth's increasing bemusement. Jane was also giving him puzzled looks. The author heaved a sigh. It was time he shared his bread with the apostles. Then they might help him bear his cross.

'A little over a year ago,' Wells explained, addressing them both, 'shortly after *The Time Machine* was published, a man came here wanting to show me a novel he had just written. Like *The Time Machine*, it was a piece of science fiction. He asked me to read it and, if I liked it, to recommend it to my editor, Henley, for possible publication.'

The young man nodded slowly, as though he had not understood yet what this had to do with him. Wells turned and began to scour the books and files lining the sitting room shelves. Finally he found what he had been looking for – a bulky manuscript, which he tossed on to the table.

'The man's name was Gilliam Murray, and this is the novel he gave me that October afternoon in 1895.'

With a wave of his hand he invited the lad to read the title page. The young man moved closer to it and read aloud clumsily, as though he were chewing each word: '"*Captain Derek Shackleton: The True Story of a Brave Hero of the Future*, by Gilliam F. Murray".'

'Yes,' confirmed Wells. 'And do you want to know what it's about? The novel takes place in the year 2000, and tells the story of a battle between evil automatons and a human army led by the brave Captain Derek Shackleton. Does the plot sound familiar?'

The visitor nodded, but Wells deduced from his confused expression that he still did not fully understand what he was getting at.

'Had Gilliam written this novel after he had set up his business, I would have had no reason, besides my natural scepticism, to question the authenticity of his year 2000,' he explained. 'But he brought it to me a whole year before! Do you understand what I'm saying? Gilliam has staged his novel, and you are its main protagonist.'

He picked up the manuscript, searched for a specific page and, to the young man's dismay, started to read aloud: '"Captain Derek Shackleton was a magnificent specimen of the human race, with his statuesque muscles, noble face and eyes brimming with ferocity, like those of a cornered panther."'

The lad blushed at the description. Was that what he looked like? Did he really have the eyes of a cornered animal? It was quite possible, for he had been cornered since birth – by his father, by life, by misfortune, and lately by Murray's thugs. He stared at Wells, not knowing what to say.

'It's a ghastly description by a talentless writer, but I have to confess you fit the part perfectly,' said Wells, hurling the manuscript back on to the table with a gesture of utter contempt.

A few moments passed in which no one spoke.

'Even so, Bertie,' Jane finally stepped in, 'this young man needs your help.'

'Oh, yes. So he does,' responded a reluctant Wells, who assumed that with his masterful exposure of Murray he had resolved the reason for the visit.

'What's your real name?' Jane asked him.

'Tom Blunt, ma'am,' replied Tom, bowing politely.

'Tom Blunt,' Wells echoed mockingly. 'It doesn't sound quite so heroic, of course.'

Jane shot him a reproachful look. She hated it when her husband resorted to sarcasm to compensate for the terrible sense of physical inferiority that usually assailed him when he was in the presence of someone bigger than himself.

'Tell me, then, Tom,' Wells went on, after clearing his throat, 'what can I do for you?'

Tom sighed. No longer a brave hero from the future, just a miserable wretch, he stared at his feet, ceaselessly wringing his hat, as though he were trying to squeeze it dry, and attempted to tell the couple everything that had happened since his pressing need to empty his bladder on the set of the year 2000. Trying not to gabble, he told them about the girl named Claire Haggerty, who had appeared out of nowhere just after he had taken off his helmet and armour, how she had seen his face, and the problems that that would cause him. He was obliged to tell them about the unpleasant ways

Murray had of assuring his cast of actors did not give away the hoax, and about what had happened to poor Perkins. His speculations caused the author's wife to gasp in horror, while Wells simply shook his head, as if he had expected as much of Gilliam Murray.

Tom then told them how he had bumped into Claire Haggerty at the market, and had made her agree to meet him, driven, he confessed shamefully, by his male instinct. He described how he was then forced to make up the story about the letters so that she would agree to go with him to the boarding-house. He knew he had done wrong, he told them, not daring to raise his eyes from the floor, and he regretted it, but they should not waste time judging his behaviour because his actions had given rise to unforeseen consequences.

The girl had fallen in love with him and, believing every word he had said to her to be true, had duly written the first letter, which she had left at Harrow-on-the-Hill. He fished it out of his pocket and handed it to Wells, who took it from him, stunned by everything he had heard. He unfolded the letter and read it aloud so that his intrigued wife could also know what it contained. He tried to speak in a modulated voice, like a priest reciting the lesson, but it caught when he read out certain passages. The emotions expressed were so beautiful he could not help feeling a pang of resentment towards the young man in front of him, who had undeservingly become the object of a love so absolute it forced Wells to question his own emotions, to reconsider his whole way of experiencing love. The look of compassion that had overtaken Jane's face confirmed that his wife was feeling something similar.

'I tried writing to her,' said Tom, 'but I can barely read. I'm afraid if there's no letter waiting for her on the hill tomorrow, Miss Haggerty might do something foolish.'

Wells had to admit it was most likely, given the feverish tone of her missive.

'The reason I came here was to ask you to write to her on my behalf,' the young man confessed.

'*What* did you say?' Wells asked, incredulous.

'Three letters, that's all, Mr Wells. It's nothing for you,' pleaded the youth, and then, after a moment's thought, he added: 'I can't pay you, but if you ever have a problem that can't be dealt with in a civilised way, just call on me.'

Wells could scarcely believe his ears. He was about to say he had no intention of getting involved in this mess, when he felt Jane's hand pressing his firmly. He turned to his wife, who smiled at him with the same dreamy expression she wore when she finished one of her beloved romantic novels. Then he looked back at Tom, who was gazing at him expectantly. He realised he had no choice: he must once more save a life using his imagination.

He stared for a long time at the pages he was holding, covered with Claire Haggerty's neat, elegant script. Deep down, he found it tempting to carry on this fantastic story, to pretend to be a brave hero from the future caught up in a bloody war against the evil automatons, and even to tell another woman he loved her passionately – with the approval of his wife. It was as though the world had suddenly decided to nurture man's deepest feelings instead of keeping them in check, resulting in a harmonious cohabitation on a planet cleansed of jealousy and prejudice, where licentious behaviour had been sublimated into tender, respectful friendship. The challenge excited him, it was true, and as he had no choice but to accept it, he cheered himself with the notion that he might find corresponding with the unknown young woman at once amusing and exciting.

'Very well,' he agreed. 'Come back tomorrow morning and you'll have your letter.'

XXX

The first thing Wells did when he was left alone in the sitting room, Jane having accompanied the young man to the door, was to place Gilliam Murray's manuscript once more out of his field of vision. Although he had not let it show, he was deeply disturbed by the appalling manner in which Murray kept his masquerade going. Naturally he had to surround himself with people who could keep their mouths shut, and although he could have achieved this with incentives, threats seemed to work much better. The discovery that Murray resorted so casually to such gruesome methods sent a shiver down his spine. Not for nothing was the man his adversary – or, at least, that was what his behaviour seemed to indicate.

He picked up the leaflet Murray sent him religiously every week and looked at it with distaste. Sickening though it was, Wells had to accept that it was his fault. Yes, Murray's Time Travel existed thanks to him, thanks to the decision he had made.

He had had only two meetings with Gilliam Murray, but for some men that was enough to establish an enmity. And Murray was one of those, as Wells had soon discovered. Their first meeting had taken place in that very room one April afternoon, he recalled, glancing with horror at the wing chair into which Murray had squeezed his bulky frame.

From the moment the man had appeared in the doorway with his visiting card and his unctuous smile, Wells had been in awe of his huge, ox-like body, although even more astonishing was the extraordinary weightlessness of his movements, as though his bones were hollow. Wells had sat down in the chair facing him, and while Jane served the tea, the two men had studied one another with polite discretion. When his wife had left the room, the stranger had given him an even broader smile, thanked him for agreeing to see him at such short notice and, without pausing for breath, showered him with rapturous adulation for his novel *The Time Machine*.

However, there are those who only admire a thing in order to blow their own trumpet, to show off their own understanding and intelligence, and Gilliam Murray belonged to that group of men. He launched into a furious eulogy of the novel, extolling with lofty speech the symmetry of its structure, the power of its imagery, even the colour of the suit Wells had chosen for his main character. Wells listened courteously and wondered why anyone would choose to waste their morning inundating him with praise when they could put it all in a polite letter, as the rest of his admirers did. He weathered the glowing tributes, nodding uneasily, as one caught in an irksome shower, praying that the tedious panegyric would soon end and he could go back to his work.

However, he soon discovered it had been no more than a preamble aimed at smoothing the man's way before he revealed the real reason for his visit. After finishing his fulsome speech, Murray plucked a voluminous manuscript from his briefcase and placed it delicately in Wells's hands, as though he were handing over a sacred relic or a new-born infant. *Captain Derek Shackleton: The True Story of a Brave Hero of the Future*, Wells read, dumbfounded. He could no longer recall how they had agreed to meet again a week later, after the giant wheedled him into reading his novel.

Wells had embarked upon the task of ploughing through the manuscript, like someone undergoing torture. He had no desire to read anything issuing from the imagination of the self-important braggart he considered incapable of interesting him, and he was not mistaken. The more he read of the pretentious prose, the more his mind fogged with boredom, and he quickly decided never again to meet any of his admirers. Murray had given him an overwritten, monotonous piece of tripe; a novel that, in common with many that were swamping bookshop windows, had copied the one he had written and targeted the fashion for speculating about the future. Such novels were veritable paper depositories of junk, which, drawing inspiration from the growing impact of science, exhibited every type of outlandish machine aimed at satisfying man's most secret longings.

Wells had read none of them, but Henley had related many of their hilarious plots to him over a meal; such as those of the New Yorker Luis Senarens, whose main characters explored the planet's far-flung territories in airships, abducting any indigenous tribe they happen across on the way. The one that had stuck in his mind was about a Jewish inventor who built a machine that made things grow bigger. The vision of London attacked by an army of giant woodlice, which Henley had described to him with contempt, had terrified Wells.

The plot of Gilliam Murray's novel was equally painful. The pompous title concealed the madcap visions of an unhinged mind. Murray argued that, as the years went by, the automatons – the mechanical dolls sold in some central London toyshops – would eventually come to life. Yes, incredible though it might seem, beneath their wooden skulls an almost human form of awareness would begin to stir, so human, in fact, that the astonished reader would soon discover that the automatons harboured a deep resentment towards man for the humiliating treatment they had endured as his slaves. Finally, under the leadership of Solomon, a steam-powered automaton soldier, they swiftly and mercilessly decided the fate of the human race: extermination. Within a few decades the automatons had reduced the planet to a mound of rubble and mankind to a handful of frightened rats, from among whose ranks, however, arose the brave Captain Shackleton. After years of futile combat, Shackleton finally put an end to the automaton Solomon's evil plans, defeating him in a ridiculous sword fight.

In the final mind-boggling pages of his already preposterous tale, Murray had the temerity to draw an embarrassing moral from his story, with which he hoped to give the whole of England – or, at any rate, the toy manufacturers – something to think about: God would punish man if he went on emulating Him by creating life – if indeed these mechanical creations could be described as possessing such a thing, Wells reflected.

It was possible a story like this might work as satire, but Murray took it terribly seriously, which only made the plot seem even more ludicrous. His view of the year 2000 was utterly implausible. In all other respects, his writing was infantile and verbose in equal measure, the characters were poorly drawn and the dialogue dull as dishwater. It was the novel of someone who believed anyone could be a writer. It was not that he strung words together willy-nilly without any aesthetic pretensions; if he had, it would have made for dull but palatable reading. No, Murray was one of those avid readers who believed good writing was akin to icing a cake – which resulted in overblown, horribly flowery prose that was full of ridiculous wordy displays, indigestible to the reader.

When Wells reached the final page he felt aesthetically nauseated. The only fate the novel deserved was to be flung on the fire; furthermore, if time travel were to become the order of the day, Wells would be honour-bound to journey into the past and beat the fellow to a pulp before he was able to disgrace future literature with his creation. However, telling the truth to Gilliam Murray was an experience he had no wish to undergo, especially since he could get out of it by handing the novel to Henley, who would certainly reject it but with none of the recriminations that would fall upon Wells.

When the day came for his next appointment with Murray, Wells still had not decided what to do. The man arrived at the house with enviable punctuality, wearing a triumphant smile, but Wells sensed barely controlled anxiety beneath the cloying politeness. Murray was plainly desperate to hear his verdict, but both men were obliged to follow the rules of etiquette. Wells made small-talk as he guided him into the sitting room, and they sat down while Jane served tea.

The author took advantage of this moment of silence to study his nervous guest, who was pressing his fleshy lips into a serene smile. All of a sudden, he was filled with a sense of his own power. He, more than anyone, knew of the hope involved in writing a novel, and the insignificance of that illusion in the eyes of others, who judged the work on its merits, not on how many sleepless nights had gone into its creation. As Wells saw it, negative criticism, however constructive, was invariably painful for a writer. It always came as a blow, whether he responded to it like a brave wounded soldier or was cast into the abyss, his fragile ego in shreds. Now, as if by magic, Wells held this stranger's dreams in his hand. He had the power to shatter them or let them live. In the end, this was the choice before him. The novel's wretched quality was irrelevant, and in any case that decision could be left to Henley. The question was whether he wanted to use his authority for good or not, whether he wanted to witness this arrogant creature's response to what was in essence the truth, or whether he preferred to fob him off with a pious lie so he could carry on believing he had produced a worthwhile piece of writing – at least until Henley's diagnosis.

'Well, sir?' Murray asked, as soon as Jane had left the room. 'What did you think of my novel?'

Wells could almost feel the air in the room tremble, as though reality itself had reached a crossroads and the universe awaited his decision to know. His silence was like a dam, holding back events.

Today Wells was not sure why he had taken the decision he had. He could have chosen either way. He was sure of one thing, though: he had not made up his mind out of cruelty. If anything, he was simply curious to see how the man sitting opposite him would react to such a brutal blow. Would he conceal his wounded pride, politely accept Wells's opinion, or break down in front of him, like a man condemned to death? Perhaps he would fly into a rage and hurl himself at Wells with the intention of strangling him, a distinct possibility Wells could not rule out. Whichever way he dressed it up, it was an empirical exercise, an experiment on the soul of that wretched man. Like the scientist who must sacrifice the rat in pursuit of his discovery, Wells wanted to measure the capacity for reaction in this stranger who, by asking him to read his manuscript, had given Wells immense power over him – the power to act like the executioner of the despicable society in which they lived.

Wells cleared his throat and replied in a courteous, almost cold voice, as though he were indifferent to the harmful effect his words might have on his visitor: 'I read your work with great care, Mr Murray, and I confess I did not enjoy any part of it. I found nothing in it to praise, nothing to admire. I have taken the liberty to speak to you in this way because I consider you a colleague and I believe that lying to you would do you no good whatsoever.'

Murray's smile vanished, and his huge paws gripped the arms of the chair. Wells studied his shifting expression even as he carried on wounding him, extremely courteously: 'In my opinion, not only have you started out with a rather naïve premise, but you have developed it in a most unfortunate way, stifling its few possibilities. The structure of your narrative is inconsistent and muddled, the episodes are linked only tenuously, and in the end one has the impression that events occur higgledy-piggledy, without any inner cohesion, simply because it suits you. This tiresome randomness of the plot, added to your writing style – worthy of some legal clerk who admires Jane Austen's romantic novels – inevitably produces boredom in the reader, or if not, a profound aversion to what he is reading.'

At this point, Wells paused to study his guest's contortions with scientific interest. He must be a block of ice not to have exploded with rage at such remarks. Was Murray a block of ice?

He watched the man's attempts to overcome his bewilderment – chewing his lip, opening then clenching his fists, as though he were milking an invisible udder – and predicted that he was about to find out.

'What are you talking about?' Murray finally burst out, seized by a rage that made the tendons on his neck bulge. 'What kind of reading have you given my work?'

No, he was not a block of ice. He was pure fire, and Wells instantly realised he would not fall apart. His visitor was one of those people whose pride was so monumental that in the long run they were morally invincible: they were so full of themselves they believed they could achieve anything through simple pig-headedness, whether this was building a bird box or writing a science-fiction novel. Unfortunately for Wells, Murray had not been content to build a bird box. He had decided to employ his efforts in showing the world what an extraordinary imagination he had, how easily he was able to juggle with the words accumulated in a dictionary, or that he had been endowed with some, if not all, of the writerly characteristics that appealed to him.

Wells tried hard to remain poised while his guest, shaking with rage, labelled his remarks foolish. Watching him wave his arms about wildly, Wells regretted the choice he had made. Clearly if he carried on in that vein, demolishing the novel with scathing remarks, the situation could only get worse. But what else could he do? Must he retract everything he had said for fear the fellow might tear his head off in a fit of rage?

Luckily for Wells, Murray suddenly appeared to calm down. He took a few breaths, twisted his head from side to side and rested his hands in his lap, in a stubborn attempt to regain his composure. His painstaking effort at controlling himself felt to Wells like a caricature of the actor Richard Mansfield's amazing transformation at the Lyceum Theatre during the performance of the play *Strange Case of Dr Jekyll and Mr Hyde* a few years earlier. He let him go on without interruption, secretly relieved.

Murray seemed ashamed at having lost his temper, and the author realised that he was an intelligent man burdened with a passionate temperament, a fiery nature that drove him to those accesses of rage he had undoubtedly learned to control over the years, achieving a level of restraint of which he should feel proud. But Wells had touched his sore point, wounded his vanity, reminding him his self-control was by no means infallible.

'You may have been lucky enough to write a nice novel everybody likes,' Murray said when he had calmed himself, although his tone was still belligerent, 'but clearly you are incapable of judging the work of others. And I wonder whether this might not be because of envy. Is the king afraid the jester might usurp his throne and do a better job as ruler than he?'

Wells smiled to himself: after the outpouring of rage came a false serenity and a change in strategy. Murray had just reduced Wells's novel – praised to the skies days before – to the category of popular fiction, and had found an explanation for Wells's opinions that bore no relation to his own lack of literary talent. However, this was preferable than having to put up with his angry outbursts. They were now entering the domain of verbal sparring and Wells felt a rush of excitement: this was an area in which he felt particularly at ease. He decided to speak even more plainly.

'You are perfectly at liberty to think what you like about your own work, Mr Murray,' he said. 'But I imagine that if you came to my house to ask my opinion it is because you deemed me sufficiently knowledgeable in such matters to value my judgement. I regret not having told you what you wanted to hear, but those are my thoughts. For the reasons I already mentioned, I doubt that your novel would appeal to anyone, although in my view the main problem with it is the implausibility of your idea. Nobody would believe in the future you have described.'

Murray tilted his head to one side, as though he had not heard properly. 'Are you saying the future I describe is implausible?' he asked.

'Yes, that's exactly what I'm saying, and for various reasons,' Wells coolly replied. 'The notion that a mechanical toy, however sophisticated, could come to life is unimaginable, not to say ludicrous. Equally implausible is the suggestion that a world war could take place in the coming century. It will never happen. Not to mention other details you have overlooked – for example, that the inhabitants of the year 2000 are still using oil lamps, when anybody can see that it is only a matter of time before electricity takes over. Even fantasy must be plausible, Mr Murray. Allow me to take my own novel as an example. In order to describe the year 802,701 all I did was to think logically. The division of the human race into two species, the Eloi, languishing in their mindless hedonism, and the Morlocks, the monsters living below ground, is an example of one possible outcome of our rigid capitalist society. By the same token, the future demise of the planet, however demoralising, is based on complex predictions made by astronomers and geologists and published daily in journals. This constitutes true speculation, Mr Murray. Nobody could accuse my 802,701 of being implausible. Things may turn out quite differently, of course, especially if other, as yet unforeseeable, factors come into play, but nobody can rule out my vision. Yours, on the other hand, does not bear up under scrutiny.'

Gilliam Murray looked at him in silence for a long time, until finally he said: 'Perhaps you are right, Mr Wells, and my novel does need a thorough overhaul in terms of style and structure. It is a first attempt, and naturally I couldn't possibly expect the result to be excellent or even passable. But what I cannot tolerate is that you cast doubt on my speculations about the year 2000. Because in that case you are no longer judging my literary abilities, you are simply insulting my intelligence. Admit it, my vision of the future is as plausible as any other.'

'Permit me to disagree,' Wells replied coldly, judging that at this point in the conversation the time for mercy had passed.

Gilliam Murray had to repress another access of rage. He twisted in his seat, as though he were suffering from convulsions, but in a matter of seconds he had recovered his relaxed, almost blasé demeanour. He studied Wells with amused curiosity for a few moments, as though he were a strange species of insect he had never seen before, then let out a thunderous guffaw. 'Do you know what the difference is between you and I, Mr Wells?'

The author saw no reason to reply, and simply shrugged.

'Our outlook,' Murray told him. 'You are a conformist and I am not. You are content to deceive your readers, with their agreement, by writing about things that might happen in the hope that they will believe them. But you never lose sight of the fact that what you are writing is a novel and therefore pure make-believe. I, however, am not content with that, Mr Wells. The fact that my speculations took the form of a novel is purely circumstantial, because all it requires is a stack of paper and a strong wrist. And to be honest, it matters very little to me whether my book is published or not, because I suspect I would not be satisfied with a handful of readers who enjoy debating whether the future I describe is plausible or not, because they will always consider it an invention of mine. No, I aspire to much more than being recognised as an imaginative writer. I want people to believe in my invention without realising it's an invention, to believe the year 2000 will be exactly as I have described it. And I will prove to you I can make them believe it, however implausible it might seem to you. Only I shan't present it to them in a novel, Mr Wells. I shall leave such childish things to you. You carry on writing your fantasies in books. I will make mine a reality.'

'A reality?' asked Wells, not quite grasping what his guest was driving at. 'What do you mean?'

'You'll see, Mr Wells. And when you do, if you are a true gentleman, you will perhaps offer me an apology.'

With that, Murray rose from his chair and smoothed down his jacket with one of the graceful gestures that startled everyone in such a bulky man.

'Good day to you, Mr Wells. Don't forget me, or Captain Shackleton. You'll be hearing from us soon,' he said, as he picked up his hat from the table and placed it nimbly on his head. 'There's no need to see me to the door. I can find my own way out.'

His departure was so sudden that Wells was left sitting in his chair, at a loss, unable to stand up even after Murray's footsteps had died away and he had heard him shut the front gate. He remained seated for a long time, pondering Murray's words, until he told himself that this egomaniac did not deserve another moment of consideration. And the fact that he heard nothing from him in the ensuing months made him forget the disagreeable encounter. Until the day he received the leaflet from Murray's Time Travel. Then Wells realised what he had meant by 'I will make mine a reality'. And, apart from a few scientists and doctors who kicked up a fuss in the newspapers, the whole of England had fallen for his 'implausible' invention, thanks in part to Wells himself having raised people's expectations with *The Time Machine*, an added irony that irritated him all the more.

From then on, every week without fail he received a leaflet inviting him to take part in one of the bogus expeditions to the year 2000. That crook would have liked nothing more than to have the very man who had unleashed the current obsession for time travel to endorse his company by sanctioning the elaborate hoax, which, naturally, Wells had not the slightest intention of doing.

The worst of it, though, was the message underlying the polite invitations. Wells knew Murray was certain he would never accept, and this turned the invitations into a mockery, a taunt on paper that was also a threat: the leaflets were delivered by hand, which suggested Murray himself, or one of his men, placed them in Wells's letterbox. In any event, it made no difference, since the objective was the same: to show Wells how easy it was to loiter around his house unseen, to make sure he knew he had not been forgotten, to remind him he was being watched.

But what most infuriated Wells in this whole affair was that, however much he wanted to, he could not denounce Murray, as Tom had suggested, for the simple reason that the man had won. Yes, he had proved that his future was plausible and, rather than sweep the pieces off the board in a fit of rage, Wells must sportingly accept defeat. His integrity prevented him doing anything while

Murray made a fortune. And the situation appeared to amuse Murray enormously, for by placing the leaflets religiously in his letterbox, not only was he reminding Wells of his victory, he was also defying the author to unmask him.

'I will make it a reality,' he had said. And, to Wells's astonishment, he had done so.

XXXI

That afternoon Wells went for a longer bicycle ride than usual, and without Jane. He needed to think while he pedalled, he told her. Dressed in his favourite Norfolk jacket, he rode slowly along the Surrey byways while his mind, oblivious to the action of his legs, reflected on how to reply to the letter penned by Claire Haggerty. According to the imaginative tale Tom had concocted in the tea room, their correspondence would consist of seven letters, of which he would write three and Claire four. In the last she would ask him to travel through time to return her parasol. Otherwise, Wells was free to write whatever he liked, provided it did not contradict Tom's story. He had to admit, the more he thought about it, the more intriguing he found the lad's tale. It was evocative, beautiful, but above all plausible – assuming, of course, the existence of a machine capable of digging holes through the fabric of time and linking eras, and also, of course, if Murray's view of the future were true.

This was the part Wells liked least: that Gilliam Murray was somehow mixed up in this, as he had been in saving the wretched Andrew Harrington's soul. Were their lives destined to carry on entwining, like creeping ivy? Wells felt distinctly odd now he was stepping into the role of Captain Derek Shackleton, the character his adversary had invented. Would he be the one responsible for breathing life into that empty shell, like the God of the Old Testament?

Wells arrived home after his ride pleasantly exhausted, and with a rough idea of what he was going to write. He scrupulously set out his pen, an inkwell and a sheaf of paper on the kitchen table, and asked Jane not to disturb him for the next hour. He sat at the table, drew a deep breath, and began penning his first ever love letter.

Dear Claire,
I, too, have been obliged to compose this letter several times over before realising that, however strange it might seem to me, I can only start by declaring my love to you, exactly as you requested – although I have to confess that to begin with I did not believe myself capable, and I used up several sheets trying to explain that what you were asking me to do in your letter was to make a leap of faith. I even wrote. How can I fall in love with you if I have never even seen you, Miss Haggerty? Yet, despite my understandable wariness, I had to face the facts: you insisted I had fallen in love with you. And why should I doubt you, since I did indeed discover your letter beside the big oak tree when I came out of the time tunnel from the year 2000. I need no further evidence, as you rightly say, to see that in seven months we will meet and love will blossom between us. And if my future self – which is still me – falls in love with you as soon as he sets eyes on you, why shouldn't I? Otherwise I would be doubting my own judgement. Why waste time postponing feelings I am inevitably going to experience?

Then again, you are only asking me to make the same leap of faith you yourself made. During our meeting in the tea room you were obliged to have faith in me: you were obliged to believe you would fall in love with the man sitting opposite you. And you did. My future self is grateful to you for that, Claire. And the self who is writing these lines, who has yet to savour the softness of your skin, can only reciprocate that trust, believe that everything you say is true, that everything you say in your letter will happen because in some way it has already happened. That is why I can only begin by telling you, Claire Haggerty, whoever you are, that I love you. I love you from this very moment until the end of time.

Tom's hand trembled as he read the author's words. Wells had thrown himself wholeheartedly into the enterprise: not only had he respected Tom's improvised tale and the history of the character he was playing but, to judge from his words, he seemed as much in love with the girl as she was with him – with Tom, that was, or, more precisely, with the brave Captain Shackleton. He knew it was only pretence, but the author's skill at deception went far beyond Tom's own impoverished feelings, even though these should have been more intense since he, not Wells, had lain with the girl.

If, the day before, Tom had wondered whether the fluttering feeling in his chest was love, now he was certain of it because he had the yardstick of the author's words to measure it by. Did Tom feel the emotions Wells attributed to Shackleton? After a few moments' reflection, Tom concluded the only answer to that tortuous question was no, he did not. He could not keep a love like that alive for someone he was never going to see again.

He placed the letter next to John Peachey's headstone and began the walk back into London. He was pleased with how it had turned out, although a little disconcerted by Wells's request to Claire near the end, which Tom considered worthy of a degenerate. He recalled the final paragraphs with deep displeasure.

I am longing as I have never longed for anything before for time to speed up, counting the seconds between now and our first meeting in seven months' time. Although I must confess that as well as being anxious to meet you, Claire, I am also fascinated to know how you will travel to my era. Is such a thing really possible? For my part, I can only wait and do what I have to do, that is to say, reply to your letters, complete my part of the circle.

I hope this first letter does not disappoint you. Tomorrow I will leave it beside the oak tree when I arrive in your time. My next visit will be two days later, and I know that by then another letter from you will await me. You may find this request impertinent, my love, but could I ask you to describe our amorous encounter to me? Remember, I must wait many months before I experience it, and although I assure you I will be patient, I cannot imagine a more wonderful way to endure that wait than to read over and over again the things I will experience with you in the future. I want to know everything, Claire, so please, spare me no detail. Describe to me the first and only time we make love, because from now I will experience it through your words, my darling Claire.

Things here are hard to bear. Our brothers perish by the thousand under the superior power of the automatons, who raze our cities as though they wanted to destroy everything we have built, every trace of our civilisation. I do not know what will happen if my mission fails, if I am unable to stop this war happening. In spite of all this, my love, I can only smile as the world crumbles around me because your undying love has made me the happiest person on earth.

D

Claire clasped the letter to her pounding heart. She had so yearned for someone to write such words to her, words that took her breath away and made her pulse quicken. Now her wish had come true. Someone was telling her their love for her transcended time itself. Dizzy with happiness, she took a sheet of paper, placed it on her writing desk, and began to describe to Tom all the things that, out of respect for their privacy, I drew a veil over:

Oh, Derek, my darling Derek: you have no idea how much it meant to me finding your letter where it was supposed to 'be', and to find it filled with such love. It was the final incentive I needed in order to accept my fate without demur. And the very first thing I will do, my love, is to comply with your request, even though I shall no doubt blush with shame. How could I refuse to share intimacies with you that are ultimately yours? Yes, I shall tell you how everything happens, even though in doing so I will be dictating your actions, the way you will behave, such is the strangeness of all this.

We will make love in a room in Pickard's boarding-house, directly opposite the tea room. I will agree to go with you there after deciding to trust you. In spite of this, you will notice how terrified I am as we walk down the corridor to the room. And this is something I would like to explain to you, my love, now that I have the opportunity. What I am about to say may surprise you, but in my own time, girls are brought up to repress their instincts, especially in well-to-do families like mine. Unfortunately, it is widely believed that the sole purpose of the sexual act should be procreation, and while men are allowed to express the pleasure they derive from physical contact, provided they do so respectfully and with moderation, we women must show perfect indifference, as our enjoyment is considered immoral. My mother has upheld this narrow-minded attitude all her life, and the same can be said of most of my married women friends.

However, I am different, Derek. I have always hated this absurd inhibition in the same way I detest crochet and needlework. I believe we women have as much right as you men to experience pleasure and express it freely as individuals. Moreover, I do not believe a woman needs to be married to a man in order to engage in intimate relations with him: in my view it is enough for her to be in love with him. These are my beliefs, Derek, and as I walked down the corridor in the boarding-house I suddenly realised the time had come for me to find out whether I was capable of putting them into practice or had merely been lying to myself, and whether my fear was only a sign of my complete ignorance of such matters.

Now you know, and I imagine that is why you treated me so gently and tenderly, but let us not get ahead of ourselves. Let me reveal everything step by step in an orderly fashion and, out of respect for you, I shall do so using the future tense as, from your point of view, none of this has as yet happened. Well, I will not put it off any longer.

The room in the boarding-house will be very small, but cosy. The winter evening will almost have set in, which is why you will first hurry to light the table lamp. I shall watch you from the doorway, unable to move a muscle. Then you will look at me warmly for a few moments, before walking towards me very slowly with a calming smile, like someone afraid of scaring off a nervous cat. When you are near me, you will gaze into my eyes, whether to read what is in them or for me to read what is in yours I do not know. Then you will lean very slowly towards my mouth, so slowly I will be able to perceive your warm breath, the warmth of the air inside you, before feeling your lips firmly and at the same time gently pressing against mine. This subtle contact will unsettle me for a few moments, and then it will be transformed into my first kiss, Derek. And although I will have spent many nights anticipating what it will feel like, I will only have imagined the spiritual side, the supposed floating feeling it gives you, but it will never have occurred to me to consider the physical side, the soft, pulsating warmth of someone else's lips on mine. But little by little I will give myself over to this sensual touch, and I will respond to you with the same tenderness, sensing that we are communicating in a much deeper, more sincere way than with words, that we are putting all of ourselves into that tiny physical space. Now I know nothing brings two souls together more than the act of kissing, of awakening desire for one another.

Then a pleasant tickling sensation will ripple over my flesh, penetrating my skin and overwhelming me inside. Is this rush of sensations what my mother and my most prudish friends try so hard to suppress? I will experience it, Derek. I will taste it, delight in it, and cherish it, my love, in the knowledge that I will be experiencing it for the first and last time, for I will know that after you there will be no other men and I must live off these feelings for the rest of my life. Then the floor will give way beneath my feet and, except for the pressure of your hands around my waist, I will almost believe I am floating.

Then you will take away your lips, leaving the imprint of your mouth on mine, and you will look at me with tender curiosity while I try to regain my breath and my composure. And then? It will be time for us to undress and lie down together on the bed, only you will seem as hesitant as I, unable to take the first step, perhaps because you think I will be afraid. And you will not be mistaken, my love, because I have never undressed in front of a man before, and all at once I will feel nervous and bashful and wonder whether taking off our clothes is really necessary. According to my aunts, my mother kept her marriage vows without my father ever having seen her naked. In keeping with the customs of her generation, Mrs Haggerty lay down in her petticoats with a hole in her undergarments revealing the scented opening where my father was permitted entry.

But it will not be enough for me simply to lift my skirts, Derek. I will want to enjoy our physical contact to the full, and therefore I will overcome my shame and begin to undress, fixing you with a gentle, solemn look. I will begin by taking off my feather hat, which I will hang on the stand. Then I will slip off my jacket, my blouse with its high-necked collar, my over-corset, my corset, my over-skirt, my skirt, my bustle and my petticoats, until all I am left wearing is my slip. Still gazing at you tenderly, I will pull down the shoulder straps so the garment slides off my body, like snow slipping from a fir tree, and lies in a furl at my feet. Then, like a final act of a long drawn-out ritual, I will slip out of my drawers, offering myself to you utterly naked, placing my body at your disposal, surrendering myself to the touch of your hands and your lips, giving myself completely, knowing it is to the right man, to Captain Derek Shackleton, the liberator of the human race, the only man with whom I could ever have fallen in love.

And you, my love, will watch the elaborate process, like someone waiting for a beautiful figure to emerge from a block of marble as it is teased out by the artist's chisel. You will see me walking towards you, and will quickly take off your shirt and trousers, as if a gust had torn them from a washing line. Then we will embrace, the warmth of our bodies mingling in a happy union, and I will feel your fingers, so accustomed to touching hard metal and weapons, exploring my body, sensitive to its delicacy, with exhilarating slowness and respectful tenderness. Then we will lie on the bed gazing into one another's eyes, and my hands will search your stomach for the scar from the bullet with which Solomon tried to kill you, and which you survived as one recovers from a fever, only I will be so nervous I won't be able to find it.

Then your mouth, moist and eager, will cover me with kisses, leaving a trail of saliva, and once you have thoroughly charted my body, you will enter it slowly, and I will feel you moving inside me with such gentleness. But despite the care you take, your intrusion will cause me to feel a sudden sharp pain inside, and I will cry out softly and even pull your hair, although immediately it will turn into a bearable, almost sweet ache, and I will become aware of something dormant inside me beginning to stir. How can I describe to you what I will feel at that moment? Imagine a harp marvelling at the notes it produces when a pair of hands plucks it for the first time. Imagine a burning candle, whose melted wax trickles down the candlestick, oblivious to the flame above, and forms a beautiful latticed pattern at the base. What I am trying to say to you, my love, is that until that moment, I will not have known it is possible to feel such exquisite rapture, the ecstatic pleasure that will radiate through my whole body from a place somewhere inside me, and although at first my bashfulness will force me to grit my teeth, to attempt to stifle the gasps that will rise from my throat, I will end up abandoning myself to that overpowering joy. I will let myself be swept away by that torrent of icy fire, and will proclaim my pleasure with passionate cries, announcing the awakening of my flesh. And I will be insatiable. I will clutch you to me, trapping you with my legs, because I want you to stay inside me for ever, because I will be unable to understand how I could have lived all that time without feeling you thrusting sweetly into me.

And when, after the final ecstasy, you slip out of me, leaving a crimson trail across the sheets, I will suddenly feel incomplete, bereft, lost. With my eyes closed, I will savour the echo of joy you have left inside me, the delicious memory of your presence, and when this has slowly faded, I will be overwhelmed by a feeling of extraordinary loneliness, but also of infinite gratitude at having discovered in myself a creature perfectly adapted to bliss, capable of enjoying the loftiest and most earthly pleasures. Then I will reach out, searching for the feel of your skin bathed in my sweat, your skin that still quivers and burns, like the strings of a violin after a concerto, and I will gaze at you with a radiant smile of gratitude for having revealed to me who I am, everything I did not yet know about myself.

Tom was so moved and surprised, he had to stop reading. Had he really unleashed all those feelings in her? Leaning back against the tree, almost out of breath, he let his gaze wander over the surrounding fields. For him, the carnal act with her had been a pleasant experience he would always remember, but Claire spoke of it as though it had been sublime and unforgettable, like the foundation stone that, as the years passed, would hold up the cathedral of her love. Feeling even more of a savage than he really was, Tom sighed and went on reading:

I was going to tell you now how I travelled to your time, Derek, but when I remember that during our meeting at the tea room you still did not know how we do it, I feel compelled to keep it secret in order not to change things that have already happened. What I can tell you is that last year an author called H. G. Wells published a wonderful novel, The Time Machine, *which made us all dream about the future. And then someone showed the machine to us. I can tell you no more than that. But I will make it up to you by saying that, although your mission in my time will fail, and the machine in which you travel here will be prohibited, the human race will win the war against the automatons, and it will be thanks to you. Yes, my love, you will defeat the evil*

Solomon in an exciting sword fight. Trust me, for I saw it with my own eyes.

Your loving,

C

Wells placed the letter on the table, trying not to show how it had aroused him. He glanced at Tom silently, gesturing almost imperceptibly with his head that he could leave. Once he was alone, he picked up the letter to which he had to reply, and flushed with excitement as he re-read the detailed account of their meeting at the boarding-house. Thanks to this girl, he finally understood women's experience of pleasure, the sensation that crept over them with intriguing slowness, overwhelming them completely or scarcely touching them. How sublime, resplendent and infinite their enjoyment was compared to that of men, so vulgar and crude, little more than a spurt of joy between their legs.

But was this the same for all women or was she special? Had the Creator fine-tuned this particular girl's sensitivity to such an astonishing degree? No, doubtless she was a perfectly ordinary creature who simply enjoyed her sexuality in a way other women would consider brazen. Her simple decision to undress in front of Tom already showed an audacious spirit, a determination to experience to the full every possible sensation arising from the sexual act.

Upon realising this, Wells felt saddened, annoyed even, by the chaste manner in which the women in his life had given themselves to him. His cousin Isabel was one of those who had resorted to the hole in the undergarment, presenting him with only her sex, which to Wells seemed like some terrifying entity, a sort of sucking orifice that appeared to have come from some other planet. Even Jane, who was less inhibited in such matters, had never allowed him to see her completely naked. No, he had never been lucky enough to meet a woman blessed with Claire's delightful nature.

There were no limits to what he could have done with a girl as easy to win over as she. It would have been enough to extol the therapeutic virtues of sex for women in order to convert her into an eager adept of carnal pleasure, a modern-day priestess ready to give and receive pleasure freely. She would have become a champion of copulation, preaching door to door that regular sexual activity improved women's physiques, gave them a mysterious glow, softened their expressions, and even rounded off any unsightly angularities. With a woman like that, he would certainly be a contented man, his appetites sated, a man who could put his mind to other things, throw himself into his interests, freed from the relentless male itch that had begun in adolescence and would stay with him until senility finally rendered his body useless.

It was no surprise, then, that Wells immediately envisaged the girl named Claire Haggerty in his bed, without any clothes veiling her slender form, allowing him to stroke her with feline abandon, intensely enjoying the same caresses that scarcely elicited a polite sigh from Jane. It seemed incongruous to him that he should understand this unknown woman's pleasure, while that of his wife remained a mystery to him. Suddenly he remembered she was waiting somewhere in the house for him to give her the next letter to read. He left the kitchen to go and look for her, taking deep breaths on the way to calm his excitement.

When he found her in the sitting room reading a book, he put the sheet of paper on the table without a word, like a poisoned chalice, then waited to see the effect it had on her. For there was no doubt the letter would affect Jane, as it had affected him, forcing her to question her approach to the physical side of love in the same way that the last letter had made her question the way she experienced its spiritual side.

He walked out into the garden to breathe in the night air, and gazed up at the pale full moon laying claim to the sky. In addition to the insignificance he always felt beneath the heavens, he was aware of his own clumsiness in comparison to the far more direct, spontaneous way others had of relating to the world, in this case the girl named Claire Haggerty. He remained in the garden for a long while, until he thought it was time to see the effect the letter had produced in his wife.

He walked slowly through the house, with almost ghost-like footsteps and, unable to find her in the sitting room or in the kitchen, he went upstairs to the bedroom. There was Jane, standing by the window, waiting for him. The moonlight framed her naked, tempting body. With a mixture of astonishment and lust, Wells examined its elements, its proportions, the supple wisdom with which her womanly parts, always glimpsed separately or divined through fabric, formed a greater landscape, creating a liberated, otherworldly being that looked as though it might fly away at any moment. He admired her soft, malleable breasts, her painfully narrow waist, the placid haven of her hips, the dark woolliness of her pubis, her feet like small, appealing animals. Jane was beaming at him, delighted to feel herself the object of her husband's astonished gaze.

Then the writer knew what he must do. As though obeying an invisible prompter, he tore off his clothes, also exposing his nakedness to the light of the moon, which instantly outlined his skinny, sickly-looking frame. Husband and wife embraced in the middle of their bedroom, experiencing the touch of each other's skin in a way they never had before. And the sensations that followed also seemed magnified, for Claire's words etched in their memories redoubled the dizzying effect of each caress, each kiss. Real or imagined, they abandoned themselves hungrily, passionately, to explore each other, to venture outside the boundaries of their familiar garden of delights.

Later on, while Jane slept Wells slipped out of their bed, tiptoed into the kitchen, took up his pen and began rapidly to fill the paper, prey to an uncontrollable sensation of euphoria.

My love,
How I long for the day when at last I shall be able to experience all the things you have described to me. What can I say except that I love you and I shall make love to you exactly as you describe? I shall

kiss you tenderly, caress you softly and reverently, enter you as gently as I can and, knowing as I do everything you are feeling, my pleasure will be even more intense, Claire.

Tom read Wells's passionate letter with suspicion. Even though he knew the author was pretending to be him, he could not help thinking those words might just as well come from both of them. Wells was evidently enjoying all this. What did his wife think of it? Tom folded the letter, replaced it in the envelope and hid it under the stone next to the mysterious Peachey's grave.

On the way back, he went on mulling over the author's words, unable to help feeling as if he had been left out of a game he himself had invented, relegated to the mere role of messenger.

I love you already, Claire, I love you already. Seeing you will simply be the next phase. And knowing we will win this bloody war gives me renewed joy. Solomon and I locked in a sword fight? Until a few days ago, I would have wondered whether you were quite sane, my love: I could never have imagined we would settle our differences with such a prehistoric weapon. But this morning, picking through the ruins of the History Museum, one of my men came across a sword. He deemed the noble relic worthy of a captain and, as though obeying your command, solemnly presented me with it. Now I know I must practise with it in preparation for a future duel, a duel from which I shall emerge victorious, for knowing that your beautiful eyes are watching me will give me strength.

All my love from the future,

D

Claire felt her knees go weak and, lying down on her bed, she luxuriated in the wave of sensations the brave Captain Shackleton's words had unleashed in her heart. While he had been duelling with Solomon he had known she was watching him, then . . . The thought made her slightly dizzy again, and she took a moment to recover.

Suddenly it dawned on her that she would receive only one

more letter from her beloved. How would she survive without them?

She tried to put it out of her mind. She still had to write two more. As she had promised, she would only tell him about their encounter in the year 2000 in her last letter, but what about the one she had to write now? She realised, somewhat uneasily, that for the first time she was free to write what she liked. What could she say to her beloved that she had not already said, especially considering that everything she wrote must be carefully examined in case it conveyed information that might jeopardise the fabric of time, apparently as fragile as glass?

After some thought, she decided to tell him how she spent her time now, as a woman in love without a lover. She sat at her desk and took up her pen.

My darling,
You cannot know how much your letters mean to me. Knowing I shall receive only one more makes me feel dreadfully sad. However, I promise I will be strong. I will never falter, never stop thinking of you, feeling you near me every second of each long day. It goes without saying that I will never allow another man to tarnish our love, even though I will never see you again. I prefer to live from my memories of you, despite the best efforts of my mother to marry me off to the wealthiest bachelors in the neighbourhood – naturally I have told her nothing of you (my love would seem like a waste of time to her, for she would see you as no more than a pointless illusion). She invites them to our house and I receive them courteously, of course, then amuse myself by inventing the most outrageous reasons for rejecting them that leave my mother speechless. My reputation is growing worse by the day: I am doomed to be a spinster and a disgrace to my family.

But why should I care a fig for what others think? I am your beloved. The brave Captain Derek Shackleton's beloved, although I have to hide my feelings for you.

Apart from these tedious meetings, I devote the rest of my time to you, my love, for I know how to sense your presence swirling around me like a fragrance even though you are many years away from me. I feel you near me always, watching me with your gentle eyes, although at times it saddens me not to be able to touch you, that you are no more than an ethereal memory, that you cannot share anything with me. You cannot slip your arm through mine in Green Park, or hold my hand as we watch the sun go down over the Serpentine, or smell the narcissi I grow in my garden, whose scent, my neighbours say, fills the whole of St James's Street.

Wells was waiting in the kitchen, as before. Tom silently handed him the letter and left before the writer could ask him to. What was there to say? Although in the end he knew it was untrue, he could not help feeling as though Claire were writing to Wells instead of to him. He felt like the intruder in this love story, the fly in the soup.

When he was alone, Wells opened the letter and began to devour the girl's neat handwriting.

In spite of all this, Derek, I shall love you until my dying day, and no one will be able to deny that I have been happy. And yet I have to confess it is not always easy. According to you I will never see you again, and the thought is so unbearable that, despite my resolve, I try to make myself feel better by imagining you may be mistaken. That does not mean I doubt your words, my love, of course not. But the Derek who uttered them in the tea room was only guided by what I am saying now, and it is possible the Derek who hurried back to his own time after making love to me in the boarding-house, the Derek who is not yet you, will be unable to bear not seeing me again and will find a way of coming back to me. What that Derek will do, neither you nor I can know, for he is outside the circle. This is my only hope, my love – a naïve one, perhaps, but necessary all the same.

I dearly hope I will see you once more, that the scent of my narcissi will lead you to me.

Wells folded the letter, put it back in its envelope and laid it on the table, where he stared at it for a long time. Then he stood up, walked round the kitchen in circles, sat down, stood up again and walked round in circles some more. Then he made up his mind. 'I'm going to London to settle some business,' he told Jane, who was working in the garden. He left the house and went to the station, where he hired a cab.

During the journey, he tried to calm his wildly beating heart.

At that hour of the afternoon, St James's Street seemed lulled by a peaceful silence. Wells ordered the cab driver to stop at the entrance to the street, and asked him to wait for him there. He straightened his hat and adjusted his bow tie, then sniffed the air, like a bloodhound. He concluded from his inhalations that the faint, slightly heady odour reminiscent of jasmine, which he detected through the smell of horse dung, must be narcissi. The flower added a symbolic touch to the scene, which pleased him, for he had read that, contrary to popular belief, the name 'narcissus' derived not from the beautiful Greek god but from the plant's narcotic properties. The narcissus bulb contained hallucinogenic opiates, and this oddity struck Wells as terribly appropriate: were not all three of them – the girl, Tom and himself – caught up in a hallucination?

He studied the long, shady street, and set off down the pavement with the leisurely air of one out for a stroll, although as he approached the apparent source of the aroma, he noticed that his mouth had dried. Why had he come there? What did he hope to gain? He was not sure. All he knew was that he needed to see the girl to give the recipient of his passionate letters a face or, failing that, to glimpse the house where she penned her beautiful letters. Perhaps that would be enough.

Before he knew it, Wells found himself standing in front of an undeniably well-tended garden with a tiny fountain on one side, and enclosed by a railing at the foot of which lay a carpet of pale yellow flowers with large petals. Since the street boasted no other garden that could rival its beauty, Wells deduced that the narcissi before him, and the elegant town house beyond, must be those of Claire Haggerty, the unknown woman he was pretending to love with a fervour he did not show the woman he truly loved. Not wishing to give too much thought to this paradox, which was none-theless in keeping with his contradictory nature, Wells approached the railings, almost thrusting his nose through the bars in an attempt to glimpse something behind the leaded window-panes that made sense of his urgent presence there.

It was then he noticed a girl looking at him, apparently perplexed, from a corner of the garden. Realising he had been caught red-handed, Wells tried to act naturally, although his response was anything but natural, especially since he realised straight away that the girl staring at him could be none other than Claire Haggerty. He tried to gather himself even as he gave her an absurdly affable grin. 'Magnificent narcissi, miss,' he declared, in a reedy voice. 'One can smell their aroma from the end of the street.' She smiled, and came a little closer, enough for the author to see her beautiful face and delicate frame. Here she was at last, before his eyes, albeit fully clothed. And she was indeed a vision of loveliness, despite the slightly upturned nose – it marred the serene beauty, which was otherwise reminiscent of a Greek sculpture – or perhaps because of it. This girl was the recipient of his letters, his make-believe lover.

'Thank you, sir, you're very kind,' she said, returning the compliment.

Wells opened his mouth as if to speak, but hurriedly closed it again. Everything he wanted to tell her went against the rules of the game he had consented to play. He could not say that, although he might appear an insignificant little man, he was the author of those words without which she claimed she could not live. Neither could he tell her he knew in precise detail her experience of sexual pleasure. Still less could he reveal that it was all a sham, urge her not to sacrifice herself to a love that only existed in her imagination, for there was no such thing as time travel, no Captain Shackleton waging war on the automatons in the year 2000. Telling her it was an elaborate lie that she would pay for with her life would be tantamount to handing her a gun to shoot herself through the heart.

Then he noticed she had begun giving him quizzical looks, as if his face seemed familiar. Afraid she might recognise him, Wells hurriedly doffed his hat, bowed politely and continued on his way, trying not to quicken his pace.

Intrigued, Claire watched for a few moments as he vanished into the distance, then shrugged and went inside the house.

Crouched behind a wall on the opposite pavement, Tom Blunt watched her go in. Then he emerged from his hiding-place. Seeing Wells had surprised him, although not excessively. The author would likewise not have been surprised to find him there. Apparently neither of them had been able to resist the temptation to look for the girl's house, the location of which she had subtly revealed in the hope that if Shackleton came back he could find her.

Tom returned to his lair in Buckeridge Street, unsure what to think of Wells. Had the author fallen in love with her? He did not think so. Maybe he had gone there out of simple curiosity. If he were in Wells's shoes, would he not also have wanted to put a face to the girl whom he addressed using words he would probably never utter to his own wife?

Tom fell back on the bed feeling completely exhausted, but his anxiety and permanent state of tension prevented him sleeping more than a couple of hours, and before dawn he set off once more on the long journey to the writer's house. These walks were keeping him fitter than the training sessions they were put through by Murray, whose hired assassin had still not appeared to punish his flagrant breaking of the rules. Even so, Tom had no intention of lowering his guard.

Wells was waiting for him on the doorstep. He did not look rested either. His face was crumpled and his eyes had dark shadows under them, although they were twinkling mysteriously. Doubtless he had been awake all night, writing the letter he now had in his hand. When he saw Tom, he greeted him with a slow nod and held out the missive, avoiding looking him in the eye. Tom took it from him, and, similarly unwilling to break the silence, which was charged with tacit understanding, turned to go back the way he had come.

Then he heard Wells say: 'Will you bring her last letter even though it needs no reply?'

Tom turned to him with a profound sense of pity, although he did not know whether he felt sorry for Wells or himself, or possibly for Claire. At length he nodded glumly and left. Only when he was at a comfortable distance did he open the envelope and begin to read.

My love,
There are no narcissi in my world, nor the least trace of any flower, and yet I swear that when I read your letter I can almost smell their fragrance. Yes, I can envisage myself standing beside you in the garden you speak of, which I imagine carefully tended by your lily-white hands and perhaps lulled by a babbling fountain. In some way, my love, thanks to you, I can smell them from here, from time's distant shore.

Tom hung his head, imagining how moved the girl would be by these words. He felt pity for her again – and, in the final analysis, an overwhelming sense of self-disgust. She did not deserve to be deceived like this. The letters might save her life, but in the end they were only repairing the harm he had so selfishly caused, merely to quench the fire between his legs. He felt unable simply to congratulate himself for preventing her suicide and forget the whole thing, while Claire was ruining her life because of a lie, burying herself alive due to an illusion.

The long walk to Harrow helped him gather his thoughts, and he concluded that the only reparation he could make that would ease his conscience would be actually to love her, to make into a reality the love for which she was willing to sacrifice herself, to bring Shackleton back from the year 2000, to make him risk life and limb for her, exactly as Claire was hoping. That was the only thing that would completely atone for his wrongdoing. But it was also the one thing he was powerless to do.

He was reflecting about this when, to his astonishment, he caught sight of her under the oak tree. He stopped in his tracks, stunned. Incredible as it seemed, Claire was there, at the foot of the tree, shielding herself from the sun with the parasol he had travelled through time to bring her. He also glimpsed the coach at the bottom of the hill, the coachman nodding off on the box. He quickly hid behind some bushes before one or other of them sensed his presence. He wondered what Claire was doing there, but the answer was obvious. She was waiting for him – or, rather, she was waiting for Shackleton to step through a hole in the air from the year 2000. Unable to resign herself to living without him, the girl had decided to act, to defy fate, and what simpler way of doing so than by going to the place where the captain emerged to collect her letters? Desperation had compelled Claire to make a move that infringed the rules of the game. And, watching her from behind the bushes, Tom kicked himself for not having foreseen this possibility, especially as she had given him ample proof of her courage and intelligence.

He remained in hiding almost the entire morning, watching gloomily as she circled the oak tree, until finally she grew tired, climbed into her carriage and went back to London. Then Tom emerged from his hiding-place, left the letter under the stone and made his own way back to the city. As he walked, he remembered the tormented words Wells had used to end his final letter:

A terrible sorrow overwhelms me when I realise this is the last letter I am going to write you, my love. You yourself told me it was, and I believe you are right about that, too. I would love nothing more than for us to go on writing to one another until we meet next May. However, if there is one thing I have learned from all this, it is that the future is predestined, and you have already experienced it. And so I can only suppose something will happen to stop me sending you more letters; possibly use of the machine will be banned and my hitherto unsuccessful mission called off.

I feel torn, as I am sure you can imagine: on the one hand, I am happy to know that for me this is not a last farewell, for I shall see you again very soon; on the other, my heart breaks when I think that you will never hear from me again. But this does not mean my love for you will die. It will live, Claire, I promise you, for one thing I am sure of is my love for you. I shall carry on loving you from my flowerless world.

D

Tears rolling down her cheeks, Claire sat at her desk, took a deep breath and dipped her pen into the inkwell.

This, too, is my last letter, my love, and although I would like to begin by telling you how much I love you, I must be honest with myself and confess to you shamefacedly that a few days ago I did a reckless thing. Yes, Derek, apparently I am not as strong as I thought, and I went to the oak tree to wait for you to appear. Living without you is too painful. I needed to see you, even if it altered the fabric of time. I waited all morning, but you did not come, and I could not escape my mother's watchful eye any longer. It is difficult enough not to arouse Peter the coachman's suspicions. He already looks at me strangely each time I ask him to take me there, but has so far kept my secret from my mother. How do you suppose he would have reacted if he had seen you step out of the oak tree as if by magic? I expect they would have discovered everything and it would have caused some sort of disaster in time.

I realise now it was foolish and irresponsible of me. Yes, for even if Peter had seen nothing, our impromptu meeting would still have changed the fabric of time. You would not see me for the first time on 20 May in the year 2000, and everything would instantly turn upside down, and nothing would happen as it is meant to. But luckily, although I would have liked nothing more, you did not appear, and so there is nothing to regret. I imagine you arrived in the afternoon, for the next day your beautiful, final letter was there.

I hope you can forgive my foolishness, Derek, which I am confessing to you because I do not wish to hide any of my faults from you. And in the hope of moving you to forgive me still further, I am sending you a gift from the bottom of my heart, so that you will know what a flower is.

After writing this, she stood up, took her copy of *The Time Machine* from the bookshelf, opened it and removed the narcissus she had pressed between its pages. When she had finished the letter, she touched the delicate petals to her lips and carefully slid the flower into the envelope.

Peter asked no questions this time either. Without waiting for her to tell him, he set off for Harrow-on-the-Hill. When they arrived, Claire walked up to the oak tree and discreetly hid the letter under the stone. Then she glanced around at the landscape, aware of saying goodbye to the place that had been the setting for her happiness those past few days, to those peaceful meadows, vibrantly green in the morning sun, to the distant cornfields, a streak of gold marking the horizon. She gazed at John Peachey's headstone, and wondered what sort of life this stranger had lived, whether he had known true love or died without experiencing it.

She took a deep breath, and almost thought she could perceive her beloved Derek's scent, as though his numerous appearances had left a trace behind in that sacred place. It was all in her imagination, she said to herself, the result of her desperate longing to see him. And she must accept reality. She must prepare to spend the rest of her life without him, to be content to listen out for the echo of his love resonating from the other side of time, for possibly she would never see him again. That afternoon, or tomorrow, or the next day, an invisible hand would seize her last letter, and after that there would be no others, only solitude unfurling at her feet like a carpet stretching to infinity.

She returned to the carriage and climbed in without giving Peter any order. With a resigned look, the coachman set off for London as soon as she was comfortably seated.

Once the carriage had vanished into the distance, Tom lowered himself from the branch he had clambered on to and dropped to the ground. From there he had been able to see her for the last time; he could even have touched her just by stretching out his hand, but he had not allowed himself to do so. And now, having indulged his whim, he must never go near her again. He took the letter from under the stone, leaned against the tree and began reading, a pained expression on his face.

As you rightly imagined, Derek, they will soon prohibit the use of the machine. There will be no more journeys through time for you until you defeat the evil Solomon. After that, you will decide to risk your life by secretly using the machine to travel to my time. But let us not get ahead of ourselves: let me at last tell you about our first meeting and what you must do afterwards.

As I told you, it will take place on 20 May in the year 2000. That morning, you and your men will mount a surprise attack on Solomon. At first glance, and despite the astute positioning of your men, you will not come out of the skirmish with the upper hand, but have no fear, for at the end of it Solomon will suggest resolving the conflict with a sword fight. Accept his offer without hesitation, for you will win the duel. You will be a hero, and this combat, which puts an end to the automatons' supremacy over the human race, will be hailed as the dawn of a new era, so much so that it will be regarded as a perfect tourist destination for time travellers from my era, who will eagerly flock there to witness it.

I will go on one of those trips and, concealed behind a pile of rubble, I will watch you fight Solomon, but when the duel is over, instead of going back with the others, I will hide among the ruins, intending to stay in your world because, as you know, my own holds no attraction for me. Yes, thanks to the dissatisfaction that has dogged me all my life, and which I never suspected would lead to anything, you and I will meet.

I must warn you, though, that our meeting will not be as romantic as it ought to have been; on the contrary, it will be rather embarrassing, particularly for you, Derek, and recalling it still brings a smile to my lips. But I suppose I should say no more about your indecorous behaviour, as I can only assume it would influence your actions. All you need to know is that, during our brief encounter, I will drop my parasol, and although you will travel across time in order to meet me and make love to me, returning it will be the excuse you give so that I agree to meet you at the tea room.

Naturally, in order for all this to happen as it is supposed to, in order to complete the circle in which we are trapped, you must appear in my time before we begin writing to each other – there would be no point in your doing so afterwards for, as you know, it is you who will encourage me to write to you. You must appear on exactly 6 November 1896 and look for me at Covent Garden Market at twelve o'clock in order to ask me to meet you that same afternoon. The rest you know. If you do as I say, you will preserve the circle, and everything that has happened already will happen once more.

That is all, my love. In a few months' time, our love story will begin for you. But for me it ends here, when I put the last full stop on this page. However, I will not say a final farewell and so deny all hope of our seeing one another again because, as I told you before, I live in the hope of you coming back to find me. All you have to do is follow the scent of the flower in the envelope.

With all my love,

C

Wells let out a sigh of dismay as he folded the letter Tom had brought him and placed it on the table. Then he took the envelope and tipped it over his open palm, but there was nothing inside. What had he expected? The flower was not for him. And, sitting in the kitchen, touched by the rays of the evening sun, he realised his expectations had been too high. Although he appeared to be, he was not the protagonist of the romance that spanned time. He saw himself, empty hand absurdly outstretched, as though checking to see if it was raining inside the house, and could not help feeling like an intruder in the story.

XXXII

Very carefully, Tom slipped the delicate flower between the pages of the only book he owned, his battered copy of *The Time Machine*. He had decided to let Wells keep Claire's letters, as a sort of thank-you gift for services rendered, but mainly because in the end he considered they belonged to the writer. In the same way, he had held on to the narcissus he found in the final envelope because he believed it was meant for him. And, after all, its perfume conveyed more meaning to him than her words.

He lay back on his bed, and wondered what Claire Haggerty would do now that the letter-writing was over and she was officially in love with a man from the future. He imagined her thinking of him each day, as she had predicted in her letters, from dawn to dusk, year in, year out, indifferent to the fact that real life, the one she ought to have been living, was slipping away from her. This cruel fate, to which he had contributed – or, rather, which he had orchestrated – made him deeply unhappy, but he could think of no way to put things right without making them worse.

His only consolation was that in her letters Claire had assured him she would die happy. And perhaps, in the end, nothing else mattered. She probably would be happier in this impossible love affair than if she married one of her insipid suitors. If so, why did it matter if her happiness was based on a lie, provided that she died without knowing she had been deceived, ended her days believing she had been loved by Captain Derek Shackleton?

He stopped thinking about the girl's fate and focused on his own. He had sworn to himself he would stay alive until he had saved Claire's life, and he had succeeded by staying hidden and sleeping outside in the fields. But now he was ready for death – he was even looking forward to it. There was nothing left for him to do in life, except struggle to survive, which felt like a terribly exhausting and, in the end, pointless exercise, and far harder to achieve with the memory of Claire piercing his heart like a painful splinter.

Twelve days had passed since his meeting with the girl in the tea room, in full view of the whole of London, and Gilliam Murray's hired assassin had still not managed to find him. He could not count on Solomon either, who apparently preferred to haunt his dreams. But someone had to kill him, or he would end up dying of hunger. Perhaps he ought to make things easier for his killer. Added to this was another consideration: rehearsals would soon begin for the third expedition to the year 2000, which was in less than a fortnight. Was Murray waiting for him to appear at Greek Street so that he could kill him in his lair with his own bare hands? Attending the first rehearsal was as good as placing his head voluntarily in the lion's mouth, but despite everything, Tom knew that that was what he would do, if only to solve once and for all the riddle of his existence.

Just then someone hammered on his door. Tom sprang to his feet, but made no move to open it. He stood waiting, every muscle in his body tensed, ready for anything. Had his time come? A few moments later, the barrage of thuds resumed.

'Tom? Are you there, you miserable scoundrel?' someone outside roared. 'Open up or I'll have to knock down the door.'

He recognised Jeff Wayne's voice. He put Wells's book into his pocket and somewhat reluctantly opened the door. Jeff burst into the room and gave him a bear hug. Bradley and Mike greeted him from the landing.

'Where have you been hiding the last few days, Tom? The boys and I have been looking everywhere for you . . . Woman trouble, was it? Well, that doesn't matter now, we've found you – and just in time. We're going to celebrate in style tonight, thanks to our good old friend Mike,' he said, pointing to the giant, who was looking as gormless as ever.

As far as Tom could gather from Jeff's muddled explanation, some days earlier Murray had paid Mike to do a special job for him. He had played the role of the infamous Jack the Ripper, the monster who had murdered five prostitutes in Whitechapel in the autumn of 1888.

'Some are born to play heroes, while others . . .' Jeff jeered. 'In any case he got the lead role and that calls for a proper splurge, wouldn't you say?'

Tom nodded. What else could he do? This was clearly not Mike's idea, but had been cooked up by Jeff, who was always ready to spend other people's money. Tom had no desire to go with them, but he knew he lacked the strength to resist. His companions all but dragged him downstairs to one of the adjoining taverns, where the trays of sausages and roast meat spread out on the table in the private room finally overcame his feeble resistance. Tom might not care for their company, but his stomach would never forgive him if he walked away from all that food. Laughing loudly, the four men sat at the table and gorged themselves, while making fun of Mike's assignment.

'It was a difficult job, Tom,' the big man groaned. 'I had to wear a metal plate over my chest to stop the bullet. It's not easy pretending to be dead trussed up like that!'

His companions burst out laughing again. They ate and drank until most of the food was gone, and the beer had begun to take effect.

Then Bradley stood up, turned his chair around and, placing his hands on the back as though leaning on a pulpit, gazed at his companions with exaggerated solemnity. There always came a time during their drunken sprees when he displayed his talent for mimicry. Tom sat back in his chair, resigned to watching the performance, thinking that at least he had satisfied his hunger.

'Ladies and gentlemen, all I wish to say is that you are about to participate in the most astonishing event of the century: today you are going to travel through time!' the lad declared in pompous tones. 'Don't look so astonished. Murray's Time Travel is not satisfied simply to take you to the future. No! Thanks to our efforts, you will also have the opportunity to witness possibly the most important moment in the history of mankind: the battle between the brave Captain Derek Shackleton and the evil automaton Solomon, whose dreams of conquest you will see perish beneath the captain's sword.'

His companions clapped and roared with laughter. Encouraged by their response to his performance, Bradley threw back his head and put on a grotesquely wistful face. 'Do you know what Solomon's great mistake was? I shall tell you, ladies and gentlemen. His mistake was that he picked the wrong lad to perpetuate the species. Yes, the automaton made a bad choice, a very bad choice. And his mistake changed the course of history,' he said, with a smirk. 'Can you imagine a more terrible fate than having to fornicate all day long? Of course you can't. Well, that was the poor lad's fate.' He spread his arms and nodded in a mock gesture of regret. 'But not only did he carry it off, he also managed to grow stronger, to study the enemy, who watched him copulating every night with great interest, before going to the city to approve the newly fabricated automaton whores. But the day the woman gave birth, the lad knew he would never see his son grow up – his son who had been brought into the world to fornicate with his own mother, thus initiating a vicious circle that would perpetuate itself through the seed of his seed. However, the lad survived his execution, brought us together and gave us hope . . .' He paused for effect, then added: '. . . only he still hasn't taught us how to fuck properly!'

The laughter grew louder. When it had subsided, Jeff raised his tankard. 'To Tom, the best captain we could ever have!'

They all toasted him. Surprised by his companions' gesture, Tom could scarcely conceal his emotion.

'Well, Tom, I suppose you know what happens now, don't you?'

Jeff said, clapping his shoulder once the cheers had died down. 'We heard a rumour about some new merchandise at our favourite whorehouse. And they've got almond-shaped eyes – do you hear me? Almond-shaped eyes!'

'Have you ever slept with an Asian woman, Tom?' asked Bradley.

Tom shook his head.

'Well, no man should die without trying one, my friend!' Jeff guffawed as he rose from the table. 'Those Chinese girls can give pleasure in a hundred ways our women know nothing about.'

They made an almighty din as they left the tavern. Bradley led the procession, vaunting the Chinese prostitutes' numerous virtues, much to the delight of Mike, who smacked his lips in anticipation. According to Bradley, Asian women were not only obliging and affectionate but had supple bodies they could contort into all sorts of positions without injuring themselves.

Tom had to suppress a groan. If he wanted any woman to make love to him just then it was Claire, even if she did not have almond-shaped eyes or an unnaturally flexible body. He remembered the intensity of her response when he had taken her, and wondered what his companions, those coarse ruffians, would think if he told them there was another way of feeling that was more sublime and exquisite than the primitive pleasure they knew.

They hailed a cab and clambered aboard, still laughing. Mike squeezed his large frame in next to Tom, almost pinning him against the door, while the other two men faced them. Jeff, who was behaving in an overexcited, rowdy manner, gave the order for the cab to set off. Reluctant to join in the general gaiety, Tom gazed out of the window at the succession of streets, alarmingly deserted at that time of night. He noticed the driver had taken a wrong turning: they were going towards the docks, not the brothel.

'Hey, Jeff, we're going the wrong way!' he cried out, trying to make himself heard above the racket.

Jeff Wayne turned and looked at him sternly, letting his laughter die menacingly in his throat. Bradley and Mike also stopped laughing. A strange, intense silence enveloped them, as though someone had dredged it up from the ocean floor and poured it into the carriage.

'No, Tom, we're not going the wrong way,' Jeff finally said, contemplating him with a sinister smile.

'But we are!' insisted Tom. 'This isn't the way to . . .'

Then he understood. How had he not seen it before? Their exaggerated high spirits, the toast that had felt more like a farewell, their tense demeanour in the cab . . . Yes, what more proof did he need? In the funereal silence that had descended, the three men looked at him with an air of false calm, waiting for him to digest the situation. And, to his surprise, Tom discovered that now the time had arrived for him to die, he no longer wanted to. Not like this. Not at the hands of these casual assassins, who were simply demonstrating Gilliam Murray's unlimited power to turn anyone into a murderer with a handful of banknotes.

He was glad at least that Martin Tucker, whom he had always considered the most decent among them, was not there, that he had been incapable of turning his back on his friend and perpetrating this cheerful collective crime.

Tom heaved a sigh, disillusioned by the fickleness of the human spirit, and gazed at Jeff with an air of disappointment. His companion shrugged, refusing any responsibility for what was about to happen. He was opening his mouth, perhaps to remark that such was life or some other cliché, when a blow to his throat from Tom's boot stopped him, crushing him against the seat. Taken aback, Jeff let out a loud grunt of pain, which in turned into a high-pitched whistle. Tom knew this would not put him out of action, but the attack had been sudden enough to take them all by surprise.

Before the other two could react, he elbowed the bewildered Mike in the face as hard as he could. The blow dislocated the other man's jaw, and a spurt of blood from his split lip hit the window.

Undaunted by Tom's violent response, Bradley pulled a knife from his pocket and pounced on him. Although supple and quick, fortunately he was the weakest of the three. Tom grabbed his arm and twisted it violently until he dropped the weapon. Then, since the move had placed Bradley's head only a few inches from his leg, Tom kneed him brutally in the face, hurling him back against his seat, where he lay slumped, blood streaming from his nose.

In a matter of seconds he had overpowered all three men, but he scarcely had time to congratulate himself on his swift, punishing action because Jeff, who had by then recovered, flew at him with a savage roar. The force of the attack flung Tom against the cab door, the handle digging into his right side like a blade. They wrestled awkwardly in the reduced space, until Tom felt something crack behind him. The door had given way. Seconds later he found himself dangling in mid-air, clutching Jeff as the cab raced on. Tom hit the ground with Jeff, the breath knocked out of him. The impact caused the two men to carry on rolling for a few moments, until they disentangled themselves from their grotesque lovers' embrace.

When everything stopped spinning Tom, whose whole body ached terribly, tried to heave himself to his feet. A few yards off Jeff, alternately cursing and howling, was trying to do the same. Tom realised it would be one against one until the others arrived, and that he must take advantage of this.

But Jeff was too quick for him. Before he was fully on his feet, Jeff charged at him, propelling him back to the ground. He felt his spine crack in several places, but even so, as his assailant's hands grappled for his throat, Tom managed to place his foot on Jeff's chest and push him off. Jeff flew backwards, but Tom felt a searing pain as his thigh muscle ripped under the strain. He ignored it and struggled to his feet, before the other man this time.

In the distance, the cab had stopped, one door hanging like a broken wing. Bradley and Mike were already rushing towards them. Quickly calculating the odds, Tom decided his best bet was to run away from a fight he could only lose. He dashed towards the busier streets, away from the deserted docks.

He had no idea where his sudden urge to live had sprung from, when only hours before he had longed for eternal oblivion. In any event, he ran as fast as his racing heart and throbbing thigh would permit, struggling to find his bearings in the pitch-black night.

Hearing his pursuers close behind him, Tom dived into the first side street he came to, which, unhappily for him, proved to be a dead end. He swore at the wall standing in his way and turned slowly, resigned to his fate.

His companions stood waiting for him at the entrance to the alleyway. Now the real fight would begin, he said to himself, and strolled casually towards his executioners, trying hard not to limp and clenching his fists at his sides. He knew he stood no chance against three of them, but that did not mean he was going to throw in the towel. Would his desire to stay alive prove stronger than their desire to kill him?

Tom walked up to them and gave an ironical bow. He did not have Captain Shackleton's sword, but he felt as though the man's spirit was beating in his breast. It's better than nothing, he thought. The dim light from the nearest streetlamp barely illuminated the scene, and their faces remained in shadow. No one said a word, for there was nothing more to say, until Jeff gave the order. The men slowly fanned out, like prize fighters sizing up their opponent.

Since none of them took the initiative, Tom assumed they were giving him the chance to initiate the one-sided combat. Who would he go for first, he wondered, as his companions circled him? He stepped towards Mike, fists raised but, at the last moment, he made a feint and threw the punch at an unsuspecting Jeff. The blow hit him full in the face, knocking him to the ground. Out of the corner of his eye, Tom saw Bradley's attack coming. He dodged the punch and, when Bradley was squarely in front of him, plunged his fist into the lad's stomach, doubling him up in pain.

He was not so lucky with Mike, whose hammer blow was deadly. The world went fuzzy, Tom's mouth filled with blood, and he had to make a superhuman effort to stay on his feet. But the giant showed him no mercy. Before Tom had time to recover, he threw another punch, this time right on the chin. There was an ominous crack and Tom went spinning to the ground. Almost immediately, he felt the toe of a boot sink ruthlessly into his side, threatening to shatter his ribs. Tom realised they had him. The fight was over.

From the hail of blows raining down on him, he deduced that Bradley and Jeff had joined in the beating.

On the ground beside him, through the dense fog of his pain, he could make out Wells's book, which must have fallen out of his pocket during the brawl. Claire's flower had escaped from its pages and lay incongruously on the filthy ground, a pale yellow brightness that looked as though it would be snuffed out at any moment, like his life.

XXXIII

When at last the beating stopped, Tom clenched his teeth and, ignoring the pain, reached out to grasp Claire's flower, but failed: at that moment someone grabbed his hair and tried to pull him up. 'Nice try, Tom, nice try,' Jeff Wayne whispered in his ear, accompanying his words with what sounded like a snigger, or perhaps a groan. 'Unfortunately, your efforts were wasted. You're going to die anyway.'

He ordered Mike to take hold of Tom's feet, and he felt himself borne aloft by his executioners to a place that, on the brink of losing consciousness, scarcely mattered to him. After a few minutes of being bumped and jolted, his companions tossed him on the ground as if he were a bundle of rags.

When Tom heard lapping water and boats knocking together, his worst fears were confirmed: they had brought him back to the docks, probably because they planned to throw him into the river. But for the moment no one did or said anything. Tom was trying to slip into oblivion, but the sensation of something soft, warm and not unpleasant touching his swollen cheeks prevented it. It felt as if one of his companions had decided to prepare him for death by wiping the blood from his wounds with a cloth dipped in tar.

'Eternal, come here at once!' he heard someone shout.

The sensation stopped, and Tom felt vibrations in the ground and heard the heavy yet delicate tread of footsteps slowly approaching the scene.

'Stand him up,' the voice commanded.

His companions yanked him roughly to his feet, but Tom's legs would not support him, causing him to slump to his knees with the almost sensual limpness of a puppet whose strings have been cut. A hand grasped his collar to prevent him keeling over completely. Once he had overcome his dizziness and could focus, Tom watched impassively from his kneeling position as Gilliam Murray made his way slowly towards him, his dog circling at his feet. He wore the slightly irritated expression of someone who has been dragged from his bed in the middle of the night for no good reason, as though it had escaped his memory that he was the one behind the ambush. He stopped a few yards in front of Tom and looked at him, smirking disdainfully, taking pleasure in his pathetic state.

'Tom, Tom, Tom,' he said at last, in the tone of someone scolding a child. 'How has it come to this unpleasant situation? Was it really so difficult to follow my instructions?'

Tom remained silent, not so much because the question was rhetorical but because he doubted he could utter a word, his lips swollen, his mouth full of blood and broken tooth. Now that he could focus, he glanced around and saw that they were indeed at the docks, only a few yards from the quayside. Besides Murray, who was standing in front of him, and his companions waiting for their orders, there seemed not another soul in sight. It would all take place in the strictest intimacy. That was how nobodies met their end, discreetly, without any fuss, like refuse tossed into the river in the middle of the night while the world is sleeping. And no one would notice his absence the next day. No one would say: 'Hold on, where's Tom Blunt?' No, the orchestra of life would play on without him, because his part had never been important to the score.

'Do you know what's so amusing about this whole thing, Tom?' said Murray, calmly, moving closer to the edge of the quay and gazing absently into the murky river. 'It was your lover who gave you away.'

Again, Tom said nothing. He simply stared at his boss, whose eyes were still contemplating the Thames, that bottomless coffer where he stored anything that posed a problem. A moment later, Murray smirked at him once more, with a mixture of pity and amusement.

'Yes. If she hadn't come to my office the day after the expedition asking for the address of one of Captain Shackleton's ancestors I would never have found out about your affair.'

He paused again to give Tom time to digest what he had told him. As Murray had suspected, the girl had never mentioned this to him. And why should she? From Tom's point of view it was unimportant, of course. For Murray it had been a fortuitous blunder.

'I had no idea what the girl's game was,' he said, walking to Tom with mincing, almost balletic, steps. 'I gave her an evasive reply and sent her packing, but I was curious so I had one of my men follow her – just to be on the safe side. You know how much I dislike people poking their noses into my affairs. But Miss Haggerty didn't seem interested in snooping – quite the contrary. Isn't that so? I confess to being astonished when my informant told me she had arranged to meet you at a tea room, and afterwards . . . Well, I don't need to tell you what happened afterwards at the Pickard boarding-house.'

Tom lowered his head in a gesture that could equally have been embarrassment or vertigo.

'My suspicions were justified,' Murray went on, amused by Tom's awkwardness, 'but not in the way I had imagined. I thought of killing you there and then, despite my admiration for the way you had used the situation to your advantage. But then you did something completely unexpected: you visited Wells's house, and that aroused my curiosity even more. I wondered what you were up to. If you intended telling the writer it was a hoax you had gone to the wrong person. As you immediately discovered, Wells is the only person in the whole of London who is aware of the truth. But, no, you had a far nobler purpose.'

As Murray spoke, he paced back and forth in front of Tom, hands behind his back. His movement made the boards on the quayside squeak unpleasantly. Eternal sat a few feet away, fixing him with a vaguely curious look.

'After leaving Wells's house, you went to Harrow-on-the-Hill. There you hid a letter under a stone, which my spy brought to me immediately. And when I had read it I understood everything.' He gazed at Tom with mock compassion. 'I have to confess I was most amused by your letters, which my informant put back before whoever was to collect them arrived. Except for the last one, of course, which you whisked away so fast I had to steal it off Wells while he was out on that ludicrous machine known as a bicycle he likes to ride around on.'

He stopped pacing and studied the river again.

'Herbert George Wells . . .' he whispered, scarcely able to contain his contempt. 'The poor fool. I can't deny I was tempted to tear up all his letters and rewrite them myself. I only refrained from doing so because Wells would never have found out, which would have been the same as if I had done nothing. But let's not talk about that any more,' he declared, suddenly brightening and turning once more to face his victim. 'You couldn't care less about petty rivalries between writers, could you, Tom? Yes, I greatly enjoyed reading your letters, one passage in particular, as I'm sure you can imagine. I believe it was very instructive to us all. However, now the final instalment has been written, the little old ladies will shed bitter tears over the lovers' tragic fate, and I am free to kill you.'

He crouched before Tom and lifted his head with almost maternal tenderness. The blood streaming from Tom's split lip soiled his fingers and he pulled out a handkerchief to clean it off, still gazing intently at Tom.

'Do you know something, Tom?' he said. 'In the end, I'm deeply grateful for all your efforts not to reveal my hoax. I realise you're partially blameless. But only partially. True, that foolish girl started everything. Yet you could have let it go, and you didn't, did you? I sympathise, believe me: I'm sure the girl was worth taking all those risks for. However, you see why I can't let you go on living.

We each have our role to play in this tale. And, sadly for you, mine consists of killing you. And how could I resist the perfect irony of giving the job to your faithful soldiers of the future?'

With these words, he gave a twisted smile at the men looming behind Tom. He studied Tom again for a long time, as though giving one last thought to what he was about to do, perhaps mulling over another possible course of action.

'I have no choice, Tom,' he said finally, shrugging his shoulders. 'If I don't kill you, sooner or later you'll look for her again. I know you will. You'll look for her because you're in love with her.'

On hearing this, Tom could not help gazing at Murray in surprise. Was it true? Was he really in love with Claire? This was a question to which he had never given much thought because, whether or not he loved her or she had just been a passing fancy, an opportunity he was loath to pass up, he still had to keep away from her. However, now he had to admit that if Murray were to let him live, the first thing he would do was look for her, and that could only mean his boss was right: he was in love with her.

Yes, he realised with astonishment, he loved her. He loved Claire Haggerty. He had loved her from the moment he had first seen her. He loved the way she looked at him, the touch of her skin, the way she had of loving him. It felt so good to let himself be enveloped by the protective mantle of that immense love, the magic cape that shielded him from life's coldness, the icy indifference of every day that made his soul tremble, the incessant wind filtering through the shutters and seeping into his innermost depths. And he wanted nothing more than to be able to love her with the same intensity, to feel he was fulfilling man's highest, most noble achievement, the one he had been born for, the one that satisfied him and made him happy: to love, to love truly, to love for no other reason than the joy of being able to do so. That was what drove him on. That was his reason for living, because although he might be unable to leave his mark on the world, he could make someone else happy, and that was the most important thing. The most important thing was to leave his mark on another person's heart.

Yes, Murray was right: he would look for her because he wanted her to be with him, because he needed her by his side in order to become someone else, to escape from who he was. Yes, he would look for her, whether to delight in the joys of spring together or to plunge into the abyss. He would look for her because he loved her. And somehow this lessened the lie Claire was living. For, in the end, the girl's love was reciprocated, and Tom's love, like Shackleton's, was also unattainable, lost in the ether, unable to find its way to her. What did it matter if they lived in the same time or even in the same city, that festering turn-of-the-century London, if they were to remain as far apart as if they were separated by an ocean of time?

'But why drag things out?' he heard Murray say. 'It would make for a worse, far less exciting ending to the story, don't you think? It's best if you disappear, Tom, for the story to end as it's supposed to. The girl will be far happier in any case.'

Gilliam Murray lifted his huge body to its full height and gazed down at Tom once more with scientific interest, as though he were something floating in a bottle of formaldehyde.

'Don't harm her,' Tom stammered.

Murray shook his head, pretending to be shocked. 'Of course I won't, Tom! Don't you see? With you out of the way the girl is no threat to me. And, believe it or not, I have my scruples. I don't murder people just for the fun of it, Tom.'

'My name is Shackleton,' said Tom, between gritted teeth. 'Captain Derek Shackleton.'

Murray burst out laughing. 'Then you needn't be afraid, for I guarantee you will rise from the dead.'

With these words, he gave Tom one last smile and gestured to his companions. 'All right, gentlemen. Let's get this over with and go to bed.'

Following Murray's command, Jeff and Bradley scooped Tom off the ground, while Mike brought over a huge block of stone with a piece of rope tied round it, which they fastened to Tom's feet. Then they bound his hands behind his back. Murray watched the proceedings with a satisfied smile.

'Ready, boys,' said Jeff, after making sure the knots were secure. 'Let's do it.'

Once more, Jeff and Bradley carried Tom shoulder high to the edge of the quay, while Mike held on to the stone that would anchor him to the riverbed. Tom gazed blankly at the murky water. He was filled with the strange calm of someone who knows his life is no longer in his own hands. Murray walked over to him and squeezed his shoulder hard. 'Goodbye, Tom. You were the best Shackleton I could hope to find, but such is life,' he said. 'Give my regards to Perkins.'

Tom's companions swung his body, and at the count of three tossed him and the stone into the Thames. Tom had time to fill his lungs with air before he hit the surface of the water. The cold came as a shock, dispelling the lethargy pervading his body. He was struck by fate's final irony: what good was it to feel so awake now that he was about to drown? He sank in a horizontal position to begin with, but the weight of the stone soon pulled him upright, and he plummeted with astonishing speed to the bottom of the Thames. He blinked several times, trying to glimpse something through the greeny-brown water, but there was not much to see, besides the bottoms of the boats floating above, and a flickering halo of light cast by the quay's only streetlamp.

The stone quickly hit the riverbed and Tom remained floating above it, suspended by ten inches of rope, like a child's kite, buffeted by the current. How long could he go without breathing? he wondered. What did it matter? Was it not absurd to struggle against the inevitable? Even though he knew it would only postpone death, he pressed his lips tightly together. Again that painful instinct to survive, but now he had understood his sudden will to live: he had discovered that the worst thing about dying was not being able to change what he had been, that when he died others would see only the repulsive tableau into which his life would solidify. He remained hanging upright for what felt like an excruciating eternity, lungs burning, temples throbbing deafeningly, until the urgent need to breathe compelled him against his will to open his mouth.

Water began to fill his throat, streaming merrily into his lungs, and everything around him became even fuzzier. Then Tom realised this was it: in a few seconds he would lose consciousness.

In spite of this, he had time to see the figure appear. He watched him emerge from the swirling fog in his brain and walk towards him along the riverbed with his heavy metal footsteps, oblivious to the water all around him. He assumed that the lack of oxygen to his brain had allowed the automaton to escape from his dreams and move around in the real world. He was too late, though. Tom had no need of him: he was quite capable of drowning without his help. Or perhaps he had come for the pleasure of watching him die, face to face in the river's murky depths.

But, to his surprise, when the automaton reached his side, he gripped Tom's waist with one of his metal arms, as if to lead him in a dance, while with the other he tugged at the rope around his feet until he loosened it. Then he heaved Tom towards the surface. Tom, still semi-conscious, saw the bottoms of the boats and the shimmering streetlamp gradually looming larger. Before he knew it, his head emerged above the water.

The night air coursed into his lungs, and Tom knew this was the true taste of life. He breathed in greedily, spluttering like a hungry infant choking on its food. He allowed his enemy to hoist his near-lifeless body on to the quayside, where he lay on his back, dizzy and numb with cold. He felt the automaton's hands pressing repeatedly down on his chest. The pumping helped him spew out the water he had swallowed. When there seemed to be no more, he coughed a few times, bringing up some congealed blood, and could feel life seeping back into his limp form. He was overjoyed to discover he was alive again, to feel life's soft pulse flowing through him, filling him voluptuously, like the river water had done only moments before. For a split second, he even felt the illusion of immortality, as though such a close brush with death, having felt the Grim Reaper's chill fingers closing around him, had in some way acquainted him with it so that its rules no longer applied to him.

Somewhat recovered, Tom forced himself to smile at his saviour, whose metallic head was floating above him, a dark spherical object lit by the single streetlamp on the quay. 'Thank you, Solomon,' he managed to splutter.

The automaton unscrewed his head. 'Solomon?' he laughed. 'It's a diving suit, Tom.'

Although his face remained in the shadow, Tom recognised Martin Tucker's voice, and was overwhelmed with happiness.

'Have you never seen one before? It lets you walk underwater, just like strolling in a park, while someone pumps air through a tube from the surface. We have Bob to thank for that and for winching us both up on to the quay,' explained his companion, pointing towards a figure out of Tom's field of vision. Then, after putting the helmet to one side, Martin lifted Tom's head and examined it with the carefulness of a nurse. ''Struth, the boys did a good job. You're in a right state. Don't be angry with them, though. They had to make it look realistic to dupe Murray. I think it worked. As far as he's concerned, they've done the job and are no doubt receiving their dues right this minute.'

Despite his swollen lips, Tom grimaced. So, it had been a charade? Apparently so. As Murray had explained to him before he had been thrown into the Thames, he had hired Tom's companions to kill him. But they were not as heartless as Tom had thought, even though they couldn't afford to refuse Murray's money. Martin must have suggested that, if they were clever, they could put on another performance – the burly fellow was now brushing back Tom's hair from his bloodied brow and gazing at him with fatherly affection.

'Well, Tom, the performance is over,' he said. 'Now that you're officially dead, you're free. Your new life begins tonight, my friend. Make the most of it, as I am sure you will.'

He patted Tom's shoulder in a gesture of farewell, smiled at him one last time and vanished from the quay, leaving an echo of metallic footsteps lingering behind him.

After he had gone, Tom lay still, in no hurry to get up, trying to assimilate everything that had happened. He took a deep breath, testing his sore lungs, and gazed at the heavens arching above him. A beautiful pale yellow full moon lit the night sky, grinning down at him, like a death's head that had threatened to swallow him only to breathe new life into him. Incredible though it might seem, everything had been resolved without him having to die. His body was racked with pain and he felt weak as a kitten, but he was alive – alive! Wild delight overwhelmed him, compelling him to get up off the cold ground – if he lay there much longer in his wet clothes he would catch pneumonia.

He struggled to his feet and limped away from the docks. His bones were bruised but not broken, and his companions must have taken care not to injure his internal organs. The place was deserted. At the entrance to the cul-de-sac where the fight had started, lying next to Wells's novel, he saw the flower Claire had given him. He picked it up and held it in the palm of his hand. The sweet, fragrant scent of narcissus, faintly reminiscent of jasmine, guided him slowly through the labyrinth of the night, pulling him, like the sea's undertow, drawing him towards an elegant house immersed in silence.

The fence around it was not too high, and a creeper seemed to adorn its façade for the sole purpose of making it easier for a daring man to climb to the window of a sleeping girl.

Tom gazed with infinite tenderness at the girl who loved him as no one had ever loved him before. From her lips came short, soft sighs as though a summer breeze were wafting through her. He noticed her right hand clutched a piece of paper on which he could make out Wells's minuscule handwriting. He was about to wake her with a caress, when she opened her eyelids slowly, as though he had roused her simply by gazing at her. She did not appear in the least surprised to see him standing beside her bed, as if she had known that, sooner or later, he would appear, guided by the scent of her narcissi.

'You've come back,' she whispered sweetly.

'Yes, Claire, I've come back,' he replied. 'I've come back for good.'

She smiled serenely at him, pushed back the bedclothes, stood up and walked into his open arms. And as they kissed, Tom understood that, regardless of what Gilliam Murray thought, this was a far more beautiful ending than the one where they never met again.

PART THREE

DISTINGUISHED GENTLEMEN

AND IMPRESSIONABLE LADIES,

WE HAVE ARRIVED AT THE

CLOSING PAGES OF OUR

THRILLING TALE.

WHAT MARVELS

ARE THERE STILL IN

STORE FOR YOU?

If you wish to find out, make sure your attention does not stray from these pages for an instant, because in an even more amazing discovery, you will be able to travel in time to your heart's content, into the past as well as to the future.

DEAR READER, IF YOU ARE NO COWARD, DARE TO FINISH WHAT YOU HAVE STARTED!

WE CAN GUARANTEE

THIS FINAL JOURNEY

IS WELL WORTH THE EFFORT.

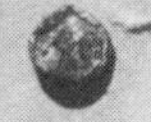

XXXIV

Inspector Colin Garrett of Scotland Yard would have been glad if the sight of blood did not make him feel so queasy that each time his job obliged him to look at a dead body he had to leave the scene to be sick – especially if the cadaver in question had been subjected to a particularly dreadful attack. However, sadly for him, this was such a regular occurrence that the inspector had even considered the possibility of forgoing breakfast, in view of how little time the meal remained in his stomach. Perhaps it was to compensate for this squeamishness that he had been blessed with such a brilliant mind. At any rate, that was what his uncle had always told him – his uncle being the legendary Inspector Frederick Abberline who, some years previously, had been in charge of hunting down the vicious murderer, Jack the Ripper.

Such was Abberline's belief in his nephew's superior brainpower that he had practically delivered the boy himself to Scotland Yard's headquarters with an impassioned letter of recommendation addressed to Chief Superintendent Arnold, the austere, arrogant man in charge of the detective squad. And, during his first year there, Garrett had to acknowledge that, to his surprise, his uncle's trust in him had not proved unfounded. He had solved a great many cases since moving into his office overlooking Great George Street, apparently with very little effort. He had achieved this without leaving his lair.

Garrett would spend long nights in his cosy refuge, collecting and fitting together the pieces of evidence his subordinates brought to him, like a child absorbed in a jigsaw puzzle, avoiding contact with the raw, bloody reality that pulsated behind the data he handled. A sensitive soul like his was unsuited to fieldwork.

Perhaps the morgue was the place that showed off the grittier side of crime to its most flamboyant effect – its tangible side, its unpleasantly real physical side, which Garrett tried so hard to ignore. Each time he was forced to view a body, the inspector would give a resigned sigh, pull on his hat and set off for the loathsome building concerned, praying he would have time to flee the autopsy room before his stomach heaved, and avoid bespattering the pathologist's shoes.

The corpse he was meant to examine that morning had been discovered in Marylebone by the local police, who had handed the case to Scotland Yard when they had found it impossible to identify what kind of weapon had inflicted the wound on the victim – apparently a tramp. Garrett imagined the bobbies doing this with a wry smile, content to give the brainboxes in Great George Street a sufficiently puzzling case to make them earn their salary.

Dr Terence Alcock had been waiting for him at the entrance to the York Street morgue, wearing a blood-stained apron, and had confessed that they were faced with a mystery he for one found completely baffling. And when a man as well versed as the pathologist, who was fond of airing his knowledge at every opportunity, admitted defeat so openly, Garrett decided he was confronted with a truly interesting case, the sort you might expect to find in a novel featuring his hero Sherlock Holmes. In real life, more often than not, criminals showed a distinct lack of imagination.

To Garrett's astonishment, the pathologist greeted him with a grim expression and guided him in solemn silence down the corridor to the autopsy room. He immediately understood that the inexplicable wound had vexed him to the point of clouding his usually excellent humour. Despite the rather alarming appearance that having only eyebrow gave him, Dr Alcock was a cheerful, garrulous fellow. Whenever Garrett appeared at the morgue, he always greeted him jovially, reciting in a sing-song voice the order in which he considered it most appropriate to examine the abdominal cavity: peritoneum, spleen, left kidney, suprarenal gland, urinary tract, prostate gland, seminal vesicles, penis, sperm cord . . . a litany of names ending with the intestines – he them left until last, he explained, for reasons of hygiene: handling their contents was a revolting job.

And I, who see everything whether I want to or not, as I have repeatedly reminded you throughout this tale, can confirm that, notwithstanding his propensity for bluster, in this instance the doctor was not exaggerating. Thanks to my supernatural ability to be in all places at once, I have seen him in this unpleasant situation, covering himself, the corpse, the dissecting table and even the floor of the autopsy room with excrement. Out of concern for your sensibilities I shall refrain from any closer description.

This time, however, as he walked down the long corridor, the pathologist had a melancholy air, and did not reel off his usual list, which Garrett, thanks to his prodigious memory, had often caught himself singing under his breath, usually when he was in a good mood. At the end of the corridor, they reached a large room where the unmistakable odour of decaying flesh lingered in the air. It was lit by several four-branched gas lamps hanging from the ceiling, although Garrett thought these were not enough for such a large room, and only made it seem even grimmer. In the semi-darkness, he could scarcely see more than two yards in front of him.

Rows of cabinets filled with surgical instruments lined the brick walls, with shelves of bottles containing mysterious opaque liquids. On the far wall was a huge basin, where on more than one occasion he had seen Dr Alcock rinsing blood off his hands, like someone practising a macabre ritual ablution. In the centre of the room, a figure with a sheet draped over it lay on a sturdy table, lit by a single lamp. The pathologist, who always wore his sleeves rolled up, which Garrett found disturbing, gestured to him to approach the table. On a stand next to the body, like a sinister still-life, lay an assortment of dissecting knives, blades for slicing through cartilage, a cut-throat razor, various scalpels, a few hacksaws, a fine chisel and accompanying hammer for boring into the cranium, a dozen needles threaded with catgut suture, a few soiled rags, some scales, an optical lens, and a bucket of pinkish water, which Garrett tried not to look at.

Just then, one of the pathologist's assistants opened the door hesitantly, but the doctor shooed him away angrily. Garrett remembered hearing him rail against the foppish youngsters they sent fresh out of university, who wielded an autopsy knife as though it were a pen, moving only their hand and wrist rather than their whole arm, and making timid little cuts as if they were preparing a meal. 'They should leave that type of slicing to the people who give public demonstrations in the amphitheatres,' Dr Alcock declared. He was a believer in bold incisions, long, deep cuts that tested the resilience of an arm or a shoulder's musculature. After heading off the interruption, the doctor drew back the sheet covering the body on the slab. He did so without ceremony, like a magician wearily performing a trick for the thousandth time.

'The subject is a male aged between forty and fifty,' he said, in a flat monotone. 'Height five foot seven, fragile-boned, with reduced amounts of subcutaneous fat and muscle tissue. The body is pale in colour. As for the teeth, the incisors are present, but several molars are missing. Most of those remaining contain cavities and are covered with a darkish layer.'

After presenting his report, he paused, waiting for the inspector to stop staring at the ceiling and to look at the corpse.

'And this is the wound,' he declared enthusiastically, attempting to coax Garrett out of his passivity.

Garrett gulped air and allowed his eyes to descend slowly towards the cadaver, until his eyes came to rest on the enormous hole in the middle of the chest.

'It is a circular opening, twelve inches in diameter,' explained the pathologist, 'which you can look straight through as if it were a window – as you will see if you lean over.'

Reluctantly, Garrett bent over the huge hole and, indeed, was able to glimpse beneath it the table the body was stretched out on.

'Whatever caused the wound, besides badly scorching the skin around the edges, pulverised everything in its path, including part of the sternum, the ribcage, the mediastinum, the lungs, the right ventricle of the heart and the corresponding section of the spinal cord. What little survived, like some pieces of lung, fused with the thoracic wall. I have yet to carry out the post-mortem, but this hole was clearly the cause of death,' the pathologist pronounced, 'only I'll be hanged if I know what made it. The poor wretch looks as if he's been pierced by a tongue of flame or, if you prefer, by some sort of heat ray. But I don't know any weapon capable of doing this, except perhaps the Archangel Michael's flaming sword.'

Garrett nodded, struggling with his rebellious stomach. 'Does the body present any other anomalies?' he asked, by way of saying something, feeling the sweat begin to pearl on his forehead.

'His foreskin is shorter than average, barely covering the base of the glans, but without any sign of scarring,' the pathologist replied, flaunting his professional knowledge. 'Apart from that, the only anomaly is this accursed hole, big enough for a poodle to jump through.'

Garrett was disgusted by the image the pathologist had conjured up. He felt as though he knew more about the poor wretch now than was necessary for his investigation. 'Much obliged to you, Dr Alcock. Let me know if you discover anything new or if you think of anything that may have caused this hole,' he said.

Hurriedly he took his leave of the pathologist and walked out of the morgue, as upright as he could. Once he reached the street, he dived into the nearest alleyway and brought up his breakfast between two piles of refuse. He emerged, wiping his mouth with his handkerchief, pale but recovered. He paused, gulped air, then breathed out slowly, smiling. The singed flesh. The grisly hole. He was not surprised the pathologist was unable to identify the weapon responsible for that ghastly wound. But he knew exactly what it was.

Yes, he had seen brave Captain Shackleton wielding it in the year 2000.

It took him almost two hours to persuade his superior to sign an arrest warrant for a man who had not yet been born. As he stood outside the door to his office, swallowing hard, he knew it was not going to be easy. Chief Superintendent Thomas Arnold was a close friend of his uncle, and had accepted him with good grace into his team of detectives, although he had never shown him anything other than distant politeness, with an occasional outburst of fatherly affection whenever Garrett solved a difficult case. When his superior walked past his office and saw him with his head down, the young inspector had the feeling he was looking at him with the same discreet satisfaction as if he were a coal stove in good working order.

The only time his affable smile faded had been the day Garrett went into his office following his trip to the year 2000 to recommend an urgent ban on the production of automatons and the confiscation of those already in circulation; he had said they should be stored where they could be watched, in a pen surrounded by barbed wire, if necessary. Chief Superintendent Arnold thought the idea was completely ludicrous. He was only a year away from retirement, and the last thing he wanted was to make life difficult for himself by advocating preventive measures against some far-fetched threat he himself had not foreseen. But because the new recruit had more than proved his astuteness, he reluctantly agreed to ask for a meeting with the commissioner and the prime minister to discuss the matter.

On that occasion, the command that had come down to Garrett from the hierarchy was a clear refusal: there would be no halt to the production of automatons or any attempt to prevent them infiltrating people's homes under the guise of their innocent appearance, regardless of whether, a century later, they were going to conquer the planet. Garrett pictured the meeting between those three unimaginative men incapable of seeing further than the end of their noses. He was sure they had dismissed his request amid scathing remarks and guffaws. This time however, things would be different. This time they could not look the other way. They could not wash their hands of the matter, arguing that by the time the automatons rebelled against man they would be resting peacefully in their graves, for the simple reason that on this occasion the future had come to them: it was acting in the present, in their own time, that very part of time they were supposed to be protecting.

Even so, Chief Superintendent Arnold put on a sceptical face the moment Garrett began to explain the affair. Garrett considered it a privilege to have been born in an era when science made new advances every day, offering him things his grandparents had never even conceived of. He was thinking not so much of the gramophone or the telephone as of time travel. Who would have been able to explain to his grandfather that in his grandson's time people would be able to journey to the future, beyond their own lifetimes, or to the past, back through the pages of history? Garrett had been excited about travelling to the year 2000 not so much because he was going to witness a crucial moment in the history of the human race – the end of the long war against the automatons – but because he was more conscious than ever that he lived in a world where, thanks to science, anything seemed possible. He was going to travel to the year 2000, yes, but who could say how many more epochs he might visit before he died?

According to Gilliam Murray, it was only a matter of time before new routes opened up. Perhaps he would have the opportunity to glimpse a better future, after the world had been rebuilt, or to travel back to the time of the pharaohs or to Shakespeare's London, where he could see the playwright penning his legendary works by candlelight. All this made his youthful spirit rejoice, and he felt continually grateful to God, in whom, despite Darwin's policy of vilification, he preferred to continue to believe. Each night, before he went to bed, he beamed up at the stars, where he imagined God resided, to indicate that he was ready to marvel at whatever He deigned to show him.

It will come as no surprise to you, then, that Garrett paid no heed to people who mistrusted the discoveries of science, still less to those who showed no interest in Gilliam Murray's extraordinary discovery, as was the case with his superior, who had not even bothered to take time off to visit the year 2000.

'Let me see if I've understood you correctly. Are you telling me this is the only lead you have in this case, Inspector?' Chief Superintendent Arnold said, waving the advertisement for Murray's Time Travel Garrett had given him. He jabbed his finger at the little illustration showing the brave Captain Shackleton shooting a hole in an automaton with a ray gun.

Garrett sighed. The fact that Chief Superintendent Arnold had not been on any of the expeditions to the future meant he was forced to fill him in on the subject. He wasted several minutes explaining in general terms what was happening in the year 2000 and how they had travelled there, until he reached the part that really interested him: the weaponry used by the human soldiers. Those guns were capable of cutting through metal, so it was not impossible to imagine that, on a human, the effect might be very similar to what he had seen on the body in the Marylebone morgue. As far as he was aware, no weapons in their own time could cause such a horrific wound, a fact he could see was borne out by Dr Alcock in his autopsy report.

At this point, Garrett presented his theory to Arnold: one of these men from the future, possibly the one named Shackleton, had stowed away on the Cronotilus when he and the others had travelled back to their time, and was now on the loose in the year 1896, armed with a lethal weapon. If he was right, they had two choices: they could search the whole of London for Shackleton, which might take several weeks, with no guarantee of success, or they could save themselves the trouble by arresting him where they knew he would be on 20 May in the year 2000. Garrett had only to go there with two police officers, and arrest him before Shackleton could travel back to their own day.

'What's more,' he added, in a last-ditch attempt to convince his superior, who was shaking his head, visibly perplexed, 'if you give me permission to arrest Captain Shackleton in the future, your department will be in line for all kinds of plaudit, because we will have achieved something truly ground-breaking: arresting a murderer before he is able to commit a crime, thus preventing it happening.'

Chief Superintendent Arnold gazed at him in disbelief. 'Are you telling me that if you travel to the year 2000 and arrest this murderer his crime will be . . . rubbed out?'

Garrett understood how difficult it was for a man like Chief Superintendent Arnold to grasp something like this. No one would find it easy to understand the implications of what he was saying, unless they stayed awake all night as he did, mulling over the paradoxes to which time travel might give rise. 'I'm convinced of it, Chief Superintendent. If I arrest him before he commits the crime, it will inevitably change the present. Not only will we be arresting a murderer, we'll be saving a life because, I assure you, the tramp's corpse will vanish from the morgue in a flash,' Garrett declared, unsure himself of exactly how this would happen.

Thomas Arnold pondered for a few moments the praise Scotland Yard would earn from such temporal acrobatics. Luckily, his limited imagination was unable to comprehend that, once the murderer was arrested, not only would the corpse disappear, but so would everything relating to the crime, including the interview taking place at that very moment. There would be no murder to solve. In short, they would earn no plaudits because they would have done nothing.

The consequences of arresting Shackleton in the future, before he travelled into the past to commit his crime, were so unpredictable that Garrett himself, as soon as he paused to analyse them, found them dizzying. What would they do with a murderer whose crime no one remembered because he had been arrested before he committed it? What the devil would they accuse him of? Or perhaps Garrett's journey into the future would also be flushed away down the giant cosmic drain where everything that had been prevented from happening disappeared? He did not know, but he was certain he was the instrument to set everything in motion.

After two hours of discussion, the dazed Chief Superintendent Arnold had ended the interview with a promise to Garrett that he would meet the commissioner and the prime minister that very afternoon and explain the situation to them as best he could. Garrett thanked him. This meant that the following day, if no problems arose, he would receive the warrant to arrest Shackleton in the year 2000. Then he would go to Murray's Time Travel to see Murray and demand three seats on the next voyage of his Cronotilus.

As one might expect, while Garrett waited he mulled over the case. On this occasion, however, rather than attempt to solve it by analysing the various elements, which was pointless as he had already found the murderer, he simply marvelled at its extraordinary ramifications, as if he were examining a web spun by a new species of spider. And for once Garrett was not sitting in his office thinking these thoughts, but on a bench on the pavement opposite a luxurious house on Sloane Street.

This was the abode of Nathan Ferguson, the pianola manufacturer, whom, unfortunately – owing to his friendship with Garrett's father – Garrett had known all his life. He had his doubts as to whether the odious fellow was in fact largely responsible for the devastating war of the future as the foul-mouthed young Winslow had suggested in jest, but he had nothing against spending the evening enjoying a bunch of grapes while he watched his house to see whether anyone suspicious came prowling around. If they did, it would no doubt save him a trip to the future. But it was quite possible, too, that Ferguson's only function in the vast scheme of the universe was as a manufacturer of pianolas, and that Captain Shackleton was at that very moment stalking someone else's house. Why else would he have killed the tramp? What could that poor wretch's life have meant to the captain? Had he been an unfortunate casualty, an accident, or was there more to the cadaver lying in the morgue than met the eye? Was it, perhaps, a key piece in the puzzle of the future?

Garret was absorbed in his thoughts, but was forced to end them when he saw the door to the house open and Ferguson step out. The inspector rose from his bench and ducked behind a tree from where he had a clear view of what happened on the pavement opposite. Ferguson paused to put on his top hat and survey the night with a triumphant expression. Garrett saw that he was elegantly turned out, and assumed he must be on his way to some dinner or other. After pulling on his gloves, Ferguson closed the door behind him, descended the flight of steps, and strolled down the street in a leisurely way. Wherever he was going must be near enough for him not to summon his carriage.

Garrett wondered whether to follow him or not. Before he had a chance to decide what action to take, just as Ferguson was passing the flowerbeds bordering the lawn in front of his house, a shadow emerged silently from among the bushes. It was wearing a long coat and a cap pulled down over its face. Garrett did not need to see who it was: he knew. He was the first to be astonished that his theory had proved correct.

With a determined gesture, the figure pulled a pistol out of its coat pocket and aimed it at Ferguson as he strolled along, oblivious of what was going on behind his back. Garrett responded with alacrity. He leaped out from behind the tree and raced across the street. He was aware that surprise was his strongest weapon against Shackleton, who was twice his size and strength. The sound of Garrett's footsteps alerted the shadow, who watched his swift approach with visible alarm, while still training the gun on Ferguson.

Garrett hurled himself at Shackleton with all his might, grabbing him round the waist. The two men fell through the bushes into the garden. The inspector was surprised by how easily he was able to pin down Shackleton, but quickly realised that this was because he was lying on top of a beautiful young woman, whose mouth was within kissing distance of his own.

'Miss Nelson?' he stammered, at a loss.

'Inspector Garrett!' she exclaimed, equally nonplussed.

Garrett's face flushed bright red. He leaped up, disentangling himself from their unseemly embrace, then helped her to her feet. The revolver lay on the ground, but neither hurried to pick it up.

'Are you all right?' asked the inspector.

'Yes,' the girl replied, gasping with annoyance. 'I don't think I've broken any bones, at any rate.'

Lucy brushed the mud off her clothes, and let down her hair from the bun it had been wound up in – it had come loose during the fall.

'Forgive me for charging at you like that, Miss Nelson,' Garrett apologised, entranced by the lovely golden cascade resting on her shoulders like honey spilling from a jar. 'I'm truly sorry, but . . . if I'm not mistaken you were going to shoot Mr Ferguson.'

'Of course I was going to shoot Mr Ferguson, Inspector! I haven't been hiding in the bushes all evening for nothing,' the girl replied sulkily.

She bent down to retrieve the pistol, but Garrett was quicker. 'I think I'd better keep this,' he said, grinning apologetically. 'But tell me, why kill Mr Ferguson?'

Lucy stared distractedly at the ground for a few moments. 'I'm not the shallow girl everyone thinks I am, you know,' she said, sounding wounded. 'I care about the world just as much as anyone else. And I intended to prove it by stopping the man responsible for the war of the future.'

'I don't think you're shallow,' said Garrett. 'And anyone who does is an ass.'

Lucy beamed, flattered. 'Do you really mean that?' she said demurely.

'Of course, Miss Nelson,' said the inspector, smiling shyly at her. 'But don't you think there are better ways of proving it than by staining those lovely hands of yours with blood?'

'I suppose you're right, Mr Garrett,' Lucy admitted, gazing at him admiringly.

'I'm so glad you agree,' said Garrett, genuinely relieved.

They stood in silence looking at each other awkwardly.

'What now, Inspector?' she said at length, her face a picture of innocence. 'Are you going to arrest me?'

Garrett sighed. 'I suppose I should, Miss Nelson,' he acknowledged reluctantly. 'However . . .' He paused to weigh up the situation.

'Yes?' said Lucy.

'I'm prepared to forget all about it if you promise not to try to shoot anyone again.'

'Oh, I promise, Inspector!' she said, overjoyed. 'Now, kindly give me the pistol so I can put it back in my father's drawer before he notices it's missing.'

Garrett hesitated, but in the end he handed it to her. When she took it, their fingers touched; they lingered for a moment sharing a sense of delight. Garrett cleared his throat as Lucy slipped the gun into her coat pocket.

'Will you allow me to walk you home, Miss Nelson?' he asked, not daring to look her in the eye. 'It is unwise for a young lady to be out alone at this hour, even if she does have a gun in her pocket.'

Lucy smiled, charmed by Garrett's offer. 'Of course I will,' she said. 'You're very kind, Inspector. What's more, I don't live far from here and it's a lovely evening. It'll make a pleasant walk.'

'I'm sure it will,' Garrett replied.

XXXV

The next morning, in the privacy of his office, Inspector Colin Garrett ate his breakfast dreamily. Naturally, he was thinking of Lucy Nelson, her lovely eyes, her golden tresses, the way she had smiled at him when she asked whether she could write him a letter. At that moment, a constable barged in with a warrant signed by the prime minister, requesting he set off for the future to arrest a man who had not yet been born. Suffering from the effects of being in love, which, as you know, more often than not puts one in a daze, the inspector did not realise the letter's significance until he found himself in the cab being driven to Murray's Time Travel.

His legs had turned to jelly the first time he had crossed the threshold of Murray's headquarters, clutching the money his father had left him, which was to be transformed into something straight out of a dream: a ticket to the future, to the year 2000. This time he did so with a resolute stride, even though he had something just as incredible in his jacket pocket: a warrant that seemed all the more extraordinary considering it was for the arrest of a phantom. And Garrett was convinced that, if time travel were to become routine, this would be the first in a long line of similar warrants enabling police officers to make arrests in different eras, provided that the crimes were committed in the same place: London.

When he had scrawled his signature on the slip of paper Garrett was carrying now in his inside pocket, the prime minister, doubtless unawares, had taken an epoch-making step – he had blazed a new trail. As Garrett had predicted, science and its amazing creations would beat the rhythm to which humanity would dance.

But this warrant would also allow Garrett certain liberties in space. Like not being forced to languish in some waiting room until that busiest of men, Gilliam Murray, deigned to see him. Invested with the power conferred on him by the paper in his inside pocket, Garrett marched straight past the secretaries guarding Murray's privacy and, ignoring their objections, went up the stairs to the first floor, then along the corridor lined with clocks and breezed into Murray's office, a bevy of breathless assistants in his wake.

Gilliam Murray was lying on the carpet playing with a huge dog. He frowned slightly when he saw Garrett come in without knocking, but the inspector did not allow himself to be intimidated. He knew his behaviour was more than justified.

'Good morning, Mr Murray. Inspector Colin Garrett of Scotland Yard,' he introduced himself. 'Forgive me for barging in like this, but there's an urgent matter I need to discuss with you.'

Murray rose to his feet very slowly, eyeing the inspector suspiciously before dismissing his assistants with a wave. 'You needn't apologise, Inspector. Any matter you deal with must by definition be urgent,' he said, offering him an armchair as he crammed his huge frame into one opposite.

Once they were seated, Murray picked up a small wooden box from the table between their two chairs, opened it and, in a brisk, friendly manner that contrasted with his initial aloofness, offered Garrett a cigar. The inspector refused politely, smiling to himself at Murray's change of attitude, reflecting how swiftly he must have concluded that playing up to an inspector from the Yard was a far better strategy than getting on his wrong side. It was thanks to this that Garrett was sitting in a comfortable armchair and not on the footstool next to it.

'So, you don't like to smoke?' remarked Murray, putting the box back on the table and picking up a cut-glass decanter containing a peculiar blackish substance, which he poured into two glasses. 'Perhaps I can tempt you to a drink.'

Garrett baulked at the dark liquid Murray was holding out to him. But Murray grinned amiably, encouraging him to try it as he took a swig of his. Garrett did the same, and felt the strange beverage sting his throat as it went down, tears starting to his eyes.

'What is it, Mr Murray?' he asked, perplexed, unable to refrain from letting out a loud belch. 'A drink from the future?'

'Oh, no, Inspector. It's a tonic made from coca leaves and cola seeds invented by a chemist in Atlanta. It's all the rage in the United States. Some people prefer taking it with a little soda, like me. I expect they'll soon be importing it over here.'

Garrett put down his glass on the table, disinclined to take another sip. 'It has a peculiar flavour. I don't imagine people will take to it very easily,' he predicted, for the sake of saying something.

Murray smiled his assent, emptied his glass and, visibly eager to ingratiate himself, asked: 'Tell me, Inspector, did you enjoy your trip to the year 2000?'

'Very much, Mr Murray,' replied Garrett, in earnest. 'What's more, I'd like to take this opportunity to say that I fully endorse your project, regardless of what some newspapers say about the impropriety of visiting a time that doesn't belong to us. I have an open mind, and I find the idea of time travel enormously appealing. I eagerly await the opening of new routes to other eras.'

Murray thanked Garrett for his comments with a timid smile, then sat expectantly in his chair, no doubt inviting the inspector to reveal the reason for his visit.

Garrett cleared his throat and came straight to the point. 'We live in fascinating but tremendously volatile times, Mr Murray,' he said, reeling off the little preamble he had prepared. 'Science drives events, and mankind must adapt. Above all, if our laws are to remain effective, we must update them to suit the changing face of the world. Even more so when it comes to time travel. We are at the dawn of an extraordinary era of discovery that will doubtless redefine the world as we know it, and whose inherent dangers are impossible, or extremely difficult, to judge. It is precisely these dangers I came here to speak to you about, Mr Murray.'

'I couldn't agree with you more, Inspector,' Murray conceded. 'Science will change the face of the world, and oblige us to modify our laws, and even many of our principles, the way that time travel is already doing. But, tell me, what are these dangers you wish to speak to me about? I confess you've aroused my curiosity.'

Garrett sat up in his chair and cleared his throat once more. 'Two days ago,' he said, 'the police discovered a man's body in Manchester Street, Marylebone. He was a tramp, but the injury that killed him was so extraordinary they handed the case over to us. The wound consists of an enormous hole twelve inches wide that goes straight through his chest and is singed at the edges. Our pathologists are baffled. They claim no weapon exists that is capable of inflicting such an injury.'

Garrett made a dramatic pause before fixing Murray with a solemn stare, and adding: 'At least, not here, not in the present.'

'What are you suggesting, Inspector?' asked Murray, in a casual manner that did not correspond with the way he was fidgeting in his chair.

'That the pathologists are right,' replied Garrett. 'Such a weapon hasn't yet been invented. Only I've seen it, Mr Murray. Guess where?'

Gilliam did not reply, but looked at him askance.

'In the year 2000.'

'Really?' murmured Murray.

'Yes, Mr Murray. I'm convinced this wound can only have been inflicted by the weapon I saw the brave Captain Shackleton and his men using. The heat ray that can pierce armour.'

'I see . . .' Murray muttered, as if to himself, staring into space. 'The weapon used by the soldiers of the future, of course.'

'Precisely. I believe one of them, possibly Shackleton, travelled back on the Cronotilus without being noticed, and is roaming our streets at this very moment. I've no idea why he killed the tramp, or where he is hiding now, but that doesn't matter. I don't intend to waste time searching the whole of London for him when I know exactly where he is.' He pulled a piece of paper from his inside pocket and handed it to Murray. 'This is a warrant signed by the prime minister authorising me to arrest the murderer on 20 May in the year 2000, before he can even commit his crime. It means I'll need to travel with two of my officers on the expedition leaving in a week's time. Once we arrive in the future, we'll separate from the others so that we can spy on the passengers from the second expedition and discreetly detain anyone who attempts to stow away on the Cronotilus.'

As he spoke, it dawned on the inspector that if he lay in wait for the passengers of the second expedition he would unavoidably see himself. He only hoped it would not repulse him as much as the sight of blood. He glanced at Murray, who was carefully studying the warrant. He was silent for so long it occurred to Garrett he might even be examining the consistency of the paper.

'But have no fear, Mr Murray,' he felt obliged to add, 'if Shackleton does turn out to be the murderer, my arresting him after his duel with Solomon won't affect the outcome of the war. It will still end in victory for the human race, and it won't affect your enterprise either.'

'I understand,' murmured Murray, without looking up from the document.

'May I count on your co-operation, Mr Murray?'

Murray slowly raised his head and looked at Garrett with what, for a moment, the inspector imagined was contempt, but he soon realised his mistake when Murray quickly beamed at him, and replied: 'Certainly, Inspector, certainly. I shall reserve three seats for you on the next expedition.'

'I'm most grateful to you, Mr Murray.'

'And now, if you'll excuse me,' said Murray, standing up and handing him back the document, 'I'm extremely busy.'

'Of course, Mr Murray.'

Taken aback by the way in which Murray had abruptly ended the interview, Garrett rose from his armchair, thanked him once more for his co-operation, and left his office. A smile played across the inspector's lips as he walked along the interminable corridor lined with clocks. By the time he reached the stairs he was in an excellent mood and began chanting to himself: 'Peritoneum, spleen, left kidney, suprarenal gland, urinary tract, prostate gland . . .'

XXXVI

Not even the touch on the skin of the delicious breeze heralding the arrival of summer, nor caressing a woman's body, nor sipping Scotch whisky in the bathtub until the water goes cold . . . In short, no other pleasure Wells could think of gave him a greater sense of well-being than adding the final full stop to a novel. This culminating act always filled him with a sense of giddy satisfaction born of the certainty that nothing he could achieve in life would fulfil him more than writing a novel, no matter how tedious, difficult and thankless he found the task. Wells was one of those writers who detest writing but love 'having written'.

He pulled the last folio from the carriage of his Hammond typewriter, laid it on top of the pile and placed his hand on it with a triumphant smile, like a hunter resting his boot on a lion's head. For Wells the act of writing was much like a struggle, a bloodthirsty battle with an idea that refuses to be seized. An idea that nonetheless originated with him. Perhaps that was the most frustrating thing of all: the eternal yawning gap between the fruit of his efforts and his initial goal, which admittedly was always more instinctive than deliberate. He had learned from experience that what he succeeded in putting down on paper was only ever a pale reflection of what he had imagined, so he had come to accept that this would only be half as good as the original, half as acceptable as the flawless, unachievable novel that had acted as a guide, and which he imagined pulsating mockingly behind each book like some ghostly presence.

Even so, here was the result of all those months of toil, he told himself, and it felt wonderful to see transformed into something palpable what had been no more than a vague premise until he had typed that last full stop. He would deliver it to Henley the next day and could stop thinking about it.

And yet such doubts never arose in isolation. Once more Wells wondered, as he sat beside his pile of typed folios, whether he had written the book he had been meant to write. Was this novel destined to figure in his bibliography or had it been engendered by accident? Was he responsible for writing one novel and not another, or was this also controlled by the fate that governed men's lives? He was plagued by doubts, although one caused him particular distress: was there a novel lurking somewhere in his head that would allow him to express the whole of what was really inside him? The idea he might discover this too late tormented him: that as he lay on his deathbed, before his last gasp, the plot of an extraordinary novel he no longer had time to write would rise from the depths of his mind, like a piece of wreckage floating to the sea's surface. A novel that had always been there, calling out to him in vain amid the clamour, a novel that would die with him, for no one but he could write it, because it was like a suit made to measure just for him. He could think of nothing more terrifying, no worse fate.

He shook his head, driving out these distressing thoughts, and glanced up at the clock. It was past midnight. That meant he could write 21 November 1896 next to his signature on the end page of the novel. Once he had done so, he blew lovingly on the ink, rose from his chair and picked up the oil lamp. His back was stiff and he felt terribly tired, yet he did not go into the bedroom, where he could hear Jane's steady breathing. He had no time for sleep: he had a long night ahead of him, he told himself, a smile playing across his face.

He padded down the corridor in his slippers, lighting his way with the lamp, and began to climb the stairs to the attic, trying to avoid making the steps creak. Shiny and magnificent, shimmering in the celestial moonlight filtering in through the open window, the machine waited for him. He had grown attached to his secret ritual, although he did not know why he derived such enjoyment from sitting on the thing while his wife was asleep below him. Perhaps because it made him feel special, even though he knew it was only a sophisticated toy. Whoever made it had reproduced every last detail: the machine might not be able to travel in time but, thanks to a clever mechanism, any date could be set on the control panel, with the fictitious destinations of impossible passages through the fabric of time.

Until now, Wells had only set the date to distant times in the future – including the year 802,701, the world of the Eloi and the Morlocks – a time so remote that life as he knew it could only appear completely alien, painfully incomprehensible – or in the past he would like to have known, such as the time of the druids. But that night, with a roguish grin, he adjusted the numbers on the control panel to 20 May in the year 2000, the date on which the impostor Gilliam Murray had chosen to stage the greatest ever battle of the human race, the pantomime by which all England had been fooled, thanks in part to his own novel. He found it ironic that he, the author of a novel about time travel, was the only person who thought it was impossible. He had made all England dream, but was immune to his own creation.

What would the world really look like in a hundred years' time? He would have liked to travel to the year 2000, not just for the pleasure of seeing it, but to take photographs with one of the new-fangled cameras so that he could come back and show the unsuspecting crowds queuing outside Murray's offices what the true face of the future looked like. It was a pipe dream, of course, but there was nothing to stop him pretending he could do it, he told himself, settling back in his seat and ceremoniously pulling the lever down, experiencing the inevitable frisson of excitement he felt whenever he performed the gesture.

However, to his astonishment, this time when the lever had come to halt, a sudden darkness fell on the attic. The flecks of moonlight shining through the window seemed to withdraw. Before he was able to understand what the devil was going on, he was overcome by a dreadful feeling of vertigo and a sudden giddiness. He felt himself floating, drifting through a mysterious void that might have been the cosmos itself. And as he began to lose consciousness, he thought that either he was having a heart attack, or he really was travelling to the year 2000.

He came to painfully slowly. His mouth was dry and his body strangely sluggish. Once he could focus properly, he realised he was lying down, not in his attic but on a piece of wasteland covered with stones and rubble. Disoriented, he struggled upright, discovering to his annoyance that each time he moved he felt a terrible shooting pain in his head. He decided to stay sitting on the ground. From there he glanced around with awe at the devastated landscape. Was this the London of the future? Had he really travelled to the year 2000? There was no sign of the time machine, as if the Morlocks had spirited it away inside the sphinx.

After his careful inspection, he decided the time had come for him to stand upright, which he did with great difficulty, like Darwin's primate crossing the distance separating him from man. He was relieved to find he had no broken bones, although he still felt unpleasantly queasy. Was this one of the effects of having crossed a century in his time carriage? The sky was covered with a dense fog that left everywhere in a pale twilight, a grey blanket dotted with red from the dozens of fires burning on the horizon. The crows circling above his head were an almost obligatory feature of the desolate landscape, he reflected. One flew down, alighting very close to where he was sitting, and made a macabre tapping sound as it pecked stubbornly at the rubble.

On closer examination, Wells saw with horror that the bird was trying to bore through a human skull. This discovery caused him to recoil a few paces, a rash response in that hostile environment.

The next thing he knew, the ground gave way beneath him, and he realised too late that he had woken up at the top of a small incline, down which he was now unhappily tumbling. He landed with a thump, coughing and spluttering as he breathed in some of the thick dust shrouding him. Irritated by his clumsiness, Wells rose to his feet. Luckily he had no broken bones, although as a crowning humiliation, his trousers had been torn in several places, leaving part of a scrawny white buttock exposed.

Wells shook his head. What more could go wrong? he thought, brushing himself down as best he could. As the dust settled, he stood stock still, aghast, contemplating the figures slowly emerging from the gloom. An army of automatons was staring at him in ghostly silence. There were at least a dozen, all with the same inscrutable, intimidating expression, even the one standing slightly to the fore, who was wearing an incongruous gold crown. They looked as though they had halted in their tracks when they saw him roll down the incline. A terrible panic gripped Wells as he realised where he was. He had travelled to the year 2000 and, amazingly enough, it was exactly as Gilliam Murray had portrayed in his novel. There in front of him, before his very eyes, stood Solomon himself, the evil king of the automatons responsible for the devastation around him. His fate was sealed: he was going to be shot by a mechanical toy. There, in the very future he had refused to believe in.

'I imagine right now you must be wishing Captain Shackleton would appear. Correct?'

The voice did not come from the automaton, although at that stage nothing would have surprised him, but from somewhere behind Wells. He recognised it instantly. He would have liked never to hear it again, but somehow, perhaps because he was a writer, he had known that, sooner or later, he would bump into Murray: the story in which they were both taking part needed a satisfying conclusion, one that would not frustrate the readers' expectations. Wells would never have envisaged the encounter taking place in the future, though, for the simple reason that he had never believed in the possibility of travelling into the future. He turned slowly.

A few yards away, Gilliam Murray was watching him, with an amused grin. He was wearing a purple suit and a green top hat, like a human descendant of those beautifully plumed biblical birds of paradise. Sitting on its haunches next to him was an enormous golden dog.

'Welcome to the year 2000, Mr Wells,' Murray said, jovially. 'Or should I say to *my* vision of the year 2000?'

Wells looked at him suspiciously, one eye on the eerily frozen group of automatons drawn up before them as though posing for a portrait.

'Are you afraid of my automatons? But how can you be scared of such an unconvincing future?' Murray asked sarcastically. He walked slowly towards the automaton at the front of the group and, grinning deliberately at Wells, like a child about to perpetrate some mischief, placed his fleshy hand on its shoulder and gave it a push. The automaton keeled over backwards, crashing noisily into the one behind it, which in turn toppled on to the one next to it until, one after another, they had collapsed on to the ground. They fell with the fascinating slowness of a glacier breaking off.

When it was finally over, Murray spread the palms of his hands as if to apologise for the din. 'With no one inside, they're just hollow shells, mere disguises,' he said.

Wells gazed at the pile of upturned automatons, then back at Murray, struggling with his dizzying feeling of unreality.

'Forgive me for bringing you to the year 2000 against your will, Mr Wells,' apologised Murray, feigning dismay. 'If you'd accepted one of my invitations it wouldn't have been necessary, but as you didn't, I had no alternative. I wanted you to see it before I closed it down. I had to send one of my men to chloroform you while you were asleep, although from what he told me, you occupy your nights with other things. He got a real shock when you came in after he'd climbed through the attic window.'

Murray's words shed a welcome light on the author's whirling thoughts, and he lost no time in tying up the necessary loose ends. He realised immediately he had not travelled to the year 2000, as everything appeared to indicate. The machine in his attic was still just a toy, and the razed city of London was no more than a vast stage set designed to hoodwink people. No doubt, on seeing him enter the attic, Murray's henchman had hidden behind the time machine and waited, unsure what to do, perhaps contemplating carrying out Murray's orders using force. Fortunately he had not needed to resort to an ignoble act of violence, as Wells himself had given the man the perfect opportunity to use the chloroform-soaked handkerchief he must have had at the ready by sitting in the time machine.

Of course, once he realised he was standing on a simple stage set and that he had not undergone some impossible journey through time, Wells felt greatly relieved. The situation he found himself in was by no means pleasant, of course, but at least it was logical.

'I trust you haven't harmed my wife,' he said, not quite managing to sound threatening.

'Have no fear,' Murray reassured him, waving a hand in the air. 'Your wife is a deep sleeper, and my men can be very quiet when they have to be. I'm sure that the lovely Jane is at this very moment sleeping peacefully, oblivious to your absence.'

Wells was about to make a riposte, but thought better of it. Murray was addressing him with the rather overblown arrogance of people in high places who have the world at their feet. Evidently, the tables had turned since their last meeting. If, during their interview at his house in Woking, Wells had been the one wielding the sceptre of power, now Murray held it between his fleshy fingers.

Over the intervening months, Murray had changed: he had become an altogether different creature. He was no longer the aspiring writer, obliged to kneel at his master's feet, but the owner of the most lucrative business in London before whom everyone grotesquely bowed down. Wells, of course, did not think he deserved any kind of adulation, and if he allowed him to use that superior tone it was because he considered Murray was entitled to do so:

after all, he was the outright winner of the duel they had been fighting during the past few months. And had not Wells used a similar tone when the sceptre had been in his hands?

Gilliam Murray spread his arms wide, like a ringmaster announcing the acts at a circus, symbolically embracing the surrounding devastation. 'Well, what do you think of my world?' he asked.

Wells glanced about him with utter indifference.

'Not bad for a glasshouse manufacturer, don't you agree, Mr Wells? That was my occupation before you gave me another reason to go on living.'

Wells could not fail to notice the responsibility Murray had ascribed to him in the forging of his destiny, but he preferred not to comment. Undeterred by Wells's frostiness, Murray invited him with a beckoning finger, to take a stroll through the future. The author paused for a moment, then reluctantly followed him.

'I don't know whether you're aware that glasshouses are a most lucrative business,' said Gilliam, once Wells had drawn level with him. 'Nowadays everyone sets aside part of their garden for these cosy spaces, where grown-ups like to relax and children play, and it is possible to grow plants and fruit trees out of season. Although my father, Sebastian Murray, had, as it were, loftier ambitions.'

They had scarcely walked a few paces when they came to a small precipice. Unconcerned about taking a tumble, Murray trotted absurdly down the slope, arms stretched out at his sides to keep his balance. The dog bounded after him. Wells let out a sigh before beginning the descent, taking care not to trip over the mangled bits of pipe and grinning skulls poking out of the ground. He did not wish to fall over again. Once was quite enough for one day.

'My father sensed the beginning of a new future in those transparent houses rich people erected in their gardens,' Murray shouted over his shoulder, 'the first step towards a world of translucent cities, glass buildings that would put an end to secrets and lies, a better world where privacy would no longer exist!'

When he reached the bottom, he offered his hand to Wells, who declined, not bothering to conceal his impatience at the whole situation. Murray seemed not to take the hint, and resumed strolling, this time along an apparently gentler path.

'I confess that as a child I was fascinated by the glorious vision that gave my father's life meaning,' he went on. 'For a while I even believed it would be the true face of the future. Until the age of seventeen, when I began working with him. It was then that I realised it was no more than a fantasy. This amusement for architects and horticulturalists would never be transformed into the architecture of the future, not only because man would never give up his privacy in the interests of a more harmonious world, but because architects themselves were opposed to glass and iron constructions, claiming the new materials lacked the aesthetic values that they claimed defined architectural works.

'The sad truth was that, however many glass-roofed railway stations my father and I built up and down the country, we could never usurp the power of the brick. I resigned myself to spending the rest of my life manufacturing fancy glasshouses. But who could content themselves with such a petty, insignificant occupation, Mr Wells? Not I, for one. Yet I had no idea what would satisfy me either.

'By the time I was in my early twenties I had enough money to buy anything I wanted, however whimsical, and as you might expect life had begun to feel like a card game I had already won and was beginning to tire of. To cap it all, around that time my father died of a sudden fever, and as I was his only heir I became even richer. But his passing also made me painfully aware that most people die without ever having realised their dreams. However enviable my father's life may have seemed from the outside, I knew it hadn't been fulfilling, and mine would be no different. I was convinced I would die with the same look of disappointment on my face. I expect that's why I turned to reading, so as to escape the dull, predictable life unfolding before me.

'We all begin reading for one reason or another, don't you think? What was yours, Mr Wells?'

'I fractured my tibia when I was eight,' said the author, visibly uninterested.

Murray looked at him, slightly surprised, then finally smiled and nodded. 'I suppose geniuses like you have to start young,' he reflected. 'It took me a little longer. I was twenty-five before I began exploring my father's ample library. He had been widowed early on, and had built another wing on to the house, probably to use up some of the money my mother would otherwise have helped him to spend. Nobody but I would ever read those books. So I devoured every one – every single one. That was how I discovered the joys of reading. It's never too late don't you agree? Although, I confess, I wasn't a very discerning reader. Any book about lives that weren't my own was of some interest to me.

'But your novel, Mr Wells . . . Your novel captivated me like no other! You didn't speak of a world you knew, like Dickens, or of exotic places such as Africa or Malaya, like Haggard or Salgari, or even of the moon, like Verne. No, in *The Time Machine* you evoked something even more unattainable: the future. Nobody before you had been audacious enough to visualise it!'

Wells shrugged off Murray's praise, and carried on walking, trying not to trip over the dog, which had the irritating habit of zigzagging across his path. Verne, of course, had beaten him to it, but Gilliam Murray need not know that.

Murray resumed his monologue, again heedless of the author's lack of interest. 'After that, as you know, a spate of authors, doubtless inspired by your novel, hastened to publish their visions of the future. Suddenly bookshop windows were crammed with science-fiction novels. I bought as many as I could, and after several sleepless nights spent devouring them in quick succession, I decided this new genre of literature would be my only reading.'

'I'm sorry you chose to waste your time on such nonsense,' muttered Wells, who considered those novels a regrettable blot on the *fin-de-siècle* literary landscape.

Murray glanced at him before letting out a loud guffaw. 'Oh, I know those potboilers have little merit,' he agreed, when he had stopped laughing, 'but I couldn't care less about that. The authors of this "nonsense", as you call it, possess something far more important to me than the ability to create sublime sentences: namely, a visionary intelligence that amazes me and which I wish I had. Most of those works confine themselves to describing a single invention and its effect on mankind. Have you read the novel about the Jewish inventor who devises a machine that magnifies things? It's a truly awful book, yet I confess the image of an army of giant stag beetles swarming across Hyde Park truly terrified me. Thankfully, they are not all like that. Such ravings apart, some present an idea of the future whose plausibility I enjoy exploring.

'And there was something else I couldn't deny: after enjoying a book by Dickens, for example, it would never have occurred to me to try to imitate him, to see whether I was able to concoct a story about the adventures of a street urchin or the hardships of a boy forced to work in a blacking factory, because it seemed to me anyone with a modicum of imagination and time would be able to do that. But to write about the future . . .

'Ah, Mr Wells, that was different. To me, that seemed a real challenge. It was an undertaking that required intelligence, man's capacity for deduction. Would I be capable of creating a believable future? I asked myself one night after I'd finished another of those novels. As you will have guessed, I took you as my example because, besides our common interests, we are the same age. It took me a month to write my novel about the future, a piece of science fiction that would display my insight, my powers of invention. Naturally I made every effort to write well, but I was more interested in the novel's prophetic side. I wanted my readers to find my vision of the future plausible. But most of all I valued the opinion of the writer who had been my guiding light. Your opinion, Mr Wells. I wanted you to be as intellectually stimulated by my novel as I had been by yours.'

The two men's eyes met, in a silence broken only by the distant cawing of crows.

'But, as you know, it didn't happen like that,' Murray lamented, shaking his head sorrowfully.

The gesture moved Wells, as he considered it the only sincere one Murray had made since they had set off on their walk.

They had come to a halt next to a huge mound of rubble, and there, hands dug into the pockets of his loud jacket, Murray paused for a few moments, staring at his shoes, clearly distressed. Perhaps he was waiting for Wells to place his hand on his shoulder and offer words of solace, which, like the shaman's chant, would soothe the painful wound Wells himself had inflicted on Murray's pride. However, the author simply studied him with the disdain of the poacher watching a rabbit struggle in a trap, aware that while seemingly responsible for what was happening, he was a simple mediator, and the animal's torment was dictated by the cruel laws of nature.

When he realised that the only person capable of alleviating his hurt seemed unwilling to do so, Murray smiled grimly and carried on walking. They went along what – to judge by the grandiose wrought-iron gates and the palatial remains of the buildings amid the rubble – had been a luxurious residential street evoking a life that seemed incongruous amid the devastation, as though man's proliferation on the planet had been no more than a divine blunder, a ridiculous flowering, doomed to perish under the elements.

'I shan't try to deny that at first I was upset when you doubted my abilities as a writer,' Murray acknowledged, in a voice that seemed to ooze with the slowness of treacle from inside his throat. 'Nobody enjoys having their work pilloried. But what most vexed me was that you questioned the plausibility of my vision, the future I had so carefully contrived. I admit my response was entirely unacceptable, and I wish to take this opportunity to apologise for having attacked your novel as I did. I'm sure you'll have guessed that my opinion of it hasn't changed. I still consider it the work of a genius,' Gilliam said, laying a faintly ironic emphasis on the final words.

He had recovered his conceited smirk, but Wells had glimpsed a chink in his armour, the crack that from time to time threatened to bring this colossus crashing down. In the face of Murray's intolerable arrogance, Wells felt almost proud to have been the cause of it.

'That afternoon, however, I was unable to defend myself other than like a cornered rat,' Wells heard Murray justify himself. 'Happily, I came to see things in a different light. Yes, you might say I experienced a kind of epiphany.'

'Really?' commented Wells, with dry irony.

'Yes, I'm sure of it. Sitting opposite you in that chair, I saw I'd chosen the wrong means of presenting my idea of the future to the world. In doing it through a novel I was condemning it to mere fiction, plausible fiction, but fiction all the same, as you had done with your future inhabited by Morlocks and Eloi. But what if I were able to put my idea across without confining it to the restrictive medium of the novel? What if I could present it as something real? Evidently the pleasure of writing a believable piece of fiction would pale beside the incredible satisfaction of having the whole country believe in the reality of my vision of the year 2000.

'But was this feasible? the businessman in me asked. The conditions for realising such a project seemed perfect. Your novel, Mr Wells, had sparked off a polemic about time travel. People in clubs and tea rooms talked of nothing but the possibility of travelling into the future. It is one of life's ironies that you fertilised the ground for me to plant my seed. Why not give people what they wished for? Why not offer them a journey to the year 2000, to "my" future? I wasn't sure I'd be able to pull it off, but one thing was certain: I wouldn't be able to go on living if I didn't try. Purely by accident, Mr Wells, the way most things happen in life, you gave me a reason to carry on, a goal that, were I to achieve it, would give me the longed-for fulfilment, the elusive happiness I could never obtain from the manufacture of glasshouses.'

Wells was compelled to lower his head to conceal his sympathy for Murray. His words had reminded Wells of the extraordinary chain of events that had delivered him into the loving arms of literature, away from the mediocrity to which his not-so-loving mother had sought to condemn him. And it had been his way with words, a gift he had not asked for, that had spared him the need to find meaning in his life, had exempted him from having to tread the path taken by those who had no idea why they had been born, those who could only experience the conventional, atavistic joy found in everyday pleasures such as a glass of wine or a woman's caress. Yes, he would have walked among those redundant shadows, unaware that the longed-for happiness he had scarcely glimpsed during his fits of melancholy lay in the keys of a typewriter, waiting for him to bring it to life.

'On my way back to London I began thinking,' he heard Murray say. 'I was convinced people would believe the impossible if it were real enough. In fact, it was not unlike building a glasshouse: if the glass part of the structure was elegant and beautiful enough, nobody would see the solid iron framework holding it up. It would appear to be floating in the air as if by magic.

'The first thing I did the next morning was to sell the business my father had built up from scratch. In doing so I felt no regret, in case you were wondering, quite the opposite, if anything, because with the money from the sale I would be able literally to build the future, which, ultimately, had been my father's dream. From the proceeds, I purchased this old theatre. The reason I chose it was because right behind it, looking out over Charing Cross Road, there were two derelict buildings that I also bought. The next step, of course, was to merge the three edifices into one by knocking down the walls to obtain this vast space. Seen from the outside, no one would think it was big enough to house a vast stage set of London in the year 2000. Yet in less than two months, I had created a perfect replica, down to the smallest detail, of the scene in my novel. In fact, the set isn't nearly as big as it looks, but it seems immense if we walk round it in a circle, don't you think?'

Was that what they had been doing? Walking round in a circle? Wells thought, containing his irritation. If so, he had to acknowledge that the intricate layout of the debris had taken him in completely, for it made the already sprawling stage set appear even more gigantic, and he would never have imagined it might fit inside a tiny theatre.

'My own team of blacksmiths made the automatons that gave you such a fright a while ago, as well as the armour worn by Captain Shackleton's human army,' Murray explained, as he guided Wells through a narrow ravine created by two rows of collapsed buildings. 'At first I thought of hiring professional actors to dramatise the battle that would change the history of the human race, which I myself had staged so that it would look as appealing and exciting as possible. I immediately discarded the idea because I felt that stage actors, who are famous for being erratic and vain, would be incapable of giving a realistic portrayal of brave, battle-hardened soldiers in an army of the future. More importantly, I thought that if they began to have qualms about the morality of the work they had been hired to do they would be harder to silence. Instead, I employed a bunch of bruisers who had far more in common with the veterans they were supposed to portray. They didn't mind keeping the heavy metal armour on during the entire performance, and they couldn't have cared less about my scheme being fraudulent. In spite of all that, I had a few problems, but nothing I wasn't able to sort out,' he added, smiling significantly at the author.

Wells understood that with this twisted grin Murray meant to tell him two things: first, that he knew about his involvement in the relationship between Miss Haggerty and Tom Blunt, the young man who had played Captain Shackleton, and second, that he was behind Tom's sudden disappearance. Wells forced his lips into an expression of horrified shock, which appeared to satisfy Murray.

Wells wanted more than anything to wipe the arrogant smirk off the man's face by informing him that Tom had survived his own death. Tom himself had told Wells so only two nights earlier when he had appeared at his house to thank him for all he had done for him, and to remind him that if Wells ever needed a pair of strong arms he could call on him.

The ravine opened on to what looked like a small square where a few gnarled, leafless trees still grew. In the middle, Wells noticed something resembling an overly ornate tramcar, whose sides were covered with a mass of chrome-plated tubes. Sprouting from these were dozens of valves and other elaborate accessories, which, on closer observation, he thought could only be for decoration.

'And this is the Cronotilus, a steam-driven tram that seats thirty,' declared Murray, proudly, banging one of its sides. 'The passengers embark in the room next door, ready to travel into the future, unaware that the year 2000 is in a large adjoining space. All I have to do is to transport them here. This distance, about fifty yards,' he said, gesturing towards a doorway hidden by fog, 'represents a whole century to them.'

'But how do you simulate the effect of travelling through time?' asked Wells, unable to believe Murray's customers would be satisfied by a simple ride in a tramcar, however ostentatious.

Murray grinned, as though pleased by his question. 'My hard work would all have been for nothing if I'd failed to find a solution to the niggling problem you have so rightly identified. And, I assure you, it gave me many sleepless nights. Evidently I couldn't show the effects of travelling into the future as you did in your novel, with snails that moved faster than hares or the moon going through all its phases in seconds. Therefore I had to invent a method of time travel that didn't oblige me to show such effects, and which, in addition, had no basis in science. I was certain that once I told the newspapers I could travel to the year 2000, every scientist up and down the country would demand to know how the devil such a thing was done. A real dilemma, wouldn't you say? And after giving the matter careful thought, I could think of only one method of travelling in time that couldn't be questioned scientifically: by means of magic.'

'Magic?'

'Yes, what other method could I resort to, if the scientific route wasn't open to me? I invented a fictitious biography for myself. Before going into the time-travel business, instead of manufacturing dreary glasshouses, my father and I ran a company that financed expeditions, like the scores of others that exist today, intent on disclosing all the world's mysteries. And, like everybody else, we were desperate to find the source of the Nile, which legend situated in the heart of Africa. We had sent our best explorer there, Oliver Tremanquai, who, after many gruelling adventures, had made contact with an indigenous tribe capable of opening a portal into the fourth dimension by means of magic.'

With these words, Murray paused, smiling scornfully at Wells's attempts to hide his disbelief.

'The hole was a doorway on to a pink, windswept plain where time stood still,' he went on, 'which was no more than my portrayal of the fourth dimension. The plain, a sort of antechamber to other eras, was peppered with holes similar to the portal connecting it to the African village. One of these led to 20 May in the year 2000, on the very day humans fought the decisive battle for the survival of their race against the automatons, amid the ruins of a devastated London. And, having discovered the existence of this magic hole, what else could my father and I do but steal it and bring it to London to offer it to the subjects of Her Imperial Majesty? So that's what we did. We locked it in a huge iron box purpose-built for the occasion and brought it here. *Voilà!* I had found the solution, a way of travelling in time that involved no scientific devices. All you had to do to journey into the future was pass through the hole into the fourth dimension aboard the Cronotilus, cross part of the pink plain, and step through another hole into the year 2000. Simple, isn't it?

'In order to avoid having to show the fourth dimension, I inhabited it with terrifying, dangerous dragons, creatures of such horrific appearance I was forced to black out the windows in the Cronotilus so as not to alarm the passengers,' he said, inviting Wells to examine the porthole-shaped windows, painted black as he had said. 'Once the passengers had climbed aboard the time-tram, I carried them away, using oboes and trombones to conjure up the roars of the dragons roaming the plain. I've never experienced the effect from inside the Cronotilus, but it must be very convincing, to judge by the pallor on many passengers' faces when they return.'

'But if the hole always comes out in this square at the exact same moment in the year 2000—' Wells began.

'Then each new expedition arrives at the same time as the previous ones,' Murray cut across him. 'I know, I know, that's completely logical. And yet time travel is still such a young idea that not many people have considered the many contradictions it can give rise to. If the portal into the fourth dimension always opens on to the exact same moment in the future, obviously there should be at least two Cronotiluses here, as there have been at least two expeditions. But, as I already said, Mr Wells, not everyone notices such things. In any event, as a precaution against questions the more inquisitive passengers might pose, I instructed the actor who played the guide to explain to them as soon as they arrived in the future, before they even stepped out of the vehicle, that we drove each Cronotilus to a different place, precisely in order to avoid this eventuality.'

Murray waited to see if Wells felt like asking any more questions, but the author appeared immersed in what could only be described as pained silence, a look of impotent sorrow on his face.

'And,' Murray went on, 'as I had anticipated, as soon as I advertised my journeys to the year 2000 in the newspapers, numerous scientists asked to meet me. You should have seen them, Mr Wells. They came in droves, barely able to conceal their contempt, hoping I would show them some device they could gleefully demolish. But I was no scientist. I was just an honest businessman who'd made a chance discovery. Most of them left the meeting indignant, frustrated at having been presented with a method of travel they had no way of questioning or refuting: you either believe in magic or you don't. Some, however, were thoroughly convinced by my explanation, like your fellow author Conan Doyle. The creator of the infallible Sherlock Holmes has become one of my most vigorous defenders, as you will know if you've read any of the numerous articles he devotes to defending my cause.'

'Doyle would believe in anything, even fairies,' said Wells, derisively.

'That's possible. As you have seen yourself, we can all be deceived if the fraud is convincing enough. And to be honest, far from upsetting me, the regular visits I received from our sceptical men of science gave me great pleasure. Actually, I rather miss them. After all, where else would I have found a more attentive audience? I enjoyed enormously relating Tremanquai's adventures over and over. As you will have guessed, they were a veiled homage to my beloved Henry Rider Haggard, the author of *Solomon's Mines*. In fact, Tremanquai is an anagram of one of his best-known characters, Quatermain, the adventurer who—'

'And none of these scientists demanded to see the . . . hole?' interrupted Wells, still disinclined to believe it had all been so easy.

'Oh, yes, of course. Many refused to leave without seeing it. But I was prepared for that. My instinct for survival had warned me to construct a cast-iron box identical to the one in my story, supposedly containing the portal to the fourth dimension. I presented it to anyone who wanted to see it, and invited them to go inside, warning them I would have to close the door behind them because, among other things, the box was a barrier that prevented the dragons entering our world. Do you think any of them dared to go in?'

'I imagine not,' responded Wells, despondently.

'That's correct,' affirmed Murray. 'In fact, the entire artifice is based on a box, in which the only thing lurking is our deepest fears. Don't you think it's both poetic and exciting?'

Wells shook his head with a mixture of sadness and disbelief at the gullibility of his fellow men, but above all at the scientists' lack of spirit, their spinelessness when it came to risking their lives in the service of empirical truth.

'So, Mr Wells, that is how I transport my customers into the future, escaping the time continuum only to plunge back into it somewhere else, like salmon swimming their way upstream. The first expedition was a resounding success,' Murray boasted. 'I confess to being surprised at how readily people were taken in by my hoax. But then, as I said before, people see what they wish to see. However, I scarcely had time to celebrate for a few days later the Queen herself asked to see me. Yes, Her Majesty in person requested my humble presence at the palace. I went there prepared to receive my just deserts for my impudence. To my astonishment, however, Her Majesty wanted to see me for a very different reason: to ask if I would organise a private trip to the year 2000 for her.'

Wells stared at him, flabbergasted.

'That's right. She and her entourage wanted to see the war of the future that the whole of London was raving about. As you can imagine, I wasn't too keen on the idea, not only because, naturally, I would be expected to organise the performance free of charge but, given the distinguished nature of our guests, it had to be carried off to perfection – in other words, as convincingly as possible. Luckily there were no mishaps. I think I can even say it was our best performance. The distress on Her Majesty's face when she saw London razed to the ground spoke for itself. But the following day, she sent for me a second time. Again, I imagined my fraud had been discovered, and again I was astounded to discover the reason for this new summons: Her Majesty wished to make a generous donation to enable me to carry on my research. It's the honest truth: the Queen herself was willing to finance my swindle. She was keen for me to carry on studying other holes, to open up other routes to other times. But that wasn't all. She also wanted me to build her a summer palace inside the fourth dimension so that she could spend long periods there, with the aim of escaping the ravages of time and prolonging her life. Naturally, I accepted. What else could I do? Although, of course, I haven't been able to finish building her palace and I never will. Can you think why?'

'It must be because the work is continually being delayed by attacks from the ferocious dragons that live in the fourth dimension,' replied Wells, visibly disgusted.

'Precisely,' declared Murray, beaming. 'I see you're beginning to understand the rules of the game, Mr Wells.'

The author refused to humour him, instead staring at the dog, which was furiously scrabbling in the rubble a few yards from them.

'Not only did the fact that Her Majesty was taken in by my deception line my pockets, it also banished my fears. I immediately stopped fretting over the letters that appeared like clockwork in the newspapers, written by scientists accusing me of being a charlatan. In any case, people had stopped paying them any attention. Even the swine that kept smearing cow dung on the front of the building no longer bothered me. Actually, at that point, there was only one person who could have exposed me, and that was you, Mr Wells. But I assumed that if you hadn't already, you never would. And I confess I found your attitude worthy of admiration, that of a truly sporting gentleman who knows when he has lost.'

With a smug grin, Murray gestured to Wells to carry on walking with him. They left the square in silence, the dog tagging along behind, and turned into one of the streets obstructed by mounds of rubble.

'Have you stopped to consider the essence of all this, Mr Wells?' asked Murray. 'Look at it this way: what if I had presented this as a simple play I had written about the future instead of passing it off as the real year 2000? I would have committed no offence, and people would have flocked to see it anyway. But I assure you that when they arrived home, none of them would have felt special, or seen the world in a different light. In reality, all I'm doing is making them dream. Isn't it a shame to think I could be punished for that?'

'You'd have to ask your customers whether they would be prepared to pay as much to watch a simple play,' replied the author.

'No, Mr Wells. You're wrong. The real question you'd have to ask them is whether they'd prefer to discover this had all been a hoax and get their money back or, on the contrary, whether they'd prefer to die believing they had visited the year 2000. And, I can assure you, the majority would prefer not to know. Aren't there lies that make life more beautiful?'

Wells gave a sigh, but refused to acknowledge that in the end Murray was right. Apparently his fellow men preferred to believe they lived in a century in which science could ferry them to the year 2000, by whatever means, than to be trapped in a time from which there was no hope of escape.

'Take young Harrington, for example,' Murray went on, with a playful grin. 'Do you remember him? If I'm not mistaken, it was a lie that saved his life. A lie in which you agreed to participate.'

Wells was about to remark that there was a world of difference between the purpose behind one lie and the other, but Murray headed him off with another question.

'Are you aware that it was I who built the time machine you keep in your attic, the little toy that pleases you so much?'

This time Wells was unable to conceal his amazement.

'Yes, I had it especially made for Charles Winslow, the wretched Andrew Harrington's cousin.' Murray chuckled. 'Mr Winslow came on our second expedition, and a few days later he turned up at my offices asking me to organise a private trip for him and his cousin to the year 1888, the Autumn of Terror. They assured me money was no object, but unfortunately I was unable to satisfy their whim.'

Murray had wandered off the main road towards a pile of debris beyond which a row of shattered rooftops was visible in the distance, darkened by a few clouds looming above.

'But Mr Winslow's reason for wanting to travel into the past was so romantic it moved me to help them,' said Murray, sarcastically, even as, to Wells's horror, he began scrambling up the hill of rubble. 'I explained to him that he could only make the journey in a time machine like the one in your novel, and together we hatched a plot, in which, as you know, you played the leading role. If Mr Winslow managed to persuade you to pretend you had a time machine, I would not only produce a replica of the one in your novel, I would also provide him with the actors necessary to play the parts of Jack the Ripper and the whore he murdered. You must be wondering what made me do it. I suppose devising hoaxes can become addictive. And I won't deny, Mr Wells, that it amused me to involve you in a pantomime similar to the one I had already orchestrated, to see whether you'd agree to take part in it or not.'

Wells was scarcely able to pay attention to what Murray was saying. Clambering up the hill was making him feel distinctly uneasy: the distant horizon had drawn so near that it was within arm's length. Once they reached the summit, he could see that what was in front of them was no more than a painted wall. Astonished, he passed his hand over the mural. Murray looked at him affectionately.

'Following the success of the second expedition, and although things had calmed down a lot, I couldn't help wondering whether there was any sense in carrying on with all this now that I had more than proved my point. The only reason I could think of to justify the effort it would take to organise a third expedition,' he said, recalling with irritation Jeff Wayne's pompous delivery of Shackleton's lines, and how scrawny he looked brandishing his rifle on top of the rock, 'was money. But I'd already made enough for a dozen lifetimes, so that was no excuse either. On the other hand, I was sure my critics would sooner or later mount a concerted attack on me that not even Conan Doyle would be able to head off.'

Murray seized the door handle protruding from the wall, but made no attempt to turn it. Instead he turned to Wells, seeming contrite.

'Doubtless I should have stopped then,' he said, with regret, 'setting in motion the plan I'd prepared even before I'd created the company. I would stage my own accidental death in the fourth dimension, eaten alive by one of my imaginary dragons before the eyes of a group of employees who, filled with grief, would see to it that the newspapers were informed of the tragic news. While I began my new life in America under another name, all England would mourn the passing of Gilliam Murray, the man who had revealed the mysteries of the future to them. However, despite the beauty of such an ending, something compelled me to carry on with my deception. Do you want to know what that was, Mr Wells?'

The writer merely shrugged.

'I'll do my best to explain, although I doubt you will understand. You see, in creating all of this, not only had I proved that my vision of the future was plausible, I had become a different person. I had become a character in my own story. I was no longer a simple glasshouse manufacturer. In your eyes I'm no more than an impostor, but to everyone else I'm a time lord, an intrepid entrepreneur who has braved a thousand adventures in Africa and who sleeps every night with his magical dog in a place where time has stopped. I suppose I didn't want to close the company because that would have meant becoming an ordinary person again – a terribly rich but terribly ordinary person.'

And with that, he turned the knob and stepped into a cloud.

Wells followed him a few seconds later, behind the magical dog, only to discover his bad-tempered face multiplied by half a dozen mirrors. He was in a cramped dressing room full of boxes and frames, hanging from which were several helmets and suits of armour. Murray was watching him from a corner, a serene smile on his lips.

'And I suppose I'll deserve what I get, if you refuse to help me,' he said.

There it was at last. As Wells had suspected, Murray had not gone to all the trouble of bringing him there simply to offer him a guided tour. No, something had happened and he had come unstuck. And now he needed his help. This was the *pièce de résistance* he was expecting his guest to swallow after having force-fed him with explanations. Yes, he needed his help. Alas, the fact that Murray had never stopped addressing him in that condescending, almost fatherly tone suggested he had no intention of begging for it. He simply assumed he would get it. For Wells it only remained to be seen what kind of threat the charlatan would use to extort it.

'Yesterday I had a visit from Inspector Colin Garrett of Scotland Yard,' Murray went on. 'He is investigating the case of a tramp found murdered in Marylebone, not exactly an unusual occurrence in that neighbourhood. What makes this case so special is the murder weapon. The corpse has a huge hole in the chest, which you can look through as if it were a window. It appears to have been caused by some sort of heat ray. According to the pathologists, no weapon capable of inflicting such a wound exists. Not in our time, anyway. All of which has led the young inspector to suspect that the wretched tramp was murdered with a weapon of the future, specifically one of the rifles used by Captain Shackleton and his men, whose devastating effects he was able to observe when he formed part of the second expedition.'

He took a rifle out of a small cupboard and handed it to Wells. The writer could see that the so-called weapon was simply a piece of wood with a few knobs and pins added for show, like the accessories on the tram.

'As you can see, it's just a toy. The automatons' woundings are achieved by tiny charges hidden under their armour. But for my customers, of course, it's a weapon, as real as it is powerful,' Murray explained, relieving Wells of the fake rifle and returning it to the cupboard with the others. 'In short, Inspector Garrett believes one of the soldiers of the future, possibly Captain Shackleton himself, travelled back to our own time as a stowaway on the Cronotilus, and all he can think of is to travel on the third expedition to apprehend him before he does so and thereby prevent the crime. Yesterday he showed me a warrant signed by the prime minister authorising him to arrest a man who, from where we're standing, hasn't even been born yet. The inspector asked me to reserve three seats on the third expedition for him and two of his men. And, as I'm sure you'll understand, I was in no position to refuse. What excuse could I have made?

'In a little more than a week the inspector will travel to the year 2000 with the intention of arresting a murderer, but in fact he'll uncover the greatest swindle of the century. Perhaps, given my lack of scruples, you think I could get out of this fix by handing one of my actors over to him. But to make that believable, not only would I have to produce another Cronotilus out of thin air, I would also have to get round the difficult problem of Garrett seeing himself as part of the second expedition. As you can appreciate, all that is far too complicated even for me. The only person who can prevent Garrett travelling to the future as he intends is you, Mr Wells. I need you to find the real murderer before the day of the third expedition.'

'And why should I help you?' asked Wells, more resigned than threatening.

This was the question they both knew would bring everything out into the open. Murray walked towards Wells with an alarmingly calm smile and, placing a plump hand on his shoulder, steered him gently to the other side of the room.

'I've thought a great deal about how to answer that question, Mr Wells,' he said, in a soft, almost sweet-sounding voice. 'I could throw myself on your mercy. Yes, I could slump to my knees and beg for your help. Can you imagine that, Mr Wells? Can you see me snivelling like a child, tears dripping on to your shoes, crying that I don't want my head chopped off? I'm sure that would do the trick: you think you're better than me and are anxious to prove it.' Murray opened a small door and propelled Wells through it with a light shove. 'But I could also threaten you by telling you that if you refuse to help me your beloved Jane will suffer a nasty accident while out on her afternoon bicycle ride in the suburbs of Woking. I'm sure that would also do the trick. However, I've decided instead to appeal to your curiosity. You and I, and the actors of course, are the only ones who are aware this is all a big farce. Or, to put it another way, you and I are the only ones who are aware that time travel is impossible. And yet someone has done it. Doesn't that make you curious? Will you just stand by and watch while young Garrett devotes all his energy to pursuing a fantasy when a real time traveller could be roaming the streets of London?'

Murray and Wells stared silently at one another.

'I'm sure you won't,' Murray concluded.

And with these words, he closed the door of the future and deposited Wells back on 26 November 1896. The writer found himself in the dank alleyway behind Murray's Time Travel, where a few cats were foraging in the rubbish. He had the impression that his trip to the year 2000 had been no more than a dream. On impulse, he thrust his hands into his jacket pockets, but they were empty: no one had slipped a flower into them.

XXXVII

The next day, when Wells called to see him at his office, Inspector Colin Garrett gave him the impression of being a shy, delicate young lad for whom everything appeared too big, from the sturdy desk where he was eating his breakfast, to his brown suit, and especially the murders, burglaries and other crimes spreading like unsightly weeds all over the city. If he had been interested in writing a detective novel, like those his fellow novelist Conan Doyle penned, he would never have described his detective as anything like the nervous, frail-looking individual in front of him, who, to judge by the excited way he shook Wells's hand, was particularly susceptible to the reverential zeal of hero worship.

Once he was seated, Wells stoically endured, with his usual modest smile, the outpouring of praise for *The Time Machine* – although, to give the young inspector his due, he ended his eulogy with a novel observation.

'As I say, I enjoyed your book enormously, Mr Wells,' he said, pushing aside his plate, as though he wished to remove the evidence of his gluttony, 'and I regret how hard it must be for you, and for all authors of futuristic tales, not to be able to continue speculating about the future now that we know what it is like. If it had remained unfathomable and mysterious, I imagine novels that predict tomorrow's world would have become a genre in themselves.'

'I suppose so,' Wells agreed, surprised: the young inspector's idea had never even occurred to him. Perhaps he was wrong to judge him on his youthful appearance.

Following this brief exchange, the two men smiled affably at one another, as the sun's rays filtered through the window, bathing them in a golden light. Finally Wells, seeing that no more praise was forthcoming, decided to broach the matter that had brought him there. 'Then, as you are a reader of my work, I imagine it will come as no surprise if I tell you I am here about the case of the murdered tramp. I've heard a rumour that the culprit might be a time traveller, and while I have no intention of suggesting I am an authority on the matter, I think I may be of some assistance.'

Garrett raised his eyebrows, as if he had no idea what Wells was talking about.

'What I'm trying to say, Inspector, is that I came here to offer you my . . . support.'

The inspector cast him a sympathetic glance. 'You're very kind, Mr Wells, but that won't be necessary,' he said. 'You see, I've already solved the case.'

He reached into his desk drawer for an envelope and fanned the photographs it contained on the table. They were all of the tramp's corpse. He showed them to Wells one by one, explaining in great detail, and with visible excitement, the chain of reasoning that had led him to suspect Captain Shackleton or one of his soldiers. Wells paid scant attention: the inspector was merely reiterating what Gilliam Murray had already told him. Instead he became engrossed in the intriguing wound on the corpse. He knew nothing of guns, but it did not take an expert to see that the grisly hole could not possibly have been inflicted by any present-day weapon. As Garrett and his team of pathologists maintained, the wound looked as though it had been caused by some sort of heat ray, like a stream of molten lava directed by a human hand.

'As you can see, there is no other explanation,' concluded Garrett, with a satisfied grin, placing everything back in the envelope. 'To be honest, I'm waiting until the third expedition leaves. This morning I sent a couple of officers to the crime scene simply for appearance's sake.'

'I see,' said Wells, trying not to show his disappointment.

What could he say to convince the inspector to investigate in a different direction without revealing that Captain Shackleton was not a man from the future, and that the year 2000 was no more than a stage set built of the rubble from demolished buildings? If he failed, Jane would almost certainly die. He stifled a gasp so that he did not betray his anguish to the inspector.

Just then, a bobby opened the door and asked to see Garrett. The young inspector made his excuses and stepped out into the corridor, beginning a conversation with his officer that reached Wells as an incomprehensible murmur. The talk lasted a couple of minutes, after which Garrett came back into the office in a visibly bad mood, waving a scrap of paper in his right hand. 'The local police are a lot of bungling fools,' he growled, to the astonishment of Wells, who had not imagined him capable of such an angry outburst. 'One of my officers found a message painted on the wall at the scene of the crime which those imbeciles overlooked.'

Wells watched him re-read the note several times, leaning against the edge of his desk.

Then the young man shook his head in deep dismay. 'Although, as it turns out, you couldn't have come at a better time, Mr Wells,' he said. 'This could almost have been taken from a novel.'

Wells raised his eyebrows and took the scrap of paper Garrett was holding out to him. The following words were scrawled on it:

The stranger came in early February, one wintry day, through a biting wind and a driving snow, the last snowfall of the year, over the down, walking as it seemed from Bramblehurst railway station.

Wells looked up at the inspector, who stared back at him.

'Does it seem familiar?' he asked.

'No,' replied Wells, categorically.

Garrett took the note from him and read it again, his head swaying from side to side, like a pendulum. 'Nor for me,' he confessed. 'What is Shackleton trying to say?'

After posing the rhetorical question, the inspector appeared to become lost in thought. Wells used the opportunity to rise to his feet. 'Well, Inspector,' he said, 'I shan't trouble you any longer. I'll leave you to your riddles.'

Garrett roused himself and shook Wells's hand. 'Many thanks, Mr Wells. I'll send for you if I need you.'

Wells nodded and walked out of Garrett's office, leaving him to ponder, balanced precariously on the corner of his desk. He made his way down the corridor, descended the staircase and left the police station, hailing the first cab he saw, almost without realising what he was doing – like a sleepwalker, perhaps, or someone under hypnosis, or, why not?, an automaton.

During the journey back to Woking, he did not venture to look out of the window even once, for fear that some stranger strolling along a pavement, or a navvy resting by the side of a road would give him a significant look that would fill him with dread. When he arrived home, he noticed his hands were trembling. He hurried straight along the corridor into the kitchen, without even calling to Jane to tell her he was back.

On the table were his typewriter and the manuscript of his latest novel, which he had called *The Invisible Man*. Pale as a ghost, Wells sat down and glanced at the first page of the story he had finished the day before, and which no one but himself had read. It began with the following sentence:

The stranger came in early February, one wintry day, through a biting wind and a driving snow, the last snowfall of the year, over the down, walking as it seemed from Bramblehurst railway station.

There was a real time traveller, and he was trying to communicate with him. This was what Wells thought when he emerged from his daze. And with good reason: why else would the traveller have written on the wall the first lines of *The Invisible Man*, a novel that had not yet been published in Wells's own time and whose existence no one but himself knew about? It was evident that killing a tramp with an unfamiliar weapon had only one purpose: to distinguish that murder from the many others perpetrated each day in the city and to attract the police's attention – but the fragment of his novel left at the scene of the crime could only be a message for him. And although Wells did not rule out the possibility that the tramp's strange chest wound had been inflicted by some present-day instrument that Garrett and the pathologists had not yet stumbled upon, no one could have known the beginning of his novel, except a man who came from the future. This fact alone dispelled any lingering doubts Wells might have had that he was dealing with a time traveller. He shuddered at the thought: not only had he discovered that time travel, which until now he had considered mere fantasy, was possible or, rather, would be in the future, but also that this time traveller, whoever he was, was trying to contact him.

He spent all night tossing and turning, unnerved by the unpleasant feeling of knowing he was being watched, and wondering whether he ought to tell the inspector everything, or whether that would anger the time traveller.

When dawn broke, he had still not come to any decision. Fortunately there was no need: almost immediately an official carriage from Scotland Yard pulled up in front of his house. Garrett had sent one of his bobbies to fetch him: another dead body had been found.

Without having breakfasted, and still wearing his nightshirt under his coat, the dazed Wells agreed to be driven to London. The coach stopped in Portland Street, where a pale-faced Garrett was waiting for him at the centre of an impressive police presence. Wells counted more than half a dozen officers trying to secure the scene of the crime against the crowd of onlookers who had flocked to the area. Among it he made out a couple of journalists.

'The victim was no tramp this time,' the inspector said. 'He was the landlord of a nearby tavern, a Mr Terry Chambers. Although he was undoubtedly killed with the same weapon.'

'Did the murderer leave another message?' asked Wells, in a faint voice, managing just in time to stop himself blurting out, 'for me'.

Garrett nodded, unable to disguise his irritation. Clearly he would have preferred Captain Shackleton to find a less dangerous way of amusing himself until he was able to travel to the year 2000 to arrest him. Clearly overwhelmed by the incident, he guided Wells to the crime scene, pushing his way through the police cordon.

Chambers was propped up against a wall, drooping slightly to one side, with a smouldering hole in his chest. The bricks behind him were clearly visible. Some words had been daubed above his head. His heart pounding, Wells tried not to step on the publican as he leaned over to read the inscription:

Left Munich at 8.35 p.m. on 1 May, arriving at Vienna early next morning: should have arrived at 6.46, but train was an hour late.

This sentence was not from his novel. Wells let out a sigh of both relief and disappointment. Was the message meant for another author? It seemed logical to think so, and he felt certain the otherwise unremarkable words formed the beginning of another as yet unpublished novel, which the author had probably just finished. It seemed the time traveller was not only trying to make contact with himself, but with someone else as well.

'Do the words mean anything to you, Mr Wells?' asked Garrett, hopefully.

'No, Inspector. However, I suggest you publish this in the newspaper. The murderer is giving us some sort of riddle, and the more people who see it the better,' he said, aware that he must do all he could to ensure this message reached the person to whom it was addressed.

While the inspector knelt to examine the corpse at close quarters, Wells gazed distractedly at the crowd on the other side of the cordon. What business could the time traveller have with two nineteenth-century writers? he wondered. As yet he did not know, but there was no doubt he would soon find out. All he had to do was wait. For the moment, the time traveller was pulling the strings.

Coming out of his daydream, he found himself looking at a young woman, who was staring back at him. She was about twenty, slender and pale, with reddish hair, and the intentness of her gaze struck Wells as odd. She was wearing an ordinary dress with a cloak over it, yet there was something about her expression and the way she was looking at him that he was unable to define but marked her out from the others.

Instinctively, Wells started towards her. But his bold gesture scared her: she turned on her heel and disappeared into the crowd, her fiery tresses billowing in the breeze. By the time he had managed to make his way through the throng, she had slipped away. He peered in every direction, but could see no trace of her. It was as though she had vanished into thin air.

'Is something the matter, Mr Wells?'

The author jumped on hearing the voice of the inspector, who had come after him, no doubt intrigued by his behaviour.

'Did you see her, Inspector?' Wells asked, still scanning the street. 'Did you see the girl?'

'What girl?' the young man asked.

'She was standing in the crowd. And there was something about her . . .'

Garrett looked at him searchingly. 'What do you mean, Mr Wells?'

He was about to respond, but realised he did not know how to explain the impression the girl had made on him. 'I . . . Never mind, Inspector,' he said. 'She was probably a former pupil of mine – that must have been why she looked familiar . . .'

The inspector nodded, but seemed unconvinced. Evidently he thought Wells's behaviour peculiar. Even so, he followed his advice, and the next day the two passages from his and the unknown author's work appeared in all the London newspapers. And if Wells's suspicions were well founded, the information would have ruined the breakfast of a fellow author. Wells did not know who at that moment was being seized by the same panic that had been brewing inside him for the past two days, but the realisation that he was not the only person the time traveller was trying to contact brought him some relief. He no longer felt alone in this. Neither was he in any hurry to learn what the traveller wanted from them. He was certain the riddle was not yet complete.

And he was not mistaken.

The following morning, when the cab from Scotland Yard pulled up at his door, Wells was already sitting on the porch steps, dressed and breakfasted. The third corpse was that of a seamstress by the name of Chantal Ellis. The sudden change in the victim's sex unsettled Garrett, but not Wells, who knew that the corpses were unimportant: they were blackboards on which the time traveller scribbled his messages. The words on the wall in Weymouth Street, against which the unfortunate Miss Ellis was propped, read as follows:

> *The story had held us, round the fire, sufficiently breathless, but except the obvious remark that it was gruesome, as, on Christmas Eve in an old house, a strange tale should essentially be, I remember no comment uttered till somebody happened to say that it was the only case he had met in which such a visitation had fallen on a child.*

'Mr Wells?' asked Garrett, no hope in his voice.

'No,' replied the author, omitting to add that the intricate prose struck him as vaguely familiar, although he was unable to identify its author.

While Garrett barricaded himself in the London Library with a dozen bobbies, intent on scouring every novel on its shelves for the one from which Shackleton, for some sinister and as yet unknown reason, was quoting, Wells made his way home, wondering how many more innocent victims would die before the traveller's riddle was complete.

The next day, no carriage from Scotland Yard came to fetch him. Did that mean the traveller had made contact with all of his chosen authors?

The answer was waiting for him in his letterbox. There, Wells found a map of London, by means of which the traveller not only indicated the meeting point, but at the same time flaunted his ability to move through the time continuum at will: the map was dated 1666 and was the work of the Czech engraver Wenceslaus Hollar. Wells admired the exquisite chart representing a city whose countenance had been transformed: months later London had been obliterated by an inferno, which, if he remembered correctly, had started in a bakery and, fanned by the neighbouring coal, timber and drink warehouses, had spread rapidly, reaching St Paul's Cathedral, then leaping over the Roman wall into Fleet Street. But what really astonished Wells was that the map showed no sign of having travelled across two centuries to reach him. Like a soldier holding his rifle aloft as he forges a river, the traveller had protected the map from the ravages of time, saving it from the stealthy caress of the years, the yellow claws of the decades and the ruinous handling of the centuries.

Having recovered from his astonishment, Wells noticed the circle marking off Berkeley Square, and next to it the number fifty. This was undoubtedly the place the three authors must go to meet the traveller. And Wells had to admit he could not have chosen a more appropriate location, for number fifty Berkeley Square was considered the most haunted house in London.

XXXVIII

Berkeley Square had a small park at its centre. It was rather gloomy for its size, but boasted some of the oldest trees in central London. Wells crossed it almost at a march, greeting with a perfunctory nod the languid nymph that the sculptor Alexander Munro had contributed to the relentless melancholy of the landscape. He halted outside a house with the number fifty displayed on its front wall. It was a modest building that looked out of place next to others bordering the square, all of which were designed by well-known architects of the period. It looked as though no one had lived there for decades, and although the façade did not appear too dilapidated, the windows on the upper floors, as well as those below stairs, were boarded up with mouldering planks to keep prying eyes from discovering the dark secrets that surely lay within.

Was he wise to have come there alone? Wells wondered, with a shudder. Perhaps he should have informed Inspector Garrett, for not only was he about to meet someone who apparently had few scruples when it came to killing ordinary citizens, but he had gone with the naïve intention of catching him and handing him to the inspector so that he would forget about going to the year 2000 once and for all.

Wells studied the austere front of the most haunted house in London, and wondered what all the fuss was about. *Mayfair* magazine had published a highly sensational piece about the strange events that, since the beginning of the century, had taken place there. Everyone who entered it had apparently either died or gone insane. For Wells, who had no interest in the spirit world, the article was no more than a lengthy inventory of gruesome gossip, rumours to which not even the printed word could lend any authority. The articles were full of maids who, having lost their wits, were unable to explain what they had seen, or sailors who, on being attacked, had leaped from the windows and been impaled on the railings below, or sleepless neighbours who, during periods when the house was unoccupied, claimed they had heard furniture being dragged around on the other side of the walls and glimpsed mysterious shadows behind the windows. This concoction of spine-tingling events had led the building to be classed as haunted, the home of a ruthless phantom, and thus the perfect place for young nobles to show off their bravery by spending a night there.

In 1840, a rake by the name of Sir Robert Warboys, who had made a virtue of scepticism, took up his friends' challenge to sleep the night there in exchange for a hundred guineas. He locked himself in, armed with a pistol and a string attached to a bell at the entrance, which he vowed he would ring if he found himself in any difficulty – he dismissed that possibility with a scornful smirk. Barely a quarter of an hour had passed when the tinkle of the bell was heard, followed by a single shot that shattered the silence of the night. When his friends came running, they found the aristocrat lying on a bed, stone dead, his face frozen in a grimace of horror. The bullet had lodged in the wooden skirting-board, perhaps after passing through the spectre's vaporous form.

Thirty years later, by which time the house had gained notoriety among the ranks of England's haunted houses, another valiant youth by the name of Lord Lyttleton was brave enough to spend the night there. He was more fortunate, surviving the phantom's assault by firing silver coins at it from a gun he had carried with him to bed. Lord Lyttleton claimed he even saw the evil creature fall to the ground, although during the subsequent investigation no body was found in the room. He had recounted his adventure in the well-known *Notes and Queries* magazine, which Wells had once read with amusement when he came across it in a bookshop.

The rumours and legends were at odds over the origin of the alleged ghost. Some claimed the place had been cursed after hundreds of children had been mercilessly tortured there. Others believed the phantom had been invented by neighbours to explain the bloodcurdling screams of the demented brother a previous tenant had kept locked in one of its rooms and fed through a trapdoor. There were also those – and this was Wells's favourite theory – who maintained that the legend began with a man named Myers, who, finding it impossible to sleep after being jilted on the eve of his wedding, spent his nights traipsing round the house with a candle. But during the past decade there had been no further reports of any disturbances, from which it was not unreasonable to assume that the ghost had descended to hell, bored with young bucks eager to prove their manliness.

However, the ghost was the least of Wells's concerns. He had too many earthly cares to worry about creatures from the other world.

He glanced up and down the street, but there was not a soul in sight, and as the moon was in the last quarter, it was absolutely dark. The night seemed to have taken on that sticky consistency so often described in Gothic novels. Since no time was specified on the map, Wells had decided to go there at eight o'clock in the evening because it was the hour mentioned in the second quotation. He hoped he was right, and would not be the only one to turn up to meet the time traveller. As a precaution he had come armed – he did not own a gun so he had brought his carving knife. He had hung it on his back from a piece of string, so that if the traveller decided to frisk him he would not notice it. He had bade Jane farewell, like the hero of a novel, with a lingering, unexpected kiss that had startled her, but which she had accepted with gentle abandon.

Wells crossed the street without further delay and, after taking a deep breath, as though he were about to plunge into the Thames, he pushed open the door, which yielded with surprising ease. He instantly discovered he was not the first to arrive. Standing in the middle of the hallway, his hands in the pockets of his immaculate suit jacket, admiring the staircase that vanished into the gloom of the upper floor, was a plump, balding man of about fifty.

Hearing him come in, the stranger turned to Wells and held out his hand, introducing himself as Henry James. So, this elegant fellow was James. Wells did not know him personally, for he was not in the habit of frequenting the sort of club or literary salon which were James's preserve and where, according to what Wells had heard, this prudish man of private means sniffed out the secret passions of his fellow members, then committed them to paper in a prose as refined as his manners. The difficulty in meeting him had not caused Wells to lose any sleep. Besides, having ploughed through *The Aspern Papers* and *The Bostonians*, he felt almost comforted to know that James lived in a world far from his own. He had concluded that the only thing he and James had in common was that they both spent their lives tapping away on typewriters. If Wells recognised any merit in James it was his undeniable talent for using very long sentences in order to say nothing at all.

Perhaps James felt similar disdain for Wells's work because he could not help pulling a face when Wells introduced himself. A number of seconds passed, during which the two men confined themselves to looking suspiciously at one another, until James obviously decided they were about to infringe some obscure law of etiquette, and hastened to break the awkward silence.

'Apparently we have arrived at the correct time. Our host was clearly expecting us this evening,' he said, gesturing towards the various candelabra distributed around the space, which, although they did not completely disperse the shadows, cast a circle of light in the centre of the hall, where the meeting was apparently to take place.

'It would seem so,' Wells acknowledged.

Both men gazed up at the coffered ceiling, the only thing to admire in the empty hallway. Luckily this tense silence did not last long, because almost at once a creaking door announced the arrival of the third author.

The man opening it with the timid caution of someone entering a crypt was also in his fifties. He had a shock of flaming red hair and a neatly clipped beard that accentuated his jaw. Wells recognised him at once. It was Bram Stoker, the Irishman who ran the Lyceum Theatre, although he was better known in the London clubs as the agent and lapdog of the famous actor Henry Irving. Seeing him creep in, Wells could not help recalling the rumours that Stoker belonged to the Golden Dawn, an occult society of which other fellow writers, such as the author Arthur Machen or the poet W. B. Yeats, were members.

The three men shook hands in the circle of light, before lapsing into a deep, uneasy silence. James had retreated into his precious haughtiness, while beside him Stoker was fidgeting nervously. Wells was enjoying this awkward meeting of three individuals who apparently had little or nothing to say to one another, even though all three, in their own separate ways, devoted their time to the same activity: dredging up their lives on paper.

'I'm so glad to see you're all here, gentlemen.'

The voice came from above. As one, the three writers glanced towards the staircase, down which the supposed time traveller was slowly descending, as though relishing the suppleness of his movements.

Wells studied him with interest. He was about forty years old, of medium height and athletic build. He had high cheekbones, a square chin, and wore a short, clipped beard, whose purpose seemed to be to soften his angular features. He was escorted by two slightly younger men, each with a peculiar-looking rifle slung over his shoulder. At least, that was what the writers assumed they were, more from the way the men were carrying them than from their appearance: they resembled two crooked sticks made of a strange silvery material. It did not take much intelligence to realise these were the weapons that emitted the heat ray that had killed the three victims.

The time traveller's ordinary appearance disappointed Wells, as though because he came from the future he ought to have looked hideous, or at the very least disturbing. Had the men of the future not evolved physically, as Darwin had predicted? A few years before, Wells had published an article in the *Pall Mall Budget* in which he envisaged the evolution of man's appearance over the centuries: mechanical devices would finally eliminate the need for limbs; advances in chemistry would render the digestive apparatus obsolete; ears, hair, teeth and other superfluous adornments would suffer the same fate. Only the two truly indispensable organs man possessed would survive this slow pruning process: the brain and the hands, which, of course, would increase in size considerably. The product of such speculation would necessarily be terrifying to behold, which was why Wells felt cheated by the mundane appearance of this man from the future standing in front of him.

The traveller – who, to add to his frustration, was dressed like his henchmen in an elegant brown suit – came to a halt and gazed at them in satisfied silence, a mischievous smile playing about his lips. Perhaps the faintly animal look in his intense black eyes and the grace of his gestures were the only qualities that delivered him from ordinariness. But such traits were not exclusive to the future either, for they could be found in some men in the present, which, thankfully, was inhabited by more athletic, charismatic specimens than most of those exemplified in the current gathering.

'I imagine this place could not be more to your liking, Mr James,' the traveller remarked, smiling sardonically at the American.

James, a past master at the art of innuendo, smiled back at him coldly but politely. 'I shall not deny you are correct, although if you will allow me, I shall defer my admission, for I shall only be able to give it truthfully if, by the end of this meeting, I consider the outcome a worthy enough recompense for the dreadful toll the journey from Rye has taken on my back,' he replied.

The traveller pursed his lips, as though uncertain if he had entirely understood James's convoluted response.

Wells shook his head.

'Who are you and what do you want from us?' Stoker asked, in a quailing voice, his eyes fixed on the two henchmen, who were looming like a pair of inscrutable shadows at the edge of the lighted area.

The traveller fixed his gaze on the Irishman, and studied him with affectionate amusement. 'You needn't address me in that timorous voice, Mr Stoker. I assure you, I only brought you here with the intention of saving your lives.'

'In that case forgive our reticence, but you will understand that murdering three innocent people in cold blood, with the sole aim of drawing our attention, leads us to doubt your philanthropic intentions,' retorted Wells, who was just as capable, when he wanted, of stringing together sentences as tortuous as those of James.

'Oh, that . . .' said the traveller, waving his hand in the air. 'I assure you those three people were going to die anyway. Guy, the tramp in Marylebone, would have been killed the following night in a fight with one of his fellow vagrants; Mr Chambers was to have died three days later when someone robbed him outside his tavern; and on the morning of the same day the lovable Miss Ellis would have been fatally knocked down by a runaway coach in Cleveland Street. In fact, all I did was bring forward their demise by a few days. Indeed, the reason I chose them was because they were doomed to die, and I needed three people I could eliminate with our weapons so that their murders, with the fragments from your unpublished novels, would be reported in the newspapers where you would learn about them. I knew that, once I had convinced you I came from the future, I had only to let you know the meeting place and your curiosity would do the rest.'

'Is it true, then?' asked Stoker. 'Do you really come from the year 2000?'

The traveller gave a wry smile. 'I come from a long way beyond the year 2000 where, by the way, there is no war with the automatons. If only those little toys were our main problem . . .'

'What are you insinuating?' said Stoker. 'Everybody knows that in the year 2000 the automatons will have conquered—'

'What I'm insinuating, Mr Stoker,' the traveller interrupted, 'is that Murray's Time Travel is nothing but a hoax.'

'A hoax?' the Irishman spluttered.

'Yes, a rather clever hoax, but a hoax all the same, although unfortunately only the passage of time will reveal that,' their host informed them, grinning. Then he looked again at the Irishman, touched by his gullibility. 'I hope you aren't one of Murray's victims, Mr Stoker.'

'No, no . . .' murmured the writer, with gloomy relief. 'The tickets are beyond my means.'

'In that case you should be happy that at least you haven't wasted your money,' the traveller congratulated him. 'I'm sorry you're so disappointed to discover the journeys to the year 2000 are no more than a charade, but look on the bright side. The man telling you so is a real time traveller. As you will have deduced from the maps I left in your letterboxes, not only do I come from the future, but I am able to move along the time continuum in both directions.'

The wind was howling, yet inside the haunted house all that could be heard were the sputtering candle flames, which cast suggestive shadows on the walls. The traveller's voice sounded oddly smooth, as if his throat were lined with silk, when he said: 'But before I tell you how I do it, allow me to introduce myself. I do not want to give you the impression that we in the future have forgotten the basic social graces. My name is Marcus Rhys, and I am, in a manner of speaking, a librarian.'

'A librarian?' said James, suddenly interested.

'Yes, a librarian, although at a very special library. But allow me to begin at the beginning. As you have seen, man will gain the ability to travel in time, but don't imagine that where I come from we have time machines like the one in your novel, Mr Wells, or that time travel is the order of the day. No, during the next century, scientists, physicists, mathematicians all over the world will become embroiled in never-ending debates about the possibility or impossibility of time travel. Theories will abound on how to achieve it, all of which will run up against the immutable nature of the universe, which, regrettably, lacks many of the physical characteristics necessary for them to test their theories. Somehow it seems as though the universe was created impervious to time travel, as though God Himself had reinforced His creation against this aberration of nature.'

The traveller fell silent for a few moments, during which he took the opportunity to scrutinise his audience with his forceful gaze, his eyes as black as two rat holes. 'Even so, scientists in my time will refuse to admit defeat, and will persist in trying to find a way of fulfilling man's deepest longing: to be able to travel along the time continuum in any direction he pleases. But all their efforts will prove in vain. Do you know why? Because in the end time travel will not be achieved through science.'

Then Rhys began to pace around the halo of light, as though to stretch his legs, pretending to be oblivious of the writers' curious stares. Finally he went back to his position and his face cracked into a smile. 'No, the secret of time travel has always been in our heads,' he revealed, almost gleefully. 'The mind's capacity is infinite, gentlemen.'

The candles continued to sputter as the traveller, with his smooth, downy voice, sympathised with them because science in their time was still a long way from envisaging the enormous potential of the human mind, having scarcely moved on from studying the skull to examining its contents in a bid to understand the functioning of the brain, albeit through primitive methods such as ablation and applying electrical stimuli.

'Ah, man's brain . . .' He sighed. 'The greatest puzzle in the universe weighs only four hundred grams, and it may surprise you to know we use only a fifth of its capacity. What we might achieve if we could use it all remains a mystery even to us. What we do know, gentlemen, is that one of the many marvels hidden beneath its cortex is the ability to travel in time.' He paused again. 'Although, to be honest, even our scientists cannot identify the exact mechanism that enables us to travel along the time continuum. But one thing is clear: man's brain is equipped with some sort of superior awareness that allows him to move through time in the same way as he moves through space. And even though he is far from being able to harness it, he can activate it, which is already a huge accomplishment, as I am sure you can imagine.'

'Our brains . . .' whispered Stoker, with childlike awe.

Rhys gazed at him fondly, but did not let this distract him from his explanation. 'We don't know exactly who the first time traveller was – that is to say, the first person to suffer a spontaneous displacement in time, as we call it – because the earliest cases were isolated. In fact, if we have any knowledge of those initial displacements it is thanks to the esoteric and other journals devoted to paranormal activity.

'However, the numbers of people claiming they had suffered such episodes began to increase steadily, although at a slow enough rate for the strange phenomenon to continue to pass unnoticed, except by a handful of mad prophets whom people usually ignore. By the middle of our century, the world suddenly experienced an epidemic of time travellers, who appeared to come from nowhere. But the fact is they existed, as if the ability to move along the time continuum were the next step on Darwin's evolutionary ladder. It seemed that, faced with an extreme situation, certain people could activate areas of their brains that snatched them from the present as if by magic, and propelled them forwards or backwards in time. Even though they were still a minority, and unable to control their ability, theirs was clearly a dangerous talent.

'As you can imagine, it was not long before the government created a department responsible for rounding up people showing this ability to study them and help them develop their skills in a controlled environment. Needless to say, registration with the department was not voluntary. What government would have allowed people who possessed a talent like that to roam free? No, *Homo temporis*, as they came to be referred to, had to be supervised.

'Be that as it may, the study of those affected did succeed in throwing some light on the strange phenomenon: it was discovered, for example, that the time travellers did not move through the time continuum at a constant speed until the inertia of the impulse was used up and they came to a halt, as in the case of Mr Wells's machine. Instead they moved instantaneously from place to place, leaping through the void, as it were, only able to control whether they landed in the past or in the future through intuition, as with the initial leap.

'One thing seemed clear: the further they travelled, the more their energy was depleted after the journey. Some took several days to recover, while others remained in a comatose state from which they never awoke. They also discovered that if they concentrated very hard, they could transport objects and even people with them on their leaps through time, although the latter proved doubly exhausting.

'In any event, once they had understood as much as they could about the mechanism in the mind that enabled people to travel in time, the most pressing question, the one that had given rise to heated debates even before time travel became a reality, still remained to be answered: could the past be changed or was it unalterable?

'Many physicists maintained that if someone travelled into the past, say, with the intention of shooting someone, the gun would explode in their hands because the universe would automatically realign itself. They assumed the universe must possess some sort of self-awareness designed to protect its integrity, which would prevent the person from dying, because they had not died. However, by means of a series of controlled experiments, based on making tiny adjustments to the recent past, they discovered time had no such protective mechanism. It was as vulnerable as a snail without its shell. History, everything that had already taken place, could be changed. And this discovery, as you can imagine, caused an even bigger uproar than time travel itself. Suddenly, man had the power to modify the past.

'Unsurprisingly, most people saw this as God's way of giving humanity a free hand to correct its mistakes. The logical thing was to prevent past genocides and afflictions, to weed out the errors of history, so to speak, for what lies ahead, gentlemen, is truly dreadful, far worse than in your innocent tale, Mr Wells. Imagine all the good that time travel could do for humanity – it would be possible to eradicate the plague that devastated London, causing a hundred thousand deaths, before the fire of 1666 ironically stamped it out.'

'Or the books in the library at Alexandria that could be saved from the flames,' suggested James.

Rhys gave a derisive smirk. 'Yes, a million and one other things could be done. And so, with the blessing of the people, the government called on a group of doctors and mathematicians to analyse the set of aberrations that made up the past in order to decide which acts deserved to be wiped out and to predict how this would affect the fabric of time – there was no reason to make things worse.

'However, not everyone was happy, and voices were instantly raised against the Restoration Project, as it was called. Some considered this happy manipulation of the past that the government was about to embark on unethical, and one section of the population did everything it could to try to sabotage it. This faction – let us call it conservative – which was gaining more followers by the day, argued that we must learn to live with the mistakes of the past, for better or for worse. Things being as they were, the government found it more and more difficult to continue with the project.

'Then everything ground permanently to a halt when the time travellers, fearful of becoming the target of a new wave of xenophobia, began fleeing through time in all directions, creating an inevitable wave of panic throughout society. All at once, the past had become soft clay in the hands of anyone who felt like altering it for personal gain or simply by accident. Suddenly, the history of the world was in jeopardy.'

'But how can we know when someone has altered the past if in so doing they change the present?' asked Wells. 'We have no way of knowing whether someone is manipulating history. We would experience only the consequences.'

'I applaud your perspicacity, Mr Wells,' said Rhys, pleasantly surprised by the author's question. 'According to the laws of time, the consequences of any change to the past are transmitted along the time continuum, modifying everything in their path, like the ripples from a stone tossed into a pond. Consequently, as you have pointed out, it would be impossible to detect any manipulation because the ripples produced by this change would affect our present as well as our memories.' He paused, then added, with a mischievous grin, 'Unless of course we had a back-up copy of the world with which to compare it.'

'A back-up?'

'Yes, call it what you will,' replied the traveller. 'I'm referring to a collection of books, newspapers and other material documenting as exhaustively as possible everything that has happened up until the present, the whole history of mankind. Like a portrait of the true face of the universe, you understand, one that enables us to detect at once any anomaly, however small.'

'I see,' murmured Wells.

'And this is something the government has been working on since the first epidemic of time travellers, with the aim of preventing anyone from unlawfully manipulating the past,' Rhys declared. 'But there was one problem: where could such an archive be kept safe from the harmful ripples caused by any changes?'

The writers gazed at him, enthralled.

'There was only one possible place.' The traveller answered his own question. 'At the beginning of time.'

'The beginning of time?' asked Stoker.

Rhys nodded. 'The Oligocene epoch, the third epoch of the Tertiary period in the Cenozoic era, to be precise, before man had set foot on the Earth, when the world was the preserve of rhinoceroses, mastodons, wolves and the earliest versions of primates. A period no traveller could go to without linking various leaps – with all the risk entailed – and where there was no reason to go because there was nothing to change.

'In tandem with the project aimed at training time travellers, the government had, in the strictest secrecy, organised what we could call an élite team, made up of the most gifted and loyal travellers. Evidently, the team's mission was none other than to transport the world's memory back to the Oligocene epoch. After countless journeys, the chosen travellers, of which, as you will have guessed, I was one, built a sanctuary there to house the world's knowledge.

'The place was also to become our home, for a large part of our lives would be spent in that epoch. Surrounded by immense grasslands we were almost afraid to step on, we would live and bring up our children, whom we would teach to use their talent, as we had done, in order to travel through the millennia, keeping watch over history, that time line which began in the Oligocene epoch and ended at the precise moment when the government decided to scrap the Restoration Project.

'Yes, that is where our jurisdiction ends, gentlemen. Any time beyond that moment is unguarded, for it is assumed that the physiognomy of the future can absorb any changes the time travellers might bring about because it occurred after they appeared. The past, on the other hand, is considered sacred and must remain immutable. Any manipulation of it is a crime against the natural order of time.'

The traveller folded his arms and paused for a few moments, studying his audience warmly. His voice sounded eager when he took up again. 'We call the place where the world's memory is stored the Library of Truth. I am one of its librarians, the one responsible for guarding the nineteenth century. In order to carry out my task, I travel from the Oligocene epoch to here, stopping off in each decade to make sure everything is in order.

'However, even I, who am capable of making jumps spanning tens of centuries, find the journey here exhausting. I have to travel more than twenty million years, and the librarians who guard what for you is the future have to cover an even greater distance. That is why the time line we are protecting is dotted with what we call nests, a secret network of houses and places where we travellers can stop off to make our journeys less exhausting. And this house, of course, is one of them. What better place than a derelict building that will stand empty until the end of the century, and is allegedly haunted by an evil ghost that keeps intruders at bay?'

Rhys fell silent again, giving them to understand he had finished his explanation.

'And what state is our world in? Have you discovered any anomalies?' Stoker asked, amused. 'Are there more flies than there should be?'

The traveller indulged the Irishman's jest, but with a strangely sinister chuckle. 'I usually find some anomaly,' he declared, in a sombre voice. 'Actually, my job is rather entertaining. The nineteenth century is one of the time travellers' preferred eras for tampering with, perhaps because in many cases their interference has extreme consequences. And no matter how many of their muddles I sort out, nothing is ever as I left it when I come back. I wasn't expecting it to be any different on this visit, of course.'

'What has gone wrong this time?' asked James.

Wells heard the note of caution in the American's voice, as though he were not completely sure he wanted to know the answer. Might it be the men's clubs, those luxurious redoubts where he took refuge from the loneliness that stuck to him like a birthmark? Perhaps they had never existed prior to a couple of time travellers deciding to found the first one, and now they would all have to close down so that the universe could go back to its original form.

'This may surprise you, gentlemen, but nobody should ever have captured Jack the Ripper.'

'Are you serious?' asked Stoker.

Rhys nodded. 'I'm afraid so. He was arrested because a time traveller alerted the Whitechapel Vigilance Committee. Jack the Ripper was caught thanks to this "witness", who chose to remain anonymous. But in reality that is not what should have happened.

If it hadn't been for the intervention of a time traveller from the future, Bryan Reese, the sailor known as Jack the Ripper, after murdering the prostitute on the seventh of November 1888, would have boarded a ship bound for the Caribbean as planned. There he would have pursued his bloodlust, murdering several people in Managua. Owing to the distances involved, no one would ever link these crimes with the murdered East End whores. Thus, for the purposes of history, Jack the Ripper would have disappeared off the face of the earth. He would have left behind him the unsolved mystery of his identity, over which as much ink would be spilled as the blood that had flowed under his knife, and which throughout the ensuing century would become the favourite pastime of researchers, detectives, and amateurs. They would all root around in Scotland Yard's archives, desperate to be the first to put a face to the shadow that time had converted into a gruesome legend.

'It may surprise you to know that some of the investigations pointed the finger of suspicion at a member of the Royal Household. It would appear that anyone can have a reason for ripping a whore's guts out. In this case, as you can see, popular imagination outstripped reality. I imagine the traveller responsible for the modification couldn't resist finding out the monster's true identity. And as you deduced, Mr Wells, no alteration was detected. Everyone fell victim to the ripple effect, like the rest of the universe, for that matter. But this is an easy change for me to sort out. In order to set history straight I need only travel back to the seventh of November to prevent the traveller alerting George Lusk's Vigilance Committee. Perhaps you don't consider this particular change to be for the better, and I wouldn't disagree, but I must prevent it all the same for, as I explained, any manipulation of the past is a criminal offence.'

'Does this mean we are living in . . . a parallel universe?' asked Wells.

Rhys glanced at him in surprise, then nodded. 'It does indeed, Mr Wells.'

'What the devil is a parallel universe?' asked Stoker.

'It is a concept that will not be coined until the next century, well before time travel ceases to be a mere fantasy of writers and physicists,' explained the traveller, still regarding Wells with awe. 'Parallel universes were meant to be a way of avoiding the temporal paradoxes that might occur if it turned out that the past was not immutable, that it could be changed. What would happen, for instance, if someone travelled into the past and killed their grandmother before she gave birth to their mother?'

'He would not be born,' replied James, hastily.

'Unless his grandmother wasn't really his mother's mother, which would be a roundabout way of finding out that his mother was adopted,' Stoker jested.

The traveller ignored the Irishman's observation and went on with his explanation: 'But how could he kill his grandmother if he was never born? Many physicists in my time will argue that the only way around this paradox would be if important changes to the past created parallel universes. After killing his grandmother, the murderer would not vanish from that universe as one would expect, he would carry on living, but in a different world, in a parallel reality sprouting from the stem of the original universe at the exact moment when he pulled the trigger, changing his grandmother's fate.

'This theory will be impossible to prove even after time travel becomes a reality with the appearance of time travellers, for the only way to verify whether changes to the past produced parallel worlds or not would be by comparing the past with a copy of the original universe, as I explained before. And if we didn't have one now, I wouldn't be here talking to you about the mystery surrounding the identity of Jack the Ripper, because there would be none.'

Wells nodded silently, while Stoker and James exchanged puzzled looks.

'But come with me, gentlemen. I'll show you something that will help you understand.'

XXXIX

An amused grin on his lips, the time traveller began to climb the stairs. The writers hesitated for a moment, then followed him, escorted by his two henchmen. On the top floor, Marcus Rhys led them briskly to a room containing a bookcase on one wall filled with dusty tomes, a couple of dilapidated chairs and a ramshackle bed. Wells wondered whether this was the bed in which Sir Robert Warboys, Lord Lyttleton and the other plucky young nobles had boldly confronted the ghost, but before he had a chance to search the skirting board for signs of a bullet, Rhys pulled a lamp attached to the wall and the bookcase opened in the middle to reveal a spacious room beyond.

The traveller waited for his henchmen to scuttle through the shadows and light the lamps in the room before he beckoned them in. As James and Stoker seemed reluctant to do so, Wells took the lead, and ventured into the mysterious place with cautious, mouse-like steps. Next to the entrance he discovered two huge oak tables piled with books, annotated notebooks and newspapers from the period; no doubt this was where the traveller examined the face of the century, in search of possible inaccuracies.

At the back of the room he glimpsed something that aroused his interest far more. It was some kind of spider's web, made of multi-coloured pieces of cord, with a collection of newspaper cuttings hanging from it. James and Stoker had also noticed the network of strings, towards which the traveller was now walking, jerking his head for them to follow.

'What is it?' asked Wells, drawing level with him.

'A map of time,' replied Rhys, beaming with pride.

Wells gazed at him in surprise, then stared once more at the shape the coloured strings made, studying it carefully. From a distance it looked like a spider's web, but now he was closer to it, the design was more like a fir tree or fish bone. A piece of white cord, approximately five feet above the floor, was stretched from wall to wall. The ends of the green and blue strings hanging from it were tacked to the side walls. Each one, including the master rope, was festooned with newspaper clippings. Wells ducked his head, venturing among the news items, hanging like washing on a line, and browsed some of the headlines. After Rhys nodded his approval, the two other writers followed suit.

'The white cord,' explained the traveller, pointing at the master rope, 'represents the original universe, the only one that existed before the travellers began meddling with the past. The universe it is my task to protect.'

At one end of the white cord, Wells noticed a photograph shimmering faintly. Surprisingly it was in colour and showed a splendid stone and glass building towering beneath a clear blue sky. This must be the Library of Truth. At the other end a cutting announced the discontinuation of the Restoration Project and the passing of a law prohibiting any change in the past. Between these two items hung a forest of clippings, apparently detailing important events. Wells was familiar with many and had lived through some, like the Indian uprising and so-called Bloody Sunday, but as the cord stretched further into the future the headlines became more and more incomprehensible. When he realised they related to events that had not yet happened, that lay in wait for him somewhere along the time continuum, he felt dizzy.

Before resuming his examination, he glanced at his companions to see whether they were experiencing the same mixture of excitement and dread. Stoker appeared to be concentrating on one particular cutting, mesmerised while, after an initial cursory glance, James had turned his back on the map. Perhaps this frightening, incomprehensible future was too far beyond his control, unlike the reality he inhabited and in which he had learned to navigate like a fish in water. The American appeared relieved to know that death would preclude him from having to live in the terrifying world charted on the map of time.

Wells also tried to tear his eyes away from the rows of cuttings, fearing his behaviour might be affected by knowledge of future events, yet a perverse curiosity compelled him to devour as many headlines as he could. He was aware that he had been given an opportunity many would kill for.

He could not help pausing to read one news item in particular, concerning one of the first ever cases of spontaneous time travel, or so he deduced from the esoteric title of the journal. Beneath the sensational headline 'A Lady Time Traveller', the article described how when employees at Olsen's Department Store had gone to open the shop on the morning of 12 April 1984, they had discovered a woman inside. At first they thought she was a thief, but when asked how she came to be in the store the woman said she had just appeared there. According to the article, the most extraordinary thing about the case was that the unknown woman claimed to have come from the future, from the year 2008, to be exact, as her unusual garments confirmed. The woman maintained her house had been broken into by burglars, who had chased her into her bedroom, where she had managed to lock herself in. Terrified by the battering on the door as her assailants tried to break it down, she had suddenly felt giddy. A second later, she had found herself in Olsen's Department Store, twenty-four years earlier, stretched out on the floor and bringing up her supper. The police were unable to interrogate the woman because, following her initial, rather confused declarations, she mysteriously disappeared. Could she have gone back to the future? the journalist speculated darkly.

'The government suspects it all began with this woman,' Rhys announced, almost reverentially. 'Have you asked yourselves why some people and not others are able to travel in time? Well, so has the government, and genetic testing provided the answer: apparently the time travellers had a mutant gene, a concept still unknown to you. I think it will be a few years yet before it comes into use after a Dutch biologist coins the phrase. But it seemed very likely this gene was responsible for the travellers' ability to connect with an area of the brain that, for the rest of the population, remained switched off. Research showed that the gene was handed down from generation to generation, meaning all the travellers shared the same distant ancestor. The government never managed to discover who the first carrier was, although they thought it might have been this woman. It is widely believed she had a child with a man who was also possibly able to travel in time, and that their offspring inherited a reinforced gene, establishing a line of time travellers who, by mixing with the rest of the population, would, decades later, trigger the epidemic of time travellers. Every effort to find her has failed. The woman hasn't been seen since she vanished from the department store, as the article says. I won't deny some of us time travellers, including myself, worship her like a goddess.'

Wells smiled, peering affectionately at the photograph of the ordinary-looking woman – obviously confused and afraid, unable to believe what had happened to her – whom Rhys had elevated to the status of Goddess of Time Travel. No doubt she had suffered another spontaneous displacement and was wandering around lost in some other distant era, unless, faced with the prospect of losing her mind, she had chosen to kill herself.

'Each of the other strings represents a parallel world,' said Rhys, requiring the writers' attention once more. 'A deviation from the path that time ought to have taken. The green strings represent universes that have already been corrected. I suppose I keep them for sentimental reasons because, I have to admit, I found some of the parallel worlds enchanting, even as I was working out ways of restoring them to the original.'

Wells glanced at one green string from which dangled several celebrated photographs of Her Gracious Majesty. They looked identical to the ones he had seen in his own time, except for one small detail: the Queen had an orange squirrel monkey perched on her shoulder.

'This string represents one of my favourite parallel universes,' said Rhys. 'A squirrel monkey enthusiast had the eccentric idea of persuading Her Majesty that all living creatures radiate a magnetic energy that can be transmitted to other beings to therapeutic effect, in particular the squirrel monkey, which, according to him, worked wonders on people suffering from digestive problems and migraines. Imagine my surprise when, browsing the newspapers of the period, I found this startling addition to the photographs of the Queen. But that was not all. Thanks to Her Majesty, it became a fad to carry a monkey around on your shoulder, and a walk through the streets of London turned into a rather amusing spectacle. Unfortunately, reality was far less exciting and had to be re-established.'

Wells looked out of the corner of his eye at James, who appeared to heave a sigh, relieved at not having to live in a world where he was forced to go around with a monkey on his shoulder.

'The blue strings, on the other hand, represent the time lines I have not yet corrected,' Rhys went on. 'This one represents the world we are in now, gentlemen, a world identical to the original, but where Jack the Ripper did not mysteriously disappear after murdering his fifth victim, thus becoming a legend, but where he was caught by the Whitechapel Vigilance Committee after perpetrating his crime.'

The writers gazed curiously at the string to which he was referring. The first cutting related the event that had caused this bifurcation: Jack the Ripper's capture. The next cutting described the subsequent execution of the sailor Bryan Reese, the man who had murdered the prostitutes.

'But, as you can see, this is not the only blue string,' said the traveller, fixing his attention on another cord. 'This second string represents a bifurcation that has not yet taken place, but will happen in the next few days. It concerns you, gentlemen. It is why you are here.'

Rhys tore the first cutting from the string and kept it momentarily concealed from his guests, like a poker player pausing before he reveals the card that will change the outcome of the game. 'Next year, a writer named Melvyn Frost will publish three novels that will bring him overnight fame and secure him a place in literary history,' he announced.

He paused, observing his guests one by one, until his eye rested on the Irishman. 'One of them will be *Dracula*, the novel you have just finished, Mr Stoker.'

The Irishman looked at him with astonishment. Wells watched him curiously. Dracula? he said to himself. What was the meaning of that strange word? He did not know, of course. Neither did he know much about Stoker, save the three or four already mentioned facts. He could never have imagined, for instance, that this unassuming, methodical man, who observed society's norms and by day adapted with tragic subservience to the frenetic social life of his conceited employer, indulged at night in drinking sessions run by whores of every condition, whose admirable aim was to alleviate the bitterness of a marriage that, following the birth of his son, Irving Noel, had turned into a sham.

'Although you do not know it yet, Mr Stoker, although you would never dare even dream of it, your novel will become the third most popular book in the English language, after the Bible and Shakespeare's *Hamlet*,' the traveller informed him. 'And your *Count Dracula* will enter by right into the pantheon of literary legends, where he will become a truly immortal creature.'

Stoker swelled with pride at the discovery that, in the future the traveller came from, his work would be regarded as a classic. His novel would elevate him to a prominent position in the first rank of present-day authors, exactly as his mother had predicted after reading his manuscript, in a note he had carried in his pocket ever since. And did he not deserve it? He had spent six long years working on the novel, ever since Dr Arminius Vambery, lecturer in Eastern languages at the University of Bucharest and an expert on the occult, had loaned him a manuscript in which the Turks spoke of the cruel practices of the Prince of Wallachia, Vlad Tepes. He had been better known as Vlad the Impaler, owing to his custom of impaling prisoners on pointed stakes and imbibing a cup of their blood as he watched them die.

'Another of Frost's novels is entitled *The Turn of the Screw*,' Rhys went on, turning to the American. 'Does the name ring a bell, Mr James?'

The American looked at him in mute surprise.

'Of course it does,' said Rhys. 'As you can tell from his response, this is the novel Mr James has just finished, a charming ghost story that will also become a classic.'

Despite his consummate skill at dissimulating his feelings, James was unable to hide his pleasure at discovering the happy fate of his novel, the first he had chosen not to hammer out with his fingers, preferring to hire the services of a stenographer. And perhaps for that very reason, because of the symbolic distance created between him and the paper, he had ventured to speak of something as intimate and painful as his childhood fears – although he suspected it might also have had something to do with his decision to give up residing in hotels and guesthouses and settle in the beautiful Georgian house he had acquired in Rye. It was only then, when he found himself in his study, the autumn sunlight shimmering around the room, a delicate butterfly fluttering at the window-pane, and a stranger hanging on his every word, that James had found the courage to write a novel inspired by a story the Archbishop of Canterbury had told him long before. It was about two children who lived in an isolated country house where they were haunted by the evil spirits of departed servants.

Watching James smile discreetly, Wells wondered what kind of ghost story it was where the ghosts were not really ghosts, and yet perhaps they were, although in all probability they were not because you were meant to think that they were.

'And Frost's third novel,' said Rhys, turning to Wells, 'could be none other than *The Invisible Man*, the work you have just finished, Mr Wells, the hero of which will also find his place in the annals of modern legend, beside Mr Stoker's Dracula.'

Was it his turn now to swell with pride? Wells wondered. Perhaps, but he could find no reason to do so. All he wanted to do was to sit in a corner and weep, and to carry on weeping until not a drop of water was left in his body: he was only able to see the future success of his novel as a failure, just as he considered *The Time Machine* and *The Island of Doctor Moreau* to have failed. Rattled off at the same speed, alas, as he felt obliged to write all his works, *The Invisible Man* was yet another novel that conformed to the guidelines set down for him by Lewis Hind; a science-fiction novel intended as a cautionary tale about the dangers of misusing scientific knowledge. This was something Jules Verne had never ventured to do, always portraying science as a sort of transparent alchemy at man's disposal. Wells, on the other hand, could not share the Frenchman's unquestioning optimism, and had therefore produced another dark tale about the abuses of technology, in which a scientist, after managing to make himself invisible, ends up losing his mind. But it was clear no one would perceive the real message in his work: as Rhys had hinted, and as he had seen for himself in the horrific news items hanging from the master rope, man had ended up harnessing science for the most destructive purpose imaginable.

Rhys handed the cutting to Wells to read and pass on to the others. The author felt too dejected to wade through the handful of tributes that appeared to make up the bulk of the article. Instead, he confined himself to glancing at the accompanying photograph, in which the fellow Frost, a small, neat man, was leaning absurdly over his typewriter, the source from which his supposed novels had emanated. Then he passed the cutting to James, who cast a scornful eye over it before handing it to Stoker, who read it from beginning to end.

The Irishman was the first to break the deathly silence that had descended on the room. 'How could this fellow have had the same ideas for his novels as we did?' he asked, baffled.

James gave him the contemptuous look he would give a performing monkey. 'Don't be so naïve, Mr Stoker,' he chided him. 'What our host is trying to tell us is that Mr Frost didn't write these novels. Somehow he stole them from us before we published them.'

'Precisely, Mr James,' the time traveller affirmed.

'But how will he stop us suing him?' the Irishman persisted.

'I'm sure you don't need me to tell you that, Mr Stoker,' replied Rhys.

Wells, who had managed to thrust aside his despair and take an interest in the conversation again, was suddenly struck by a ghastly thought. 'If I'm not mistaken, what Mr Rhys is trying to tell us,' he said, with the aim of dispelling the fog the others were in, 'is that the best way to silence a person is by killing him.'

'By killing him?' declared Stoker, horrified. 'Are you saying this fellow Frost is going to steal our works and then . . . kill us?'

'I'm afraid so, Mr Stoker,' Rhys confirmed, accompanying his words with a solemn nod. 'When, after arriving in your time, I came across the news item about a mysterious fellow named Melvyn Frost, who had published these novels, I hastened to learn what had become of you, their real authors. And I'm sorry to have to tell you this, gentlemen, but all three of you are going to die next month. You, Mr Wells, will break your neck in a cycling accident. You, Mr Stoker, will fall down the stairs of your theatre. And you, Mr James, will suffer a heart attack in your own home, although, needless to say, your death, like those of your colleagues, will also be murder. I don't know whether Frost plans to carry out the deeds himself or to hire someone else, although judging from his frail physique, I would incline towards the latter.

'In fact, Frost is a typical instance of a time traveller who, afraid to return to his own time, chooses a particular period in the past in which to settle down and build a new life. All perfectly understandable and legitimate. The problem arises because the majority of these time exiles consider earning a living in the traditional sense – that is to say, by the sweat of their brow – which is utterly absurd when their knowledge of the future could make them rich. Most give themselves away when they modify the past in order to implement their money-making schemes, like this fellow Frost. Otherwise it would be impossible for us to trace them.

'But I didn't bring you here to torment you with tales of your imminent demise, gentlemen, rather to try to prevent it happening.'

'Can you do that?' Stoker asked, suddenly hopeful.

'Not only can I, but it is my duty, for your deaths represent a significant change to the century I have been assigned to protect,' replied Rhys. 'My sole aim is to help you, gentlemen. I hope I've convinced you of that. And that includes you, Mr Wells.'

Wells gave a start. How did Rhys know he had come to the meeting filled with misgivings? He found the answer when he followed the direction in which the traveller and his two henchmen were looking. All three were staring at his left shoe, where the knife he had strapped to his back was peeping out. It seemed the knot he had tied had been a little loose. Shamefaced, Wells picked up the knife and slipped it into his coat pocket, while James shook his head disapprovingly.

'All of you,' the traveller went on, attaching no further importance to the matter, 'will live for many more years in your original universe, and will continue delighting your faithful readers, of whom I consider myself one, with many more novels. Forgive me, though, if I refrain from telling you any details about your future. It is so that once we have resolved this small matter you will continue to act naturally. In fact, I ought to have intervened without revealing myself to you, but this fellow Frost is devilishly clever and will eliminate you so stealthily that the information I need to prevent your deaths, such as the exact time you were pushed down the stairs, Mr Stoker, will not appear in the newspapers. I only know the days on which you will suffer your respective accidents, and in your case, Mr James, I won't even know that because no one will notice you are dead until a neighbour discovers your body.'

James nodded ruefully, perhaps aware for the first time of his entrenched loneliness, which would make his death a silent act, unseen by the world.

'Let us say that bringing you here was a desperate measure, gentlemen, for I could think of no other way to prevent your deaths than by asking for your co-operation, which I feel sure will be forthcoming.'

'Naturally,' said Stoker, hastily, apparently physically ill at the thought he could be dead within a few days. 'What do we have to do?'

'Oh, it's quite simple,' said Rhys. 'Providing this fellow Frost cannot find your manuscripts, he won't be able to kill you. I therefore suggest you bring them to me at the first opportunity. Tomorrow, if at all possible. This simple act will create another bifurcation in the time line, because Frost will not have killed you. Once I am in possession of the novels, I shall travel forward to the year 1899, and take another look at reality. Then I shall decide what to do next.'

'I think it's an excellent plan,' said Stoker. 'I shall bring you my manuscript tomorrow.'

James agreed to do the same, and although Wells had the impression they were mere pawns in a game of chess between Rhys and this fellow Frost, he had no choice but to consent. He felt too disoriented by events to think of a better way than the one Rhys was proposing. And so, like the others, he agreed to bring his manuscript the next morning, although if Rhys finally apprehended Frost and unravelled the muddle of the future, it did not guarantee that he would be able to ride his bicycle in complete safety without first resolving the matter pending with Gilliam Murray. To do this he had no choice but to help Inspector Garrett catch Rhys, the very man who was trying to save his life.

* * *

But if there was a more difficult undertaking than capturing a time traveller, it was undoubtedly catching a cab in London in the early hours of the morning. James, Stoker and Wells spent almost an hour trawling the area around Berkeley Square without success. Only when they decided to walk towards Piccadilly, shivering with cold and cursing their luck, did they catch sight of a berlin. They started as it emerged from the thick fog that had settled over London, rolling along the street towards them almost solely thanks to the horse's efforts, because the driver was half asleep on his box. It would have passed straight by them, like a visitation from the beyond, had the driver not finally noticed the red-headed giant blocking the street and waving his arms wildly.

After the cab came to a hasty halt, the three men spent what seemed like eternity trying to explain their itinerary to the driver: first he would take Stoker to his house, then drop James at his hotel, and finally leave London for Woking, where Wells lived. When the man signalled that he had understood the route by blinking a couple of times and grunting, the three men clambered into the carriage and flopped on to the seats, like castaways reaching shore after days in a lifeboat.

Wells longed for some peace and quiet so that he could reflect on the events of the past few hours, but when Stoker and James launched into a discussion about their respective novels, he realised he would have to wait a little longer. He did not mind them leaving him out; in fact, he was relieved. Apparently, they had nothing to say to a writer of escapist literature who in addition came to meetings with a kitchen knife strapped to his back. He was not in the slightest bit interested in what they had to say either, so he gazed through the window at the turbulent swirls of mist. He soon realised that Stoker's voice, when its owner was not cowed by fear, was too loud to ignore even if he wanted to.

'What I'm trying to achieve with my novel, Mr James,' the Irishman explained, waving his arms in the air, 'is a deeper, richer portrayal of that elegant embodiment of evil, the vampire, whom I have attempted to divest of the burden of the romantic aesthetic that turned him into little more than a grotesque sex-fiend, incapable of inspiring in his victims any more than a sensual frisson. The protagonist of my novel is an evil vampire, whom I have endowed with the original attributes found in the myth of folklore, although I confess to having added a few of my own, such as him not having a reflection in mirrors.'

'But if you embody it, Mr Stoker, evil loses most of its mystery and its potency!' exclaimed James, in an offended tone that took his fellow writer by surprise. 'Evil should always manifest itself in the subtlest way. It must be born of doubt, inhabit the shadowy realm between certainty and uncertainty.'

'I'm afraid I don't really understand what you mean, Mr James,' murmured the Irishman, once the other man appeared to have calmed down.

James let out a long sigh, before agreeing to expand a little more on the sensitive subject, but Wells could tell from the bewildered look on Stoker's face that the Irishman grew increasingly confused as the other man spoke. It was no surprise, then, that when they stopped in front of Stoker's house, the red-haired giant had the air of someone punch-drunk as he stepped out of the cab. The situation only grew worse after Stoker's desertion (for this was precisely how Wells experienced it) as the two men found themselves brutally exposed to silence. A silence that the urbane James naturally felt obliged to break by engaging Wells in a shallow discussion about the different kinds of material that could be used to upholster carriage seats.

When Wells was finally alone in the cab, he gave thanks to heaven, then eagerly became lost in his deliberations as they left the city behind. He had many things to think about, he told himself. Yes, matters of great import, ranging from the future he had glimpsed in the clippings, which he was unsure whether to forget or to commit to memory, to the exciting idea that someone had thought of charting time as though it were a physical space. Only this was a region that could never be properly charted, because there was no way of knowing where the white cord ended. Or was there? What if the time travellers had journeyed far enough into the future to discover the edge of time, the end of the thread, just as the traveller in his novel had tried to do?

But did such a thing exist? Was there an end to time, or did it carry on for ever? If it did end, then it had to happen at the exact moment when man became extinct and no other species was left on the planet: what was time if there was no one to measure it and nothing to experience its passing? Time could only be seen in the falling leaves, a wound that healed, a woodworm's tunnelling, rust that spread, and hearts that grew weary. Without anyone to discern it, time was nothing, nothing at all.

Although, thanks to the existence of parallel worlds, there would always be someone or something to make time believable. And there was no doubt that parallel worlds existed. Wells knew this for sure now: they sprouted from the universe like branches from a tree at the minutest change to the past, just as he had explained to Andrew Harrington in order to save the young man's life less than three weeks earlier. And discovering this gave him more satisfaction than any future success of his novel, because it spoke of his powerful intuition, the effective, even precocious workings of his brain. Perhaps his brain lacked the mechanism that enabled Rhys to travel in time, but his powers of reasoning set him apart from the masses.

He recalled the map the traveller had shown them, the figure made of coloured strings representing the parallel universes Rhys had untangled. It suddenly struck him that the map was incomplete because it included only the worlds created by the travellers' direct interventions. But what of our own actions? The parallel universes not only grew from their wicked manipulations of the hallowed past, but from each and every one of our choices. He imagined Rhys's map with this new addition, the white cord weighed down by a sudden flowering of yellow strings representing the worlds created by man's free will.

Wells emerged from these reflections as the cab pulled up in front of his house. He climbed out and, after tipping the driver generously for having made him leave London in the small hours of the morning, he lifted the gate's latch and entered the garden, wondering whether it was worth going to bed or not, and what effect it might have on the fabric of time if he decided to do one thing or the other.

It was then he noticed the woman with the fiery red hair.

XL

Thin and pale, her reddish hair glowing on her shoulders, like embers escaped from a fire, she looked at him with the peculiar gaze that had caught his attention a few days before, when he had noticed her among the crowd of onlookers milling around the scene of Rhys's third crime.

'You?' exclaimed Wells, stopping in his tracks.

The girl said nothing. She simply walked as silently as a cat to where he was standing and held something out to him. The author saw it was a letter. Puzzled, he took it from her lily-white hand. *To H. G. Wells. To be delivered on the night of 26 November 1896*, he read on the back. So this girl, whoever she might be, was some sort of messenger.

'Read it, Mr Wells,' she said, with a voice that reminded him of the early-afternoon breeze rustling the net curtains. 'Your future depends on it.'

With that, she walked away towards the gate, leaving him motionless in the doorway, his face frozen in a frown. When he managed to rouse himself, Wells ran after her.

'Wait, Miss . . .'

He came to a halt halfway. The woman had disappeared: only her perfume lingered in the air. And yet Wells could not recall having heard the gate squeak. It was as though after handing him the letter she had literally vanished without trace.

He stood stock still for a few moments, listening to the silent throb of night and breathing in the unknown woman's perfume, until finally he decided to enter the house. He made his way as quietly as possible to the sitting room, lit the little lamp and sat down in his armchair. He was still startled by the appearance of the woman, whom he might have mistaken for one of Conan Doyle's fairies had she measured eight inches and worn a pair of dragonfly wings on her back. Who was she? And how had she suddenly vanished? But it was foolish to waste time surmising when he would no doubt find the answer in the envelope he was holding.

He tore it open and took out the pages it contained. He shuddered when he recognised the handwriting. His heart in his mouth, he began to read:

Dear Bertie,

If you are reading this letter then I am right and in the future time travel will be possible. I do not know who will deliver this to you. I can only assure you she will be a descendant of yours, and of mine, for as you will have guessed from the handwriting, I am you. I am a Wells from the future. From a very distant future. It is best you assimilate this before reading on. Since I am sure the fact that our handwriting is identical will not be enough to convince you, as any skilled person could have copied it, I shall try to prove to you that we are one and the same person by telling you something only you know about. Who else knows that the basket in the kitchen full of onions and potatoes is not just any old basket? Well, is that enough, or must I be crude and remind you that during your marriage to your cousin Isabel you masturbated thinking about the nude sculptures at Crystal Palace? Forgive me for alluding to such an upsetting period of your life, only I am certain that, like the secret meaning the basket has for you, it is something you would never mention in any future biography, proving beyond doubt that I am not some impostor who has found out everything about you. No, I am you, Bertie. And unless you accept that, there is no point in reading on.

Now I shall tell you how you became me. The three of you will be in for a nasty surprise tomorrow when you go to give Rhys your manuscripts. Everything the traveller has told you is a lie, except that he is a great admirer of your work. That is why he will be unable to stop himself smiling when you deliver his precious haul to him in person. Once this is done, he will give the order to one of his henchmen, who will fire at poor James. You have already seen what their weapons can do to a human body so I shall spare you the details, but it is not hard to imagine that your clothes will be sprayed with a grisly spatter of blood and entrails. Then, before either of you has a chance to react, the henchman will fire again, this time at a stunned Stoker, who will suffer the same fate as the American. After that, paralysed with fear, you will watch as he takes aim at you, except that before he pulls the trigger Rhys will stop him with a gentle wave of his hand. And he will do this because he respects you enough not to want to let you die without telling you why. After all, you are the author of The Time Machine, *the novel that started the vogue for time travel. At the very least he owes you an explanation, and so, before his henchman kills you, he will go to the trouble of telling you the truth, even if it is only to hear himself recount aloud how he managed to outsmart the three of you. Then he will confess to you, as he bounces round the hallway in that ridiculous way of his, that he is not a guardian of time, and that in fact, had it not been for a chance encounter he would have known nothing of the existence of the Library of Truth or that the past was being guarded by the state.*

Rhys was an eccentric millionaire, a member of that select group of people who go through life doing only what they wish to, and who had been obliged to let the government study him when they opened the Department of Time. He had not found the experience too objectionable, despite being forced to rub elbows with people from all walks of life. It was a small price to pay for finding out the cause of his ailment (which is what he assumed it was, after suffering a couple of spontaneous displacements at moments of extreme tension) and, above all, discovering the exciting possibilities it opened up.

When the department was closed down, he decided to hone the skills he had already learned to control remarkably well by doing some sightseeing through time. For a while, he devoted himself to travelling back into the past at random, wandering through the centuries until he grew tired of witnessing historic naval battles, witches being burned at the stake and fecundating the bellies of Egyptian whores and slave girls with his seed of the future. It was then that it occurred to him to use his talents to take his passion for books to the limit. Rhys had a fabulous library in his house, containing a fortune in sixteenth-century first editions and incunables, but suddenly his collection seemed to him ridiculous and utterly worthless. What good was it to him to own a first edition of Lord Byron's Childe Harold's Pilgrimage *if the verses he was reading could be perused by anyone else? It would be quite different if he possessed the only copy in the world, as if the poet had written it exclusively for him.*

With his newly discovered abilities, this was something he could achieve quite easily. If he travelled back in time, stole one of his favourite author's manuscripts before he published it, then killed the writer, he would be able to build up a unique library of works no one else knew even existed. Murdering a handful of writers to add a private literary archive to his library did not trouble him in the slightest, for Rhys had always thought of his favourite novels as originating out of nowhere, independently of their authors, who were human beings, and, like all human beings, pretty despicable. Besides, it was too late for him to start having scruples, especially since he had amassed his fortune in a way conventional morality would doubtless have deemed criminal.

Happily, he no longer needed to judge himself by others' moral codes, for he had long ago elaborated his own morality. He had been obliged to do so to be able to get rid of his stepfather in the way that he had. Still, even though he had poisoned him when the man had included Rhys's mother in his will, that did not stop him going to put flowers on his grave every Sunday. After all, he had him to thank for who he was.

The vast fortune he had inherited from this brutal, uncouth man was nothing compared to his legacy from his real father: the precious gene that enabled him to travel in time, placing the past at his feet. He began dreaming of his unique library, on whose shelves Treasure Island, The Iliad *and* Frankenstein, *or his three favourite novels by Melvyn Aaron Frost, would sit secretly side by side. He picked up a copy of* Dracula *by Frost and studied his photograph carefully. Yes, the sickly little man with eyes that oozed corruption, showing he was as riddled with vices and weaknesses as any other, would be the first of a long list of writers who would meet their end in a series of freak accidents that would help Rhys amass his phantom library.*

With this in mind, he travelled to our time accompanied by two of his men, arriving a few months before Frost's rise to fame. He needed to find him, make sure he had not delivered his manuscripts to his editor, and force him at gunpoint to hand over the only thing that differentiated him from all the other wretches who gave the world a bad name. Then he would end Frost's ridiculous life by staging some sort of accident. But, to his surprise, he could find no trace of Melvyn Frost. No one seemed to have heard of him. It was as though he had never existed. How could he possibly have guessed that Frost was also a time traveller and would reveal his identity only once he was in possession of your works?

But Rhys had no intention of leaving empty-handed. This was the writer he had chosen to start his literary bloodbath, and he would find him come hell or high water. His plan was not notable for its subtlety: the only thing he could think of to force Frost out into the open was to kill three innocent bystanders and write the opening sentence of each of his three novels at the scene of each crime, lifting them from the published copies he had brought with him. This could not fail to arouse Frost's curiosity.

As Rhys had predicted, it was not long before the passages appeared in the newspapers. But still Frost did not come forward, seemingly not taking the hint.

By turns desperate and infuriated, Rhys lay in wait day and night with his men at the scenes of the crimes, but to no avail

– until a man in the crowd caught his eye. It was not Frost, yet his presence gave Rhys a similar frisson of excitement. He had been staring like any other spectator at Miss Ellis's slender corpse, which, hours before, he himself had propped against the wall, and at the inspector from Scotland Yard, standing next to the dead woman, when he noticed the middle-aged man on his right. He was wearing all the typical accoutrements of the period: an elegant blue suit, a top hat, a monocle and a pipe hanging out of his mouth, all of which revealed themselves to Rhys as a deliberate disguise. Then he noticed the book the man was carrying. It was Melvyn Frost's hitherto unpublished novel The Turn of the Screw. *How could this man possess a copy of it? Clearly he was a fellow time traveller.*

Scarcely able to contain his excitement, Rhys discreetly watched as the man compared the beginning of the novel with the passage he had scribbled on the wall, then frowned, surprised to find they were identical.

When he slipped the book into his pocket and began to walk away, Rhys decided to follow him. Unawares, the stranger guided him to a deserted-looking house in Berkeley Square, which he entered after making sure no one was watching. Seconds later, Rhys and his men forced their way inside. In no time they overpowered the stranger. It took only a few blows for him to confess how he had come to be in possession of a book that did not yet exist. This was when Rhys found out about the Library of Truth and everything else. He had travelled there in order to murder his favourite author and become his only reader, but had ended up discovering much more than he had bargained for.

The name of the fellow in front of him, with the bloody nose and two black eyes, was August Draper, the real librarian responsible for guarding the nineteenth century. He had gone there in order to repair changes made to the fabric of time when a traveller named Frost murdered the authors Bram Stoker, Henry James and H. G. Wells and published their novels in his own name. Rhys was astonished to find that Melvyn Frost was not the real author of his favourite novels, that they were the works of the three writers his hostage had mentioned. In Rhys's reality they had died just as they were becoming famous, but in the original universe they had gone on to write many more novels.

He was almost as astonished to learn that Jack the Ripper had never been caught. He felt an almost metaphysical revulsion when he realised he had been simply travelling between parallel universes created at will by other travellers like him, but who, unlike him, had not been content merely to fornicate with Egyptian slave girls. However, he tried to put it out of his mind and concentrate on Draper's explanations.

The stranger planned to rectify the damage, warning the three authors of what was about to happen by leaving a copy of their respective novels published under the name of Melvyn Frost in each of their letterboxes, with a map showing them where they could meet him. He was about to set his plan in motion when news of Rhys's mysterious murders appeared in the papers, which led him to the scene of one of the crimes. You can imagine what happened next: Rhys killed him in cold blood and decided to step into his shoes and pass himself off to you as the real guardian of time.

These are the facts, and if you study them carefully, certain things become clearer. For example, did it not strike you as odd that Rhys chose such an indiscreet way to contact you: reports in the press and alerting every policeman in the city by brutally murdering three innocent people – who, by the way, I doubt very much were going to die in a few days' time. But what you think now is irrelevant, actually: you should have thought of it then, and you did not. You cannot imagine how much it pains me to tell you this, Bertie, but you are not as intelligent as you think you are.

Where was I? Oh, yes. You will listen to Rhys's explanation, eyes fixed on his benchmen's weapons pointing at you, as your heart beats faster and faster, the sweat starts to pour down your back, and you even begin to feel overcome with a strange dizziness. I imagine if you had been shot as promptly as James and Stoker were, nothing would have happened. But Rhys's lengthy explanation had enabled you to 'prepare yourself', so to speak, and when he had finished his little talk, and his benchmen took a step forward and aimed at your chest, all of your built-up tension exploded, and a flood of light enveloped the world.

For a split second, you became weightless, released from your own body, which felt more than ever like an unnecessary shell, a focus for pain and futile distractions. You had the impression of being a creature of the air. But a moment later the weight of your body returned, like an anchor securing you to the world, and although you were relieved to feel solid again, it also left you with a vague sense of nostalgia for the fleeting experience of being out of your body. You found yourself once more trapped inside the organic casing that contained you while blinkering your vision of the universe. A sudden surge of vomit filled your throat, and you released it with violent retching.

When your stomach stopped heaving, you dared look up, unsure if Rhys's benchmen had already fired or were relishing drawing out the moment. But there was no weapon aimed at you. In fact, there was no one around you, no trace of Rhys, or his benchmen, or Stoker, or James. You were alone in the darkened hallway, for even the candelabra had disappeared. It was as if you had dreamed the whole thing.

But how could such a thing have happened? I'll tell you, Bertie: simply because you were no longer you. You had become me.

So now, if you have no objection, I shall carry on narrating events in the first person. To begin with, I did not understand what had happened. I waited for a few moments in the by-now pitch-black hallway, trembling with fear and alert to the slightest sound, but all around me was silence. The house was apparently empty. Presently, as nothing happened, I ventured out into the street, which was equally deserted. I was utterly confused, although one thing was clear: the sensations I had experienced were too real to have been a dream. What had happened to me?

Then I had an intuition. With trepidation, I plucked a discarded newspaper out of a refuse bin. After verifying the date with amazement, I realised my suspicions were true: the unpleasant effects I had felt were none other than those of spontaneous time travel. Incredible though it may seem, I had travelled eight years back in time to 7 November 1888!

I stood in the middle of the square for a few moments, stunned, trying to take in what had happened, but I did not have much time. I suddenly remembered why that date seemed so familiar: it was the day Jack the Ripper had murdered young Harrington's beloved in Whitechapel and was subsequently captured by the Vigilance Committee, who had gone to Miller's Court after being alerted by a time traveller who . . . Was it me? I wasn't sure, but there seemed to be every indication it was. Who else could have known what was going to happen that night?

I glanced at my watch. In less than half an hour the Ripper would commit his crime. I had to hurry. I ran in search of a cab, and when at last I found one I told the driver to take me to Whitechapel as fast as he could. As we crossed London towards the East End I could not help wondering whether it was I who had changed history: had I made the whole universe abandon the path it was on to take this unexpected detour represented by the blue string, moving further and further away from the white cord, as Rhys had explained to us? If so, had I done it of my own free will, or simply because it was pre-ordained, because it was something I had already done?

As you will imagine, I arrived in Whitechapel in a state of extreme agitation, and once there I did not know what to do: naturally I had no intention of going to Dorset Street alone to confront the bloodthirsty monster; my altruism had its limits. I burst into a busy tavern crying out that I had seen Jack the Ripper at the Miller's Court flats. It was the first thing that came into my head, but I suspect whatever I had done would have been the right thing to do.

This was confirmed to me when a stocky fellow with a shock of blond hair named George Lusk sprang out from among the throng of customers gathered round me and, twisting my arm behind my back and pressing my face against the bar, said he would go and look, but that if I was lying I would live to regret it. After this display of strength, he released me, gathered his men together and marched towards Dorset Street in no particular haste. I went as far as the door, rubbing my arm and cursing the brute who was about to take all the credit. Then, among the crowd out in the street, I glimpsed young Harrington. Pale as a ghost, he was stumbling through the throng, a dazed expression on his face, burbling incoherently and shaking his head. I understood that he must just have discovered the disembowelled corpse of his beloved. He was the image of despair.

I wanted to comfort him; I even took a few steps towards him, but I stopped when I realised I had no memory of having performed this kindly gesture in the past. I confined myself to watching him until he disappeared at the end of the street. My hands were tied: I had to follow the script, any improvisation on my part could have had an incalculable effect on the fabric of time.

Then I heard a familiar voice behind me, a silky voice that could belong to only one person: 'Seeing is believing, Mr Wells.' Rhys was leaning against the wall, clutching his rifle. I looked at him as though he had stepped out of a dream. 'This is the only place I could think of to look for you, and I was right to follow my instinct: you are the traveller who alerted the Vigilance Committee, which then captured Jack the Ripper, changing everything. Who would have thought it, Mr Wells? Although I imagine that's not your real name. I expect the real Wells is lying dead somewhere. Still, I'm beginning to grow accustomed to the masked ball into which time travellers' actions have transformed the past. And the fact is I couldn't care less who you are. I'm going to kill you anyway.'

With that, he smiled and aimed his gun very slowly at me, as though he were in no hurry to finish me off, or wanted to savour the moment.

But I was not going to stand there and wait for him to blast me with his heat ray. I wheeled round and ran as fast as I could, zigzagging down the street, playing the role of quarry to the best of my ability in that game of cat and mouse. Almost at once, a ray of lava shot over my head, singeing my hair, and I could hear Rhys's laughter. Apparently he meant to have some fun before murdering me. I continued running for my life, although as the seconds passed this felt like an ever more ambitious endeavour. My heart was knocking against my chest and I could sense Rhys advancing casually behind me, like a predator intent on enjoying the hunt. Luckily, the street I had run down was empty, so no innocent bystanders would suffer the deadly consequences of our game.

Then another heat ray passed me on the right, shattering part of a wall; after that I felt another cleave the air on my left, blowing away a streetlamp in its path. At that moment, I saw a horse and cart emerge from a side street and, not wanting to stop I speeded up as fast as I could, just managing to pass in front of it. Almost at once, I heard a loud explosion of splintering wood behind me, and I realised Rhys had not hesitated to fire at the cart blocking his way. This was confirmed to me when I saw the flaming horse fly over my head and crash to the ground a few yards ahead of me.

I dodged the burned carcass as best I could, and leaped into another street, aware of a wave of destruction being unleashed behind me. Then, after turning down another side street, I caught sight of Rhys's elongated shadow thrown on to the wall in front of me by a streetlamp. Horrified, I watched him stop and take aim. I realised he was tired of playing with me. In less than two seconds I would be dead, I told myself.

It was then that I felt a familiar dizziness coming over me. The ground beneath my feet vanished for a moment, only to reappear a second later with a different consistency, as daylight blinded me. I stopped running and clenched my teeth to prevent myself vomiting, blinking comically as I tried to focus. I succeeded just in time to see a huge metal machine bearing down on me. I hurled myself to one side, rolling several times on the ground.

From there, I saw the fiendish machine continue down the street while some men who were apparently travelling inside it shouted at me that I was drunk. But that noisy vehicle was not the only one of its kind. The whole street thronged with the machines, hurtling along like a stampede of metal bison. I picked myself up off the ground and glanced about me, astonished, but relieved to see no sign of Rhys. I grabbed a newspaper from a nearby bench to see where my new journey in time had brought me, and discovered I was in 1938. Apparently, I was becoming quite skilled at it: I had travelled fifty years into the future this time.

I left Whitechapel and began wandering in a daze through that strange London. Number fifty Berkeley Square had become an antiquarian bookshop. Everything had changed, and yet happily it still seemed familiar. I spent several hours wandering aimlessly, watching the monstrous machines criss-crossing the streets; vehicles that were neither drawn by horses nor driven by steam – whose reign, contrary to what people in your time imagined, would end up being relatively brief. No time had passed for me, and yet the world had lived through fifty years. Yes, I was surrounded by hundreds of new inventions, machines testifying to man's indefatigable imagination, even though the director of the New York patent office had called for its closure at the end of your century. He claimed there was nothing left to invent.

Finally, weary of all these marvels, I sat down on a park bench and reflected about my newly discovered condition of time traveller. Was I in Rhys's future where there would be a Department of Time I could turn to for help? I did not think so. After all, I had only travelled fifty years into the future. If I was not the only time traveller there, the others must have been as lost as I was.

Then I wondered whether, if I activated my mind again, I could travel back to the past, to your time, to warn you about what was going to happen. But after several failed attempts to reproduce the same impulse that had brought me there, I gave up. I realised I was trapped in that time. But I was alive, I had escaped death, and Rhys was unlikely to come looking for me there. Should I not be happy about that?

Once I had accepted this, I set about finding out what had happened to my world, but above all what had become of Jane and all the other people I knew. I went to a library and, after hours spent trawling through newspapers, I managed to form a general idea of the world I was living in. With great sorrow, I discovered not only that the entire world was moving stubbornly towards war, but that there had already been one some years earlier, a bloody conflict involving half of the planet in which eight million people had died. Few lessons had been learned, and now, despite its graveyards piled with dead, the world was once more teetering on the brink.

I recalled some of the clippings I had seen hanging from the map of time, and understood that nothing could prevent this second war, for it was one of those past mistakes that the people of the future had chosen to accept. I could only wait for the conflict to begin, and try my best to avoid being one of the millions of corpses that would litter the world a year from then.

I also found an article that both bewildered and saddened me. It was the twenty-fifth anniversary of the death of Bram Stoker and Henry James, who had died attempting to spend the night confronting the ghost at number fifty in Berkeley Square. That same night another equally tragic event in the world of letters had occurred: H. G. Wells, the author of The Time Machine, *had mysteriously disappeared and was never seen again. Had he gone time travelling? the journalist had asked ironically, unaware of how close he was to the truth.*

In that article, they referred to you as the father of science fiction. I can imagine you asking what the devil that term means. A fellow named Hugo Gernsback coined it in 1926, using it on the cover of his magazine Amazing Stories, *the first publication devoted entirely to fiction with a scientific slant in which many of the stories you wrote for Lewis Hind were re-edited, together with those of Edgar Allan Poe and, of course, Jules Verne, who competed with you for the title of father of the genre.*

As Inspector Garrett had predicted, novels that envisaged future worlds had ended up creating a genre of their own, and this was largely thanks to his discovery that Murray's Time Travel was the biggest hoax of the nineteenth century. After that, the future went back to being a blank space no one had any claims on, and which every writer could adorn as he liked, an unknown world, an unexplored territory, like those on the old nautical maps, where it was said monsters were born.

On reading this, I realised with horror that my disappearance had sparked off a fatal chain of events: without my help, Garrett had been unable to catch Rhys and had gone ahead with his plan to visit the year 2000 and arrest Captain Shackleton, thus uncovering Murray's hoax, resulting in him going to prison. My thoughts immediately turned to Jane, and I scoured hundreds of newspapers and magazines, fearing I might come across a news item reporting the death of H. G. Wells's 'widow' in a tragic cycling accident.

But Jane had not died. She had gone on living after her husband's mysterious disappearance. This meant Murray had not carried out his threat. Had he simply warned her to convince me to co-operate with him? Perhaps. Or perhaps he had not had time to carry out his threat, or had wasted it searching for me in vain all over London to ask why on earth I was not trying to discover the real murderer. Despite his extensive network of thugs, he had failed to find me. Naturally, he had not thought to look in 1938. In any case, he had ended up in prison, and my wife was alive. Although she was no longer my wife.

Thanks to the articles about you, I was able to form an idea of what her life was like, what it had been like after my sudden upsetting departure. Jane had waited nearly five years in our house in Woking for me to come back, and then her hope ran out. Resigned to continuing her life without me, she had returned to live in London, where she had met and married a prestigious lawyer by the name of Douglas Evans, with whom she had a daughter they named Selma. I found a photograph of her as a charming old lady who still had the smile I had become enamoured of during our walks to Charing Cross. My first thought was to find her, but this, of course, was a foolish impulse. What would I say to her? My sudden reappearance after all this time would only have upset her otherwise peaceful existence. She had accepted my departure, why stir things up now? I did not to try to find her, which is why from the moment I disappeared I never again laid eyes on the sweet creature who must at this very moment be sleeping above your head.

Perhaps my telling you this will prompt you to wake her with your caresses when you finish reading the letter. It is something only you can decide: far be it from me to meddle in your marriage. But, of course, not looking for her was not enough. I had to leave London, not just because I was afraid of running into her or into one of my friends, who would recognise me immediately since I had not changed, but purely for my own protection: it was more than likely Rhys would carry on trawling the centuries for me, searching through time for some trace of me.

I assumed a false identity. I grew a bushy beard and chose the charming medieval town of Norwich as the place where I would discreetly start to build a new life for myself. Thanks to what you had learned at Mr Cowap's pharmacy, I found work at a chemist's, and for a year and a half I spent my days dispensing ointments and syrups, and my nights lying in bed listening to the news, alert to the slow build-up of a war that would redefine the world once more. Of my own free will I had decided to live one of those redundant, futile lives that I had always been terrified my mother's stubbornness would finally condemn me to, and I could not even compensate for its simplicity by writing for fear of alerting Rhys. I was a writer condemned to live like someone who had no gift for writing. Can you imagine a worse torture? Neither can I. Yes, I was safe, but I was trapped in a dismal life, which made me wonder at times whether it was worth the trouble of living.

Happily, someone came along to brighten it up: she was called Alice and she was beautiful. She entered the chemist's one morning to buy a bottle of aspirin – a preparation of acetylsalicylic acid marketed by a German company that was very popular at the time – and when she left she took my heart with her.

Love blossomed between us amazingly quickly, outstripping the war, and by the time it broke out Alice and I had much more to lose than before. Luckily, it all seemed to be taking place far away from our town, which apparently presented no threat to Germany, whose new chancellor intended to conquer the world under the dubious pretext that the blood of a superior race pulsed through his veins. We could only glimpse the terrible consequences of the conflict through the ghastly murmurings carried to us on the breeze, a foretaste of what the newspapers would later report. I already understood this war would be different from previous ones, because science had changed the face of war by presenting men with new ways of killing one another.

The battle would now take place in the skies. But do not think of dirigibles firing at one another to see who could burst the enemy's hydrogen balloons first. Man had conquered the skies with a flying machine that was heavier than air, similar to the one Verne had envisaged in his novel Robur-the-Conqueror, *only these were not made of papier-mâché glued together, and they dropped bombs. Death came from above, announcing its arrival with a terrifying whistle.*

And although, because of complex alliances, seventy different countries had been drawn into the atrocious war, in no time England was the only country left standing, while the rest of the world contemplated, astonished, the birth of a new order. Intent on breaking England's resistance, Germany subjected our country to a remorseless bombardment, which to begin with was confined to airfields and harbours (in keeping with the curious code of honour that sometimes underlies acts of war) but soon spread to the cities. After several nights of repeated bombing, our beloved London was reduced to smoking rubble, from which the dome of St Paul's Cathedral emerged miraculously, the embodiment of our invincible spirit.

Yes, England resisted, and even counter-attacked with brief sallies over German territory. One of these left the historic town of Lübeck, on the banks of the river Trave, partially destroyed. In angry retaliation, the Germans decided to increase their attacks two-fold. Even so, Alice and I felt relatively safe in Norwich, a town of no strategic interest whatsoever. Except that Norwich had been blessed with three stars in the celebrated Baedeker guide, and this was the one Germany consulted when it resolved to destroy our historic heritage. Karl Baedeker's guide recommended visiting its romanesque cathedral, its twelfth-century castle and its many churches, but the German chancellor preferred to drop bombs on them.

The intrusion of the war took us by surprise as we listened to Bishop Helmore's sermon in the cathedral. Sensing it would be one of the enemy's prime targets, the bishop urged us to flee the house of God, and while some people chose to remain – whether because they were paralysed by fear or because their faith convinced them there could be no safer refuge, I do not know – I grabbed Alice's hand and dragged her towards the exit, fighting my way through the terrified crowd blocking the nave.

We got outside just as the first wave of bombs began to fall. How can I describe such horror to you? Perhaps by saying that the wrath of God pales beside that of man. People fled in all directions, even as the force of the bombs ripped into the earth, toppling buildings and shaking the air with the roar of thunder. The world fell down around us, torn to shreds. I tried to find a safe place, but all I could think of as I ran hand in hand with Alice through the mounting destruction was of how little we valued human life.

Then, in the middle of that frenzied running, I felt a familiar dizziness steal over me. My head began to throb, everything around me became blurred, and I realised what was about to happen. Instantaneously, I stopped our frantic dash and asked Alice to grip my hands as tightly as she could. She looked at me, puzzled, but did as I said, and as reality dissolved and my body became weightless for a third time, I gritted my teeth and tried to take her with me. I had no idea where I was going, but I was not prepared to leave her behind as I had left Jane, my life, and everything that was dear to me.

The sensations that subsequently overtook me were the same as before: I felt myself float upwards for a split second, leaving my body then returning to it, slipping back between my bones, except that this time I could feel the warm sensation of someone else's hands in mine. I opened my eyes, blinking sluggishly, struggling not to vomit. I beamed with joy when I saw Alice's hands still clasping mine. Small, delicate hands I would cover with grateful kisses after we made love, hands joined to slender forearms covered with a delightful golden down. The only part of her I had managed to bring with me.

I buried Alice's hands in the garden where I appeared in the Norwich of 1982, which did not look as if it had ever been shelled, except for the monument to the dead in the middle of one of its squares. There I discovered Alice's name, among many others, although I always wondered whether it was the war that killed her, or Otto Lidenbrock, the man who loved her. In any event, it was something I was condemned to live with, for I had leaped into the future to escape the bombs. Another forty-four years: that seemed to be as far as I could jump.

The world in which I now found myself was apparently wiser, intent on forging its own identity and displaying its playful, innovative spirit in every aspect of life. Yes, this was an arrogant world that celebrated its achievements with a child's jubilant pride, and yet it was a peaceful world where war was a painful memory, a shameful recognition that human nature had a terrible side that had to be concealed, if only under a façade of politeness. The world had been forced to rebuild itself, and it had been then, while clearing the rubble and gathering up the dead, while putting up new buildings and sticking bridges back together, patching up the holes that war had wreaked on his soul and his lineage, that man had become brutally aware of what had happened, had suddenly realised that everything which had seemed rational at first had become irrational, like a ball in which the music stops.

I could not help rejoicing: the zeal with which those around me condemned their grandfathers' actions convinced me there would be no more wars like the one I had lived through. And I will tell you I was also right about that. Man can learn, Bertie, even if, as with circus animals, it has to be beaten into him.

In any event, I had to start again from scratch, to build another wretched life from the very beginning. I left Norwich, where I had no ties, and went back to London where, after being astounded by the advances of science, I tried to find a job that might be suitable for a man from the Victorian age going by the name of Harry

Grant. Was I doomed, then, to wander through time, floating from one period to another like a leaf blown in the wind, alone for ever? No, things would be different this time. I was alone, yes, but I knew I would not be lonely for very long. I had a future appointment to keep, one that did not require me to travel in time again. This future was close enough for me to wait until it came to me.

But apparently, before that, the mysterious hand of fate had made another appointment for me, with something very special from my past. And it happened at a cinema. Yes, Bertie, you heard right. It is hard to exaggerate the extent to which cinema will develop from the moment the Lumière brothers first projected images of workers leaving their factory at Lyon Monplaisir. No one in your time had any inkling of the enormous potential of their invention. However, once the novelty wears off, people will soon tire of images of men playing cards, scampering children and trains pulling into stations – everyday things they can see from their windows and with sound – and they will want something more than dull social documentaries accompanied by the absent tinkle of a piano. That is why the projector now tells a story on the empty screen.

To give you an idea, imagine one of them filming a play that does not have to take place on a stage raised in front of rows of seats, but can use anywhere in the world as its setting. And if in addition I tell you that the director can narrate the story using not just a handful of painted backdrops but a whole arsenal of techniques, such as making people vanish in front of our eyes by means of manipulating images, you will understand why the cinema has become the most popular form of entertainment in the future, far more so than music hall. Yes, nowadays an even more sophisticated version of the Lumière brothers' machine makes the world dream, bringing magic into people's lives, and an entire industry commanding enormous sums of money has grown up around it.

I am not telling you this for pure pleasure, but because sometimes these cinema stories are taken from books. And this is the surprise, Bertie: in 1960, a director named George Pal will turn your novel The Time Machine *into a film. Yes, he will put images to your words. They had already done this with Verne, of course, but that in no way diminished my joy. How can I describe what I felt when I saw the story you had written take place on screen? There was your inventor, whom they had named after you, played by an actor with a determined, dreamy expression, and there, too, was sweet Weena, played by a beautiful French actress whose face radiated a hypnotic calm, and the Morlocks, more terrifying than you could ever have imagined, and the colossal sphinx, and dependable, no-nonsense Filby, and even Mrs Watchett, with her spotless white apron and cap. And as one scene succeeded another, I trembled with emotion in my seat at the thought that none of this would have been possible if you had not imagined it, that somehow this feast of images had previously been projected inside your head.*

I confess that, at some point, I looked away from the screen and studied the faces of the people sitting near me. I imagine you would have done the same, Bertie. I know more than once you wished you had that freedom: I still remember how downcast you felt when a reader told you how much they had enjoyed your novel, without you being able to see how they had responded to this or that passage, or whether they had laughed or wept in the proper places, because to do so you would have had to steal into their libraries like a common thief. You may rest assured: the audience responded exactly as you had hoped.

But we must not take the credit away from Mr Pal, who captured the spirit of your novel brilliantly – although I will not try to hide the fact that he changed a few things in order to adapt it to the times: the film was made sixty-five years after the book was written, and part of what for you was the future had already become the past. Remember, for example, that despite your concern over the ways man might use science, it never even occurred to you that he might become embroiled in a war that would engulf the entire planet. Well, he did, not once but twice, as I have already told you. Pal made your inventor witness not only the First and Second World Wars, he even predicted a third in 1966, although fortunately in that case his pessimism proved unfounded.

As I told you, the feelings I experienced in that cinema, hypnotised by the swirling images that owed so much to you, is beyond words. This was something you had written, yes, and yet everything that appeared on the screen was unfamiliar to me – everything, that is, except the time machine, your time machine, Bertie. You cannot imagine how surprised I was to see it there. For a moment I thought my eyes were playing tricks on me. But, no, it was your machine, gleaming and beautiful, with its graceful curves, like a musical instrument, betraying the hand of a skilled craftsman, exuding an elegance that the machines in which I had been cast adrift had lost. But how had it ended up there, and where could it be now, more than twenty years after the actor called Rod Taylor, who played you, first climbed out of it?

After several weeks spent scouring the newspapers at the library, I managed to trace its eventful journey. I discovered that Jane had not wanted to part with it and had taken it with her to London, to the house of Evans the lawyer, who would contemplate with resignation the intrusion into his home of the absurd, seemingly useless piece of junk, which, to cap it all, was a symbol to his new wife of her vanished husband. I pictured him unable to sleep at nights, circling the machine, pressing the fake buttons and moving the glass lever, to satisfy himself it did not work, and wondering what mystery was contained in the object his wife referred to as the time machine, and why the devil it had been built. I was sure Jane would have explained nothing to him, considering the machine part of a private world that Evans the lawyer had no business knowing about.

When, many years later, George Pal began preparations for his film, he ran into a problem: he did not find convincing any of the designs his people had come up with for the time machine. They were clunky, grotesque and over-elaborate. None of the models bore any resemblance to the elegant, stately vehicle in which he envisaged the inventor travelling across the vast plains of time. That was why it seemed to him nothing short of a miracle when a woman named Selma Evans, close to bankruptcy after squandering the small fortune she had inherited from her parents, offered to sell him the strange object her mother had dusted every Sunday in a languid, ceremonious manner that had made little Selma's hair stand on end.

Pal was stunned: this was exactly what he had been looking for. It was beautiful and majestic and had the same lively air as the toboggans he had ridden as a boy. He remembered the wind whipping his face as he sped down the slopes, a wind that had taken on a magical quality over time, and he imagined if you travelled through time in that machine you would feel the same wind lashing your face. But what really decided him was the little plaque on the control panel that said: 'Made by H.G. Wells'. Had the author really built it himself? And, if so, why?

This was an insoluble mystery, as Wells had disappeared in 1896, just as he was becoming famous. Who knows how many more remarkable novels he might have given the world? However, although he did not know why the machine had been built, Pal sensed it could not be put to better use than in his film, so he persuaded the production studio to buy it. That was how your machine gained the fleeting immortality of the silver screen.

Ten years later, the studios organised a public auction of scenery and other props from several of its productions, including the time machine. It sold for ten thousand dollars, and the buyer went round the United States showing it in every town, until finally, after getting his money's worth from it, he sold it to an antiquarian in Orange County.

And that was where Gene Warren, one of the technicians on Pal's film, stumbled on it in 1974. It was sitting in a corner, rusty and neglected, with all the other junk. Its seat had long since been sold. Warren bought it for next to nothing, and set about lovingly restoring the toy that had come to mean so much to everyone working on the film: he repainted all the bars, repaired the broken parts, and even made a replacement seat from memory. Once fully restored, the machine was able to continue its journey, being displayed in fairs and events with a science-fiction theme, and even occasionally driven by an actor dressed as you. Pal himself appeared sitting on it on the front cover of Star Log, *smiling like a boy about to ride his toboggan down a snowy slope. That year, Pal even sent out Christmas cards to his friends of Santa Claus riding on your time machine.*

As you can imagine, I followed its progress like a loving father contemplating the adventures of a son who has lost his way, knowing that sooner or later he will return to the fold.

And on 12 April 1984 I kept my appointment at Olsen's Department Store. There she was, confused and scared, and it was I who whisked her out from under the noses of the press, holding her hand and whispering in her ear, 'I believe you because I can also travel in time.' We left the store through the emergency exit, taking advantage of the ensuing chaos. Once in the street, we scrambled into the car I had hired, and made our way to Bath, where a few weeks before I had acquired a charming Georgian house. There I intended us to make our home, far from London and all those time travellers from the future, who would doubtless be searching for her under orders from the government, which had decreed to sacrifice her was the only way to eradicate the root of the problem.

At first, I was not sure I had done the right thing. Should I have been the one to rescue her from Olsen's, or had I usurped the role of another time traveller from the future who had proclaimed himself the saviour of the Madonna of Time? The answer came a few days later, one bright spring morning. We were painting the sitting-room walls when suddenly a little boy of three or four materialised on the carpet, gave a loud chortle, as though tickled with joy, then disappeared again, leaving behind a piece of the puzzle he had been playing with. Following that brief and unexpected glimpse of a son we had not yet conceived, we understood that the future began with us, that we were the ones who would produce the mutant gene that years, or possibly centuries, later would enable man to travel in time. Yes, the epidemic of time travellers Rhys had told us about would quietly originate in that secluded house, I said to myself, stooping to pick up the piece of puzzle, an unconscious gift from our son.

I kept this fragment of the future in the larder, among the tins of beans, knowing that in a few years' time it would help me understand the puzzle someone would give to the boy at the precise moment they were supposed to.

After that there is not much more to tell. She and I lived happily ever after, like the characters in a fairy tale. We enjoyed life's small pleasures, attempting to live as quiet and uneventful a life as possible so that neither of us would suffer an inopportune displacement that would separate us in time. I even indulged myself and bought your time machine when Gene Warren's son put it up for sale, although I had absolutely no need of it: I travelled through time like everyone else now, letting myself be swept along by the delightful flow of the days, while my hair began falling out and I found it more and more difficult to climb the stairs. I suppose a mark of the calm happiness we enjoyed was our three children, one of whom we had already met.

Needless to say, their gift for time travel was far greater than ours. They were never in complete control of their ability, but I knew their descendants would be, and I could not help smiling when I saw our genes begin to propagate as they went out into the world. I did not know how many generations it would take before the government finally noticed the time travellers, but I knew it would happen sooner or later.

That was when I had the idea of writing you this letter with the aim of entrusting it to one of my grandchildren, who in turn would pass it down to one of his, until it reached someone who would be able to carry out my request: to deliver it to the author H. G. Wells, the father of science fiction, on the night of 26 November 1896. And I imagine that if you are reading it now then I was right about that too. I have no idea who will deliver this letter to you but, as I said before, he or she will be our own flesh and blood. And when that happens, as you will have guessed, these words will already be the voice of a dead man.

Perhaps you would have preferred it if I had not written you any letter. Perhaps you would have liked it better if I had let you meet your fate unprepared. After all, what awaits you is not all that bad, and even contains moments of happiness, as you have seen. But if I wrote to you it is because somehow I feel this is not the life you should live. Indeed, perhaps you should stay in the past, living happily with Jane and turning me into a successful writer who knows nothing about journeys through time, not real ones anyway.

For me it is too late, of course. I cannot choose a different life, but you can. You can still choose between your life and the life I have just recounted to you, between going on being Bertie or becoming me. In the end that is what time travel gives us, a second chance, the opportunity to go back and do things differently.

I have given a great deal of thought to what might happen if you decide not to go to the meeting with Rhys tomorrow. If you do not go, no one will point a gun at you, your brain will not be activated, and you will not travel through time. Therefore you will neither bring about the Ripper's capture, nor meet Alice, nor flee the German bombardment, nor rescue any woman at Olsen's Department Store. And, without you, the mutant gene will not be created, so there will be no time travellers and no Rhys to travel into the past to kill you.

I imagine everything that happened from the moment he murdered the tramp in Marylebone will disappear from the time continuum as though a huge broom had swept it away. All the coloured strings dangling from the white cord of the map of time will vanish, for no one will have created any parallel universe where Jack the Ripper had been caught, or where Her Gracious Majesty went around with a squirrel monkey on her shoulder. Good God, the map of time itself will disappear! Who will be there to create it?

As you can see, Bertie, if you decide not to go you will annihilate an entire world. But do not let this put you off. The only thing that would remain unchanged would be her appearance at Olsen's Department Store in 1984, although no one will take her by the hand and lead her away to a beautiful Georgian house where she will live happily ever after.

And what will happen to you? I imagine you will go back to the moment just before your life was altered by your own time travelling. Before Murray's thug chloroforms you? Almost certainly, because if

Rhys never travelled to your time and did not kill anyone, Garrett would never suspect Shackleton, and Murray would not send his thug to abduct you so that you could save his bacon. Therefore no chloroform-soaked handkerchief would be placed over your face on the night of 20 November 1896. Be that as it may, however far back you go, I do not imagine you will experience any of the physical effects of time travel: you will simply disappear from one place and reappear in another as if by magic, without being aware of any transition, although, of course you will remember nothing of what you experienced after that moment.

You would not know that you had travelled in time, or that parallel universes exist. If you decide to change what happened, this is what will occur, I fear: you will know nothing of me. It would be like reversing the moves in a game of chess until you find the one that began the check mate. At that point, if instead of the bishop you ought to move you decide to use your rook, the game will take a different turn, just as your life will tomorrow if you do not go to the meeting.

And so everything depends on you, Bertie. Bishop or rook? Your life or mine? Do what you believe you have to do.

Yours ever,
Herbert George Wells

XLI

And what about predestination? Wells wondered. Perhaps he was fated to travel in time, first to 1888, then to the beginning of the atrocious war that would involve the entire planet, and so on, exactly as he had told himself in the letter. Perhaps he was fated to produce the first race of time travellers. Perhaps he had no right to change the future, to prevent man being able one day to travel in time because he refused to sacrifice his own life, because he wanted to stay with Jane in the past it had taken him so long to arrange to his liking. For wanting to go on being Bertie.

However, this was not only a consideration about the morality of his choice, but about whether he really had a choice. Wells doubted he could solve the problem simply by not turning up at the meeting, as his future self had suggested. He was certain that if he did not go, sooner or later Rhys would find and kill him in any case.

In the end, he was sure that what he was about to do was his only choice, and clutched to him the manuscript of *The Invisible Man*, as the cab skirted Green Park on its way to Berkeley Square, where the man who intended to kill him was waiting.

After he had finished reading the letter, he had put it back in the envelope and sat for a long time in his armchair. He had been irritated by the tone of mocking condescension that the future Wells had used to address him – although he could hardly reproach him for it, given that the author of the letter was himself. Besides, he had to recognise that if he had been in the future Wells's shoes, considering all he had gone through, he would have found it difficult to avoid that patronising tone towards his callow past self, someone who had scarcely taken his first steps in the world.

But all that was immaterial. What he needed to do was assimilate as quickly as possible the astonishing fact that he himself was the author of that letter, in order to focus on the really important question: what he should do about it. He wanted his decision to take into account what he thought was the almost metaphysical principle of the matter. Which of the two lives branching off beneath him was the one he ought to live? Which path should he venture down? Was there any way of knowing? No, there was not. Besides, according to the theory of multiple worlds, changes to the past did not affect the present, but created an alternative present, a new universe that ran alongside the original, which remained intact. Accordingly, the beautiful messenger who had crossed time to give him the letter had slipped into a parallel universe, because in the real world no one had walked up to him outside his house. Consequently, even if he did not go to the meeting, in the world in which he did not receive the letter he would. His other life, then, the one in which the jocular future Wells had lived, would not disappear. It was redundant therefore to regard the act of not bowing to fate as some sort of miscarriage of time.

He must simply choose the life that most appealed to him without splitting moralistic hairs. Did he want to stay with Jane, write novels and dream about the future, or did he aspire to the life of that distant, future Wells? Did he want to go on being Bertie, or to become the link between *Homo sapiens* and *Homo temporis*? He had to admit he felt tempted to surrender quietly to the fate described in the letter, to accept that life punctuated by exciting episodes such as the bombardment of Norwich, which – why deny it? – he would not have minded experiencing, secure in the knowledge he would come out of it alive. It would be like rushing around calmly while bombs dropped out of the sky, admiring the terrifying force of man's insanity, the hidden depths of beauty in that display of destruction. Not to mention all the wonders he would be able to see on his journeys into the future, brimming with inventions even Verne could not have imagined.

But that would mean giving up Jane and, more importantly, literature, for he would never be able to write again. Was he prepared to do that? He thought about it for a long time, before finally making up his mind. He went up to the bedroom, woke Jane with his caresses and, in the anguished, oppressive darkness of the night, which felt exactly like being down a mole hole, he made love to her as if for the last time.

'You made love to me as if for the first time, Bertie,' she said, pleasantly surprised, before falling asleep again.

And hearing her breathe softly by his side, Wells had understood that, as so often happened, his wife knew what he wanted much better than he did, and that if only he had asked her, he could have saved all that time he had taken coming to a decision that, in addition, now proved to be the wrong one. Yes, he had told himself. Sometimes the best way to find out what we want is to choose what we do not want.

He pushed aside these thoughts when the cab pulled up in front of number fifty Berkeley Square, the most haunted house in London. Well, the moment had finally arrived. He took a deep breath, climbed out of the carriage and made his way slowly towards the building, savouring the aromas floating in the afternoon air, still with the manuscript of *The Invisible Man* tucked under his arm.

On entering, he discovered Stoker and James already there, engaged in a lively conversation with the man who was about to kill them in the halo of light cast by the candelabra dotted about the hallway. From then on, every time he heard some columnist praising the American's uncanny powers of observation, he would be unable to stop himself guffawing.

'Ah, Mr Wells,' cried Rhys, on seeing him. 'I was beginning to think you weren't coming.'

'Forgive the delay, gentlemen,' Wells apologised, glancing despondently at Rhys's two henchmen, who were firmly planted at the edge of the rectangle of light on the floor, waiting for Rhys to give them the order to finish off the foolish trio.

'Oh, that doesn't matter,' said his host. 'The important thing is you've brought your novel.'

'Yes,' said Wells, waving the manuscript idiotically.

Rhys nodded, pleased, and pointed at the table beside him, signalling to him to leave it on top of the two already there. Rather unceremoniously, Wells added his own to the pile, then stepped back a few paces. He realised this placed him directly in front of Rhys and his henchmen, and to the right of James and Stoker, an ideal position if he wanted to be shot first.

'Thank you, Mr Wells,' said Rhys, casting a satisfied eye over the spoils on the table.

He will smile now, thought Wells. And Rhys smiled. He will stop smiling now and look at us, suddenly serious. And he will raise his right hand now.

But it was Wells who raised his. Rhys looked at him with amused curiosity. 'Is something wrong, Mr Wells?' he asked.

'Oh, I hope nothing is *wrong*, Mr Rhys,' replied Wells. 'But we'll soon find out.'

With these words, he let his hand fall in a sweeping motion – as he had little experience at making gestures of this kind, it lacked authority, looking more like the action of someone swinging a censer.

Even so, the person who was supposed to receive the message understood. There was a sudden noise on the upper floor, and they raised their heads as one towards the stairwell, where something, which for the moment they could only describe as vaguely human, came hurtling towards them. Only when the brave Captain Shackleton landed on the floor in the middle of the circle of light did they realise it was a person.

Wells could not help smiling at the position Tom had taken up, knees bent, muscles tensed, like a wild cat ready to pounce on its prey. The light from the candelabra glinted on his armour, the metal shell covering him from head to toe, except for his strong, handsome chin. He struck a truly heroic figure, and Wells understood now why he had asked his former companions to get him the armour, which they had stolen from Gilliam Murray's dressing room that very morning.

While the others were still trying to understand what was going on, Shackleton unsheathed his sabre, performed a perfect flourish in the air and, following the movement through, plunged the blade into one of the two henchmen's stomachs. His companion tried to take aim, but the distance between them was too short for him to manoeuvre, which gave the captain ample time to draw the sword from his victim's stomach and swing round gracefully.

The henchman watched with horrified fascination as Shackleton raised his sword, slicing the man's head off with a swift two-handed blow. Still gaping in terror, the head rolled across the floor, disappearing discreetly into the gloomy edge of the circle of light.

'Have you brought an assassin with you, Wells?' James exclaimed, scandalised by the bloody spectacle taking place before him.

Wells ignored him. He was too busy following Tom's movements. Rhys finally responded. Wells saw him retrieve one of his men's weapons from the floor and aim it at Tom who, gripping his bloody sabre, was that very moment turning towards him. They stood at least four paces apart, and Wells realised with horror that the captain would be unable to cover this distance before the other man fired. And he was not mistaken: Tom barely managed to take a step before he received the full blast of the heat ray in his chest. His armour shattered, like a crab shell hit by a hammer, and he was thrown backwards, his helmet flying off as he fell. The force of the shot sent him rolling across the floor until he finally came to a halt, a smouldering crater in his chest, his handsome face lit by the nearby candelabra. Blood trickled from his mouth, and only the candle flames glinted now in his beautiful green eyes.

Rhys's roar of triumph broke the silence, forcing Wells to take his eyes off Tom and fix them on him. Rhys surveyed the three corpses strewn around him with amused incredulity. He nodded slowly, then turned towards the writers, huddled together on the far side of the hallway.

'Nice try, Wells,' he said, walking over to them with his springy gait, a ferocious grin on his face. 'I have to admit you took me by surprise. But your plan has merely added a few more bodies to the count.'

Wells did not reply. He felt suddenly dizzy as he watched Rhys raise his weapon and point it at his chest. He assumed the sensation announced that he was about to travel through time. So he would be going to the year 1888 after all. He had done his best to prevent it, but apparently his fate was sealed. There probably did exist a parallel universe where Shackleton had been able to finish off Rhys, and where he would not travel in time and could go on being Bertie, but unfortunately he was not in that universe. He was in one very similar to that of the future Wells, where he would also travel eight years into the past, but where Captain Shackleton had died, pierced by a heat ray.

Realising he had failed, Wells could only smile sadly, as Rhys slid his finger towards the trigger. At that very moment, a shot rang out, but a shot fired from an ordinary pistol. Then it was Rhys's turn to smile sadly at Wells. A moment later, he lowered his weapon and let it drop to the floor, as though he had suddenly decided it was worthless. With the languid voluptuousness of a puppet whose strings have been cut one by one, Rhys slumped to his knees, sat down, and finally toppled over on to the floor, his blood-spattered face still smiling. Behind him, a smoking gun in his hand, Wells saw Inspector Colin Garrett.

Had the inspector been following him all along? he wondered, bemused by the young man's sudden appearance. No, that was impossible: if Garrett had been spying on him in the original universe – that is to say, in the universe where Wells would inevitably travel in time and would write himself a letter, the inspector would have burst in and seized Rhys once Wells had vanished into thin air, and even if Rhys had succeeded in escaping, whether through time or space, Garrett would have discovered everything. Wells knew this was not the case because his future self had read a news item reporting the strange deaths of the authors Bram Stoker and Henry James after a night spent at the haunted house in Berkeley Square. Evidently, if Garrett had seen what had happened, that article would not have existed. Accordingly, Inspector Garrett had no business being in that universe any more than he had in the previous one.

The only new card on the table was Shackleton, whom Wells had enlisted in his battle with fate. Garrett's presence, therefore, could only have been determined by Shackleton, leading the writer to conclude that he was the person the inspector had followed there.

And, incidentally, he was correct in this assumption, for I, who see everything, can confirm that not two hours before, after a delightful stroll in the company of Miss Nelson, Garrett had bumped into an enormous fellow in Piccadilly. Following the violent collision, the inspector had turned to apologise, but the man was in too much of a hurry even to stop. His strange haste was not the only thing that aroused Garrett's suspicion: he was also puzzled by the curious solidity of his body, which had left his shoulder smarting painfully. Such had been the force of the blow that Garrett had even thought the fellow must be wearing a suit of armour under his long coat.

A minute later, this thought had not seemed so foolish. Gazing down at the stranger's bizarre footwear, he had realised with a shudder who he had just bumped into. His jaw had dropped – he was scarcely able to believe it. Trying to keep calm, he had begun to tail Shackleton cautiously, his trembling hand clasping the pistol in his pocket, unsure of what to do next. He had told himself the best thing would be to follow Shackleton for a while, at least until he discovered where he was going in such a hurry. By turns excited and calm, Garrett had followed him down Old Bond Street, holding his breath each time the dead leaves rustled like old parchment under his feet, and then down Bruton Street, until they reached Berkeley Square.

Once there, Shackleton had paused in front of what looked like a deserted building. Then he had scaled its façade until he disappeared through a window on the top floor.

The inspector, who had watched his climb from behind a tree, was unsure how to proceed. Should he follow him in? Before he had time to answer his own question, he noticed a carriage pull up in front of the dilapidated building and, adding to his surprise, out of it stepped the author H. G. Wells, who walked very calmly up to the house and went in through the front door. What was going on between Wells and the man from the future? Garrett was perplexed.

There was only one way to find out. He crept across the street, scaled the front of the building and climbed in through the same window Shackleton had used moments before. Inside the darkened building, he had witnessed the entire scene unnoticed. And now he knew Shackleton had not come from the future in order to perpetrate evil with impunity, as he had first thought, but to help Wells do battle against the time traveller named Rhys, whose wicked plan, as far as the inspector could tell, had been to steal one of Wells's works.

Wells watched the inspector kneel beside Tom's corpse and gently close his eyes. Then Garrett stood up, grinned his inimitable boyish grin, and said something. Wells, though, could not hear him, because at that very moment the universe they were in vanished as if it had never existed.

XLII

When he pushed the lever on the time machine forward, as far as it would go, nothing happened. Wells only needed to glance about him to see that it was still 20 November 1896. He smiled sadly, although he had the strange sensation that he had been smiling like that long before he touched the lever, and confirmed what he already knew: that despite its majestic beauty, the time machine was simply a toy. The year 2000 – the genuine year 2000, not the one invented by that charlatan Gilliam Murray – was beyond his reach. Like the rest of the future, in fact. No matter how many times he performed the ritual, it would always be make-believe: he would never travel in time. No one could do that. No one. He was trapped in the present from which he could never escape.

Gloomily, he climbed off the machine and walked over to the attic window. Outside, the night was quiet. An innocent silence enveloped the neighbouring fields and houses tenderly, and the world appeared exhausted, terribly defenceless, at his mercy. He had the power to change the trees around, paint the flowers different colours, or carry out any number of outrageous acts with total impunity for, as he gazed out over the sleeping universe, Wells had the impression that he was the only man on Earth who was awake. He had the feeling that if he listened hard enough he could hear the roar of waves crashing on the shores, the grass steadily growing, the clouds softly chafing against the membrane of the sky, and even the creak of age-old wood as the planet rotated on its axis. And his soul was lulled by the same stillness, for he was always overcome with an intense calm whenever he put the final full stop to a novel, as he had just done with *The Invisible Man*.

He was back at the point of departure, at the place that filled writers with dread and excitement, for this was where they must decide which new story to tackle of the many floating in the air, which plot to bind themselves to for a lengthy period. And they had to choose carefully, study each option calmly, as though confronted with a magnificent wardrobe full of garments they might wear to a ball, because there were dangerous stories, stories that resisted being inhabited, and stories that pulled you apart while you were writing them – or, what was worse, fine-looking clothes fit for an emperor that turned out to be rags.

At that moment, before reverently committing the first word to paper, he could write anything he wanted, and this fired his blood with a powerful sense of freedom, as wonderful as it was fleeting, for he knew it would vanish the moment he chose one story and sacrificed the others.

He contemplated the stars dotted across the night sky with an almost serene smile. He felt a sudden pang of fear. He remembered a conversation with his brother Frank a few months before, during his last visit to the house in Nyewood where his family had washed up, like flotsam. When the others had gone to bed, he and Frank had taken their cigarettes and beer out on to the porch for no other reason than to stand in awe under the majestic sky studded with stars like a brave general's uniform.

Beneath that blanket, which allowed them a somewhat immodest glimpse of the universe's depths, the affairs of man seemed painfully insignificant and life took on an almost playful air. Wells swigged his beer, leaving Frank to break the atavistic silence that had settled over the world. Despite the blows life had dealt him, whenever Wells came to Nyewood he always found his brother brimming with optimism, perhaps because he had realised it was the only way he could stay afloat; he sought to justify it in tangible ways – for example, in the pride any man should feel at being a subject of the British Empire.

Perhaps this explained why Frank had begun to extol the virtues of colonial policy, and Wells, who detested the tyrannical way in which his country was conquering the world, had felt compelled to mention the devastating effects of British colonisation on the five thousand aborigines in Tasmania, whose population had been decimated. He had tried to explain to an inebriated Frank that the Tasmanians had not been won over by values superior to those of their own indigenous culture, but had been conquered by a more advanced technology. That had made his brother laugh. There was no technology in the known world more advanced than that of the British Empire, he had declared, with drunken pomposity.

Wells did not bother to argue, but when Frank had gone back inside, he remained gazing uneasily up at the stars. Not in the known world, perhaps, but what of the others?

He studied the firmament once more now with the same sense of unease, in particular the planet Mars, a tiny dot the size of a pin-head. Despite its insignificant appearance, his contemporaries speculated about the possible existence of life on the red planet. It was shrouded in the gauze of a thin atmosphere, and although it lacked oceans, it did have polar ice caps. Astronomers everywhere agreed that, of all the planets apart from Earth, Mars possessed the conditions most advantageous for the creation of life. And for some this suspicion had become a certainty when, a few years earlier, the astronomer Giovanni Schiaparelli had discovered grooves on its surface that might be canals: undeniable evidence of Martian engineering.

But what if Martians existed and were not inferior to us? What if, unlike the indigenous tribes of the New World, they were not a primitive people eager to welcome a missionary visit from Earth, but a more intelligent species than man, capable of looking down their noses at him as he did at monkeys and lemurs? And what would happen if their technology allowed them to travel through space and land on our planet, motivated by the same conquering zeal as man? What would his compatriots, the great conquerors, do if they encountered another species that sought to conquer them, to destroy their values and their self-respect, as they did those of the peoples they invaded, applauded by those like his brother?

Wells stroked his moustache, reflecting on the potential of this idea, imagining a surprise Martian attack, steam-propelled cylinders raining down on Woking's sleepy commons.

He wondered whether he had stumbled upon the theme of his next novel. The buzz of exhilaration he felt in his brain told him he had, but he was worried about what his editor would say. Had he heard right? A Martian invasion was what he had come up with, after inventing a time machine, a scientist who operated on animals to make them human, and a man suffering from invisibility? Henley had praised his talent after the excellent reviews of his last book, *A Wonderful Visit*. Agreed, Wells did not do science the way Verne did, but he used a kind of 'implacable logic' that made his ideas believable. Not to mention his prodigious output of several novels a year.

But Henley seriously doubted whether books pulled out of a hat like that were true literature. If Wells wanted his name to endure longer than a new brand of sauce or soap, he must stop wasting his considerable talent on novels that, while undeniably a feast for the imagination, lacked the necessary depth to impress themselves on his readers' minds. In brief: if he wanted to be a brilliant writer, and not just a clever, competent storyteller, he must demand more of himself than dashing off little fables. Literature was more than that, much more. True literature should rouse the reader, unsettle him, change his view of the world, give him a resolute push over the cliff of self-knowledge.

But was his understanding of the world profound enough for him to unearth its truths and transmit them to others? Was he capable of changing his readers with what he wrote? And, if so, into what? Supposedly into better people. But what kind of story would achieve that? What should he write in order to propel them towards the self-knowledge of which Henley had spoken? Would a slimy creature with a slavering mouth, bulbous eyes and slippery tentacles change his readers' lives? In all probability, he thought, if he portrayed the Martians in this way the subjects of the British Empire would never eat octopus again.

Something disturbed the calm of the night, stirring him from his meditations. This was no cylinder falling from the sky but the Scheffer boy's cart. Wells watched it pull up in front of his gate, and smiled when he recognised the sleepy young lad on the driver's seat. The boy had no objection to getting up early to earn a few extra pennies. Wells made his way downstairs, grabbed his overcoat and left the house quietly, so as not to wake Jane. He knew his wife would disapprove of what he was doing, and he could not explain to her why he had to do it, even though he was aware that it was not the behaviour of a gentleman.

He greeted the lad, cast an approving eye over the cargo (he had excelled himself this time) and clambered on to the driver's seat. Once he was safely installed, the lad snapped the reins and they set off towards London.

During the journey they exchanged a few pleasantries. Wells spent most of the time silently absorbed in fascinated contemplation of the drowsy, defenceless world around him, crying out to be attacked by creatures from space. He glanced out of the corner of his eye at the Scheffer boy, and wondered how such a simple soul, for whom the world probably only extended as far as the horizon, would react to an invasion of extra-terrestrials. He imagined a small huddle of country-folk approaching the place where a Martian ship had landed, nervously waving a white flag, and the extra-terrestrials responding to the innocent greeting by instantaneously annihilating them with a blinding flame, a sort of heat ray that would raze the ground, leaving a burning crater strewn with charred corpses and smouldering trees.

When the cart reached the slumbering city he stopped imagining Martian invasions to concentrate on what he had come to do. They drove through a maze of streets, each more deserted than the last, the clatter of hoofs shattering the silence of the night, until they reached Greek Street. Wells could not help grinning mischievously when the boy stopped the cart in front of Murray's Time Travel. He glanced up and down the street, pleased to see no one was about.

'Well, my boy,' he said, climbing down, 'let's go to it.'

They each took a couple of buckets from the back of the cart and approached the front of the building. As quietly as possible, they plunged the brushes into the buckets of cow dung and began daubing the walls round the entrance. The repellent task took no more than ten minutes. Once they had finished, a nauseating stench filled the air, although Wells breathed it in with great delight: it was the smell of his rage, the loathing he was obliged to suppress, the never-ending directionless anger bubbling inside him. Startled, the boy watched him inhale the foul odour.

'Why are you doing this, Mr Wells?' he ventured to ask.

For a moment, Wells stared at him with furious intent. Even to such an unthinking soul, devoting one's nights to a task that was as eccentric as it was disgusting must have appeared ridiculous.

'Because between doing something and doing nothing, this is all I can do.'

The lad nodded in bewilderment at this gibberish, no doubt wishing he had not ventured to try to understand the mysterious motivations of writers. Wells paid him the agreed sum and sent him back to Woking, telling him he still had a few errands to run in London. The boy nodded, visibly relieved at not having to consider what these might be. He leaped on to his cart and, after geeing up the horse, disappeared at the end of the street.

XLIII

Wells contemplated the ornate façade of Murray's Time Travel and wondered again how this modest theatre could possibly contain the vast stage set Tom had described to him of a devastated London in the year 2000. Sooner or later he would have to try to get to the bottom of the mystery, but for the moment he must forget about it if he did not want his adversary's unarguable shrewdness to put him in a bad mood. Determined to push the thought aside, he shook his head and stood admiring his work for a few moments.

Then, satisfied with a job well done, he began to walk in the direction of Waterloo Bridge. He knew of no better place from which to observe the beautiful spectacle of morning. Cracks of light would soon begin to appear in the dark sky as dawn broke, and there was nothing to stop him dallying to witness the colourful duel before he went to Henley's office.

In fact, any excuse was good enough to delay his meeting with his editor, for he felt certain Henley would not be overly pleased with the new manuscript. Of course he would agree to publish it, but this would not spare Wells from having to listen to one of Henley's sermons aimed at steering him into the fold of authors destined to pass into the annals of literary history – and why not accept his advice for once? he suddenly thought. Why not give up writing for naïve readers easily convinced by any adventure story – or any story that shows a modicum of imagination – and write for more discerning readers, those, in short, who reject the entertainment of popular fiction in favour of more serious, profound literature that explains the universe and even the precariousness of their existence in centuries to come. Perhaps he should resolve to write another kind of story altogether, one that would stir his readers' souls in a different way, a novel that would be nothing short of a revelation to them, just as Henley wanted.

Immersed in these thoughts, Wells turned down Charing Cross Road and headed for the Strand. By that time, a new day was slowly dawning around him. The black sky was gradually dissolving, giving way to a slightly unreal dark blue that instantly paled on the horizon, taking on a soft violet tint before turning orange. In the distance, he could make out the shape of Waterloo Bridge growing more and more distinct as the darkness faded, slowly invaded by the light. A series of strange, muffled noises reached his ears, making him smile contentedly. The city was beginning to stir, and the isolated sounds hanging in the air would soon be transformed into the honest, relentless flow of life, an ear-splitting din that might invade the outer reaches of space transformed into a pleasant buzz of bees, revealing that the third largest planet in the solar system was very much inhabited.

Although, as he walked towards the bridge, Wells could see nothing beyond what was in front of him, somehow he felt as though he were taking part in a huge play, which, because every single inhabitant of the city was cast in it, seemingly had no audience. Except, perhaps, for the clever Martians, busy studying human life in the way that man peered down a microscope at the ephemeral organisms wriggling in a drop of water, he reflected. And, in fact, he was right for, as he threaded his way along the Strand, dozens of barges loaded with oysters floated in eerie silence along the ever more orange-tinted waters of the Thames, on their way from Chelsea Reach to Billingsgate wharf, where an army of men hauled the catch on to land.

In wealthy neighbourhoods, fragrant with the aroma of high-class bakeries and violets from the flower-sellers' baskets, people abandoned their luxurious houses for their no less luxurious offices, crossing the streets that were filling with cabriolets, berlins, omnibuses and every imaginable type of wheeled vehicle, jolting rhythmically over the cobblestones, while above them, the smoke from the factory stacks mingled with the mist rising from the water to form a shroud of dense, sticky fog. An army of carts drawn by mules or pushed manually, brimming with fruit, vegetables, eels and squid, took up their positions at Covent Garden amid a chaos of shouts.

At the same hour, Inspector Garrett arrived – before finishing his breakfast – in Sloane Street, where Mr Ferguson was waiting to inform him rather anxiously that someone had taken a pot shot at him the night before, poking his pudgy thumb through the hole it had made in his hat. Garrett examined the surrounding area with a trained eye, searching among the bushes around Ferguson's house, and could not prevent a tender smile spreading across his face when he discovered the charming kiwi bird someone had scratched in the soil. He glanced up and down the street to make sure no one was watching, then quickly erased it with his foot and emerged from the bushes, shrugging his shoulders.

Just as he was telling Ferguson with an expression of feigned bewilderment that he had found no clues, John Peachey, the man known as Tom Blunt before he had drowned in the Thames, embraced the woman he loved in a room at a boarding-house in Bethnal Green, and Claire Haggerty let herself be wrapped in his strong arms, pleased he had fled the future, the desolate year 2000, to be with her. At that very moment too, standing on a rock, Captain Derek Shackleton declared in a grating voice that if any good had come of the war it was that it had united the human race as no other war had ever done before. Gilliam Murray shook his head mournfully, telling himself this was the last expedition he would organise, that he was tired of fools and of the heartless wretch who kept smearing his building with dung, that it was time to stage his own death, to pretend he had been devoured by one of the savage dragons that inhabited the fourth dimension – dragons between whose razor-sharp teeth Charles Winslow was that very instant being torn to ribbons in his dreams, before he woke with a start, bathed in sweat, and alarmed with his cries the two Chinese prostitutes sharing his bed, at the same time as his cousin Andrew, who was just then leaning on Waterloo Bridge watching the sun rise, noticed a familiar fellow with bird-like features coming towards him.

'Mr Wells?' he enquired, as the man drew level.

Wells stopped and stared at Andrew for a few moments, trying to remember where he had seen him before.

'Don't you remember me?' said the young man. 'I'm Andrew Harrington.'

As soon as he heard the name, Wells remembered. This was the lad whose life he had saved a few weeks before, preventing him killing himself, thanks to an elaborate charade that had allowed him to confront Jack the Ripper, the murderer who had terrorised Whitechapel in the autumn of 1888.

'Yes, Mr Harrington, of course I remember you,' he said, pleased that the young man was still alive and his efforts had not been in vain. 'How good it is to meet you.'

'Likewise, Mr Wells,' said Andrew.

The two men stood in silence for a moment, grinning idiotically.

'Did you destroy the time machine?' asked Andrew.

'Er . . . y-yes, yes,' stammered Wells, and quickly tried to change the subject. 'What brings you here? Did you come to watch the dawn?'

'Yes,' the other man confessed, turning to look at the sky, which just then was a palette of beautiful orange and purple hues. 'Although in actual fact I'm trying to see what's behind it.'

'What's behind it?' asked Wells, intrigued.

Andrew nodded. 'Do you remember what you told me after I came back from the past in your time machine?' He was rummaging for something in his coat pocket. 'You assured me I'd killed Jack the Ripper, in spite of this newspaper clipping contradicting it.'

Andrew showed Wells the same yellowed cutting he had presented to him in the kitchen of his house in Woking a few weeks before. *Jack the Ripper strikes again!* the headline announced, going on to list the ghastly wounds the monster had inflicted on his fifth victim, the Whitechapel prostitute whom the young man loved. Wells nodded, unable to help wondering, as everyone has done ever since, what had happened to the ruthless murderer, why he had suddenly stopped killing and had disappeared without a trace.

'You said it was because my action had caused a bifurcation in time,' Andrew went on, slipping the cutting back into his pocket. 'A parallel world, I think you called it, a world in which Marie Kelly was alive and living happily with my twin. Although, unfortunately, I was in the wrong world.'

'Yes, I remember,' said Wells, cautiously, uncertain what the young man was driving at.

'Well, Mr Wells, saving Marie Kelly encouraged me to forget about suicide and to carry on with my life. And that is what I am doing. I recently became engaged to an adorable young woman, and I am determined to enjoy her company and to savour the small things in life.' He paused and looked up at the sky again. 'And yet I come here each dawn to try to see the parallel world you spoke of, and in which I am supposedly living happily with Marie Kelly. Do you know what, Mr Wells?'

'What?' asked the writer, swallowing hard, afraid the young man was about to turn and punch him, or seize him by the lapels and throw him into the river, out of revenge for his having deceived him in such a childish way.

'Sometimes I can see her,' said Andrew, in an almost tremulous whisper.

The author stared at him, dumbfounded. 'You can see her?'

'Yes, Mr Wells,' the young man affirmed, smiling like one who has had a revelation. 'Sometimes I see her.'

Whether or not Andrew believed this, or had chosen to believe it, Wells did not know, but the effect on the young man appeared to be the same: Wells's fabrication had preserved him. He watched the young man contemplating the dawn, or perhaps what was 'behind' it, an almost childlike expression of ecstasy illuminating his face, and could not help wondering which of them was more deluded: the sceptical writer, incapable of believing the things he himself had written, or the desperate young man who, in a noble act of faith, had decided to believe Wells's beautiful lie, taking refuge in the fact that no one could prove it was untrue.

'It's been a pleasure meeting you again, Mr Wells,' Andrew said, turning to shake his hand.

'Likewise,' replied Wells.

After they had said goodbye, Wells watched the young man cross the bridge unhurriedly, swathed in the golden light of dawn. Parallel worlds. He had completely forgotten about the theory he had been obliged to make to save the young man's life. But did they really exist? Did each of man's decisions give rise to a different world? In fact, it was naïve to think there was only one alternative to each predicament. What about the unchosen universes, the ones that were flushed away? Why should they have less right to exist than the others? Wells doubted very much that the structure of the universe depended on the unpredictable desires of the fickle, timid creature called man. It was more reasonable to suppose that the universe was far richer and more immeasurable than our senses could perceive, that when man was faced with two or more options, he inevitably ended up choosing all of them, for his ability to choose was an illusion. So the world kept splitting into different worlds, worlds that showed the breadth and complexity of the universe, worlds that exploited its full potential, drained all of its possibilities, worlds that evolved alongside one another, perhaps only differentiated by an insignificant detail such as how many flies were in each, because even killing one of those annoying insects implied a choice: it was an insignificant gesture that gave birth to a new universe all the same.

And how many of the wretched creatures buzzing around his windows had he killed or allowed to live, or simply mutilated, pulling off their wings while he thought about how to resolve a dilemma in one of his novels? Perhaps that was a silly example, reflected Wells, as such an action would not have changed the world in any irreversible way. After all, a man could spend his entire life pulling off flies' wings without altering the course of history. But the same reasoning could be applied to far more significant decisions, and he could not help remembering Gilliam Murray's second visit. Had Wells not also been torn between two possible choices and, intoxicated with power, had he not opted to squash the fly, giving rise to a universe in which a company offering trips to the future existed, the absurd universe in which he was now trapped?

But what if he had opted instead to help Murray publish his novel? Then he would be living in a world similar to the one he was in now, only in which the time travel company did not exist, a world in which one more book would have to be added to the necessary bonfire of scientific novels: *Captain Derek Shackleton: The True and Exciting Story of a Hero of the Future*, by Gilliam F. Murray.

And so, since an almost infinite number of different worlds existed, Wells reflected, everything that could happen did happen. Or what amounted to the same thing: any world, civilisation, creature it was possible to imagine already existed. Which meant there was a world dominated by a non-mammalian species, another by birdmen living in huge nests, another in which man used an alphabet to count the fingers on his hand, another in which sleep erased all memory and each day was a new life, another in which a detective called Sherlock Holmes really did exist, and his companion was a clever little rascal called Oliver Twist, and still another in which an inventor had built a time machine and discovered a nightmarish paradise in the year 802,701. Taking this to its limit, there was also somewhere a universe governed by laws different from those Newton had established, where there were fairies and unicorns and talking mermaids and plants, for in a universe where anything was possible, children's stories were no longer inventions but copies of worlds their authors, by some quirk of fate, had been able to glimpse.

Did no one invent anything, then? Was everyone merely copying? Wells pondered the question for a while – and given that it is becoming clear this particular tale is drawing to a close, I shall use the time to bid you farewell, like an actor waving goodbye to his audience from the stage. Thank you very much for your attention, and I sincerely hope that you enjoyed the show . . .

But now let us return to Wells, who recovered with a start, owing to an almost metaphysical shudder running down his spine: his wandering thoughts had led him to pose another question. What if his life were being written by someone in another reality, for instance in the universe almost exactly like his own in which there was no time travel company and Gilliam Murray was the author of dreadful little novels?

He gave serious thought to the possibility of someone copying his life and pretending it was fiction. But why would anyone bother? He was not material for a novel. Had he been shipwrecked on a tropical island, like Robinson Crusoe, he would have been incapable of making so much as a clay gourd. By the same token, his life was too dull for anyone to transform it into an exciting story. Although, undeniably, the past few weeks had been rather eventful: in a matter of a few days, he had saved Andrew Harrington and Claire Haggerty's lives by using his imagination, which Jane had taken care to point out in a somewhat dramatic manner – as though she had been addressing a packed audience he could not see in the stalls.

In the first case, he had been forced to pretend he possessed a time machine like the one in his novel, and in the second that he was a hero from the future who wrote love letters. Was there material for a novel in any of this? Possibly. A novel narrating the creation of a company called Murray's Time Travel, in which he, unfortunately, had played a part, a novel that surprised its readers towards the middle when it was revealed that the year 2000 was no more than a stage set built with rubble from a demolition (although this, of course, would only be a revelation to readers from Wells's own time).

If such a novel survived the passage of time, and was read by people living after the year 2000 there would be nothing to reveal, for reality itself would have given the lie to the future described in the story. But did that mean it was impossible to write a novel set in Wells's time speculating about a future that was already the author's past? The thought saddened him. He preferred to believe his readers would understand they were meant to read the novel as if they were in 1896, as if they, in fact, had experienced a journey through time.

Still, since he did not having the makings of a hero, he would have to be a secondary character in the novel, someone to whom others, the story's true protagonists, came for help.

If someone in a neighbouring universe had decided to write about his life, in whatever time, he hoped for their sake that this was the last page, as he very much doubted his life would carry on in the same vein. He had probably exhausted his quota of excitement in the past two weeks, and from this point on his life would carry on in peaceful monotony, like that of any other writer.

He gazed at Andrew Harrington, the character with whom he would have started this hypothetical novel, and, as he saw him walk away bathed in the golden glow of dawn, perhaps with a euphoric smile playing about his lips, he told himself that this was the perfect image with which to end the tale. He wondered, as if somehow he were able to see or hear me, whether at that very moment someone was not doing precisely that, then experiencing the rush of joy every writer feels when finishing a novel, a happiness nothing else in life can bring – not sipping Scotch whisky in the bathtub until the water goes cold, not caressing a woman's body, not the touch on the skin of the delicious breeze heralding the arrival of summer.